# T
# JUGO
# BOX

## CLIO GRAY

Clio Gray is the award winning author who first came on the scene in 2004, gaining the Harry Bowling First Novel Prize, and in 2006 the Scotsman/Orange Award.
In 2015 she was nominated for the Man Booker.
In 2016 she was Long Listed for the Bailey's.
In 2022 she was Short Listed for the Cinnamon Award.
For the past 30 years she has lived in the Highlands of Scotland with her dogs, and has continued to work in the Public Library Service that she loves and has dedicated her working life to.
She hopes you will enjoy her book.

First published 2023 by Thornborough Press

Thornborough
Press

Copyright © Clio Gray

ISBN 978-1-7397042-6-1

By the same author

*The Stroop Series*
Guardians of the Key
The Roaring of the Labyrinth
Envoy of the Black Pine
The Brotherhood of Five

*The Scottish Series*
Deadly Prospects
Burning Secrets
Hidden Pasts

*The Troubadours Series*
Stumblestone
The Fifth Face of Fear

*The Bookfinders Series*
Legacy of the Lynx
The Juggler's Box

*Other books*
The Anatomist's Dream
Archimimus
Types of Everlasting Rest
Peder and the Skincatcher

# Prologue

## Out of the Pierced Mountain

### Vettie's Giel, Norway, 1800

A NETSUKE NIGHT, CLOSED and tight: line of river etched by the nail-scratch of a new moon. Hela staring out her window at the familiar landmarks of Vettie's Giel: stone-tumbled valleys; scree-ridden, grey-sheeted cliffs; the fist of Torghatten Hill on its island rising up from the foam-bitten fjords at its feet.

She swung herself from her scratchy straw-stuffed pallet, wriggled stockinged feet into clogs, climbed down the ladder from the loft where she slept. The goats in the room below jostling and wakening as she alighted, waiting expectantly for their pen to be swept, their detritus shovelled into pails ready for the midden, for Hela to strew out clover-scented hay and softened cakes of beet, refill their basin with fresh water. Goats bleating belligerently as Hela did none of it. Hela instead reaching for her cape, pulling it about her shoulders, going out the door. Began to wind her way through the night-blinkered street, clogs tapping on the

1

cobbles like the heavy hail that so frequently fell upon Vettie's Giel.

Glancing upwards as she went, seeing clouds to the north bunch and push across the sky ready to let forth rain, send it down fleet and heavy, to gather in torrents, rip through gullies and ginnels like angry tail-whipping snakes.

Didn't have long.

Vettie's Giel a place apart, closest township being Bergenstift: thin track from the former to the latter folding like a bird's leg down the cliff and across a bridge of turf and birch swinging several hundred feet above Kokende Chasm, water thundering below, plummeting between narrow splits and spills of rocks. Terrifying to the newly appointed pastor, who'd swayed for mere moments upon the first few slats before drawing back, declaring he would go no further; that anyone on the other side needing his services would have to walk their own bones down to Bergenstift because he wasn't going anywhere near Vettie's Giel.

Not the first, nor the last.

Pastors born and bred in cities not stern enough stuff to suffer the like. Folk wanting marrying or baptising having the whole village packing themselves off down to the churchyard in Bergenstift the neglectful pastors had made their own. Dead folk wrapped in linen, strapped to a plank, two men carrying, one in front, one behind, for that was as wide as path and bridge could take them. And in truth, the folk of Vettie's Giel were glad they had no pastor to chide and chastise them. Pleased to be left to their own.

Hela crossing the bridge many times, although never in darkness and never when the wind was roaring down the gully scouring those water-whipped serpents on, as no sane person would. Slats of the bridge ready to writhe and buck, throw anyone off its back into Kokende's maw.

Such a wind on its way now: those malevolent northern clouds already halfway across the sky in a morning not quite dawned. No netsuke night when they reached her, and no way down to Bergenstift when they did.

She quickened her steps, heading for the tiny chapel and its tinier manse in which lived the boy who'd left Vettie's Giel before Hela was born. Returned a man mysterious: bent-backed, cracked lips spilling over with tales of where he'd been, what he'd seen with those dark eyes of his that glinted like crowberries sparkled over with dew. A man who had half the village enthralled; eschewed by the other half - by those who'd known him as a boy – who'd warned against him. Troubled by his leaving, more so by his return. A man who, in his youth, had crossed to Torgett Island on his home-made raft , despite his parents' insistent protestations. Sat vigil in the cleft that sundered Torghatten Hill through and through so you could see light from one side to the other, as through the eye of a needle. A boy, returning to Vettie's Giel on his near-collapsing raft, transformed; who had packed his small life up into a single back-pack and left; never heard of from that day until the night the villagers saw a thin screel of smoke coming from the one-roomed manse the previous pastor had abandoned and the new one had never set foot in.

*As if he knew,* the older members of Vettie's Giel had whispered, *as if he knew.*

*Eerie,* the word some used; *too convenient by half,* said others.

How the different circumstances hung together they could not fathom, but you didn't live in Vettie's Giel without having a healthy regard for superstition. Seasons came and went; crops burgeoned - given the right amount of sunshine and rain - or straggled and bolted into weedy unproductivity if not. Livestock bred more livestock, mothers looking after their offspring unless they found those offspring unfit, unworthy of investing milk and time in. Like Stefan's cow, who had splurged out her offspring and promptly walked away, afterbirth still spooling from her uterus. Wobbly-legged calf unable to stand or follow. Stefan gently leading mother back to calf, mother giving her calf a kick that broke its ribs, made it mewl like a punctured toad. Stefan kneeling down and palpating the calf, unwilling to let it go. But it went anyway. Stefan curious, Stefan cutting open the carcass prior to chopping it into usable pieces – for meat was meat, and this the youngest and tastiest you could ever have - Stefan finding the calf had a herniated intestine and would never have thrived.

*As if she knew,* he told friends and neighbours, as he handed them their portions of meat, share and share alike. *Eerie it was. As if she knew.*

Hela not so bound by these conventions and superstitions.

Hela knowing more than most.

Bent-backed man, previous absconding boy of Torghatten, selecting Hela from his young story-sucking-up acolytes precisely because she was not so bound. Hela strong, hardened, alone. Keeping her farmstead together these last few years since mother and brother had died. Hela, who had a cape fringed with the ears of the forty nine hares she'd harried and caught, slaughtered and smoked, cooked and eaten, since her brother had gone over a ledge whilst hunting them and not been able to get out. Revenge on her mind, blaming those long men in the grass for Jule's dying.

Hela, who had one small space on the fringe of her cape for the very last hare needed to complete it.

*Complete this task I'm giving you,* the boy, the man, who'd returned so unexpectedly had told her, *and all your other tasks will be at an end.*

Hela believing him.

Hela pulling her almost-finished cape about her shoulders on that night-soon-to-become-morning as she abandoned goats and farmstead, clip-clopped her way through the only street of Vettie's Giel, hurrying onwards, needing to keep ahead of those threatening clouds.

*One task, to end all others.*

Bent-backed man's words in her head as she scuttled forward, reached the chapel, the tumbled-down walls about it. The need strong in her to get on, get her bones down the skinny track rounding rocks and basalt outcrops as it cricked-cracked down the hill towards the rickety bridge.

Only one thing to do before she took that journey.

Hela's fingers going habitually to the ears fringed about her cape. Nothing like a hare's ear to give comfort in times of stress. So unexpectedly soft and long. Heart beating hard as she saw the door of the manse open, the man waiting for her a step within, apparently knowing she would come despite her prevarications the night before. Decision made suddenly when she had awoken and listed all the things needed doing: see to the goats, the fields, the dairy; get the butter churned, check on the cheeses, turn the meat above the fire, make sure the fire was smoking properly to smoke the meat.

All too much for Hela.

Had been too much for far too long.

Hela having difficulty getting up some days. Turning her face to the wall, not caring about the goats, the farm, the fields; all those things needing doing that went on and on and on, never an end in sight. The whole of Vettie's Giel telling her she was long past the age for marriage, needed to do the right thing to keep herself and her homestead, her family name, alive. Prospective matches the ones she'd always known would be on the list, bar the few she might have considered earlier in her life when things had been simpler, when she'd had a parent and a brother and a passable stab at a dowry. Not so now. Only dregs left for her: men who weren't considering her at all, only the pitiful farmland in her possession.

A life she could see rolling on ahead of her like a field unharrowed of stones.

Hard, bleak, and unrelenting.

A life she didn't want.

The bent-backed man giving her the chance of getting out, doing as he had done before her.

*Take it, Hela*, he said. *Take it, and don't look back. This is your time.*

Hela taking the package from his hands.

Hela going down the path, across the bridge.

New life beckoning.
Hela on her way.

# 1

## Bad Days Getting Worse

### *Bad Salzbaum, Germany November 1809*

MATHILDE STOSS ROLLED herself from her bed, looked out of the single window. A dreary morning staring back at her: grey drifts of light eking from a low-lying mist, drizzle swaying in the slight breeze. The vast wooden scaffolding surrounding the Salt hedges darkly immobile, as menacing as the trolls who'd scattered themselves through the fairy tales of her youth; trolls disguised as piles of rocks that came alive when least expected. Mathilde taking an involuntary step backwards as the topmost part of the structure rippled, hand going to her throat as an eerily silent line of rooks unfolded into uncoordinated flight.

'Heaven's sake!' she swore quietly, annoyed to have been so feared if only momentarily; gave her long grey hair a quick brush before tying it into a bundle on top of her head, secured it beneath her cap.

'Holger,' she said, eager to wake her husband, not be alone in this forbidding morning. 'Holger,' she prompted again, Holger groaning, turning onto his side, coughing spasmodically until he threw up a lump of phlegm that he spat into his handkerchief.

'No need to raise the rafters,' Holger croaked, swinging his legs from the bed and sitting on its edge, rubbing his eyes with calloused knuckles, fumbling for his boots with his feet.

'You know you've to be there early, what day it is,' Mathilde remonstrated, getting to the fire, poking its embers back to life, giving a little light to the room. Holger screwing up his face, needing no reminder. Worst part of his job, no matter it only came about once or twice a decade. But had to be done. Every stook and stack of the blackthorn bundles in the hedges needing hoiking out and replacing, and them hedges the height of five tall men and seven times as long as them were high.

Was going to take him and his pal from dawn to dusk to unpack them, and another day to get them restocked again. Interrupted by a sharp rapping at the door and the round robust face of Piet Hoost poked in, all smiles and crooked teeth and sticky-up hair.

'Ready for the off? Can't wait to get started!' Piet announced, effervescent optimism in every syllable. 'Sorry, missus,' he apologised, taking in the scene. Mathilde on her knees by the hearth, skirts hoisted to avoid the worst of the ash as she riddled the stove, Holger still trying to get his boots on.

'It's fine, Piet,' Mathilde motioning the young man in. 'Just got to make you two a bite of food to take with. Beef and horseradish do you?'

'Do us grand,' Piet agreed, taking a chair at the table, there being no other place to sit. Accommodations weren't great here in Bad Salzbaum, but a fine bit better than back at home where six folk would have to do in a place as small as this.

Mathilde smiled at the lad who emanated cheer with every step, every word. Nothing could daunt him. A lad like a spaniel whose only goal in life was to fetch the gnawed old bone thrown for him and who woke up waiting for that bone, lived every minute in constant expectation of the next and of it being better than the last.

She retrieved a skinny hank of beef from the meat safe, fetched up the jar of creamed horseradish, scowled briefly at the bread she'd unshrouded from its towel.

'Yesterday's,' she apologised, putting it on the table, began to slice. 'No time to do today's yet, seeing as you're so early started. I'll bring you some fresh-made and warm when it's done.'

'Thanks, Missus,' came Piet's earnest reply. Mathilde smiling again at that hope, that expectation, that bone she'd promised to fling – no matter how paltry.

'I'm really looking forward to the hedge dressing,' Piet added.

'That'll soon wear thin,' Holger grumbled, snapping braces onto his shoulders, finished lacing his boots. 'Worst job in the world.'

Piet laughed - an airy sound, like a flock of fieldfares rising from a haw tree.

'Not for me!' he said. 'Really want to see how it all goes together.'

Mathilde glancing out of the window at the enormous Salt hedges – not so formidable now the sun had tipped its way above the horizon and Piet was warming her house with his smiles. Mathilde seeing only what she saw every day. Salt hedges rising like the walls of a cathedral, the dark passageway a nave between where the sick and gouty went in hope of reprieve; the silvery glint of water in the aqueducts that ran over their tops, designed to drip-feed the water down the length and height of the dead hedges, caking them in crystalline salts that shone like frost in the glimmers of the dawn; rooks and trolls forgotten.

Turning back to her tasks, once Piet and her husband had left, thinking through the day and evening that would follow when they would return, partake of whatever repast she'd managed to conjure up. A game of cards, a few throws of dice on the rickety table, the warmth of Piet's youth sucked into her like oil to a wick. Piet her only light in the darkness, especially now Holger was failing - and no idea what was going to happen when all that came out. She'd lived in this shack for thirty odd years, but the shack was tied to the hedges. Sever that link and where would she be? Dirt and ditches all she could see ahead of her. No children to take care of her, take her and Holger in. Only Piet, bright beacon that he was. Only Piet, who might be able to save them.

Talk about spaniels and bones.

# 2

## Grim and Grime

### *Gronau November 1809*

A GRIMY STREET, A GRIMY shop, another grimy window.

Ruan Peat rubbed at the muck on its outer surface, held his hand over his eyes as he gazed inside, ennui slowing every movement. He might have been looking at his own life: narrow stacks and shelves of book needing ownership, his job to provide them. Employed by folk to track down various volumes, discover in them lost learning, provenances of works of art or jewellery. Business brisk since the incursions of the French, the Low Countries redesignated as Batavia. Rumours abounding that it wouldn't be long before they were absorbed stick and stone into France, national identities entirely lost. Hard-taken by the Dutch, angry men in coffee houses bridling against the rapaciousness of the incomers. Ruan's last mission, before this one, being to trace the ancestry of some minor member of the aristocracy holed up in the Palace at Apeldoorn, seeking out ancient documents proving how grand and great he was before scarpering over the water to England to butt his way into their gentry and the life he believed he deserved.

A situation that couldn't help but remind Ruan of Greta Finnerty. The Dutch against the French, the Irish against the English. At least the Irish had had the guts to fight back. Ten years since he'd seen her, and every second of every day of those ten years regretting he'd not snatched her up when he'd had the chance, stayed with her, fought with her.

Ruan pulled himself away from the window, angered by those old thoughts, pushing them away, replacing them with his immediate goal.

'Caro!' he called, Caro instantly by his side, and some comfort in that – not that it had always been the way. 'Looks like it's going to be another long day,' Ruan sighed.

'But ain't they always the best?' Caro replied happily, pushing open the door to the haphazard book-shop, stepping inside, lost to view.

'Mr. Peat?'

A voice Ruan didn't recognize.

'Mr. Ruan Peat?'

Ruan seeing in the grimy window's reflection a tall man made comically taller by his ostentatious top hat, a long rectangular face below the brim with a ridiculous wisp of beard at his chin. *Looks like a goat in men's clothing,* Ruan thought uncharitably as he turned to the stranger, found a calling card shoved into his hand.

'Professor Ottelius Jorn,' Ruan read slowly. 'Spa Proprietor, Bad Salzbaum. What can I do for you?'

Hoping it was a commission that would take him away from Gronau for he'd no care for it at all, finding it uncomfortably claustrophobic, a shambling provincial border-town halfway German, halfway Dutch, unable to make up its mind which to be. The exact sort of place the French could creep into when no one was looking, begin expanding their empire town by town, city by city. The Holland he'd settled in already beginning to lose the tolerance and liberalism that had been its benchmark for centuries. A land taking in intellectuals of all stripes, from John Locke to Descartes, when they'd nowhere else to go.

It felt like the world he knew was about to end.

'I've a rather delicate matter to discuss with you,' the Professor began. 'Not entirely usual.'

'Not entirely usual is my stock in trade, sir,' Ruan replied shortly. 'But unless you explain there'll be no way I can aide you. Be frank, sir, please.'

Conversation stalled by Caro coming excitedly back out the door.

'They found it straightaway! Had it ready for us, got your letter before...Hold up,' Caro interrupted himself. 'What's going on?'

'Gentleman's just about to enlighten us,' Ruan said easily, taking from Caro the small book they'd come in search of, tucking it away in his satchel. Nothing urgent. It could wait.

'Have you heard of the Salt hedges of Bad Salzbaum?' Professor Jorn asked, as the three moved off down the street towards the coffee house on the corner.

'No, Sir, I have not,' Ruan replied with weariness.

'Nor me,' Caro chipped in. 'But they sounds interesting!'

'That they are, young man.'

Caro possibly twenty-one, by his own reckoning; small-framed, thin-boned, younger looking than he was.

'They're part of the spa,' Professor Jorn went on. 'We've several mineral springs in the vicinity, one of which we pump out and drip over the hedges, covering them with precipitate. Very healthy, many believe.'

*I rather doubt that's why you've come in search of us*, Ruan thought, as Professor Jorn pushed open the door of the coffee house and directed his guests inside. The three immediately enveloped by a fug of tobacco smoke and the acrid smells of long boiled coffee and over-ripe sweat. Ruan and Caro sitting while the Professor got a jug of coffee and an unappetizing plate of pastries no one touched.

'What you mayn't know about the hedges,' the Professor explained, 'is that every few years they need replacing,' holding up a finger to allay the question already on Caro's lips. 'They're not living hedges. The calcification would kill them. They're built from bundles of blackthorn, up to a height of thirty feet.'

'Sounds amazing!' Caro commented, sipping at the coffee, grimacing. Nothing like the good stuff they had back in Deventer, eager as Ruan to be gone from Gronau, especially when it saw fit to serve up coffee as bad as this.

'Plainly we're not packers of hedges,' Ruan asked. 'So where do we come into it?'

A little of the old Ruan coming to the surface. Caro twisting out half a smile, for the old Ruan had been insufferable. The change in him after Deventer a small miracle. Although saving lives, Caro's included, could do that to a man. Either way, Caro was thankful to still be with him, and the constant struggle Ruan underwent to keep himself in check was daily sport for Caro.

'The point, sir, as you so eloquently put it,' Professor Jorn went on, 'is that we very recently unpacked our hedges and found something... completely unexpected.'

HOLGER AND PIET HAD closed the sluice gates, shutting off the water from the wheel; wooden paddles creaking as they came to rest, water draining from their slats, emptying the aqueducts atop the hedges. Piet admiring the simple mechanics of it.

Holger not admiring it at all, arthritic fingers throbbing as he went at the winch.

Next job being to squirrel their way up the graduation towers at one end of the hedges, remove the aqueducts from their tops section by section.

Easy part over. Next came the hard labour of manipulating the rods to hoik out the packed bundles of blackthorn making up the height and breadth of the hedge. Top few levels not too bad, Holger and Piet throwing them to the ground with easy gusto. The deeper they got the more difficult it became, rods getting progressively longer, hooks stouter and more vicious. Despite Holger's grumbling he was excellent at his task, had done it five times during his employment at the spa. Piet quick to learn how to gauge the dropping of the rods, the adept flick of the wrist needed to get the hook beneath the rope of the bundles and bring them out without them tilting and dropping back again, when it was so much more complicated to grab up a second time.

Last few courses got at from ground level, wriggling their bodies between the scaffolding keeping the Salt hedges from buckling and tipping. Only short-armed rods needed now, Piet carrying on enthusiastically as Holger began to rake all the bundles together, expertly manipulating them into a massive heap ready for the burning.

'Holger!' Piet's voice loud and excited. Holger looking over, seeing Piet's habitually ruddy face redder than ever with the day's exertions.

Holger sighing, hoping to heaven there wasn't going to be some hitch like that the bottom-most blackthorn bundles had rotted and would need scraping out with rakes along with the mice and rats who'd chewed the rotten stems into nests, which was a slow job and dirty.

'What?' he asked, as he closed on Piet whose cheeks had puffed out like robins' breasts on cold Winter mornings.

Piet said nothing, instead pointed his rod towards the base of the hedge, its empty hook a grinning question mark. Holger leaning forward, back clicking as he went in for a better look.

'Well I'll be...' he murmured. 'How the devil?'

Piet withdrew his rod and shrugged, for how the devil indeed.

# 3

## How to Put Your Neck in a Noose

Walcheren Peninsula, Holland

November 1809

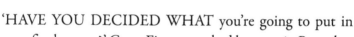

'HAVE YOU DECIDED WHAT you're going to put in your final report?' Greta Finnerty asked her cousin Peter, her ginger hair as short and spiky as it had been during her time with the United Irish back in 1798. Greta dressed once more in men's clothing, as she had then, so as to fit in better with the troops. She could no longer pass as a boy any more than the sun could have pretended to be the moon but, with her cap on and her army fatigues as muddy and stained as the rest, no one gave her a second glance as she moved through the garrison, gathering the stories of the men who'd been deployed on this disastrous British mission to Holland.

'Got to tell it like it is,' Peter pronounced, puffing manically at his pipe, hand scribbling frantically across the page. 'I'm not going to whitewash it, no matter what they'd have me do.'

Greta expecting nothing less.

'Gonna land you in a big pile of shite, but hey ho.'

'Hey ho, indeed,' Peter agreed. 'But someone's got to say it. It's an utter shambles. How did the English imagine they'd do better here than the French? And all for taking Flushing and Antwerp. What an absolute human waste.'

'Read me what you've got so far,' Greta asked, Peter flashing her a smile.

'You're not going to like it. But here goes.'

He put down his pipe, ran his finger under the lines as he read them out.

*You know, from my previous reports, that the British forces decided in July of this year to mount an offensive on the ports of Holland to aid the beleaguered forces of Austria there - an expedition I was invited to attend – objective being to halt the French by utterly destroying the ships and shipyards of Antwerp and taking Flushing. First foothold falling on the peninsular of Walcheren, with forty thousand men and fifteen thousand horses to put field artillery into play. The leisurely approach of Army Commander, the Earl of Chatham, has seen to it that the main objective has failed: Flushing taken by a hair, Antwerp completely lost, and we've news that after their defeat at Wagram the Austrians have anyway capitulated. This pointless campaign has cost English tax-payers eight million pounds, according to my sources. It is well that a mere one hundred and six men fell in battle, but here is the worst part of the bargain, dear readers. Here on Walcheren we are witnessing a catastrophic, needless and completely foreseeable waste of life: four thousand men dead these last few months from the local form of malaria, almost half that amount about to go the same way and that amount again permanently invalided by the same disease. Medical assistance is at best utterly inadequate, at worse obscenely negligent. It is only by God's grace I am left alive to tell you what the English Government will not do: that Walcheren is a charnel house, and we are running out of places to bury the dead.*

Greta drew in a breath as Peter finished his recitation. He'd always been impassioned against the English, as was she. You didn't come through the brutalities of the Irish Rebellion without being so.

'Chatham is going to skin you alive when he reads this,' she said quietly, shaking her head, Peter smiling up at her through the remnants of pipe smoke hovering about the small tent in wisps and wraiths.

'What can I say? Old habits die hard.'

'They might really hang you this time around,' Greta not so flippant.

'They were the ones asked me on this expedition,' Peter reminded her. 'Why would they do that unless they wanted me to tell the truth?'

Greta shook her head.

'You're such a numbskull. They asked you precisely so you wouldn't tell the truth. They want to make an example of you, tell every other upstart Irish journalist that even the great Peter Finnerty would eventually toe the line. Why can't you see that?'

Peter thumped his fist on the table.

'I will never be their lackey! Never! No matter how much it costs.'

'Even if it's your neck? And mine too, seeing as I'm your supposed secretary?'

Greta hadn't meant to be so harsh but it was true. High time Peter started thinking on something other than the failed Uprising in Ireland. Jesus. He knew how much she'd been through back then. What she'd had to do because of it. The person she'd given up in the hope of carrying on the cause, carrying on Peter's printing press while he was in prison, even when it became obvious the cause had all but had the life throttled out of it. Greta's throat closing up, might have cried had she not been so angry. Peter holding up his hands in conciliation.

'I didn't mean...'

Greta unable to hold her tongue.

'That's just it! You never do. You never blasted well think things through, see what the consequences might be for other people. Remember all that shite you wrote about the United Irish joining forces with the French? Those heroes' names you bandied about? Remember how badly that went?'

Peter dropped his hands, for of course he remembered. The Irish Legion captured to a man by the English not long back, shipped over the water. Not a few of those prisoners singled out because of the many articles he'd written back in the day holding them up as saviours to the cause. No idea anyone in the English establishment had paid his articles any mind, jotted those names down for future reference. Which was exactly what they'd done. Many of those men likely executed because of it.

'A few managed escape,' he gave his weak argument. 'Lawless and O'Reilly got back to French lines and are about to receive the Légion d'Honneur...'

A mistake on his part, Greta looking ready to throw him into the nearest slurry pit alongside the most recent English dead.

'Well that makes it just dandy then,' she hissed, had had enough, walked out of the tent, fists clenched inside the too long sleeves of the tattered bespattered uniform she despised.

# 4

## A Gorgon's Work is Never Done

### Bad Salzbaum, Germany

'I'VE NEVER SEEN THE like,' Ruan observed, as Professor Jorn led him into the cellar of his spa's hotel. 'It's somewhat...disturbing.'

'Looks like a side of salted cod,' Caro added.

'The body is covered with precipitate,' the professor told them. 'Spring-waters and petrifying wells such as our own have mineral salts dissolved in them: calcium carbonate, lime, magnesium, various others that will coat any object they drip over for any length of time and...'

'Didn't you say he was in the bottom courses of the hedge?' Ruan interrupted. 'And the hedge last laid years back? Wouldn't that mean he'd have had time to rot away before the water got to him?'

'*Au contraire,*' pronounced the professor with a distinctly continental flourish, as irritating a man as Ruan had ever met. Regretting taking him up on his offer, but Bad Salzbaum a stone's throw from Deventer so had little to lose.

'The imperative of water, like gravity,' the professor continued, 'is always to descend. When we pump the water over our hedges it will of necessity drip downwards, collect in the most compacted places if it can't escape...'

'In a hot Summer, for example,' Ruan interrupted what promised to be another interminable flow of explication.

'Precisely,' the professor ground on. 'Soil below the hedges hard and unable to drink up the excess. Instead is evaporated by the sun, like in a salt pan.'

'Exactly like salted cod,' Caro triumphant.

'Exactly like in some respects,' Professor Jorn explicated precisely. 'The salts drawing out all bodily fluids before covering the exterior, sealing him tight.'

And it did appear to be a he, given the outline of body and clothes, a man literally gorgonized, laid out like a crude sculpture waiting for hammer and chisel to knock off the edges and make it sing, become an object admired instead of pitied.

Caro thinking of those gorgons: *their heads with hair of snakes and tusks of boar, hands of brass, wings of gold.*

Petrifying monsters. What he was looking at seeming monstrous indeed.

Ruan seeing the stillness overtaking Caro, knowing Caro's pockets of empathy were tailored deeper than most. Hard to believe there'd been a time when he'd not liked the boy. Caro a brother to him now. Only family either of them had left.

'Implying what, Caro?' Ruan broke the spell. Caro's thoughts veering away from myth and monsters, went instead tick-tacking along the logic-lanes Ruan had taught him to follow over the years, weighing up the information given him, taking it to reasonable conclusion.

'Presumably put into the hedge during a hot Summer,' Caro said quietly, 'or a hot spell at the very least. Possibly the bottom sections of the hedge pulled out and him put in, or,' he bit his lip, looked at Ruan.

'Or?' Ruan asked.

Professor Jorn getting in first.

'Obviously he was put in, or got himself in, when the hedge was last laid. Had to have been.'

*And so no blame on me,* he was thinking. *Before my time.*

'It's certainly intriguing,' Ruan said.

'Intriguing or otherwise,' Jorn continued sharply, sweeping a hand towards the straw bales on which the calcified body lay curled like a frozen frond of fern. 'This... this... thing... isn't your concern. Nor is it mine. What I need to know about is what we found him with, what I have employed you to explore. The rest is not worth a pile of pins. I take it we have a bargain? Necessary expenses to be paid on top of your normal fee?'

Ruan hesitating, if only for a moment, for this was undoubtedly a puzzle and a challenge. And both he and Caro liked a puzzle and a challenge.

'We do,' Ruan therefore replied. Swift handshake sealing the bargain.

Professor Jorn removing himself, glad to take his way up the stone steps and into sunlight. A lot more on his mind than this carapace of a man drawn out of his hedge. Bonfire to be lit that very evening. A spectacle pulling in towns folk, fairs folk, and a great many visitors who might, next season, become paying customers at his spa. Spas quite the fashion. Well-heeled people, like the famous author Goethe, frequently spending four months of the year in their favoured spots. As far as he was concerned this calcified homunculus could be thrown onto that same bonfire and be burned into oblivion. He'd no curiosity how this situation had come about. Happening before his time. Professor Jorn nominal manager of the hotel back then, but not of the grounds; himself not even in Bad Salzbaum during the hedge-laying; away on a fact-finding mission visiting other spas, and therefore was personally unaccountable. Professor Jorn well-versed in pushing the uncomfortable into dark corners where it could not be seen. All thoughts of the dead body shoved into one of those shadowy corners the moment he left the cellar.

Ruan and Caro not so sanguine.

'We can't just let this be,' Caro said, 'no matter what old goat-face had to say.'

Ruan clapping Caro's thin shoulder.

'Never a truer word said. And no, we'll not. We're investigators, you and me. We've not investigated a body before but no reason this shouldn't be our first. And people, like books, always leave traces. We're being paid to investigate the books but we'll do more.'

Caro straightening the stoop his shoulders had fallen into as his mind drifted backwards.

'Have you ever thought how odd it is,' he asked, 'how two of the gorgon sisters were immortal and the other wasn't? How does that make any sense?'

As if Greek myths ever made any sense.

Caro and Ruan spending evenings and idle days discussing whatever treasures they'd uncovered on their travels. Brothers of the book. One of their latest being a collection of Ancient Greek writers: Homer, Euripides, Hesiod, Apollodorus...

A list as endless as it was arbitrary, as was the distinction of being gifted mortality or otherwise.

'I don't think it matters,' Ruan said. 'What matters now is what we do.' Greek gods to be trusted on no account. 'We've to crack him open. Knock off as much of that precipitate as we can. Find out who he was and how he got in there. But, before we do, there's one avenue we've yet to explore.'

Rewarded by a smile from Caro.

'Are you ready to be an investigator of bodies instead of books?' Ruan bellowed, as if firing up competitors in a boxing match. Caro understanding, taking the stone steps from the cellar two by two, recognising the challenge. Relieved Ruan was enlivened, as he'd not been in Gronau. Ruan sometimes finding his life so bleak and bad all he wanted to do was hole up in his bed, let the days pass, let life go on without him. Caro the blink of light forcing him up and out. Caro the needling younger brother requiring help and guidance.

*Need you to look at the prinklings in the snow,* he'd say, *tell me what animal's made them.*

*Need you to come look at this book, tell me the provenance of the handwriting in the margins.*

*Need you to get out of that blasted bed and get a shave. You look like a badger's arse and, got to say it, you stink far worse.*

Only Caro able to lift him from those melancholic places of regret Ruan sometimes sank into.

Only Caro able to see beyond what Ruan could not.

Wise old man in a young man's body.

Wise old man, who often saw what others never bothered to look for.

As Professor Jorn was not doing now.

'You know I am!' Caro called as he went. Ruan grinning, pushing his way up the stairs, catching Caro up as they reached the top and pushed the door closed behind them, sliding home the bolt.

'You don't even know where we're going,' Ruan admonished, Caro tipping his head, raising his eyebrows.

'Want to take a bet on that?' he asked, and was off. 'I'll fly like the wind!' Caro added, running full tilt across the grass towards the hedges. 'I've wings on my back! I'm Pegasus, son of Medusa the gorgon! See if you can catch me!'

Such was Caro. Ruan's self-appointed gonfalonier of light on bad days and freedom on the better ones, such as this had just become. Ruan tugging off his hat, ignoring everything and everyone about him as he ran after Caro and laughed and laughed.

'GRETA FINNERTY, AS I live and breathe!'

Brother Joachim hobbled across the yard of the Servants of the Sick to greet her, astonished how little she appeared to have aged, an impression aided by her being once more in men's clothing, hair clipped short, as when he'd first met her.

Greta giving the old monk a hug, the two walking together through the monastery gates, taking the path towards the polders leading to St Drostan's Well. Sitting on the stone bench there, with a broad view of the sea.

Joachim glad of the breeze blowing in from the west. The Servants on the tip of Walcheren, the English holed up in the environs of Vlissingen – or Flushing as they insisted on calling it. Winds blowing from the east bringing with them the stench of dirt and disease from their ranks, unpleasant and unmistakable.

'I'm sorry I never came before,' Greta apologized, squeezing the old man's hand, feeling the lumps and gnarls grown on knucklebones and finger joints. 'It's been difficult.'

Joachim nodded.

'It's a tragedy,' he said, 'what's happened here. Anyone on Walcheren could have told the English what would happen if they chose to wage their campaign during the Summer months. But of course, they never asked.'

'I know,' Greta agreed, watching the ever-changing lines of long-legged birds digging their beaks into the sands about the mudflats . 'And I'm sorry the Servants got dragged into it.'

Servants of the Sick the only people who'd done anything to stem the ague inflicting the soldiers, handing out all they could of pills that could prevent or allay it. Not enough for everyone, forty thousand men too many for anyone. Most hogged by the officers, who cared for themselves far more than for their men.

Grave-space running a bit short on Walcheren, as both Joachim and Greta knew.

And Greta's sympathy for the English even shorter. A sentiment shared by many of his fellow monks, most notably the Abbot who had agreed the Servants be part of the chain for Irish exiles fleeing to Germany and France this last decade, precisely to fight once more against those same English.

'Heard your Irish Legion did good,' he said, 'before being captured.'

'And then escaping again,' Greta corrected. 'Some of them at least.'

'Which is why it's so timely you're here,' Joachim stated, casting a quick glance at Greta, seeing that yes, she had aged but in a good way, unlike him. Her face fuller and rounder, enhancing the dimples in her cheeks. A good-looking lass on every count, if not a normal one by any means. Time to tread with care, gentle as the redshanks lifting their feet from the mud of the estuary and placing them back down again. 'I've news of Ruan.'

Greta lowering her head to hide the blush spreading across her cheeks. No point thinking about that now, about what might have happened.

'How's he doing?' she asked. Joachim splayed his fingers over his knees and looked towards the sea, towards the great rollers that had been coming in for the past two weeks, the moon working with the sun to bring in spring tides that had come higher and higher up the dunes until they'd littered the paths with seaweed and detritus. At pause now. The sea at its furthest way off.

'He writes to me now and again,' he offered. 'Got a letter a while back saying he'd just finished a job for one of those French exiles holed up in Apeldoorn.'

'I don't know where that is,' Greta said, lifting her head, trying to envisage Ruan somewhere in the unfathomable vastness of war-torn Europe. No way to find him, even if she wanted to. And she still hadn't made her mind up about that; although, if she was truthful, it was part of the reason she'd come with Peter to Walcheren. For the merest chance of it, for if anyone might know of Ruan's whereabouts it had to be Joachim.

All over in Ireland years back. She and Peter exiled to London. English enacting the Union in August 1800. Hope rising briefly when Robert Emmet took up the reigns of rebellion, stood his ground for several years; might have stood it longer if he hadn't come out of hiding in the Wicklow Hills to visit his sweetheart. Emmet promptly delivered into enemy hands, tried on September 19$^{th}$ 1803, hung the following morning.

The English always swift when dealing with their Irish upstarts. Not ones to hang around.

Unlike on Walcheren, where it seemed hanging around was all they'd done.

'He's gone into business as a finder of missing manuscripts and books,' Joachim informed her.

'You've got to be joking!' She couldn't help herself. 'He'd no more interest in books than I have in...well, I don't know, the latest fashions.'

'Nevertheless,' Joachim went on, 'that's the profession he's chosen for himself, and I gather he's rather good at it.'

Greta quiet a few moments, heart beating too quickly as she formed her next question.

'So he sold his place in Scotland?'

Remembering his words:

*I'll go back, if you come with me.*

And how brutal had been their parting, Greta's last words to him:

*What, and stop myself up in some hole in the middle of nowhere while my country burns? It's not over, Ruan. The fight's not over, and I'm going back to see it done whether you come with me or no.*

And no answer from Joachim.

Greta looking out over the sea, listening to the shooshing of the waves upon the sand. Its surface beyond the breakers caught by some unseen current, making it satin-smooth, blurred reflections of clouds captive on its surface. So like the sea to present such contradictions. So like herself in that respect.

'There has to be hope, Greta,' Joachim said, recalling the last line of Ruan's latest letter.

*Do you ever hear from her? Please let me know, no matter the news.*

'There might be a way,' he said, 'if you're willing to try.'

'What do you mean?' Greta asked shortly. Greta calculating the odds. The English forces due to ship out of Walcheren the following week, Greta never liking retreat – even if it wasn't her own. Completely and suddenly aware she didn't want to go back to England. London might be fine for Peter, definitely not for her. Every inch of her desperate to break out of such confinement, to go her own way, fight her own fight. Do or die, test her mettle, needing adventure of whatever kind.

'You said before that several of the Irish Legion had escaped?' Joachim asked.

Greta turning towards Joachim for so much was old news.

'We've one of them arrived here not long since,' Joachim went on. 'Pretty big cog as it happens. A man needing help. Your help, if you're up for it.'

# 5

# The Approach Of Strangers

---

'ANY IDEAS?' PIET ASKED Holger, the two tucking into their beef and horseradish sandwiches as they hunkered down in the work hut, latest duties completed. Hedges emptied and refilled, bonfire piled and ready for the off.

Holger shook his head, chewed his bread, swallowed with difficulty. He simply couldn't understand how it could have come about, that man in the hedge. It made no sense. How could he not have noticed?

And now people were coming.

Sweat gathering in his armpits, dreading what would must be. Had in his head fractured sentences of what he was supposed to say, words Piet and Mathilde had coached him in. Couldn't keep them straight. Kept stumbling over the worst possible scenarios: what would happen to Mathilde if he was accused, sacked, maybe even arrested. Their marriage always a little rocky and no wonder, given the life they'd had to lead. But he'd always loved her, since the first few days of refuge a lifetime ago, her hair a glistening chestnut plait wrapped twice about her head. Fierce joy to recall the

34

first time she'd allowed him to unpin it, stroke it free, comb through the kinks, splay the strands of it through his fingers. Her face still having a profile that set his heart on fire when he caught it now and then as she sat perfectly still by the fire darning socks, or sewing a patch onto a smock or retying a button. That curve to her forehead, the gentle slope of her nose, the outline of lips and chin, the slight asymmetry of her face leant by one eyebrow being arched as if in constant surprise. He loved every part of her and had never said it often enough.

*No need to raise the rafters, woman.*

Hoped those weren't the last words she'd remember him saying, no memory that he'd spoken to her several times since he'd uttered them.

'Oh Lord,' Holger whispered, getting to his feet, legs weak with worry, heart going like the clappers in his chest. Piet's hand on Holger's arm holding him back, as the two strangers neared their door.

'What can we do for you?' Piet moving forward, taking a step out of the shack to greet the visitors.

'My name is Ruan Peat, and this here is Caro,' the dark-haired man announced, a little out of breath from his running. 'Please excuse us disturbing you, but we've questions we need answers to.'

'Anything,' Piet said, not a whiff of worry in that expansive smile. 'Are you guests at the spa? We'd be glad to tell you all about the hedge laying if that's...'

The blonde companion, with the pinched face and a nose like a tree-creeper's beak, leaned in; looked inside the shed at the tools hanging from the walls. Saws of varying designs and purpose, drainage scoops, shovels, spades, scythes, axes, sharp-pronged forks.

'Would you look at that! What're they all used for?'

'Holger can tell you,' Piet said. 'He's the Master Groundsman here. Knows everything about anything to do with hedges, lawns and topiary.'

Quick wink at Caro, who took him at his word and dodged by Piet into the shack.

Holger blinking, heart subsiding now he was on steadier ground.

'That there's a billhook,' Holger began, 'used for coppicing and layering.'

'Had something similar on the ships,' Caro said, fingering the curve of the blade, 'for slicing through ropes when the nets got tangled.'

Caro dipping his head at Ruan as Ruan led the other man away. Not a conscious plan on their part to separate the two parties, merely what they always did to glean maximum information. Usually to do with books. This time with a corpse.

Piet going willingly, no real belief in him this was a spa guest. Could have scraped up something more tidily and appropriately dressed from the bottom of his boot.

'I'm guessing this is about what we found when we emptied the hedges?'

'It is,' Ruan agreed. 'I also have to tell you I'm only asking out of curiosity. Your Professor Jorn brought us in to look at what's in the crate. He's no interest at all in the person you found.'

Piet drawing in a breath of pure relief. No harm to come to Holger after all.

'I can't tell you much,' he said, 'but I'll tell you what I can.'

Ruan nodding. Asking when the hedges had last been laid, whether there was any possibility someone could have got into it at any time since. If anyone had gone missing in any of that time. Piet giving him the information he and Mathilde had managed to squeeze out of Holger the previous night.

'We're reckoning it was laid seven years back. I hadn't joined Holger then. He had a lad with him called Ignace, who only stayed that one Summer. Found it all a bit hard-going, I gather.'

'So the last hedge was laid in Summer?' Ruan asked. 'Is that usual, given this time around it's being laid in November?'

Piet stumped. He didn't know, and hadn't thought to ask.

CARO HAVING NO MORE luck with Holger, who was fine talking tools and billhooks. Vague about everything else.

'We usually do it late on in the year,' Holger told Caro, 'so the branches have sunk and don't easily collapse. Makes the bonfire all the more spectacular. But seem to mind there was some reason that year...'

He trailed off, couldn't recall why. Hadn't been able to recall so much these last couple of years. Kept going out of the cottage on the trail of something or other and forgetting what he'd been looking for. Taking a tool from its hook in the work-shed and setting off to perform some duty, getting halfway there and turning back because he'd no idea why or where he'd been heading. Piet a godsend, never commenting or doubting, merely getting Holger back on track.

'Back coppice?' he'd prompt, or 'thought we was off to clear out the spring?'

Mathilde the same, now Holger thought on it.

*Don't forget we're off to market tomorrow, Holger. Get some new handles for the hoes and dibbers...*

*Mind we've to go the blacksmiths, get them scythes sharpened good and proper and replace that blade on the shovel...*

Holger having a sudden chill shrivelling his chest to realise he'd no idea what had happened during the last laying of the hedge, couldn't recall it at all. Whole tranches of his past slipping through the cracks and disappearing.

Piet and Holger saved by Mathilde, who came hurrying out of her small homestead a hundred yards or so from the work-shed, smiling and frowning all at the same time, bustling up to the two strangers, steering them to her home.

'Come!' she was effusive, perhaps excessively so. 'I've coffee and some bites to eat.'

Piet whispering into her ear all Ruan had asked him, what little he'd said in reply.

Mathilde rubbing her hands together, eager to help now the threat to her household seemed less imminent. Mathilde seating Ruan and Caro on two of the three available chairs, Piet taking the last, Holger perching on the edge of the bed. Mathilde quickly pouring out coffee, taking from her small oven the batch of biscuits swiftly whipped up from flour, sugar and lard the moment she'd seen the strangers approaching. Ten minutes cooking all they needed.

'I'm guessing you're wanting to know about the last hedge-laying,' Mathilde took over, smiling quickly at her husband. Holger hot with relief and shame.

'It is,' Ruan agreed. 'Seven years ago, Piet was telling me. And in the Summer?'

'It was,' Mathilde said. 'A week or so after our anniversary of arriving here.'

*That's right!* Holger thought, wondering how he could have forgotten. Such a grand day they'd had. Ignace, for once, coming to the fore, allowing Holger the whole day off. He and Mathilde walking by the river through the centre of Bad Salzbaum, past the posh houses, over the three-arched bridge to the tea-shop where they'd had a fine spread. Him giving Mathilde a small tin locket containing their silhouettes, her giving him a new Winter jumper she'd managed to knit without him knowing. Jumper donned at first only on special occasions, soon employed every day during the cold seasons as she'd intended. A little baggier now; the words at its hem skew-whiff with wear, but still going strong: *Long years together, never a day regretted.*

'It was an unusual time,' Mathilde providing the details she'd not briefed Holger nor Piet with, knowing Holger would only recall the essentials if anything at all. 'First off we had a load of them millennium noodle-heads coming in from Münster, them being chucked out of there, and quite right too. Kept holding meetings in the marketplace saying the calendar had got it wrong and it was really the millennium all over again. Can't think why folk get so excited about the turning of the years. Numbers is just numbers, far as I'm concerned.'

Ruan took a sip of coffee, a nibble of biscuit – both remarkably good – remembering well the millennialists who, immediately before 1800, had predicted the end of the world. Nothing momentous happening. One day ticking into the next, life going on as usual. The world apparently not caring how the human cargo upon its back divvied up their timespans.

'And the year after that, in 1801,' Mathilde added, 'we got took over briefly by those damn Prussians who brought a load of POWs with them. Then, the following March, there was the peace treaty that sent all the Prussians off again.'

Ruan remembered it. A bit of a shuggle-up after the Russian Tsar, Paul I, was assassinated. The English, as usual, taking advantage of political chaos, launching a brief and devastating attack on the Danish fleet in Copenhagen harbour, which led to the dissolution of the pact of neutrality between Russia and the Scandinavian countries. Leading, in turn, to the Prussians joining the Northern Convention against the English and marching on Hannover with intent to head towards the North Sea to protect ports there from English incursion.

'A memorable time, then,' Ruan Peat commented. 'And the hedge laid early? Why was that?'

'Ah,' Mathilde held up a finger, looked over at Holger in case he was able to supply the answer which, now he'd the prompts from Mathilde, he was.

'Because of the Prussians leaving, and the appointment of the new mayor,' Holger said happily, scratching his cheek, all those lost memories bubbling back to the surface. 'Didn't really understand the whys and wherefores of the politics and that, but they wanted a big end-of-Summer bash in celebration and thought the hedge-laying would be perfect for it.'

'And a hot Summer?' Ruan prodded.

'Oh heavens, yes,' Holger agreed, glancing at his wife, hoping he'd not got it wrong, muddled up one Summer with another.

'Very hot,' Mathilde agreed. 'So hot poor Ignace got heat-stroke with all the work.' Mathilde laughing at the memory. 'Right on top he was, hoiking out the blackthorn bundles. Would've toppled right off if Holger hadn't caught him. Got brought into this cottage all rambling rubbish, and some of the things he said could've made a stevedore blush!'

Looking over at Holger, who didn't seem inclined to go on.

'Last sight we had of the boy,' she added, for Holger's benefit. 'Never came back to work.'

'So maybe it's this Ignace fellow you found in the hedge,' Caro mused. Mathilde putting him straight.

'I don't see how. He was here for a couple of days getting back to rights. But now that I think on it, his almost falling off halted the work a bit because the spa folk were worried what the new mayor might think if he'd gone and plummeted to his death. Remember, Holger?'

Holger screwed up his eyes, tried to push through the clouds ebbing up once more between that time and this.

'I do,' he finally got out. 'Had a man come over looking at what we was doing and how. Asked if I needed help now Ignace was out of action, which I did. Brought in someone...can't mind the name. Big-shouldered chap. Foreign fella. Couldn't understand a word he said. One of the Frenchies that came in with the Prussians though, I'm sure of that.'

Brought to the edges of his memory and could go no further.

'Holger's right,' Mathilde coming to his rescue. 'Can't mind his name neither. Only met him the once when he came to fetch Holger first morning he was here. And the hedge-laying was only stopped for the rest of that first day because the mayor decided he wasn't going to put back his festivities. And there were festivities. Fireworks enough to blow out the sky. Never seen anything like it before nor since.'

Glancing at Holger, worrying what she might have provoked by her mention of fireworks. Holger's face blank as the sky had been back then, fingers at the hem of his jumper, fiddling at the skew-whiff words embroidered into it.

'Is there anyone keeps records of the hedge-laying?' Ruan asked. 'Records that might pinpoint the day, who your new helper was?'

'Suppose,' Holger's one word dull, inanimate and uninformative.

'Must be someone you go to with your finances,' Ruan suggested, 'when you've to buy a new tool, or receive wages?'

Holger didn't look up, mumbled a reply.

'Goes through the Dieters at...well, not entirely sure where.'

'Of course it does!' Piet agreed. 'We should have thought of it before.'

'So they'll have mention of any pay given to the French labourer who helped you out,' Ruan stated. 'Did he stop with you long?'

Holger shaking his head, staring at his boots.

'Just for the hedge-laying. Was on me own a while after that, biggest job being done and Autumn then Winter coming on soon after. Them baking hot Summers,' he said, surprising himself, 'always bring the cold quick on their heels.'

'And this crate your professor wants me to see to. How was it found exactly? I mean was it underneath the body? Above it? Side by side?' Ruan asked.

Holger screwed up his eyes, trying to picture the scene as it had been when Piet first hollered at him and he'd come running.

'Aside him,' Piet put in for Holger, 'like he'd shoved it in before him. Tried to hide it. Although the whole situation is mighty odd. Like when he got himself in there. Suppose he might've thought it a good place to hide if he was on the run. But why would anyone be on the run and lug with him a heavy crate? And it was heavy.'

'And why didn't any of us hear him?' Mathilde asked. 'We walk past that hedge every day, as do all the visitors. If he'd got himself stuck, for a prank or whatnot, he would've called for help.'

Ruan highly doubtful pranks were involved.

'Maybe he was already partway dead,' he said, 'or all the way.'

'Which implies that Piet's original surmise might be the right one,' Caro added, 'and that it was not himself he was trying to hide but the crate he had with him. Which in turn means he couldn't have been dead, and whomever he was hiding from never found him. Else why didn't whoever put him in there take the bally crate?'

'Excellent question, Caro,' Ruan said, getting to his feet, thanking his hosts. Thinking questions were like sheep: set one running and a whole load more come on behind.

'Where next?' Caro asked, as he and Ruan walked by the newly repacked salt hedges, dark and spiky with fresh bundles of blackthorn, no water yet flowing, no precipitate, no shining salts.

'Find out from the professor where this firm of Dieters is,' Ruan replied, although seemed abstracted, had lost his earlier exuberance from running after Caro across the grass. Caro not replying. Caro well attuned to Ruan's moods, how they could shift and darken, lift and lighten, on the turn of a single word. Caro waiting for that word, which came a few moments later.

'She called me a noodle-head once,' Ruan stated. 'Well, several times, if truth be told.'

No need to tell Caro of whom he was talking.

Caro saying nothing.

Caro linking his arm through Ruan's in solidarity as they went back towards the hotel at a considerably slower pace than they'd left it. Caro hoping Ruan wasn't going to sink into that all too familiar mire and morass for, when that happened, it was damned hard to pull him out. Caro rehearsing in his mind what he assumed was running through Ruan's. First and foremost he would be thinking of Greta. Secondly – it always happened like this - would be the image of his old home in Scotland. He didn't talk about it often and, when he did, it was with the utmost regret. He would be thinking of his departure from that house, his fingers twitching – as they were now – as he remembered how they'd fixed planks over every window before they'd left, bolted every door, kept the house tight and tidy to await a return that never came. Ruan recalling the awful guilt of how eager he'd been to depart, how he'd cursed the house without a backward glance; how Ruan had regarded it back then as a decrepit useless old man in the sticks, the grey waters of Loch Eck hemming it in on one side, wild moors at each remaining point of the compass. And he'd be fearing for that old man house, how it had fared with the battering of successive storms and shrieking Winter winds, the clinkerbells and shockles of ice that would have stoppered up gutters, eked below tiles, sagged the eaves with their freezing and thawing. He'd be imagining the planks against the windows thinned and worn, bolts raddled and rusted, snow-bones lying on the moors, on the edges of the loch. He'd be seeing the house as an isolated widower collapsing on the banks of the water with no one to care for it, the thousands of books inside it rotting away word by word, line by line, page by page.

'Maybe it's time,' Caro said quietly. 'Time to let go the house.'

Wise old man talking.

Ruan thinking he was right.

Ruan looking up at the hedges as they passed them by. Hedges emptied and refilled every seven or so years to keep them to their true and rightful purpose, whereas he had allowed the house of the shores of Lock Eck to rot. A day of decisions.

Time to put what was left of the old house onto the sale-books and be done with it.

Had sworn he'd not return without Greta by his side. The chances of that happening slim as a blade of grass lost amongst the many. Grief back in him that he'd let Greta go, hadn't joined her, hadn't believed in her, had let her swerve on along her dangerous path alone.

Unable to forgive himself, then or now.

'You're right,' Ruan sighed.

Years, Caro had been waiting to hear this agreement; and years he'd been practicing what to say when it came. Caro adding a caveat to his oft repeated exhortation.

'You've to promise me one thing,' Caro said, squeezing Ruan's arm within his own. 'Before you sell old man house,' Caro said, 'we've to make one last foray, find out about Greta, what happened to her.'

Heart aching for Ruan, to witness the small tear trickling from the corner of Ruan's eye as he recognized the time had truly come.

# 6

## Places, and People, Apart

GRETA TOOK IN A BREATH. Let it out on one single word.

'Who?' she asked.

Joachim supplying the answer.

Greta closing her eyes, shaking her head.

'You're wrong. It can't be. He's dead, I'm sure of it.'

'Apparently that was the plan,' Joachim spoke softly, distressed by Greta's distress, but no time for niceties. Time to take her to this latest Irish exile to come to the Servants' doors, who was sat in the refectory awaiting news. A man as dark and bleak as a storm cloud, who'd looked the same since he was a nipper and grown into a man without grace, elegance or humour. Had a face flat and wide, as if he'd been struck with an anvil, carrying an expression of perpetual wariness as if expecting that same anvil to strike again at every turn. And struck he'd been, many times, by fists and pikes, blasts from exploding English shells, if not by anvils. Living through more battles than anyone had a right to survive. Clinging on when almost every other leader of the United Irish had been captured, imprisoned, executed.

Which made it all the more odd how nervous this ex-leader was to meet Greta Finnerty after all this time. Back in the day he'd known her passably well: her flitting between Irish encampments up and down country, passing on strategic information, gathering evidence of what was really going on, getting it to her cousin Peter and his printing press in Dublin - the only antidote to the lies manufactured up by the Loyalists, spewed out in their own broadsheets to discourage further resistance. Not that Mick had read any of them. No call for book learning where he came from, nor for his parents before him.

Not many folk living through those years still believing in the cause, still willing to rise up and fight the fight. Mick only lately learning Greta had been one of those few, going back to Ireland a few months after the disaster of Vinegar Hill, trying to start it all up again, do her running once more between the few pockets of rebellion that remained. A man not given to introspection, wouldn't have known what the word meant if it was shouted in his face, yet realized here was the seed of his anxiety: that he'd stayed hidden, allowed everyone to believe he was dead, removed his way from Irish soil, while the likes of Greta had carried on.

Mick back on Walcheren to right those wrongs; thank the people, the nation, the Servants, who'd got him away first time around. Repay the favour, gain favour in return. He twiddled his fingers. Picked up the empty cup, put it to his lips for the fourth or fifth time. Put it down again. Looked nervously towards the refectory door, scratched his beard. Heard the commotion of feet fast approaching, saw the flinging back of the door. Saw Greta Finnerty in mud-clarted trousers and jerkin, clipped red hair alight with Winter sun making her look like the avenging angel he'd been dreading. Mick Malloy getting to his feet as Greta strode towards him, Joachim tripping on her heels. Joachim aghast when Greta held up her hand and gave the hardest-looking man he'd ever met a smart blow across the face with all the strength she could muster.

'Glad to see you too,' said Mick, taking the blow, rubbing his bristly cheek with the back of his hand.

'How could you?' Greta exclaimed, holding her ground, pointing tingling fingers at him in accusation. 'How could you let us think you were dead?'

'Let's all sit down,' Joachim tried.

Greta ignoring him.

'How could you? Mick?' Greta asked again. 'Don't you know what it did to us?'

Mick unable to look Greta in the eye. So difficult to explain how tired he'd got after so many years of plotting and fighting had all gone to shite.

'How could you give up on us, after everything we did?' Greta twisting in the knife.

'I'm not sure that's quite fair...' Joachim began, cut off by Greta, green eyes glinting.

'And what would you know about it? Were you there?'

'Well, no,' Joachim started.

'Well no,' Greta went on for him. 'But I was, an' I saw what was left afterwards. Stuck around, tried to get folk planning and fighting back. And I know folk were hanged, that them English didn't have a morsel of pity in 'em. But Jesus, Mick. You were the only one could've got everyone back together, and instead you scarpered like a filthy rat down a vennel.'

Words meant to sting, meant to shame.

'Why didn't you stay, try to save us?'

Mick shook his head.

'Guess I'd had enough of saving people,' sounding like he'd a ball of thistles in his throat. 'And of killing them,' he added, 'and of fighting.'

'Still fighting now, if not for your own people.' Greta couldn't help it, could not forgive his betrayal.

'Aye, well,' Mick said. 'Kinda different when you're just one of the troops, following instead of leading. What the beggeration else was I s'posed to do, Greta? It was finished.'

Greta thinking on that, realizing he was right. And she'd deserted too, once it was clear the Uprising was as dead as Mick would have been if he'd stayed. Black kettles, black pots.

She sat down, asked her last question. Belligerence dissipated.

'Where did you go?'

'Here,' Mick answered simply. 'To the Servants. And from here to Hamburg.' Mick sitting too as he tried to explain. 'Lots of rebels going the same way, and a load of us in that city for a good few years. Tried to get another rebellion going from there...but. Well. English put pressure on the authorities, got a load of us put in prison, including Napper Tandy and Corbett. After that, the French Irish Legion didn't seem so bad a way to go.'

'So you didn't give up entirely,' Greta stated, wondering how she could have doubted him. Mick a man as solid as a tree bole and as unbending. Mick seeing her belief in him rekindling, straightening his shoulders, knotting his fingers together on his thighs.

'I did not,' he said; small stab of guilt at the lie for, in truth, after Hamburg, he had given up, came to the belief that the only way to hound the English out of Ireland was to have the French do it for them. They'd never cared for Irish freedom. Valued the Uprising only because, had it succeeded, Ireland would have been a convenient jumping-off point for a French attack on English soil. Tremors travelling through him to see Greta believed his lie, believed in him, believed him to be a better man than he was. Tips of his ears reddening as she smiled up at him.

Joachim immensely relieved the two appeared to have reached a truce.

'We've something to ask of you, Greta,' Joachim stated. 'I'd been trying to think of a way to get you here, and now, thank the Lord, here you are. We need your help, like I said before. But I'll warn you, it isn't going to be easy.'

RUAN WAS DEPOSITED without argument by Caro in the cellar of the spa hotel while Caro went off to find out about the Dieters.

Ruan, on the way there, thinking on that conversation with Mathilde and Holger. A detail popping into his head regarding the Battle of Copenhagen in 1801.

*There was silence deep as death, as the oldest held their breath.*

A line from a poem in a book he'd stumbled across years ago describing that same battle, words staying packed tight inside his head, unspooled in Greta's voice whenever he thought of them. Words woven through with the desolation of her own battles and comrades lost. The page worn thin at the edge, so often had he thumbed it. As was another, once he'd moved on from that opening poem, skimmed the contents, caught the title *Exile of Erin*.

Read those verses repeatedly.

*Erin, my country, sad and forsaken,*
*In my dreams I visit your sea-beaten shores.*
*But alas, in a far foreign land I awaken,*
*Sighing for friends who can meet me no more.*

The book a constant companion ever since. Its poetry a refuge in which Ruan sank on dark nights, able to recite every word of the preface to that last poem.

*While tarrying at Hamburg I made acquaintance with some of the refugee Irishmen concerned in the rebellion of 1798. Amongst these was Anthony McCann, an honest, excellent man who commanded respect whether he was rich – as he was then - or poor, as he is now. It was in consequence of meeting him one evening on the banks of the Elbe, lonely and pensive at the thoughts of his situation, that I wrote this poem,* Exile of Erin.

Might have been writing of Greta.

Greta likely having known Anthony McCann, as she knew so many of the main players in Ireland, most dead by now; the lucky few – like McCann – achieving exile.

The author of that poem one Thomas Campbell, son of a Glasgow tobacco merchant bankrupted by the American Wars of Independence, by the tariffs thereafter imposed; a poet who'd railed against the iniquities of the slave trade, the partitioning of Poland, the consequences of the French Revolution.

Thomas Campbell, who'd left Scotland hoping for adventure exactly as Ruan had done. Campbell going to Germany, to Regensburg, arriving three days before the French stampeded in and took over, Thomas lucky to find refuge in a nearby Scottish monastery.

Thomas going from there to Hamburg where he met his Irish exiles, maybe even met Greta - for who knew where she'd ended up.

If she was still alive.

If she'd not died sighing for friends no longer to be met, including Ruan - if Ruan had by then still been considered a friend.

Joachim coming to mind, as they neared the spa hotel.

Memory of sitting with him by St Drostan's Well, calm green polders going down to the sea; the brimskud haze rising up from the waves as they broke upon the sand.

Joachim saying the sea always calmed him because the sea, unlike men, could never be swayed by even the strongest will; took its commands from sun, moon and wind, unless God chose to take a hand in it which, as far as Joachim knew, he'd never had need to do.

The parting of the Red Sea coming into the conversation.

Joachim dismissing it.

*It wasn't a sea of water. Sea of Suph, in Hebrew, meaning reeds. Red because of the colour of the sedge. Don't dismiss me because I'm a Servant, Ruan. I don't need miracles to believe what I believe.*

Joachim so certain, so sure.

*Walcheren, my perfect place,* Joachim had said. *And you can find the same, if only you choose to look.*

But no place for Ruan perfect without Greta in it.

Ruan's longing so intense he stumbled, couldn't get his breath.

Caro helping him back up.

Caro always helping him back up.

Ruan taking a deep breath.

*That's the last time,* he told himself. *The very last time Caro has to do this.*

*I will not be weak, I will be strong.*

*I will not cause Caro to have the constant worry of trying to save me from myself.*

*I will banish all thoughts of Greta until this is done, until we set off to find her.*

*I will become like Joachim sitting by the sea, choose to see the world as he sees it.*

*Ever changing, under no one's control.*

Joachim's last words that morning before Ruan left Walcheren for the last time:

*Men can't change the sea, Ruan, but men can change men. Think on that as you go into the world.*

Men can change men. As can women.

Time to take action, be the man she had chided and deserted him for not being.

He would get back to Deventer, involve himself in partisan rebellion, if it existed.

He'd never concerned himself with politics, had willfully blinded himself to battle news shouted about in the broadsheets. Only one he could clearly remember, because of Thomas Campbell, which was the second vicious Battle of Copenhagen, the newly emergent Danish fleet hammered below the water by the English as before.

One strange fact, one strange name, stored up in his head because of its oddity: that this second Copenhagen victory - or defeat - of 1807, designed specifically to prevent the Danish obediently adopting Napoleon's Continental System, had also prompted the English to commandeer a mazy Danish outpost in the form of an island barely eight miles wide, stranded forty miles off-shore.

Heligoland: nothing about it but storm-stirred seas, and another tiny island. The quietened strait between the two providing safe haven for vessels up to twelve feet draught.

An astonishing place, a place apart.

A place that should not exist.

A place that had to be the flattened apex of an enormous mountain whose masse sank right down to the bottom of the North Sea and into its bed.

They had boggled him, those few facts, and beguiled him. Had jotted them down in the margin right next to Campbell's verses on the first attack on Copenhagen that weren't by any means complimentary to the English. Thomas Campbell a Scot, as was Ruan; despising English claims on their land, viewed by their inhabitants as their own place apart. Separated from their enemies by eighty odd miles of shaky, shifting borderlands, if not by forty miles of sea.

*Silence deep as death, as the oldest held their breath.*

A sentiment undoubtedly shared by the islanders of Heligoland when the English fleet dropped anchor off their homeland. HMS Majestic at its fore, seventy-four canons and guns trained on their town, and the Majestic only one of many.

*Heligoland: this a place I want to go.*

Ruan's pencil jotting out his small desire on the blank expanse at the edge of Thomas Campbell's printed words.

*This a place I mean to see.*

A desire entirely forgotten until now.

Until Caro had made him promise that before he sold old man house on Loch Eck he would at the very least find out if Greta was alive or dead.

# 7

## Conundrums At Every Quarter

JOACHIM RIGHT. IT WAS not going to be easy. Taking Mick Malloy up country, seeing as she had a grasp of the language as Mick did not, no simple task. Would mean breaking through both French and English lines in and around Walcheren. Obvious plan of action being to take a boat from Walcheren over the Schelde to the mainland and all would be solved. A plan neither Mick nor Joachim approved of.

'I don't get where the urgency is,' Greta therefore said. 'Where's the threat? Why all the secrecy?'

Joachim and Mick exchanging glances. Joachim the one to answer.

'Have you ever heard of the Continental System?' he asked.

Greta thinking, coming up empty.

'It's Napoleon's ban against trading with the English,' Joachim explained. 'And for us, for the Low Countries, it will mean disaster. It means breaking all ties of banking, agriculture, textiles, pottery. Even the mail between us and England will be stopped dead in its tracks.'

'Doesn't sound good,' Greta commented, not really understanding.

'It isn't,' Joachim agreed. 'We're a bit isolated here on Walcheren, but we do get the odd trade ship arriving from England, as do all the ports up and down the country. And if that's stopped? If it's banned? It's going to hurt a lot of people, ordinary people; take away their livelihoods both sides of the channel.'

'Getting to sound worse and worse,' Greta said.

'We have King Lodewijk on side,' explained Joachim. 'For the past few years he's absolutely refused to adopt the System, knows what it would do to us if imposed. But he's weak. Won't go into outright conflict with his brother and is about to leave us belly up, ready for the gutting.'

Greta frowned.

'You've lost me,' she said. 'Why would this Lodewijk be feared of his own brother?'

Unaware that history was strewn through with fratricides, matricides, patricides, sororicides, where power bases were concerned. And Lodewijk's brother more concerned with power than most.

'Because Lodewijk is Louis,' Mick weighed in, 'youngest brother of Napoleon.'

Greta seeing the light. She'd once thought Napoleon the greatest of the great, a man come from nowhere to challenge the indolence of kings, create republics where all men and women would be equal; where no one would be left to starve on the streets, considered of less worth than the buttons they crafted from ivory and bone for the clothes of the rich. An idolatry stripped away and replaced by the hatred the betrayed have for the betrayer as she'd come to realise how little Napoleon cared for anyone but himself and his newly Imperialized family.

Peter had railed on about it often enough, how Napoleon had divvied out Europe to his own: *Here's the crown of Naples! Here's the crown of Spain! Sisters, nieces, nephews, here are marriages that will make you the greatest leaders of the land!*

So much for equality. Napoleon proving himself as bad as the English when it came down to it. The downtrodden still downtrodden, the rich still as rich as they'd ever been, if not more so. A miracle any of them – meaning Lodewijk/ Louis, King of Holland – had held out against him for so long.

'So where do we fit in?' she asked. 'Surely if it's done then it's done.'

Joachim withdrew his hands from the table, held them over his chest as if in prayer.

'Because it's not done. Not yet. A slim chance we can avert this implementation if we get word to Apeldoorn. There's a man there knows Mr. Malloy, a man tied in with the Duke of Brunswick. His little army from Silesia and Bohemia were beaten back by French troops, got as far as Bremen and from there to England. And they're there now, waiting for a reason to come back.'

'You mean us to consort with the English?' Greta blurted out, hot blood suffusing her cheeks, blotting out her myriad freckles.

'You don't understand, Greta,' Mick broke in. 'If we can get them back we can...'

'We can do bloody nothing!' Greta was having none of it. 'I'll not be an informer or a collaborator, not ever!'

Joachim lowered his hands, leaned across the table.

'Not even to save the Servants? To save me and mine?'

All the while Joachim had been talking he'd been finding it peculiar to be in the position of maybe saving a nation, but there were more personal issues involved.

'The French Revolutionaries have no love of religion,' he said sadly. 'And Napoleon may no longer be of the Revolution but he's adopted some of their values. The moment the English leave Walcheren the French will come in from Antwerp. And where better to barrack up than here? Won't trouble them a second to chuck us all out on our heels, and the malaria won't touch them in the Winter.'

Greta took pause, for the Servants were dear to her.

'Did you know the Pope excommunicated Napoleon not long back?' Mick sprinkled on the salt. 'And in return he had the Pope arrested and imprisoned?'

Greta didn't know, and was shocked. Saw Joachim flicker a brief smile.

'He won't yield,' he said. 'Has refused to consecrate the bishops Napoleon wants to put in place.'

Greta having to rethink her position, rethink this entire situation.

'What's to do with this Brunswick fellow?' she asked. 'If you can get word to him?'

Mick seeing his in and getting it said.

'Then we can get his soldiers back over the water from England. Get him to hold the Hollandish ports, take the seat of government at Apeldoorn before the French arrive in droves.' Mick cleared his throat. 'And in return all we'll ask is that they help the Servants, give them somewhere protected to go. We owe them, Greta. Without them hardly any of our exiles would have survived, including me.'

*And me,* thought Greta.

'But giving information to the English?' she asked, rubbing her hands together. 'It don't seem right.'

'Maybe not for you, my dear,' Joachim put in, 'but very right for us: for the Servants, for Holland, for the Low Countries as a whole. We're at war, Greta. This whole country is on the edge of an abyss and we're about to fall in.'

Greta shook her head, but couldn't stop a smile as she looked over first at Joachim before fixing her gaze on Mick.

'Jeez, man. You don't change. Always one for battle plans and strategies. Guessing this one's all yours and that you're kinda missing them.'

Guessing right and understanding, for she missed them herself.

Mick straightening his back, galvanized. Greta on side.

'So what's the plan from here on in?' Greta asked, plain and simple. 'Got to assume you got one, else we wouldn't all be sat here about this table.'

Mick smiling grimly inside his beard, Brother Joachim breathing out his relief for yes, they had a plan, although it was all a bit risky and without Greta they wouldn't stand a chance.

'It's the third strand gives strength to the cable,' Joachim toting out the old Dutch proverb, 'and our third strand is you. But we also need the second, so here's what we need you to do.'

CARO RETURNED WITH the address of the firm of Dieters Accountancy who oversaw the financial runnings of the spa, surprised to find Ruan pacing the floor, eager to be gone. Ruan's new resolve pushing his steps fast across the flags now he had direction. Wanted this Bad Salzbaum job done with, wanted to get on with all he had decided must take place instead. He said nothing to Caro, although Caro – as always – divined Ruan's changing mood and kept up beside him as they gained the steps, without need for interrogation.

They reached the edge of the spa's grounds and moved into the streets of Bad Salzbaum, soon got directions to Dieters. Met there by a stern and no-nonsense woman in her thirties, hair swept back, so tightly bound it pulled her forehead into immobility. A woman as small, neat and precise as the handwriting in her ledgers, her lines of numbers ordered as a General would, in a perfect world, choose to keep his troops.

'Summer, 1802,' she said, in answer to Ruan's questions. 'Grounds-work: Holger Stoss. Hedge removal and relaying...'

She licked a finger, turned a page, cast a quick smile at Ruan who flickered one back, uncertain what that smile meant.

'Well here it is, and no mistake,' she said. 'Fabian Guichot, a prisoner of war, worked with Herr Stoss for two days and two days only, pulled from the excavations for the new mill-workings when Holger's previous assistant was no longer able to assist.'

'Mill-workings?' Ruan asked, scratching his ear that had gone a little hot as Frau Dieter flashed that smile at him again. Such certainty in it, and so like Greta's. This woman in a world very likely undervaluing her as it had undervalued Greta. Ruan pushing down thoughts of Greta. A vow taken, and one he meant to stick to. No thoughts of her until all this was done, when he would seek her out with more urgency than he had sought out any book.

Frau Dieter happily filling in the blanks.

'A project I managed to inveigle out of our mayor, who was new back then. And the mill-workings quite magnificent – modelled on the Roman ones at Barbegal near Arles. Basically a long aqueduct leading from more of our area's natural springs to a chain of mills going down the side of the hill outside town.'

She stood, took Ruan to a window, pointed out the workings running dark through the snow; two arms of the aqueduct settled high in the hills leading to a single chute from which water sped and jostled into a mill race rushing from high to low; ten blocked buildings equally spaced on its downward fling: ten water-wheels spinning splash-white with the water's momentum.

'Capable of producing two tons of flour a day, at full capacity,' Frau Dieter informed Ruan with evident pride. 'The water powering conical basalt millstones of ninety centimeters in diameter, to use the new French system of measuring, and the water never fully freezing, even in the worst of Winters, because of the salts in it. Provides flour for the town all year round.'

'Impressive,' Ruan said as Frau Dieter returned to her seat, Ruan going with her.

'It is,' she agreed, 'and all done within budget I'm glad to say, seeing as I oversaw the finances, with most of the investment coming from Napoleon himself.' A quick preen of her hair, a touch to straighten her collar. 'You won't know it, but Napoleon came to visit in 1805 to see the outcome, along with his brother. And very charming men they were. Complimented me on my book-keeping.'

Ruan, given his new found interest in politics, so surprised he bit his tongue. The most he knew of Napoleon, although knew nothing of the brother, coming from Greta who'd regarded the man as a hero of the free world, a great leader and practically a saint. And sitting across the table from him was a woman who'd consorted with the man himself. Another addition to the storehouse he kept partitioned in his head of all the things he'd tell Greta if he ever met her again. A storehouse, he reminded himself, needing to be boarded up and locked down like about-to-be-sold old-man house rotting on the shores of Loch Eck, for the while at least.

'It was because of Napoleon,' Frau Dieter went on, 'that we dressed the hedge early that year. Our mayor – who, like I said, was newly appointed back then – decided that because of Napoleon's interest in our project our yearly hiring fair should be shifted to the first Sunday after the fifteenth of

August which is, of course, the Emperor's birthday. And he wanted a spectacle to mark it, and Hedge Dressing is always a spectacle.'

'Because of the bonfire,' Caro chimed in.

'Exactly, my young sir. Because the bonfire always comes with the emptying and relaying of the hedges, and with it the drawing in of people from far and wide.'

'And this Guichot fellow?' Ruan asked. 'Is he still around?'

Frau Dieter looked at him like a buzzard zeroing in on a mouse it was about to skewer.

'He might or he might not,' she was evasive. 'Either way, why would you need to know?'

An odd reaction to a straightforward question, one both Ruan and Caro picked up on. Their reaction to her evasion not lost on Frau Dieter.

'There's something you're not telling me,' Frau Dieter stated.

Ruan not wrong to compare her to Greta. Frau Dieter as much an anomaly to what was normal for females as was Greta. Frau Dieter plain Elise back in the day, the only girl of a brood of ten, who'd singled out where her parents' farming strategies had been going wrong, offering solutions that doubled their profits within three years of implementation. Elise thereby shoved on in school, earning a scholarship to a better one where she excelled in mathematics, logic and philosophy. After which she was denied access to any further education. *No women here,* said the universities, *and not about to start now.*

All Frau Dieter's doing that she'd sought out and married Herr Dieter who – thank her lucky stars – had died not long after their marriage, bequeathed her his business. Herr Dieter enlightened, believing in his wife, knowing her worth and acting upon it. The aqueduct for the mills all Frau Dieter's scheme, with the help of the Prussians' ex-prisoner Fabian Guichot. And Frau Dieter not about to give Fabian up until she understood the circumstances surrounding these questions being lobbed at her by people she didn't know.

'Who are you anyway?' she added to her previous question. 'You said Professor Jorn sent you. Is that the case? For if not, then I will ask you both to vacate the premises immediately.'

Ruan suppressing a smile as Frau Dieter sat ramrod straight in her chair, shoulders squared, long neck stretched to give height to her chin, eyes intense and boring right into him.

'He did and he didn't,' Ruan her equal when it came to being evasive. 'Have you heard what was found in the hedges when they were unpacked?'

Not a movement from Frau Dieter, the merest flicker of interest in her marl-hard eyes.

'I have not,' she replied. 'But if there was anything amiss with the last hedge-laying then it is Herr Stoss you should be talking to, not the man who was a mere assistant for a couple of days, and a newcomer at that.'

Ruan raised his eyebrows. Her defence of some paltry prisoner odd, to say the least.

'They found a body,' Caro put in, 'in the lower courses. 'Dead as dead can be. Professor Jorn doesn't care a fig about him, but we do.'

Frau Dieter's gaze shifting from Ruan to his companion with the slightest twist of her head upon her slender neck.

'And you are whom? You've been singularly lax in introducing yourselves to any informative degree, and I'll not say another word until you do so.'

Aware she was being obstructive, logic dictating she be exactly that until she understood what was really going on here. She'd fought long and hard to keep the Dieter name of high standing in this town, which had not been easy. Every project, every accounting partner, every single job in which she had a hand, needing to be seen by the outside world as being ultimately managed not by her but by someone more substantial. No one in this blinkered town yet prepared for a manager to be other than a man, and certainly not the peacock-fancy who was Professor Jorn. And she had need of the spa contract, needed to step carefully.

Unaware that Ruan perfectly caught the cause of her concern.

Ruan coming clean.

'We're Finders of Missing Books, Frau Dieter. Sought out by Professor Jorn because the dead man in the hedge was in possession of a crateful of them. And although he has employed us solely to investigate the books, in case any are of value, it seems to us he is entirely overlooking the larger question. Namely how both the man and his books came to be in the hedge in the first place, when and why. Which is, it has to be said, a conundrum.'

Frau Dieter unbending, leaning forward in her chair, for she was a woman who loved conundrums and was good at solving them. Back in her studying days she'd been presented with Sun Tzu's third century Classic Problem: *We've a pile of oranges but we don't know how many oranges we have. We do know that if we count them by threes we get a remainder of two; if we count by fives we get a remainder of three; if we count by sevens we have two again left over. So how many oranges do we have?*

Elise having the answer long before anyone else in the class, which is twenty-three. Elise understanding intuitively the key lay in totaling the three divisors, using successive multiplications and subtractions to reach the correct result.

'Well now,' she said, 'that is intriguing. And Professor Jorn knows nothing of this little side-line you're venturing into?'

'Nothing,' Ruan said. 'And if it's all the same to you, Frau Dieter, we'd prefer to keep it that way.'

# 8

## Behemoths and Toads

FABIAN GUICHOT HAULED the Word Board into place and secured it.

*Wallow in the Warmth of our Mineralization Mud-baths: Efficacious in the Treatment of Rheumatism, Arthritis, Gout, Skin Sores and Psoriasis, amongst many other Common Ailments too numerous to mention.*

The mud-baths Frau Dieter's latest project, built on the edge of the grounds of the spa with Professor Jorn's blessing – as long as he got a cut of the profits - and about to be opened to the paying public. Fabian as proud of the mud-baths' construction as he was of the mills, his own blessings reserved for one person and one person only: for Frau Dieter.

Fabian deposited in Bad Salzbaum as a prisoner of a war he'd wanted no part in; drafted into a labour-force abandoned by the Prussians when they decided they'd better things to be doing. Fabian set to digging out the first ditches in the hills for the mills; Fabian not slow to see how ineptly the foreman was directing the diggings: all at wrong depths and wrong angles. Fabian witnessing Frau Dieter once or twice having heated arguments with the man, shaking her imperious head upon her slender neck. Took a while to figure out she was ultimately in charge and not her incompetent foreman, took a chance when next she'd visited. Approached her, spoke to her in his back-then shaky German about his concerns; Frau Dieter astonishing him by replying in the faultless French of his native tongue. Frau Dieter astonishing him over and over since that day. Frau Dieter dismissing the foreman on the spot, replacing him with Fabian. The two spending many days together planning how the mill-workings should really go, and now the mud-baths too.

He'd never met a woman like her.

She a fresh Spring breeze blowing away the darkness of Winter.

Always felt a little shaky and dizzy when she was near, and she was near now: grey silk skirts skimming across the grass, skirts soon trailing in the mud – not that she cared. Another reason to prize her, for she'd never minded getting skirts or hands dirty, pitching in whenever she was needed, wearing workmen's gloves far too large as she held a piling post steady while he hauled up a sledgehammer and brought it down with the strength of an ox. Always feeling stronger when she was around, feeling a need to prove her belief in him right.

Had a swift panic all was not ready.

Thought through his tasks, if he'd directed them rightly done.

Two days since she'd been to check on things, trusting it all to him. A trust treasured and not to be squandered. The pilings deep and solid, as were the frameworks above; the channels that would contain the mud tidily tiled along base and sides, as were the walkways between. At his suggestion the entire area had been enclosed, ceiling and walls plastered so the whole resembled a luxurious Roman abode. The steam engine that would heat the spring-water, warm and dilute the mud, primed and ready, sited at just such a distance so its noise would not disturb the visitors.

Everything as planned.

Everything ready and fit for purpose.

Only two additions had Fabian made that he'd not yet told Frau Dieter of.

Ideas he'd harboured, secretly engineered and installed after the other labourers had gone to their beds.

Fabian working by candlelight in the enclosed emporium.

Fabian having goosebumps at the thought - the hope - these additions would delight, evoke one of her rare unguarded smiles that had Fabian humming like a hive of bees.

And now here she was, two unknown companions in tow. Frau Dieter quickening her pace as she neared. Fabian opening the door to the enclosure and in she came. And there the smile he'd been longing for as she looked about her and gasped.

'Oh my! But would you look at this!'

Pivoting on her heels as she took in all the frescos Fabian had spent many nights painting, ignoring her visitors as she went rapturously from one to another. 'Here's Narcissus gazing into his pool, and John the Baptist on the banks of the Jordan, and there's the Four Rivers of Paradise...and this one...what's this one?'

She moved forward, read out the scrolled legend beneath.

'Moses striking the rock to produce the water of Meribah. Oh Fabian, this is breathtaking. I'd no idea you could paint. Why did you never say?'

Frau Dieter placing her hands upon her breast, heart beating too fast within. Engineer and artist. Lights under bushels. Wondering what else there was to find.

'There's one more,' Ruan said, as impressed as she. Ruan lifting his head, pointing upwards.

'The naiads,' she murmured.

'The Maidens of the Rheingold, I think,' Ruan corrected pedantically. 'And that one in the middle looks uncommonly like...' he creased his brows, arched his head further back on his neck, Caro getting in first.

'It's you, Frau Dieter!'

Fabian closing his eyes, face as hot as if he'd shoved it into a scalding-pan. He'd not thought anyone would notice, least of all Frau Dieter. Dizzy and shaky all over again until Frau Dieter spoke, and not in her usual clipped businesslike tones but soft as blown seed-wisps from rosebay on late Summer days.

'I don't know what to say. It's...it's...'

*Say it's nothing,* Fabian wanted to get out, *a nonsense. An appreciation of everything you've done for me.* No words coming. Fabian acutely thankful when one of the strangers took over.

'It's magnificent, is what it is,' said Ruan, 'and to make the whole look like a Roman mansion is a stroke of genius. You undoubtedly get a load of folk visiting your aqueduct, and now you'll get those same folk here too.'

Frau Dieter frowned, gave a quick glance at Fabian who shook his head, as perplexed as she. Caro laughing lightly.

'I've always said the cleverest people can be the dimmest,' he said.

'He has,' Ruan agreed, 'most often of me.'

'You've one Roman installation in the aqueduct and now you've another,' Caro explicated. 'Folk who come to one will naturally go see the other. Hope you're charging people to look around the mills.'

Frau Dieter had not, although would have guides in place by the morning and an entry booth and, when Fabian had the time, a huge introduction board.

She couldn't figure how she'd never thought of something so obvious before.

'Forget the blessed bonfire,' she said. 'This opening is going to be magnificent, and all because of you.'

Fabian Guichot almost felled by the merriment in Frau Dieter's grey-green eyes.

Fabian wondering if he had the nerve to tell to her of the other secret addition he, engineer, artist and ardent admirer, had planned.

FORCED DEPARTURE FROM the refectory came when
a couple of monks arrived to prepare for evening repast.
Conspirators heading into an afternoon on the cusp of
night, rounding hummocks of red-gold clouds luminous in
the west, crepuscular canopy darkening above their heads.
Shadows deepening between the inlets and geos of
Walcheren's short cliffs, waves thrumming, softly booming
against rocks shining like mirrors, wet with spray.

Greta glad for it.

Glad for the sand-blow and sea-froth quivering across
the bay, for the dry and twitchy wind blowing little pluffs
of dust before subsiding. Long time since she'd experienced
anything so soul-refreshing. Five months cooped up on
Walcheren in filth and scurr, sentries on guard to stop
anyone wandering, sentries lax now they knew they were
soon for the off. Lax enough to allow her out to visit the
Servants and be graced by this glimpse of the wider world
going on in disregard of camps and warring men. Unnerved
when a huge flock of geese took sudden flight at their
approach, heard Joachim's whispered words behind her.

*Behold the land, shadowed by whirring wings.*

Geese whiffling up, white tail-bars like fans, circling
thickly before moving noisily off to the other side of the
peninsula where they would settle again, tuck themselves in
for the night.

Approaching St Drostan's Well she thought back over
the last of their conversation at the Refectory. She'd assumed
it would be a simple matter to leave Walcheren by boat. Told
unequivocally it would not be so. English lookouts along the
Eastern Schelde specifically to stop such escapades. Fearful

of spies infiltrating, or informers getting out. French patrolling the Western Schelde, fearful of the same. Only way out, therefore, being to punch through English lines and broach the skinny neck of Walcheren, then bypass the French. No wonder Joachim had said it would be dangerous. She'd chewed her lip as she'd thought about it, offered an alternative. Suggested they stay hidden at the Servants until the English decamped then take that initial boat she'd mooted; knocked back once more, informed that the second the English departed the French would come flooding down the isthmus and bar every point of escape.

Hazardous seemed too generous a word.

Success resting on furtiveness and secrecy, scampering through unknown territory during the dark fist of night. Skills previously honed in Ireland, Greta hoping they'd not been entirely lost during her indolent, ennui-filled London years.

The three of them reaching the Well, sitting on the small seats provided. Joachim taking up the cup lying at the end of the wooden pipe looping the water into the small spring pool and scooping it full, offering it to Greta who took it, put it to her lips and drank. A blessing to find it fresh and cool, the opposite of the rancid bilge slopped up to them in the camp.

Mick too took his draught as did Joachim and then, as the wind stuttered about them and the waves beat on and the evening darkened and the camp lights winked alive a way down the coast, they restarted their ruminations.

'There's something we've not yet told you,' Joachim began, Mick ostentatiously clearing his throat, getting ready for the axe to fall. Everything so far hammered out between himself, Joachim and the Abbott. Greta no part of their earlier plans. They knew she was here for she'd written to Joachim, but her getting out of the camp had been impossible until now, until the English realized their only option was retreat. Her appearance heaven-sent, making what had previously seemed the slimmest of slim chances an actuality instead of a possibility. Ruan not the only one to write letters. Peter knowing all about the Servants and their links to the Irish Legion. Peter feeding them what facts he could from the start. The Servants his back-up plan, keeper of all his reports in case he was silenced on his return – or never returned at all - giving specific names and places to send those reports to if he succumbed to the fever, or was gagged and imprisoned once the true nature of his broadcasts was learned. One name coming up in his latest report that made Mick's chances of success in Apeldoorn a hundred-fold more likely if, by some miracle, they could get that certain person of interest on side. And, now they had Greta, that hundred-fold increase might be in reach.

'There's someone else we need to take with us, if we can,' Mick said, into the mellowing afternoon.

'One of the Irish Legion?' Greta was excited. 'Anyone I know?'

Malloy coughed.

'No, Greta. Not one of us at all. Young bloke called Ivor Merrill.'

Greta narrowed her eyes, pushing at a nearby stone with her foot.

'Sounds suspiciously English,' she said, 'and...vaguely familiar...'

Kicking that stone into the pool. Memory of a blond young man in ragged uniform sneaking furtively from their tent as she'd approached. Peter's cautious words as he'd departed.

*Thank you, Ivor. I'm sure I don't need to tell you not to say a word to anyone you've been here.*

She'd thought nothing of it at the time. Peter doing his usual poking and prying, gleaning sources wherever he could.

Malloy pulling uncomfortably at his collar.

'He might well be familiar,' he said. 'He's one of the English officers, high up and high born. But he's a conscience for all that. Doesn't like what's been done on Walcheren. Has spoken to your Peter about it.'

'And high born is exactly right,' Joachim put in quickly. 'He's family links to the Duke of Brunswick we talked about earlier. And please don't dismiss this, Greta,' seeing the twitch of her shoulders, the set of her mouth. Collaboration with the English never her favourite pastime. 'If we can get him on his way with you and Mick it would mean the difference between... well. To put it bluntly: if we get him, we get the ear of the high up folk in Apeldoorn. If you get there. And we all know that's a big if. And we're both aware what we're asking of you. If it's too much, then tell us. We'll understand.'

Greta picked up the cup, took another scoopful of St Drostan's water. The whole plan beginning to seem mad and undoable. Even if she and Mick managed out of Walcheren, got to Apeldoorn, who the hell was going to listen to a couple of stragglers like them? They'd not even get past the gates. Mick might have some lowly contact there, but how on earth Mick thought he could have done it all by himself was beyond her. Her turning up at the Servants the merest coincidence.

All chance and circumstance.

Which was Mick all over.

Always a bugger for taking risks and damn the consequences.

Having Greta with him would certainly ease his passage; having an English toff with them would really tip the cards in their favour. Biggest problem being how they could get this Ivor fellow to agree to their slapdash scheme. Greta couldn't see how that would go. How they could present it as a viable reason for him to desert, because that's what it would mean for him. And no one liked a deserter. Bullet to the head the swiftest resolution to that particular crime, no matter whose side you were on. Far more likely being this Ivor going to his superiors the moment he caught wind of what they were about, get Mick charged with war crimes against the English – for either Ireland or the Irish Legion, take your pick – her cast as co-conspirator.

No difficulty seeing how that scenario would end: swift and very public trial to maximize their wickedness, the two condemned and executed. Probably the very same day Ivor Merrill got his new and shiny medal pinned to his new and shiny upgraded uniform for his heroic acts to the motherland.

Greta clicking her tongue as Joachim trotted out the argument he and Mick had come up with in their defence.

'He's been speaking very recently to Peter,' Joachim said. 'The only officer prepared to kick up a stink about the entire campaign here on Walcheren, how badly planned it was. How bad has been the outcome.'

Brief admiration for the man; Greta spending her days filtering through the lower ranks, getting their life stories: how they'd come to be here, what and whom they'd left behind. Everyone critical of the conduct of this campaign, yet never once had a single member of the officer class spoken out against it, and never once had they admitted her into their circle. For one of them to go sneaking off to Peter therefore implied a person of mettle.

'There's no way he's going to go for it,' she said. 'What could he possibly gain by coming in with me and Mick? And how could we spirit him away?'

Although - right as she said those last words - she could see one solution.

One more slimmest of slim chances dependent entirely on the man himself, what he was made of. And to find that out she needed to return to camp, sound him out by ear, put to him a possible pathway that would lead not to disaster and desertion but to glory, the possible saving of the Servants and of Holland itself.

Big thoughts.

Big problems.

Possible resolutions.

'I need to speak to him,' she said. 'We can't do anything until I've done that. Can you trust me on this?'

Mick and Joachim had no choice, and so they said.

'Either way,' Greta concluded, 'with him or without, me and Mick leave Walcheren before the English decamp. We're going to need a missive from the Abbott. Something we can take with us to Apeldoorn that might get us through the gates if neither Mick, nor this Ivor, can do it for us.'

Thoughts tumbling through Greta's head like acrobats across the boards. Needing to get those acrobats in order.

Slim chances.

Big returns if they paid off.

And how she'd missed all this: the fight, the furore, the never knowing if you were going to live or die with the turn of the next card, the next walk around a corner, the next door you knocked upon to ask for help.

Life-blood to her and those like her. Folk like Mick.

Greta looking towards the polders, last of the light almost gone. Just enough to see a solitary black-tailed godwit digging into the sand with its spear of a beak, a bird choosing to stay on Walcheren for the Winter instead of heading south. Just enough light for Greta to see herself in that lone bird, staying on in a foreign country after all its more level-headed brethren had rightly fled.

PROFESSOR JORN TOOK a few minutes to spruce himself up, studying his figure in the vast mirror he'd installed across the wall of the landing of the hotel's main staircase: a shimmering pool of silver reflecting a secret world of green sculptured topiary laid out like chess pieces leading to the spa's famous maze. He flicked a handkerchief over his shoulders to remove some tiny specks of dandruff, brushed the nap on his hat before replacing it on his head, straightened his cravat.

*All in all, not too bad.*

Not a handsome man, noteworthy by his stature and neatly tailored clothing. Face a tad long and rectangular, an impression he'd tried to soften with carefully coiffured sideburns and the merest whiff of a beard. Satisfied, he descended the last of the staircase, strode from the ornate glass doors at the hotel's entrance and out through the topiary garden, checked the outer and inner walls of the maze were clipped neat and tidy – which they were.

Professor Jorn having a jab of excitement at the night to come: his first hedge-dressing, needed it to be a spectacle of the first order, given the profligate amount of money he'd spent advertising the event. His breath catching in his throat as he turned from the maze towards the hedges and saw a black behemoth rising behind them from the shadows of the afternoon. Took a couple of seconds of quick breathing to realise what it was; couldn't comprehend how it could be so huge and intimidating: an ogre of expertly piled blackthorn bales built up from the grass, grazing past the height of the hedges and twice as broad as the two of them put together.

The bonfire.

Not so much excitement now as trepidation.

Hoping to God Holger Stoss knew what he was doing, for once this giant was given life it was anyone's guess how it would go if it got out of hand. One strong gust of wind and the hedges would be done for, and maybe the hotel not far behind. Holger Stoss himself emerging from behind the ogrous pile, face worn and worried, which worried Professor Jorn the more.

'All going well?' Jorn asked, a huge lump growing in his throat to realise how much he was asking of this man who was, now he looked at him closely, perilously old and a little vacant about the eyes. Cursing himself for not looking further into the previous hedge-dressings, blithely assuming it had been done before without incident and would therefore be done again the same under his own command. Away studying in France when the very first dressing had been made into a public spectacle and gone so spectacularly wrong. Same reason Holger's brow and mouth were puckered for it was all he could think about, could still taste the aftermath of it on his tongue. He might not be able to recall what he'd had for breakfast but there was nothing about that night he would ever forget: the wind hie-ing up over the hills from the west without warning; his master – Holger an apprentice back then – yelling *Get back, you all! Get back! Holger! Turn on the pumps! Open the sluice gate! Get in the hoses!* Holger's knees cracking as he ran, shoulders almost pulled out of their sockets as he got the hoses into the lett and dragged their other ends back again, spraying water into the heart of the bonfire to extinguish it. Not in time to prevent a shower of sparks falling onto nearby stalls setting several of their awnings alight, and set up one man too: the sparks catching his hair, the back of his woollen coat, as he fought to pack up his gear instead of legging it as the others had done. A man who had lit up like a human torch and began skittling and wailing, screaming through the crowds, setting several women alight - skirts catching and burning up to their waists and then to their skin.

It had been a massacre.

Five people horribly burned and one man dead, and only Holger's hoses to thank there hadn't been more.

Holger unable to shake the terror of that night, nor the stink as he'd turned his hose upon the man writhing, kicking and charring a few yards from his feet. Still heard the horrid whistling coming from the man's lips even as those lips were sizzled right off his face. And the women. God, the women.

The dreams he'd had, the nightmares, coming on strong every hedge-dressing since.

No one to know about it except Mathilde who'd stay awake those nights, ready with cold compresses soaked in lavender oil to soothe him; Mathilde watching Holger's eyes, his face, trying to divine when he was seeing it all again, jolting him awake, holding him to her as he shook and wept. Worst for Holger was never learning the dead man's name. No one seeming to know. Just another itinerant who'd set up shop hoping to rake in the wally on this greatest of Bad Salzbaum's days.

'He must have had a family,' he'd greet, Mathilde cradling him in her arms. 'And they'll never know, Mathilde. They'll never know.'

He and Mathilde the only people at the graveside of the unknown man who'd burned to death in Bad Salzbaum when what little remained of him was shovelled into the earth.

No chance of that happening these days.

Holger already having commanded the stall-holders to pull themselves back, pitch themselves at more of a distance.

'Dunno why,' one grumbled, about to hammer in his rope-stays. 'Closer to the crowds, more money we're going to make.'

'Just get it done,' Holger said, in no mood to prevaricate. 'If you ain't back past the line you'll no be here at all.'

Stall-holders obeying, albeit grudgingly.

Holger stepping away. Holger turning to see Professor Jorn bearing down on him.

'All going well?' the Professor asked.

Holger looking, Holger calculating, Holger not yet lost.

'All well,' he said. 'Got everyone at a good distance.'

Holger having that ghastly oily taste in his mouth again, and the urgent need to spit.

Professor Jorn regarding the behemoth of the bonfire.

'Sure you know what you're doing, Holger?'

Holger pinching the nape of his nose with his fingers, swallowing the mucous gathering at the back of his throat.

'I do,' he got out. 'No need to worry, Professor. All will go as planned.'

Bonfire staved and supported, blackthorn bales laid as precisely as they had previously been in the hedges. Apex narrowed so it would quickly burn away, the rest designed to fall in upon itself as it went. Hoses in the lett, pumps at the ready – just in case.

'And lads are putting up the stage now.'

'Excellent!' Jorn commented, the stage being an addition of his own from where himself and the mayor could make their speeches, sit in splendour.

Hedge-dressing a great to-do in Bad Salzbaum, four celebrations strong. Disaster of the first one forgotten for the sake of the spa which was what brought folk to their doors, and all the money those folk brought with them. This year no different. Every last man jack who made their living from the spa soon to congregate in a noisy crowd along with all the other visitors.

Holger couldn't bring himself to ask Professor Jorn about the man found in the hedge, although it snagged at Holger's heart. Couldn't bear to bury another corpse who had no name. Tried to drum up the courage to ask, but Professor Jorn was already on the move, heading for the stage, shouting at the boys to shift one chair here, another there. Professor Jorn running through his speech in his head. No space for anything else.

Holger left behind to worry, harbour dark thoughts as the edge of the night fell upon the last of the afternoon and the shadow from the hedges crept towards him across the grass, the great black menace of the bonfire an enormous toad squatting at his back.

# 9

## Mills, Mud And Men

RUAN WAS TOTTING UP various dates and times in his head, needing to get them straight.

On the way to the mud-baths Frau Dieter had volunteered several details of the mills' construction.

'I had the idea of it a good while back,' she'd said. 'My husband generous enough to allow me to pursue it. We started up the workings when the POWs arrived with the Prussians. All going well, until my husband died and all the financial avenues we'd explored collapsed. Except, as luck would have it, the following month - January 1802 - Napoleon's brother Louis got married.'

Ruan failing to see the relevance.

'He was rather sickly, was Louis,' Frau Dieter confided. 'Prone to epileptic fits. Sought out every spa in the environs in hope of a cure. And of course by then Napoleon had Flanders and Holland in his sights, declared them the Kingdom of Batavia.'

Ruan once again regretting his active blindness to what had been going on in Europe.

'And us being right on the border between Germany and Holland seemed a good fit to our new mayor. No one more a Francophile than he, and a great friend of my husband. So we cooked up a plan.'

Ruan lost. Frau Dieter lighting his way.

'We had the idea of providing the perfect wedding gift for Louis and his new bride by inviting them here. To Bad Salzbaum.'

Ruan suspecting it had been Frau Dieter's idea.

'He'd never been before, and couldn't resist. First encounter he'd had with salt hedges, and apparently found them of some efficacy because that's when his brother - Napoleon himself - offered us the financing for the mills.'

1802 an auspicious year for Frau Dieter and Bad Salzbaum.

Napoleon declaring himself Consul for Life of his self-forged Empire on August $2^{nd}$ that same year.

August also Napoleon's birth month.

Hedge-dressing therefore shifted to late Summer in honour of Napoleon and his financing. August 1802 therefore had to be when the man had got into the new hedge and remained there.

Dates, times, explanations, milling around in Ruan's head seeking connections.

Ruan lining up his questions once the tour of the mud-baths was at its end, Frau Dieter choosing to formally introduce Ruan to the man those questions would be aimed at.

'This is Fabian Guichot,' she said. 'My colleague and my friend.'

So Fabian no mere POW, and no wonder Frau Dieter had not been keen to throw him to the first wolf of Winter to come along.

Fabian so flabbergasted he dropped his hat, looked like his heart might implode with shock.

'It's the truth, Fabian,' Frau Dieter added. 'I know it would do us detriment to say so in certain circles, but these two gentlemen are not in those circles and I'm glad at last to say it out loud.'

Fabian retrieving his hat, straightening slowly, trying to compose himself.

'They need to know about the hedge-dressing you took part in years back,' she went on, 'when you helped Holger Stoss. Was there anything unusual you recall?'

'I don't think so,' he got out. 'Then again I only did it the once so wouldn't know if it was usual or not.'

He'd an odd way of speaking, Ruan noted, no doubt due to the cleft palate he'd been born with - given the scar going from upper lip to nose taking some of that upper lip with it.

'Did you stop at any time?' Ruan asked.

'Well yes and no,' Fabian answered, getting back on an even track. 'Which means no, not after I got there.'

Casting back through his memory, throwing a spinner into the still water of it, dragging it home.

'There was something,' he said, air leaking from soft palate into nose, worsened by his stress, giving a slight slur to his speech, rubbing away the hard edges of his consonants. 'Never thought on it till now.'

'Which was what?' Frau Dieter prompted.

'Well we were only partway through the workings for the mills on the hillside,' he explained, 'and back then our accommodations were a little, well, they weren't too good. Prisoners of War and all that.'

Fabian glancing at Frau Dieter, who knew all about it; outraged to see how the men had been bivouacked, forced to sleep in the ditches they'd spent their days digging; no proper sanitation, no cover if it rained. Her first stamp of authority on that first incompetent foreman being to have the men build themselves proper quarters before any more work was carried out. The vitriol that man had spewed when she'd challenged him vile and unforgettable.

*They're little more than animals! They're cannon fodder. The most of them are fucking French, godammit, excuse my language, and nobody anybody is going to miss.*

Excuse him she had not, not then, not since. A great joy when Fabian spoke up to her about how wrong things were going so she could finally chuck that pig of a foreman out on his ear, let it be known his replacement would be one of those animals, that cannon fodder, who someone must have missed because she would miss this Fabian Guichot if he ever left her. Colour rising in her cheeks to realise that maybe there was someone back in his homeland wondering where he was, how he was doing, why he'd never returned. Maybe children sitting about a chilling fire because their papa had gone missing and they'd not enough food on their plates.

'Holger came up to the workings to fetch me,' Fabian continued his narrative. 'Or not exactly me. Just anyone who had experience with salt hedges or anything like. And I was the only one who did. Worked at St Armand's spa in Flanders in my early days, although it wasn't so grand as this.'

Telling Ruan how they'd refilled one hedge and the first courses of the second that afternoon and half the evening, for it was light enough; how proud he'd been at doing more than expected, Holger hurrying to catch up the previous day lost. Holger not a talker, except to explain how things were to be done; Holger tipping his hat at him when they'd finished for the night, invited him in to eat with him and Mathilde, telling him he could sleep in the work shed instead of tramping all the way back to the mill-workings so they could start all the earlier the next day. How his shoulders had ached with the hoiking and packing, how quickly he'd gone to sleep after such a long day's work. And also how early he'd woken, maybe an hour or so before dawn, had gone outside for a pee and heard a kind of gurgling, like a disgruntled frog or the night herons back in the marshes outside St Armand.

Woken, pissed, heard, and gone back to sleep for the last hour before Holger came tapping at his door.

The relevance of that sound only now apparent.

'There was something,' Fabian said, chewing his lower lip, 'although don't know if it means anything.'

Animation amongst his companions as he gave his tidbit of news, mulling it over, pointing out the possibilities.

'So could have been when he got into the hedge, the one that hadn't yet been filled. Maybe he'd been in there a few hours when Fabian heard him, but by then couldn't get himself out,' said the younger lad.

'You said several courses had been laid in that second hedge?' the older asked. Fabian nodding. 'And how loose are they when they first go in?'

Fabian chewing at his lip again, seeing where this was going.

'Packed pretty tight, to stop too much subsidence once the ones above are laid,' he explained. 'Although not so tight a determined man couldn't lift up a bale and get in, although mighty scratchy it would have been.'

Ruan shaking his head.

'Even if he did get in, how is it possible no one saw him? Or notice the bales had bulged with him burrowing beneath one or another? And not just him but his crate? It seems incredible, but what could be the alternative?'

Frau Dieter stepping in with a question offering possible solution.

'How many bales are laid for the width of a hedge?' she asked Fabian, finding herself fascinated by the mechanics of the hedge-filling as she'd never been before.

'Five, laid lengthwise side by side,' Fabian answered. 'Any larger would make the bundles too difficult to manipulate.'

'And so it's possible,' Frau Dieter got in, before Ruan or Caro had the chance to speak, 'that he squirrelled himself in between those inner bales of the second hedge the night after the first had been filled. Only a few layers laid. Got himself in, got himself hidden, pulled the bales about him...'

Fabian thought, Fabian construed, Fabian running back through his memories of filling that second hedge. How he'd woken once again when Holger fetched him from the work-shed; how they hadn't tarried, got themselves straight to work and straight up top the hedges because there was no time to lose. No need to inspect the lower bales of that second hedge, for Holger had already done so the previous evening. Straightaway up top sending in the next layers, pushing them down hard as they could.

Skin prickling at the implication, the faintest echo of the suffering a man must have gone through with all those sharp thorns sticking into skin, scalp and body as more bundles came down upon him, tamped ruthlessly into place by the squared metal plates welded to poles wielded by the men – by himself and Holger - up top.

*It had to have been agony.*

An agony surely no man could have endured without crying out, if he'd been able.

*Except that if he had,* Fabian thought, Fabian said, *we'd not have heard him. We were thirty foot up, or else were barrowing bales back from the blackthorn copse, trip after trip.* Until Holger stated they had enough, by which time the concealed man must have suffered a death excruciating and unstoppable. Would have bled to death or suffocated, or both.

'It's unthinkable,' Fabian whispered. Unbearable to believe he'd been there on the spot, could have averted such torture and tragedy if only he'd had the wit to interpret better what he'd heard on that pre-dawn evacuation of his bladder. 'What would make a man do that?' he added.

The others looking at Fabian, understanding. Someone dying under his watch, despite that watch not being entirely his. Not understanding – as Fabian did - how those bales were not so peaceful and neat as bundled straw, were spiky jagged enemies manipulated by hooks and heavy tampers that could give you no way out, not once you'd got in.

And someone had got in.

Fabian saw it clear as day.

First hedge filled right to the top, to the gunwales.

Second hedge only several courses up.

Someone so desperate they'd seen no other way to go and had hauled themselves over the first few courses, burrowed into the centre, maybe dragged the blackthorn about him to make himself invisible. Someone who'd willingly subjected himself to the saws and harrows of the salt hedge, which must mean the alternative he'd been hiding from was dire indeed.

'Did anyone go missing at that time, from the mill-workings for example?' Ruan ploughed on regardless.

Fabian shaking himself, trying to concentrate on anything other than the man in the hedge. A trickier question than Ruan understood, for men back then had gone missing all the time. POWs no longer under the supervision of their Prussian captors, yet neither were they free; effectively indentured to the Bad Salzbaum authorities who'd volunteered to keep them fed and sheltered in exchange for their labour. A bad bargain, but no alternative: no money nor means for them to get back home, given they weren't paid actual wages. And for most no idea where home was, relative to where they'd ended up.

Bound to Bad Salzbaum tight as staves about a barrel, hammered into a hard life that at least gave them food and a place to sleep, and companionship. Many wanting nor needing anything more, nor any better than they would get elsewhere. Others desperate to return to family and homeland; a few political agitators keen to rejoin the French, carry on the expansion of the Empire. Absconders leaving under cover of night, usually performing small acts of burglary in the town to help them on their way. The drip-dripping of a tap tainting those who stayed with a bad reputation that further hemmed them in, made their shifting into normal town life impossible, portrayed them as untrustworthy thieving foreigners who thought about no one but themselves.

A reputation not entirely erased even once mills and aqueduct were completed and the ex-POWs were farmed out as day labourers to anyone who would take them. Several reckoned of worth enough to be taken on permanently, a few marrying into one family or another, yet still now – years later – the majority returning at night to those same quarters Frau Dieter had caused to be built in the hills, which to them was the best home they were ever going to get.

Outsiders to a man, and no one but their immediate pals to miss them if and when they went. And not a one of them in possession of a crate of books, that much Fabian was certain of, for he was one of those still in that home-of-sorts in the hills where no one's business was hidden, everyone's doings the gossip of everyone else. The odd book making the rounds here or there amongst those who could read – and most could not – Fabian himself in possession of the most. His paltry shelf of volumes hardly able to line the bottom of a crate, let alone fill it up.

Fabian explaining all this in his stuttering, soft-whistled words and, once he'd got through it and everyone understood the problem, he posed two simple questions of his own.

'Can I see him?' he asked, given the faintest possibility he might recognize the man. 'And can you show me where he was found?'

Eminently reasonable questions Ruan could not dismiss. Ruan leading the posse away from the mud-baths, past the hedges – pointing out the relevant place where the body had been discovered. All skirting the enormous bonfire, taking stock of those old bundles covered in precipitate, some with spines extant, sharpened and honed, turned to stone. All seeing too Professor Jorn fussing and fittling on his stage, directing this seat to go here and that one there, how the lectern should be placed.

All of them thinking him unforgivably callous for not giving a cuss about the man who, in Fabian's earlier words, had found himself in such dreadful circumstance his only option had been to burrow his way into a prison of spine and spite, and stayed there until the world collapsed in on him, Holger and Fabian tamping down their new bundles, burying him alive.

# 10

# Let's All Join The Puppet Theatre!

'WHAT D'YOU RECKON?' Greta was asking Peter. 'Will he go for it?'

Peter listening as Greta spilled out her proposition, his face a shifting panorama of amusement, overtaken by alarm and concern as she got to the nub.

'This is Mick Malloy we're talking about? *The* Mick Malloy?' Peter knowing the man's past actions during the Uprising, his reputation for taking wild bets with his men's lives that most would consider insane.

'Same exact,' Greta supplied happily, unaware of Peter's misgivings.

'He's dangerous,' Peter said slowly. 'Are you sure you can trust him?'

'Trust him with my life and this Ivor's too, come to that.'

Greta puzzled by Peter's prevarications. Obviously helping the English went against the grain, and he'd no connection to the Servants or Holland like she had, but he had to see the upside: in the long run perhaps the Dutch, unlike the French, proving a better ally to Ireland when they rose up to fight another day.

Peter shook his head.

'There's huge risks involved,' he said, looking at Greta. 'What's going to happen if you're caught? Have you even thought on that?'

'It never stopped you,' Greta said simply, Peter having to admit as much. He and Greta animals of similar stripe in that regard. And she wasn't a child anymore, had earned the right to make her own decisions.

'I'll get Ivor Merrill here soon as,' Peter sighed. 'Although he's going to take some convincing.'

'Thought about that already,' Greta said.

'Of course you have,' Peter replied, a smile coming unbidden to his lips. 'So come on my lass, spill it out.'

And so Greta did. Greta ending with confidence, Greta well used to weighing people up quick and accurate when it was essential you knew who was on side and who was not. And she'd lay good odds this Ivor would be enough on side - given all that Peter had just told her about his past - to at least not betray them, even if he didn't join them. Floppy blond hair never a plus in her experience, but she'd tailed him all day as he'd stalked the camp, seen how he'd swallowed his rage and disgust, burying it deep and turbid where it would twist and turn in his guts like a mole running through its holes, waiting to dig its way to the surface.

'I think he'll go for it. I'll break all his fingers if he don't,' she added happily. 'Although I suspect it'll only take the one.'

GOD, THE STINK OF THE Surgeon's tent was appalling, more disturbing the undercurrent of groans rising and falling as you passed it by: a dreary monotone punctuated unpredictably by out of kilter wails and screams sending the hairs on the back of your neck to swift attention. Everyone avoiding it if they could, crossing themselves bleakly if they could not, holding hands against mouths and noses to avoid contagion. No one trusting the Servant's statement that it was mosquitoes which passed on the sickness. Fear of it their constant companion, far more than any skirmish with the French. Ivor Merrill no exception, going near now only because it was on his route to Peter Finnerty's tent, both on the outskirts of the encampment.

He'd not seen much action; first engagement being the Battle of Corunna back in January that had forced the English to evacuate Spain with their tails between their legs. A defeat that rankled, particularly as Ivor hadn't been with Wellesley on their comeback when Oporto had been taken, spearheading the campaign back into the North West. Ivor not there because three fingers had been blown off his left hand at Corunna, Ivor retreating with the rest of the wounded. An option given him because he'd connections to the top, an option he'd taken, too callow, too horrified by his first taste of battle, his first battle wounds, to refuse.

An option regretted ever since.

The looks the men under his command had given him as he'd prepared for departure never leaving him: narrow-eyed suspicion, outright animosity; worst of all the few who'd regarded him with compassion. Could still feel the slap on the back one had given him: *Get yerseln out whilst the going's good, lad. No one'll hold it agin you.* Which of course they had. He'd been a coward. He'd abandoned his men. He might have lost three fingers, but many of his own had lost far worse - half a leg here, an arm wrenched uncleanly from its socket, one man with the bottom part of his jaw shot clean off so all you could see was a bloody hole going from the base of his chin to his top mandible where a few teeth – unnervingly - yet remained. Most of the wounded dying vilely, chucked overboard before they got to Portsmouth.

Not so Ivor Merrill, who'd shame leaking out of him ever since, who'd wriggle those three missing fingers every day to remind himself he'd betrayed his men; those three missing fingers a part of him even if they were gone, feeling them move and itch and touch, had pain in them when the weather was damp, could feel the creaking of their invisible joints, the snagging of their fingernails when he scratched the lice bites on his skin. The Walcheren Campaign was to have been his redemption, given him the chance to lead his men to victory. Instead it had all been a mis-planned mess, and now here he was in the midst of yet another retreating army. Ivor bitter and angry, swearing, as he put his boot down and the mud ploutered and threatened to keep it there.

"God-damn!' he muttered, pulling his boot free from the slurping stinking slurry. Stink in his nostrils ever since he'd been in this god dammed place, stink in his heart – if that was possible, although he truly felt it was.

'Need a hand to get on?'

Ivor looking up to see a red-headed recruit standing in his path, humiliated to have been spotted in such ignominy.

'Got two of the blasted things already, so no.'

Voice gruff as he waggled his hands in exasperation to demonstrate the fact.

'Looks like you'll no be going into puppet theatre real soon,' commented his interlocutor. Ivor taking a deep breath, about to turn tail and head off in another direction, until he focused in on the person speaking to him. No recruit this, red-headed or otherwise, but Peter's cousin. He'd seen her once or twice when he'd been leaving Peter's tent, and knew all about her tending the men on Walcheren on Peter's behalf, getting their stories down whether they were sick or no, in fact caring especially if they were sick or dying, sitting at their sides as if she didn't care if she caught the ague. And now he was really riled up, because she represented everything he was not: brave, empathetic, unafraid in the face of danger.

'And what the blazes would you know about puppet theatres?'

A weak riposte. Ivor concentrating on wiping his boot on the grass to free it from clag and clart. Greta watching him, weighing him up, seeing the boiling inside him as if he were a pot of water on the stove.

'Only that I hear there's real good ones further up country,' she replied mildly. 'Going there myself. Could maybe take you with, if you're willing to take a chance.'

Ivor pulling himself back, looking at the girl – or young woman, as she clearly was on further inspection.

'Puppet theatres?' was all Ivor could muster. 'What the hell are you on about?'

Greta looking pointedly at his hand, at the thumb and little finger and the ravaged stump between.

Ivor outraged, and then obscurely amused as he got the joke; Ivor feeling the quiver of hysterical laughter in his throat, for she had it exactly right. No job waiting in puppet theatres for him. Ivor wondering what sort of person could see his injury in such a jovial light. Ivor bedeviled to realise this obscure woman was of so much more worth than him that she made him want to scream and, more than that, made him want to be like her. Wanted to exceed her, needing to exceed her, if he was to count himself of value to be alive.

Such is what war does to a man: forces him to measure himself against his fellow soldiers. Not that Greta was a fellow solider exactly, although Ivor convinced – once he'd entered Peter's tent and she'd laid out her proposition - that she'd been a braver soldier in her war than he had been in his. And by Christ that irked him, stirred him up in soul and mind so much that once the feelers had been put out and Greta and Peter deemed it time to lay out the plan in its entirety before him like a game of knucklebones, he'd not cared about anything except besting her.

Ivor immediately agreeing, saying *yes* when the obvious commonsense answer had to be the opposite. Ivor positing one slight change to the plan.

'Why don't we just go to the Army Commander, get it all explained? He could give us passage...'

Drying up as he saw the looks on both Greta's and Peter's faces.

'Well, he could,' Ivor said lamely. 'Why wouldn't he? This is a mission to aid our fight against the French.'

Peter the first to respond.

'You really think your Earl of Chatham, the man responsible for this entirely catastrophic campaign in Walcheren, would sanction one of his own officers, namely you, to go gallivanting off with an escaped Prisoner of War who was supposedly under his purview?' Peter began, then hammered home the nail. 'And an Irish Prisoner of War at that? You do know Chatham's the brother of your blasted ex-Prime Minister William Pitt who forced unification with Ireland nine years back, and all the backlash that entailed?'

Ivor blenched. So much so true. William Pitt – the youngest Prime Minister England had ever had – dying three years back, sickly as he'd always been. A man Ivor had met but never envied; who'd done his duty as well as he could and yet exited this world alone, friendless, and in debt. Younger brother of the man leading this failed campaign in Walcheren, and God only knew how Chatham would apportion the blame to come out of this latest debacle.

'You're right,' he agreed in hindsight. 'John would never go for it.'

Missing the eye-rolling from Greta as Ivor unwittingly allied himself with the upper-classes, the elite, by his familial use of the name. No Earl of Chatham for Ivor, merely John. A man he obviously knew better than most.

Missing a whole lot more, until it was spelled out to him.

'The point being,' Peter explained, 'is that we're going to need subterfuge.'

'And what Peter means by that,' Greta chipped in, 'is that we need you dead.'

# 11

## Jack-in-the-Box

THE CELLAR COOL AND dark, the entire length and breadth of the hotel up above.

Cavernous, struck through with the pilings keeping the building upstanding. No other divisions. Emptiness yawning away into gloom: shadows of wine barrels hunched like goblins; racks of wine, glass necks glinting in the pinches of light coming from their lanterns; long thin shelves holding pickled vegetables, syruped fruits, jams and chutneys; alarming hooks bearing down from the ceiling with sausage-strings whose skins blossomed with faintly luminescent mould; sides of cured and salted meats split down rib and sternum, halved heads grimacing with extant teeth although the tongues – thankfully - had been removed for potting; salamis set to slow motion by the breeze stealing in behind them before they closed the door.

The man from the hedge curled on his bed of straw not dissimilar to those haunches. Dehydrated flesh coated and infiltrated by the minerals Professor Jorn had drawled on about, explications briefly reiterated for these new visitors so they understood what they were looking at.

'What do you think?' Ruan asked, as he ushered Fabian and Frau Dieter towards the body. 'Do you recognize him?'

Fabian finding it hard to breathe. He'd never seen the like: a man calcified in stone, yet no statue this. Only a couple of centimeters of precipitate hiding his features which ran into one another liked warmed wax.

Frau Dieter not so circumspect. Frau Dieter leaning in, peering at the calcified face, putting out a hand to touch it.

'It's rather beautiful, in its way,' she said, 'and yet horrifying, all at the same time.' Lifting off her hand. 'There's really a human being inside all this?'

'There really is,' Ruan replied. 'So you see why we're perplexed. Do you recognize him?'

Frau Dieter making it her business to know all her POWs, although no earthly reason this should be one of them.

'I don't,' she said. 'Then again, how could anyone?'

Fabian took a breath, embravened by Frau Dieter, and moved closer, put out his own hand, ran it across the man's brow and down his cheek, repelled by the clammy hardness beneath his fingers yet having the need to feel it for himself.

'What about you, Fabian?' Ruan asked, noting how quiet the man had become, how troubled his expression, how Fabian had at first abjured the touch and then gone into it with the tenderness normally reserved for a parent to a child.

'I'm not sure,' Fabian said. 'I'm really not sure.'

The thought in his head nonetheless: *it could be Constantine. It kind of looks like Constantine.*

Fabian choking, dashing through his memories like a sled down a snow-slide of when Constantine had been with them, of when Constantine had left. Constantine their youngest conscript, a boy really, and such a happy one, such joy in him every day and so conscientious at his work. A favourite of Fabian's. Constantine, who'd talked non-stop about how happy he was he'd ended up in Bad Salzbaum, how blessed to have Fabian and Frau Dieter looking out for him. Constantine, who'd carved a rudimentary nativity scene from left-over wood for the camp the first Christmas they were there; Constantine also fashioning three amulets: one for himself, one for Fabian and another for Frau Dieter, earnestly explaining the two circles surrounded by twelve stars he'd carved into his little roundels of wood.

*It's the sun and the moon, which means Jacob and his wife and their twelve children, the twelve tribes of Israel. The sun also being you, Frau Dieter, and Fabian the moon, and us POWs all the stars you've gathered around you.*

Frau Dieter had found it a touching gesture, symbolic of her care for the POWs – although they'd numbered far more than twelve.

Fabian, by contrast, blushing and stuttering out his thanks, finding the implication of Frau Dieter being his wife unbecoming and embarrassing, especially considering Jacob's twelve progeny. Fabian reluctant to enlighten Constantine, tell him they'd not been born of one wife but four - the latter two hardly more than bed-meets, servants given to Jacob when the first two could no longer reproduce.

It had made Fabian consider the boy in a new light, and how young he was: far too young to be in any war, so young he needed to seek out mother and father figures in this new situation he'd found himself.

Fabian's toes curling in his boots in this cold cellar looking on what might or might not be Constantine because, Good Lord, he'd actually allowed himself – however briefly – to consider himself and Frau Dieter as sun and moon: his Jacob to her Leah-Rachel-Bilhah-Zilpah, all rolled into one. Frau Dieter the equal of four, eight, ten thousand women, as far as he was concerned. His amulet kept in his pocket ever since, becoming smoother, more rounded, surface polished like a pebble in a stream.

'Fabian?' Frau Dieter asked. 'You've an idea. Who do you think this is?'

Fabian remembering the night Constantine had disappeared along with several older POWs. A young lad like Constantine an asset: nimble fingers, small lithe body, quick to get into buildings or store-houses and out again without being noticed, unlike his lumbering companions. Frau Dieter and Fabian conversing about his disappearance at the time, both certain he would not have departed under his own steam, but nothing – literally nothing – they could do about it. No way to track the escapees or bring them back and, even if they had, they'd have been ear-marked as deserters – Constantine included - and flung into jail. Fabian wondering about the boy occasionally, if he'd ever got back home, although it seemed unlikely. Constantine one more notch on the tally-stick of history whose story would never be fully known.

Fabian shifting from foot to foot.

'He always wore it,' he said, swallowing hard. 'At least before he left.'

Hand drifting from the hedge-man's chin to his neck, to his chest.

'Wore what?' Ruan asked. 'What did he wear?'

Halted by Frau Dieter taking a sharp gasp of air.

'I won't believe it,' she whispered. 'It can't be him. Not Constantine. Oh God, Fabian, please tell me it's not him.'

But Fabian could not.

Fabian's fingers coming to rest on the small bulge rising like an understated hillock by the dead man's breastbone, a hillock shifted slightly to one side so it overrode where his heart must once have beaten, where his dead heart still must be.

Fabian fumbling in his pocket for his own worn medallion, laying it on the straw.

'Like this,' he said. 'One just like this.'

FROM ONE DEAD BODY to another.

Ivor contemplating his own imminent demise. Ivor shaking his head slowly, trying to find a flaw. Ivor finding several, Greta countering them all.

'Gist is then,' he said, 'I fall sick.'

The others nodding.

'Very sick, very quick,' Greta agreed, 'so Peter whisks you off to the Servants 'cos it wouldn't do at all to have the likes of Mr. Ivor Big Fellow stuffed into the surgeons' tent with all the other muck.'

Quick sour grin at that, knowing both she and Peter would be considered muck, probably so mucky even the surgeons' tent was too good for the likes of them.

'And then the Abbott tells the English, via Joachim,' Peter went on, 'that poor Ivor's kicked the bucket, carried off like all the rest. And the English'll be in a such a flurry for decamping they'll be begging Joachim on hand and knee to bury him right.'

'By which time,' Greta put in the punchline, 'we three'll be off and yonder.'

Mick Malloy twisting his lips beneath his beard, chuckling in admiration. This the first time he'd heard this particular part of the plan.

'God, lass, you've still got it. That you have.'

Not given to humour, but damn, it felt good to be doing what he did best, energized right down to his boots.

Ivor not so eager. Hating to be the damp squib, but needing to get it said.

'What if someone wants to come pay their last respects, or visit me when I'm sick? Or take my body home?'

'Pah!' Greta was right back at him. 'It's the timing. We do it right when your lot are about to leave. High up or no, once you've the lurgie you're as contagious as anyone and no one will want to be holed up with you on a ship. Only sane thing to do being to put you in quarantine, stuff you away in the Servants.'

Ivor chewed his bottom lip. He didn't like to admit it but Greta had it right. High up or no, and he was higher up than most, there wasn't a single person he could think of who would bother enough to come visit, or feel the need to bring his contagious body back with them on their retreat. Least of all Earl John blasted Chatham, who hadn't wanted Ivor with him on Walcheren in the first place. Ivor besmirched by the Spanish campaign and his utter cowardice that was still muttered about in the ranks and gave all the higher-ups a bad name, reinforcing the general feeling of Them and Us that did nobody any good. Ivor never a popular officer in Corunna – a wet-behind-the-ears greenback who'd not earned his stripes.

Not then, nor here on Walcheren.

Now maybe Ivor's chance to prove the lot of them wrong.

THEY CRACKED OPEN THE hedge-man.

They started with his chest.

They set to with chisels and hammers borrowed from Piet and Holger.

They uncovered first the amulet – Fabian proved right, for there it was: dormant, encased, extant. No doubt about it. Frau Dieter closing her eyes, for she couldn't understand how it could have come about that Constantine – lost from herself and Fabian in the Winter of 1801, not long after Christmas – had ended up eight months later trapped in the hedge-laying of August 1802, fleeing for his life with a box of books coming from who knew where, a box of books he'd apparently deemed valuable enough to protect with everything he'd got. Her husband dying not long before, yet Constantine's loss she'd grieved for more.

It made no sense, no sense at all.

And it hurt her heart to imagine how terrible must have been his dying.

Young Constantine: bright light, bright soul, brought to this.

She'd always known he'd never have left unless coerced, and it seemed imperative now she remember who must have coerced him, who else had gone missing at the same time. She'd made note of it then, and needed to consult those notes.

Couldn't bear to look on this scene anymore, couldn't bear to see these two strangers cracking Constantine open like an over boiled egg.

'I need to go,' she said, the dark-haired man not reacting, concentrating on where the next chisel point should be put, the next hammer blow taken. The younger lad smiling up at her, making her stomach heave because oh Lord he was so like Constantine. Not in looks, not at all, but in that brightness, that open optimism, that face that said *I've got all my life to live, and thank you for looking out for me.*

'Thank you for all your help, Frau Dieter,' said Caro, as if he'd read her thoughts, as if he was pushing a scalpel through her guts.

'Fabian, will you come with me?' she asked, clutching up a lamp from the hay bales and then setting it down again as Ruan drew his brows together at the shifting of the light.

Fabian also keen to get away. Fabian cupping Frau Dieter's elbow with his hand because she looked so pale and shaky, so unlike he'd ever seen her before.

Frau Dieter gladdened by his touch, emboldened by his nearness. Frau Dieter getting out a last few words before they left.

'We've records,' she said, 'of who deserted and when. And we know precisely the day when Constantine...' she swallowed, couldn't go on, rubbed a hand to her forehead, put her fingers to the cool silk of her dress, wished that like Fabian she'd kept Constantine's amulet with her instead of placing it in the box of her other Christmas doo-das to be brought out only once a year. And had brought it out every year since. Merely another bauble to hang on a tree while she fussed over the candles as the plum pudding steamed in its basin. Tree and pudding to be enjoyed by no one but herself. Another regret she added to all the rest. So much she'd done, so much achieved; Christmas and plum pudding shared with the camp inmates that first Christmas when Constantine had been with them because he was a boy, a youngster who'd reveled in it. Not shared with anyone since.

*It may not be him. It cannot be him.*

Words repeated over and over in her head, and next on her lips as she and Fabian retreated from the cellar.

'It may not be him. It cannot be him,' she whispered, her skirts dragging, catching on a crack in the step. She tugged at her dress impatiently, tearing the hem, sending a small rivulet up the shimmering material.

Not that she cared.

# 12

## Wine And Worries

PETER POURED THE WINE Greta had brought back from the Abbey. Good stuff, unlike the dregs folk like him and the men in the ranks were routinely doled out. Minded of the strange fact Ivor had offered him during their first meeting: William IV, stadholder of Holland, going into battle against the Bishop of Utrecht armed with 176 pounds of sweetmeats, exclusively for personal use. No thought of those under his command, and not much changed since. Peter, pushing the scabid mugs about the stained table, regarding his strange bedfellows.

Mick Malloy: closed-down face, skewed nose, dark monobrow cowling eyes creased from years of being screwed up against the odds.

Ivor Merrill: slim and febrile, shoulders squared, no longer looking like a bashed-about package trying to fold itself into a smaller lot.

Greta: grown into her dead brother's boots, sure and focused, an eye-glass funneling light onto one particular spot, everything else excluded from her care.

Only a couple of days before all would be enacted.

Peter re-evaluating Greta's masterplan: a shaky construct now he saw it in the round, regretting his earlier enthusiasm. Aware that when he got to England, published his coruscating reports, he'd be arrested and imprisoned and had prepared for it. Had garnered influential support over the years from enlightened literati who would soon put a petition in place for his release.

Greta having no such network, and nothing he could do for her if she was caught.

He gulped at his wine, plonked his mug down on the table.

'Are you sure you all want to go through with it?' he asked.

Harsh guttering bark from Mick Malloy.

'No choice for me, man. French won't take me back. Too long away. They'll take me for a turncoat, hang me out on hooks until my ins are on the out.'

Peter looking at Ivor who nodded dumbly, shifting a dirty blonde screen of hair across his forehead.

Greta speaking for them all.

'It'll be fine. Stop your worrying.'

Peter worried all the more by this trio's nonchalance.

'Getting through Antwerp is going to be dangerous, and the more I think about it the more I'm thinking it a bad idea.'

Peter ready to call a halt to the hare-brained scheme, drag Greta bodily back with him to London. Ivor piping up in their defence.

'I've been doing a bit of poking, think I've a way around it. Discovered something about the folk of Ghent, just along from Antwerp. And pretty interesting it is too.'

Peter worrying about that poking; Mick and Greta leaning in to hear what would come next.

'Historically those Ghenters,' Ivor explained, 'have always been a bit contrary far as the English and French are concerned. Sided with one and then the other, whichever went least against the grain. And at the moment they're with us, seeing as how the French have taken Antwerp and presume themselves not long behind.'

'So what?' Greta demanded brusquely.

Ivor colouring, going on

'Fact is, they knew we'd be in trouble the moment we got here. Got word over, established a clandestine supply line coming in from Ternauzen to our side at Ellewoutsdjik Point.'

Peter sceptical. This had all the makings of a trap. A lie given to Ivor by his superiors to take down Greta, recapture Mick, remove both back to England as the only prizes to come out of this shambolic campaign.

'It's not possible,' Peter argued. 'The French have been patrolling the Western Schelde specifically to stop such a thing happening.'

Ivor smiled, wan features flaring into life.

'Like I said – clandestine,' Ivor animated. 'Firstly they sent a man over under cover of night, swimming the whole of the way if you can believe it. Nearly a mile from Ternauzen to the sand bank, and another two from the sand bank to Ellewoutsdjik...'

'You're not suggesting we swim,' Greta began, for she'd never swum further than one side of a river to the other on a hot sunny day as a bairn, and the idea of Mick Malloy chucking himself into the briny was laughable. Ivor shaking his head, smiling again, a brightness to his eyes that had Greta considering him with renewed interest.

'Of course not,' Ivor chided. 'But that lone swimmer brought with him a method we've apparently been using ever since. I've always although it odd we had regular rations of fresh food, so I asked one of the cooks.'

Ivor looking around for some appreciation of his sneaky interrogation methods. Getting nothing but a scowl from Greta, fresh foodstuffs never doled out to the rank and file, nor to her and Peter. William stadholder and his sweetmeats all over again.

'And this works how?' Peter plugging the gap. Ivor gratefully switching his gaze from Greta to her cousin.

'They've a man their side in Ternauzen sits look-out every evening, and if we've need we contact them. Use a beach-fire – like fishermen have going all the time – and a mirror. Three flashes our side, then nothing; three flashes then nothing; us carrying on until someone responds from their side. Then three flashes their side to say they've seen, four flashes our side to say we've understood. Them bringing over a small boat at midnight and we tell them what we're needing.'

'All this from a cook?' Peter looking for the downside, Peter wanting the entire madness quashed. Ivor shrugging his shoulders, slumping under Peter's disbelief.

'An under-cook, as it happens,' attempting bravado. 'I interrogated him as an officer in command, so why would he lie?'

Sighs on all sides. Ivor's naivety apparent for all to see.

'Who else have you spoken to about what we're at?' Peter asked quietly. Ivor taking a second to realise he was being rounded on. Accused. Blood suffusing cheeks.

'No one!' he said hotly. 'And certainly not to an under-cook. What do you take me for?'

Ivor brushing a hand through his insipid hair so it stood at tilt.

*Hair like a robber's dog,* thought Greta, although dogs of robbers never at fault for what their masters did. Ivor only trying help, and helpful it could be. Ternauzen men and Ghenters would have no knowledge the English were about to decamp, and therefore would still be on the look-out.

'I'm with Ivor,' Greta said. 'No reason for us to disbelieve him or his cook. Feeling a little sickly?'

Greta casting a quick grin in Ivor's direction.

Ivor frowning, before catching Greta's drift.

Taking his final decision. Bit parts be damned. He wanted in. And Greta believed in him, even if the others didn't.

'Think I might be coming down with the ague,' he said, running the fingers of his good hand across his forehead in overly dramatic fashion. 'Might want to take me to the Servants, get me suited and booted in case I sadly succumb to the grave.'

# 13

## Swing And Swerve

NIGHT.

Dark.

Ivor, Mick and Greta waiting on the beach.

After their talk in Peter's tent they'd signaled over to Ternauzen and got the requisite signal back, a boat coming soon afterwards and all explained: Brethren out first, on Mick's suggestion – a plan pleasing to everyone. Ghent men bringing over more vessels under cover of darkness, shipping the Servants out; boats dangerously overloaded and no room for more until this night, this last night.

Only Joachim and the Abbott waiting at Ellewoutsdjik Point on Walcheren with Mick, Greta and the recently deceased Ivor Merrill - that part going better than expected. Grave dug and covered, wooden cross its only marker. No one from the English encampment caring to check all had been done correctly; but someone needing to be there, just in case. Joachim and the Abbott the obvious choices, being the only Servants knowing what was truly going on.

Two days into the English retreat, one more to go; the French shaking themselves awake in Antwerp as they got news the English were on their way out. Jubilation for them, troops readying themselves in Antwerp to stamp along the road to the Servants where they would make barracks – exactly as Joachim had predicted – for no handier base for taking Vlissingen once the English departed.

On Ellewoutsdjik beach they waited, the last remaining English amassed further up the coast at Flushing, eager to be gone.

'I don't see no boat,' Greta anxious, biting her lip. Already past three in the morning, a full hour after the agreed-upon pick-up time.

'They'll be here,' Ivor staunch, despite the gnawing in his stomach.

Joachim's soft voice calm and unconcerned.

'We've no need to panic yet. We knew the French would get wind the moment the English started off Walcheren, send a party to check it out. But they've no cause to come down here, so all will be fine.'

Greta lifting her head, catching sounds she knew well of men and horses moving under cover of night. Greta certain the French were conducting a classic pincer manoeuvre: coming out of Antwerp, coming down Walcheren and very likely also to Ghent on the other side of the Schelde and if the French took Ghent it would make their escape plan no escape plan at all.

'Can't be more than a cupla miles away,' Greta whispered, Ivor putting out his hand and laying it over hers;

the oddness of it, given his missing fingers, a little disturbing, so she didn't immediately shake it off.

'They'll be here,' Ivor repeated, scanning the dark seas, seeing nothing, fearing Greta was right, that all was up...and then, oh thank Christ! There it was. A wink of light, a fishing ketch not far off shore and he was up and running, the others too, all of them charging into the water right up to their waists and being hauled in oversides.

'Hold up! You're gonna bloody tip it!'

The boatman tried to stop their precipitous entry without success, yet soon all were aboard and they were on their way.

'Gonna wanta temper that enthusiasm,' the boatman commented, his drouked passengers getting themselves sat, 'else we're really gonna dive.'

Everyone settling, dripping onto their seats, taking sharp breaths of relief, grinning at the pale outlines of each other's faces.

'You don't know what a great service you're doing for us,' the Abbot said in formal speak, flapping his wet garb about knees and ankles, feeling the scratch of salt and sand.

'What, like saving the Servants?' the boatman replied mildly, puffing at his pipe. 'But hold up...French abroad...'

Snuffing out the small lantern on the stern, turning the boat witherwise as a massive bulking hulk bore down on them: a twenty-four gunned frigate the French had pulled into Antwerp following news of the English departure.

'Don't say nothing,' the boatman advised. 'Don't even squeak.'

Letting go the rudder, allowing the boat to turn with the current, be sucked out with the tide past Ternauzen and on towards the open sea. Greta gripping at the wood as the boat slewed wildly, rocked haphazardly; Greta concentrating on the regular rhythm of the boatman puffing at his pipe, not about to change his smoking habits for anyone. Greta sucking in her cheeks as the boatman suddenly grabbed the rudder and aimed the boat to the left between one sandbank and the next so they ended up zooming down a narrow current parallel to the shore. Walcheren no longer visible on the other side of the Schelde.

Soft chuckle from the boatman's throat.

'No getting us now, friends, even if they was on our trail. Vessel that big's gotta go the other side if they don't want to ground themselves on the sand. Gonna have to make land a bit way over,' the boatman stated. 'Might do you well. Heard tonight – reason I'm late – that the French are within a spit of Ghent, but can get you up coast and around a bit afore I lands you.'

Joachim sending thanks into the night. One thing to believe your God will save you, another to witness it being done by the quick wit of a good boatman who knew how to ply a slice of wood through the sea.

No miracle in that. Saved all the same.

# 14

## Chip, Chip; Knock, Knock

HEDGE-MAN REVEALED, as much of him as could be. Ruan and Caro going at it long after Frau Dieter and Fabian had departed, chipping and knocking away the precipitate to reveal clothes thin on flesh, flesh thinner on bones as if the latter had sucked the former into themselves for last protection. They'd been careful about the face, since both Fabian and Frau Dieter had appeared to give it a name, although neither Ruan nor Caro were convinced. Possession of a precipitate-caked amulet not enough, not until they uncovered it properly, had left it soaking in a bowl of dilute acid to do precisely that.

The face itself squashed some way off its axis by the weight of the hedge bearing down on him.

No way to be entirely certain what he'd looked like in life.

Ruan having a thought.

'Perhaps if we inject saline solution deep under the skin we could plump him up a little, make him more like he used to be?'

'Perhaps,' Caro doubtful, didn't like the idea. Had one of his own. 'Think maybe we should go the other way,' he suggested. 'Remember those bog-bodies we saw a couple of years back? They were reckoned to be thousands of years old, and I know they looked like hide on bones but I'd swear if anyone was still alive who'd known them they'd have found them recognizable.'

Ruan plucking at his bottom lip.

'Now that, young Caro, is a very good idea.'

'Got to be a tanning works in town,' Caro suggested, 'and we'll only need a couple of gallons of the strong stuff.'

Ruan smiling.

'Quite right too. So do you want to chop off his head, or will I?'

FRAU DIETER AND FABIAN had departed from the cellar, crossed the grass, spying Professor Jorn standing on his podium, one hand tucked into his waistcoat, practicing his speech to a non-existent audience.

'That man,' muttered Frau Dieter, casting a scornful glance in his direction. 'Can you believe he's more concerned with impressing the townsfolk than finding out who that poor soul is in the hedge?'

Fabian saying nothing, for yes, he could well believe it. Scratched his cheek, spoke half-heartedly in Professor Jorn's defence.

'The bonfire's an important event. He'll maybe have more concern tomorrow, when it's over.'

Frau Dieter snorted.

'Well yes, maybe. Probably not.'

'Probably not,' Fabian agreed. 'But at least someone cares.'

The book-finders, whose names he didn't know, a little inquisition all to their own.

'Do you really think it was Constantine?' Frau Dieter asked. Fabian seeing the quiver running through her, like a sparrow sheltering in a Winter hedge. Let out a long breath, shook his head.

'I don't know,' he answered honestly. 'But if anyone can find out, I believe it will be them.'

Frau Dieter putting a cold hand to her brow, seeing the great behemoth of the bonfire heaving itself up from the ground. Coming to a stop on the damp grass, envisioning in those tangled scribbles of piled-up branches her own neat handwriting in her ledger, last day of 1801 when she'd summed up the year's work and tallied the figures.

'I've remembered the names,' she said. 'The ones who deserted when Constantine... when they took Constantine with them. Friedrich Auslander, Ricard Gericault, and the two Hungarian brothers, Mokush and Zsolt...'

'Polovtsy,' Fabian finished for her.

Friedrich Auslander tall and thin, spiky as a pitchfork, always grumbling at orders, always arguing at nothing. Always capitulating with bad grace.

Ricard Gericault younger than Auslander, in the same work cadre, become petulant in a quieter way as Auslander's grumbles rubbed off on him, made him discontent, shifty as a pebble at the bottom of a fast running stream.

The Hungarian brothers of a different humour, seemingly upbeat, eager to please. Ingratiating themselves with anyone and everyone at every turn.

The two pairs coalescing into a unit of friendship-four after a few months of stuttering through their various languages, settling into German as their common pattern – as did everyone else. Bad Salzbaum their new abode for the foreseeable future and needing to get along with the locals and their fellows. Ricard occasionally lapsing into French when speaking to Fabian, although not often and not at all by the end of that first year of their suborned labour. Not entirely unexpected when the friendship-four had legged it, although huge upheaval to discover Constantine gone with them.

No need for Fabian to ask Frau Dieter if she was sure about those names. Frau Dieter always sure and accurate when it came to her men. Could imagine her writing down those four names neatly in her ledger, alongside the fifth. The page - had he been writing - would have been splotched and blotched as he pressed the nib too hard against the paper in his anger: not that they'd left, but because they'd taken Constantine with them. A betrayal twisting and turning within him then as now to have drawn that joyful lad into their darkness with the easy unconcern of snuffing out a candle. A rage impotent, with no one to direct it at once the culprits had left the scene. Rage firing back up in him, because if that was Constantine in the hedge – and he hoped to God it wasn't, but if it was, well. Maybe the others had stuck around Bad Salzbaum for those eight months, in between their absconding after Christmas in 1801 and the hedge-laying in August the following year. And if that was the case, if they'd been here that long, there had to be traces, someone who had seen them, maybe aided them. The two gangles of Auslander and Gericault and the jolly jackanapes who were the brothers Hungarian. He should have looked harder at the time. Should have tramped the streets calling out Constantine's name. Should have raked through every house and barn in search of him, instead of consigning the boy to the loss column of Frau Dieter's book of accounts.

The curse of hindsight hammering through him like a nail through bad wood.

About to speak to Frau Dieter on it, find out if what he suspected was true, if there was any means to find those four black-hearted men after these intervening years. Intentions cut short by a young man running across their path as they drew parallel to the hedges, the young man panting, out of breath, having run full-tilt from seeing to the bonfire that was about to go up.

'Holger!' Piet called out, Fabian looking up to see the old groundsman he'd once worked with teetering on the top of the newly filled hedge, boots a lick over the edge.

'Sit down, Holger,' Piet pleaded, beginning to scramble his way up the scaffolding.

Frau Dieter taking a step towards Fabian.

'What's going on?' she asked, although Fabian was at a loss. The two standing in the hedge's shadow, gazing up as Piet gained the top and took a few quick steps across the planking.

'Please sit down, Holger,' they heard Piet say again, saw Piet taking Holger's elbow, easing him back from the edge.

Fabian and Frau Dieter dismayed to realize what had been about to happen: that the old groundsman had been considering flinging himself from the top of the hedge and having done with it.

Fabian and Frau Dieter seeing Holger's face in the fast-failing afternoon before Piet drew him back, a face blotched and swollen like he'd been crying; a face that so mirrored their own internal miseries they could not move. Watched Holger snuffling back the tears that had started at random ever since he'd started the hedge refilling; Holger feeling like a mosaic whose pieces kept moving of their own accord, skittering from one scene into another, mostly of the night the man had been set on fire. The sight of it blurring over what he was actually seeing when he least expected it; the smell of it strong in his nostrils making him gag, making him anxious, making him want to go home and curl up in his bed. And since the stall-holders had begun to arrive and started setting up, and Professor Jorn had taken to his podium and begun to rehearse his speech, he just couldn't bear it. Couldn't bear to see another bonfire go up, couldn't bear what more visceral sights and smells he would have to endure because of it. Couldn't bear that his memory had gaps in it you could sink a boat in. Couldn't bear that he was going to be dragged away, accused of murder. Had already forgotten this was no longer a possibility. Couldn't bear what was going to happen to Mathilde because of it.

'Come on, Holger,' Piet spoke softly, wrapping his arm about Holger's shoulders as he eased him back against the planking.

Holger complying, eyes tracking the movements of the stall-holders, zeroing in on inconsequential details: the patterned blues and whites of their awnings, the grain of the wood on which they were setting out their wares, the boys who were erecting benches about the bonfire from bales of straw and planks, the flutter of bunting about the dais as a breeze played in from the west, the last slants of light stepping inch by inch across the roof of his home – of his and Mathilde's home.

'I can't do it anymore, Piet,' Holger murmured. 'I think I'm done. And I mean really done.'

Piet aghast, didn't know what to do. Looked down on the bonfire and the stall-holders and Professor Jorn on his dais, eyes settling on Fabian and Frau Dieter, people he knew by sight if not by name: the people responsible for the mill-workings and the about-to-be opened mud-baths.

'Could do with some help,' he called down softly, hoping he was heard which he was.

'Tell us what to do,' Fabian called back, unnerved, the old groundsman plainly having intended to do as a few of the POWs had over the years: men who'd thrown themselves from the highest cliff workings from the guilt of being captured, or guilt they'd survived their battles and others hadn't; or because they saw no way out of their servitude, never able to find their way home even if this servitude ended; or that there was nothing to go back to, too long passed, that wives and sweethearts would not have waited, and children – if they had them – calling someone else *papa* instead of themselves.

'Can you see that cottage over yonder?' Piet answered Fabian's question.

Fabian taking a few yards, reaching the end of the hedges.

'I see it,' he called upwards, eager to help.

'That's Holger's home,' Piet explained, incredibly relieved someone was here to give aid. 'His wife is there. I really need you to bring her out.'

Fabian on his way.

Mathilde just finished putting the next day's sourdough into its pan to rest and rise overnight when the soft tap came at her door. Mathilde opening it to a man she vaguely recognized. Mathilde fearing the worst, that Holger was about to be sacked. She knew how much Holger's mind had been slipping its mooring ropes of late, how badly the hedge-laying had affected him. How it might go. Fears aggregated by what the stranger said.

'Frau Stoss. I need you to come with me.'

Mathilde's face flushing with anxiety.

'Is it Holger? Is he all right? Has something happened?'

'He's need of you,' was all Fabian said, Mathilde whipping off her apron.

'Take me,' she commanded, Fabian obliging. Mathilde remembering her fear on waking the morning they'd found the body in the hedge; how everything, for those few moments, had seemed so unworldly: the rooks rising up as they'd done, the fear she'd had of trolls hiding in the shadows.

Sharp stab back to Torghatten where she'd grown up, and young Håkon Tryggvason choosing to spend several days and nights in the pierced hill. Of him telling her, on his return, that life was not so straightforward nor so solid as a stone rolling inexorably down a hill; life instead a succession of transient screens shifting and slotting, now here now there, going backwards as well as forwards. Words and notions inexplicable to her, if not to Håkon who'd always been a little out of kilter within their tiny world of Torghatten. Håkon, who'd left soon afterwards and whom she'd never seen again, and yet Håkon the reason she'd the courage to leave when she did after that fishing ship had foundered on the fjords by Torghatten Hill and she'd first met Holger, and Holger had carried her away.

Mathilde experiencing the shift and slot of those screens as she came out from her cottage at the Frenchman's back – Fabian suddenly recognized as the man who'd helped Holger with that last hedge-laying - the sun a dark red circle on the hill, upper-most mill-workings scratching the sky with their scrawny necks, shadows spilling with menace down the hill, racing across the flat bottom of the valley like a malevolent mist, hedges looming before her and, right up top, two figures silhouetted against the brief red sun whose lower arc was already below the hill, dragging the rest of the day down with it.

Breath catching in her throat.

Hand going to her locket.

'What are they doing up there?' she whispered. 'Is something wrong with the hedges?'

'Very likely,' Fabian said, grasping at this suggestion. 'It seems Holger's had a bit of a turn,' he improvised. 'Got a little dizzy, I expect.'

So much better than the truth, yet Fabian embarrassed by the lie.

'Talk to him,' he added, as she came alongside. 'Reassure him if you can.'

Missing Mathilde's frown at these words that belied the lie, and yet taking the line he'd given her, calling up to her husband.

'Holger. It's me, it's Mathilde. Come on down, love. I've your dinner baked and ready, and we can spend the evening playing whist with Piet. I've your slippers warming by the fire...'

Mathilde stopping abruptly for oh Lord, how she wished she'd not said that last word as she saw her husband stutter and shake up there on the hedge, saw Piet's hands dragging at Holger's arms and elbows, saw Holger's feet moving forward, one of Håkon's screens shifting as she recognized the scene for what it was.

'Holger!' she called out. 'It's all right, my darling. You're not going to be sacked, and no one believes you a murderer! We've folk here, remember? Those two young men who've come to sort everything out. And Frau Dieter's here too,' she added, casting a desperate glance at Frau Dieter who'd drawn up close beside her. 'If you don't believe me, believe her.'

Frau Dieter blinking quickly as Mathilde clutched at her arm.

'Please say it's so,' Mathilde urged. 'I know Holger's not what he used to be and I'll tell you everything. We'll leave, we'll be gone, but please, please, not like this.'

Frau Dieter having no idea what Mathilde had to tell, but wasn't going to let any man step off a thirty foot high hedge to land and splatter on the grass at her feet. The day already too disturbing.

'Your wife's entirely right, Herr Stoss,' Frau Dieter assured, in the sternest most business-like voice she could muster. 'There is absolutely nothing for you to worry about. And whist? Good Heavens, I haven't played whist in years. I'd be most glad if you'd reintroduce me to the rudimentaries.'

'Of course he will, won't you Holger?' Mathilde pleaded. 'And you need to bring Piet down with you. You know how dangerous it is up there in the dark.'

Up top the hedge Piet's upper lip was sweating. He was young and strong, but Holger was older, stronger and determined. He'd got Holger away from the edge, both leaning against the wooden aqueduct that would drip the spring's water onto the hedge once the pumps were turned back on, but Holger was straining against Piet's grasp, Piet holding onto the water channel with one hand, Holger with the other.

Piet letting out a soft breath once Mathilde had arrived and Holger appeared to relax, air going out of Holger like a toad deflating, but only for a moment, and then Holger tensed once more and began to pull away.

'What about it, Holger?' Piet asked. 'Good supper, warm slippers, game of whist with a new player you can fleece like you fleeced me early doors?'

Holger shook his head slowly.

'Me heart feels like it's a hole punched through it,' he whispered, 'and me head's a big empty place where all the paths have got lost.'

And the tears began again to fall, confusion flooding him, forcing him back into the tunnel that had only one way out. Holger making a break for it, wrenching free from Piet's grasp, about to call out to Mathilde, beg forgiveness for what he was about to do, when his coat was grabbed, arms about his shoulders and locked beneath his chin.

'Let me go!' Holger cried in desperation, but Fabian would not release him, Fabian having scarpered up the graduation tower swift as a stoat.

'This isn't the way,' Fabian assured. 'I know it doesn't seem like it, but this blackness will ease once we get you back home.'

Holger letting out a heart-rending, soul-piercing wail that had those down below putting hands to breasts and mouths. Holger's last choice gone as Piet joined forces with Fabian and they manhandled him towards the tower at the hedge's end.

Frau Dieter sighing with relief, Mathilde likewise. Mathilde breathing hard to slow her heart. Mathilde saying to Frau Dieter

*You'd be very welcome for a game of whist, if you felt it appropriate.*

Frau Dieter smiling, patting Mathilde's hand.

*I could twist the two of you like yarn through a Spinning Jenny at any game of cards you put to me.*

Both laughing softly, moving over the damp grass companionably. Halted abruptly by the unwelcome intrusion of the twitchy-footed, top-hatted Professor Jorn, who'd spied something wrong from his podium and decided to personally intervene.

'What the devil is going on here?' he demanded loudly. 'Is that Holger Stoss up there? If there's something amiss with the hedges I need to know, and I need to know right now.'

Frau Dieter bit her lip in irritation.

'This is not a good time,' she reprimanded, 'nor is it appropriate.'

She could not see Professor Jorn's face, for by now it was quite dark, but she could imagine it: thin lips contracting, eyebrows lifting, long face getting longer as he opened his mouth again.

'It's a damn good time,' he replied tartly, 'and appropriate or not, it is none of your business. But if Herr Stoss has been slipshod at his duties then, my good Frau Dieter, it is very much mine.'

Professor Jorn a disliker of women, mainly because experience had taught him they disliked him, and no more was he a man to pass over other men's failings lightly. And it seemed to him failing was in the air. Why else would his Master Groundsman be on top of the blasted hedge when he should already be elsewhere?

'Stoss!' Professor Jorn called out loudly. 'Get yourself down here soon as! I've stall-holders all set up and the town's folk will be here any minute. We've a spectacle to lay on, in case you've forgotten. Biggest night of the year. Pumps to prime, bonfires to light!'

'Oh, you shouldn't have said that,' Holger's wife bleated at his side, grabbing Professor Jorn's arm. Jorn in no mood for female fittling, swatting Mathilde away and taking a swift step forward.

'Did you hear me, Holger?' he bellowed. 'You've to get that beggaring fire going or I'm going to sack you on the spot!'

*Stall-holders, sack me, fire...*

All Holger heard from Professor Jorn's outburst, anxiety swallowing him whole.

Holger pushing away from his captors, who'd relaxed their grasp believing the danger over.

Holger running from them both.

Holger seeing the straight black line of the hedge, the skinny aqueduct guiding him on as Piet's voice squalled behind him, calling his name.

Holger not caring.

Holger knowing there was only one way all his gnawing doubts and disturbances could come to an end.

Holger having a fleet faint gasp of memory in his head of when his ship had ploughed on down the coast of Norway, pushed in yard by yard with every furlong taken as the ice of the green-backed sea solidified and hummocked, shoved them further and further into the coast until they had nowhere else to go. Ship crushed in sight of the island with that weird hill that had a hole punched through it from one side to the other. Like the one through his heart.

*My light at the end of the tunnel.*

Words he'd spoken to Mathilde the first time he'd had the courage to speak to her of how he felt.

*And you mine,* she'd said, although not straightaway.

The men there for days, weeks, months, until that wicked Winter did its worst and a ship from back home was summoned to grab them up, their own by then a pitiful pile

of splinters floating on the thawing surface of the sea, by
which time Holger had decided that Mathilde was his be all
and everything. And told her so. And by some miracle she
had agreed to come away with him.

*My light, and you mine.*

Oh Jesus. Holger's heart, hole or not, was pumping as he
ran, and only twenty three yards to go.

He didn't want to leave Mathilde, didn't want to leave
anything, but couldn't bear to face another fire, couldn't
stand that his mind was slipping away from him like an eel
down a stream.

'Holger, no!'

Mathilde.

Mathilde desperate.

But what else for him, and what else for her?

At least this way she'd have his pension, or what little
Professor whatsis name would agree to settle on her. Almost
thirty years he'd been in this job, sea-faring no longer for
him after he'd been wrecked, met Mathilde, been rescued.
Thirty odd years since he'd been apprenticed at his uncle's
heel, taken all the jibes that came in its wake: gone off to be
a sea-faring lad, returning two years later with a wife and a
different attitude on life.

No need to be a Håkon Tryggvason to realise which side
your bread was buttered.

Hanging thread in Holger's head to conjure up the name
of that man as he ran, the boy Mathilde had mentioned every
now and then.

*I'd not have gone with you if it hadn't been for him.*

*How so?*

*Because he saw life so differently. Because he told me once that life is not a stone rolling down a hill; that you can change its course, that...well, I'm not exactly sure what he was telling me, only that it seemed he was saying I should take a chance when it came. See what it throws at you. And that chance is you.*

*Is it enough?*

*It's enough, Holger.*

'Enough, Holger,' someone grabbing hard at Holger's arm. 'You've a wife to think of.'

Fabian Guichot the man of the moment.

Fabian not wasting a second once Holger had broken free. Fabian racing off over the hedge as if there was solidity to either side and not empty air, catching Holger in the nick of time. Fabian expecting a struggle as he got hold of Holger, and getting one.

'I can't do it anymore!' Holger wailed. 'I can't, I can't...'

Holger heaving with sobs, Fabian's arms a vice about Holger's waist. Fabian pulling the two of them back along the hedge. Piet coming to meet them, the two of them vigilant this time until Holger was funneled down the tower and they reached base, were back on the grass.

Professor Jorn the first to meet them.

Professor Jorn stabbing his finger hard into Holger's chest.

'This is a disgrace, Stoss,' Jorn stated, his glasses steaming up with the annoyance contained in his clipped words. 'You're finished. You and your wife can pack up and go. You'll get two weeks wages, no more, no less. And you,' he turned on Piet. 'You've to leave this old ditherer and get to the bonfire right now, unless you want to go the same way.'

And with that parting command he was off. Piet hovering on the grass, uncertain what to do, Fabian retreating a few steps with Holger secured.

'Go,' Mathilde said, fingers shaking as she patted Piet's arm. 'Do as the Professor asks. Get that wretched heap up in flames.'

'I'm not sure I'm ready, and I certainly can't do it alone.'

Piet couldn't quite get to grips with what was going on.

Unthinkable that Holger had been sacked so peremptorily. Feeling his own small hole panging through his own young heart.

'You'll be fine,' Mathilde said. 'We've talked it through a thousand times. We both knew Holger mightn't be able to go through with it, not with his mind scattering to the four corners of the earth.'

First time she'd ever said it out loud, even to Piet.

First time Piet had actually acknowledged it as a reality.

'But you're right,' Mathilde added. 'You'll need help. Get those two men from the hotel, Ruan Peat and the other one. Perhaps, Frau Dieter, you'd lend us your man to fetch them?'

Frau Dieter nodding her agreement, casting a quick smile at Fabian.

'There's something you're both overlooking,' she said. 'My man, as you have so elegantly labelled him, my Mr. Fabian Guichot, has done all this before.'

Mathilde putting a hand to her neck, looking properly at Fabian.

'It is you, then,' she said. 'Please, please, will you do it again?'

Fabian clearing his throat.

'I'll do all I can.'

Remembering how nervous Holger had been around the bonfire, how he'd visibly sweated and swayed, how he'd got himself together and put the process in motion; Holger dipping in his thumb to measure the rate of the waters of the spring and then again at the sluice gates as he got them opened. Holger next heading to the tower, commanding Guichot up onto the second platform while he took the first; Holger holding up an arm, cocking his head as he listened to the water-wheel building speed, waiting, waiting as the water came gurgling into the pool at the base of the tower and began to fill the tubes; Holger loosening his valves, shouting to Fabian to unloose his own. Fabian's time with Holger short, Fabian unappreciative how skilled Holger had been at his task. Especially now, when everything was recumbent on him when all Holger had used was his thumb, his ears, his acumen and experience.

'I think we'll fetch the others anyway,' he said. 'Got the feeling we'll need all the help we can get.'

Mathilde eager to get Holger away, looking at Frau Dieter whose face – normally so stern – was creased with concern.

'Don't you worry,' Frau Dieter assured. 'We'll get it done exactly as your Holger would have, if he'd been able.'

'Thank you, thank you all,' Mathilde said quietly. 'Now get you gone.'

Piet leaning over, kissing her cheek.

'I'll be back soon as. Look after Holger.'

Mathilde managing a weak smile.

'I always have,' she said. 'And I always will.'

Piet away on a run, Fabian off too. Mathilde leading her broken Holger home.

Frau Dieter gazing after them.

*I'll tell you everything. We'll leave, we'll be gone, but please, please, not like this.*

And not like this was precisely what it would not be.

She'd been dealing with the Stoss's ever since she'd taken over her husband's firm, and knew Holger had been working as groundsman at the spa for a long long time; had admired the Stoss's, saw them welded together like the willow tree out at the mill-workings which was not one tree but two, both sprouting from the same root, growing up stem by stem, bough by bough, the one winding into the other until they were indistinguishable.

She'd envied them that closeness. And the paltry two weeks wages Professor Jorn had assigned them a pittance so derisory Frau Dieter would absolutely not let it stand. A curse on Professor Jorn, and all men like him, who believed women should be inside walls and never let out. And a curse on Professor Jorn to believe that Holger Stoss could be let go with no more concern than kicking a flea-bitten dog out the door, never to be let back in.

She'd leverage, had Frau Dieter, as did all accountants.

And this circumstance she would not let lie.

# 15

# Other Dramas, Other Considerations

ON THE SANDS OF KNOKKE, the boatman landed his cargo.

'Done you a favour, that French frigate,' he commented, 'by driving us around the corner.'

'How so?' Greta asked. 'We're miles from where we should've been.'

Looking around her in the breaking dawn, seeing nothing but grey sand stretching off to the right, and a load of grass with a few windmills up behind as the dunes straggled towards the houses of Knokke-Heist. Sea calm and glassy, clouds so low they trailed veils right down to the surface giving the odd impression the two were communing, exchanging information, the old suspicions of seeing spies around every corner returning to the fore.

'Because you're in Flemish land,' the boatman informed her, shoving out his boat, leaping in. 'And up that way is Zeebrugge,' pointing with the stem of his pipe. 'Biggest port hereabouts afore the waterways from it to Bruges silted up. Still has ships calling in and out to England and up the way.

And no Frenchies there, far as I know, nor no English, so you can get on any boat you choose.'

Greta and Mick exchanging glances, Ivor letting out a breath.

'He's right,' Ivor chided himself. 'Should have thought on it sooner. All that stuff about getting around Antwerp? Stupid. Stupid!'

'Didn't hire you as no military analyst,' Greta tried to soften the blow.

'Going up the way to go down,' Mick commented. 'Ain't the most natural of deductions.'

Joachim creaking beside Greta with relief and the strictures of sodden habits.

'God's blessings come unexpectedly,' he stated, as if it was fact, helping up the Abbott who'd been the first unloaded and subsided to the sands.

'And you'll be all right?' Greta asked. 'What if the French have already taken Ghent?'

Joachim smiling.

'We'll be fine. Rest of the Brothers will have found a place to hide by now if that's so, and the Ghenters will help. And have to admit, I'm glad you've better options than you had before.'

'Done and dusted,' Mick said. 'We're here, we've a new plan, so let's get jumping.'

Mick looking down the long ribbon of beach towards Zeebrugge, seeing ketches pushing out on the back of the dawn, scribbles and shadows at the moment, and probably an hour or two's walking to get there but, once arrived, no hard shakes to hire someone to take them to Holland proper.

'Take care of yourself,' Joachim whispered as he hugged Greta. 'And maybe take a fly by Deventer. You never know...'

Greta hugging him back.

'Think it's been too long,' lump forming in her throat.

Joachim releasing her, holding her out, looking at Greta Finnerty - as brave and honest a person as he'd ever met - and wished her well.

'There's always hope until there isn't,' he said. Which platitude he left her with, as he and the Abbott headed off up the dunes towards the hamlet of Knokke-Heist, and from there to Ghent to rejoin the rest of the rescued Servants brought over by the men of Ternauzer. Joachim wondering what would happen to Greta and Ruan when, if, they met again.

*Always hope.*

Until there isn't.

Last sight of Greta being her, Ivor and Mick Malloy heading off at a good pace across Knokke Bay.

'God's speed,' he whispered, as he crossed himself. 'And God's help. I think you'll be needing it.'

'HAVE WE MONEY ENOUGH to gain passage?' Ivor asked.

'Abbott gave me some funds,' Mick informed.

'Just as well,' Ivor replied, feeling light and merry, nowhere near as dead as he was supposed to be. 'For I've nothing but a couple of spare buttons in my pockets.'

Greta frowning, Greta always prepared; Greta carrying with her a small survival kit consisting of tinder and flint, candles, a sharp knife, a pot of blackened grease in case movement at night was necessary, grease doubling as wound-disinfectant, imbued with comfrey, honey and whatever astringent herbs she'd come across on her way. A few coins sewn into one of the seams.

Greta saying nothing, although Ivor sensed her scorn. Finding Greta's disappointment humiliating, wondering how many more times she could be so withering. Ivor humiliated all over again when Mick Malloy spoke out in his defence.

'No reason you should have,' Mick said, casting a quick glance at Greta. 'Can't expect anyone to be battle-ready unless battle-honed.'

Ivor's face rhubarb-red as Mick and Greta dismissed him, headed off up the sand on their battle-ready, battle-honed heels - until he caught a jitter of movement to his left and the blood drained down to his boots.

'Get down!' he urged, grabbing at Greta's arm, Mick ducking by reflex at his words then bobbing up his head for a second, retracting it quicker than a snail sprinkled with salt.

'Soldiers,' he said succinctly 'Line of them up top o' the bay.'

'For why? Can they be looking for us?' Greta whispered urgently.

Mick sanguine, determined, Mick alive in the moment, calculating the odds.

'Maybe us, maybe not. But no way back,' he stated. 'Time to bluff or be bluffed, and if they don't swallow it whole, well then. We're done for.'

Ivor's heart battering in his chest for release, aware this was truly do or die.

Ivor no longer in uniform, dressed in Servants' dregs, seeing a way out. Not a great one, but could see no other.

'I speak it,' he whispered, 'the language. And we're right on the border, like the boatman said. We can do this! We can!'

Ivor standing, calling out in his best French accent.

'Can you tell us if we're on the right track to Zeebrugge?'

Mick cursing worse than Greta had ever heard, the two of them obliged to raise their heads as Ivor shouted out his plea.

'Got a Dutch girl with me!' Ivor couldn't stop himself. 'My fiancé, and her father too.'

'He's bloody done it now,' Mick growled. 'If it's Dutch I'm supposed...'

'Bit doolally, her dad,' Ivor went on, the soldiers advancing towards them. 'Taking him to town, get him fixed before the wedding. Heard there's a head doctor there can work wonders.'

Soldiers tired and dusty.

'Name,' the first demanded wearily as he closed on them.

'Horace de Saussure,' Ivor replied, name as French as he could make it – an Alp-climbing geologist whose adventures he'd been reading about a few weeks previously.

'Got any papers?' the soldier asked, looking Ivor over, at the tattered ex-Servants' garb, the muddled mop of blonde hair, the colour rising up Ivor's throat.

'Um, no,' the faux Horace replied. 'Didn't think we'd need them. Only off on a day's jaunt.'

'Doesn't anybody around here know we're at war?' another of the soldiers sighed, disgusted. 'Got a load of English decamping just over the water. Could be sending spies out left, right and centre, and you're just off to take old pop to see the mad doctor?'

Spitting out of one side of his mouth, the gob landing not far from Mick's boot, the soldier looking at Mick and raising his eyebrows, daring him to object. Mick standing fast and looking right back, not that the soldier could tell it from the squint in Mick's eye.

'Hell, the lad's right,' another soldier said. 'Does look a bit bonkers, this one.'

Mick grinding his teeth, trying to keep his face still. He mayn't be able to speak French like a native - as Ivor apparently could - but he'd not spent the last nine years in Napoleon's Irish Legion without picking up a fair bit of the lingo.

'What's going on?' Greta asked in her Dutch, pulling at Ivor's sleeve, anxiety unfeigned.

'Pretty little minx,' a third soldier said, licking his lips. 'Although don't get why she's done up in boy's clothing.' Narrowing his eyes, looking hard at Ivor, twitch of suspicion at this mismatched brood who'd appeared so suddenly on the sand before them. 'So why is that, exactly?'

Ivor's colour deepened.

'Bit of a story there,' he mumbled, frantically trying to conjure one out of thin air.

'Probably one of them nancy boys,' another of the soldiers offered, 'what likes their girls to look like boys when they can't get the real thing.'

The soldier laughing, poking his pistol into Ivor's chest.

'That what it is? That what really gets your juices going?'

Too long in the army, this one, too many years making cruder and cruder jokes to disguise the fact that at heart he felt nothing anymore, not for women, nor for men, not for anyone. Only thrills he got being from combat up close and personal, the bloodier the better. Everything else about him scoured away.

Mick saw it in him clear as a boulder stranded naked on a hill, worrying what the clean-cut Ivor would do at the jibe. But Ivor didn't rise. Ivor took it, Ivor blushed to his roots, as would any man whose betrothed had been so insulted. Ivor straightening his shoulders and letting rip, in the most gentlemanly fashion imaginable.

'I apologize if we've disrupted your day,' Ivor said, pushing the gun barrel away, grabbing Greta's hand, pulling her close. 'And I'm glad my girl being garbed so as to carry out the work her father can't has given you some amusement. We all know the war is no joke,' letting out a breath, 'and Heaven knows we're glad for the order you're trying to bring to everywhere hereabouts. But all I want right now is for me and Gretel to get married like normal people,' lowering his voice, quick tilt of his head at Mick. 'Which we can't do, not if we can't get him fixed, or maybe locked away, which would be a blessing.'

Ivor uncomfortably aware the soldiers had encircled them, had them trapped, smelling Mick's sweat as Mick stood like a monolith beside him. Ivor regarding the lead soldier, how dull were the buttons of his uniform, how grimy the frayed cuffs of his sleeves, how worn the leather of his boots. No polish to these soldiers; men who'd seen action, come out the other side alive. Admiring them, despite his precarious situation, more so when their leader ordered a perfunctory search, as protocol required.

'Shake `em down and let `em go,' the man said, turning away, leaving the ribald spit-gobbing man and his companions to perform the deed, which was quickly done; only hiatus coming when they found Mick's bag of coins.

'Well, will you look at this,' the gob-spitter commented as he raised it aloft. 'Some kind of prize, I should say.'

Ivor horrified, seeing all their plans melting away.

'For the doctor,' he pleaded. 'It's all we have. We've saved and saved and...'

Glimmer of humanity in the commander of this small French troupe; glimmer of humanity pared from his companions, discarded as useless dross. He hated all this. Hated being here in the Lowlands. Hated being in the army. Hated all he'd been forced thereby to do, what he'd seen, what he'd caused to be perpetrated.

He was tired, was the honest truth, and he saw in this weird wedding group something of the normal and oh my, how he longed for normal.

'Give it back,' he commanded, much to the gob-spitter's chagrin, who surreptitiously extracted a few coins and put them in his pocket before handing the pouch over.

'Get yourselves gone,' the trio were advised. 'Zeebrugge's a couple of hours walk up the coast. Do yourselves a favour: get wed there and stay there, idiot father-in-law or no.'

Shaking his head. Too worn out for anything else. For why the hell should everyone have to suffer because blasted

Napoleon was rampaging himself across every country from here to Spain and across the water in Egypt? Not every French soldier thinking Napoleon the best thing to have ever come along. This particular French soldier believing the opposite. Revolution one thing: beginning good, ending bad. Worst of it being the apparently unstoppable rise of Napoleon Bonaparte. This particular French soldier giving Ivor, Greta and Mick leave to go off into the morning; this particular French solider leading his men back on their march to Ternauzen where, rumour had it, a line to the English had been established. No point hurrying. English already in retreat. No point at all in the mission, as he saw it. Chiding the gob-spitter as they went.

'Will you never let up?' he sighed. 'God's sake, Alfonse, what were you thinking? Pinching money off folk just going about their way? And don't think I didn't see it. Bear in mind we're trying to keep people here on side. That we're soldiers of the Empire and have standards.'

His subordinate narrowing his eyes in contempt, livid at the reprimand. First chance he got he'd blow the principled head off his upright, forward thinking, irritatingly moral leader. No care for either Revolution and the Empire. Would have shot those three interlopers on the spot for the hell of it, for being the tiniest bit suspicious.

But shit and sideways, not his call.

# 16

## The Chest Of Books

AMULET IN ITS BATH of weak acid.

Hedge-man's head in a bucket of strong solute of tannin.

Nothing more Ruan could do about them until morning.

Time to get to what Professor Jorn had employed them to do: break into the hedge-man's crate of books, ascertain if any were of value and, if they were, get them on the market. Crate under lock and key in Professor's Jorn's study, a copy of the key in Ruan's possession.

They'd chipped off as much precipitate as they could from the wood without damaging it, for wood could tell you as much about provenance as the contents. From what they'd uncovered they'd come to the conclusion the chest was made of cherry. Hard, lightweight - perfect for carrying anything heavy, like books – and spent a while sanding the last of the precipitate off one corner, just to make sure, cherry having a shine, a lively grain scattered through with rays and pores reflecting light. Smelling of roses when freshly cut.

He'd wondered how Jorn had known what was in there. Soon clear on closer examination: breathing holes bored into the wood below the leather strops holding lid to base. Strops cut through, leather old and worn, not as conducive to the settling precipitate as the wood itself. Not much help in getting the lid off, but enough to look through the holes to see what was inside, which was plainly books.

So a crate of books not meant to go over the water. For, had that had been the case, there would be no breathing holes, and elm used instead of cherry; elm tough and waterproof, used to fashion water pipes and coffins. Elm bleeding its red-bark dye into bodies buried so when, for whatever reason, those bodies were dug up folk thought them revenants, made a song and dance about stabbing those blood-guzzling corpses through the heart before reinternment in unconsecrated ground.

*So much, so ordinary*, Ruan thought, placing his chisel beneath one of the lock plates and having at it with his hammer.

'Almost there,' he said.

'Another couple of hits,' Caro advised.

'I've nearly got it,' Ruan added. 'Just got to give it one more bash...'

Interrupted at their task by Fabian Guichot flinging open the door, calling them out.

'We've a problem,' Fabian never one to dissemble. 'And we really need your help.'

———— ⬡ ————

TEN MINUTES BEFORE eight.

Evening dark and calm.

Gentle breeze fluttering and lifting the bunting.

Glimmers in the gloom as Professor Jorn ordered his lads to light the lanterns around the podium; clickety-clack as the stall-holders got their boards together and got their own lanterns going, poked their braziers into life.

Everything perfect as Professor Jorn swept up the steps onto the dais, no thought in him how Holger Stoss was doing, nor how Piet was going to manage the entire event on his own. Piet's problem, not his.

'Ladies and Gentlemen, welcome!' the Professor's voice loud and jubilant, body bowing to the great and good of Bad Salzbaum seated about him; vague rustling between podium and stalls where people from town and hinterland had gathered for this grandest of grand nights.

Piet making several rounds of the bonfire, noting the starting boughs Holger had thrust in at regular intervals about its circumference - light and dry, providing a quick and even burn. Piet immensely relieved to see the vanguard arrive: Ruan, Caro, Fabian and Frau Dieter.

'Thank you for coming,' Piet said, gratitude glistening on his round face. 'I don't know how Holger ever managed this by himself. It's all so complicated, and we've not much time left.'

'What's needed doing?' Ruan asked for them all, Piet rubbing his hands through his hair, making it as untidy as the nest of a negligent crow.

'Easiest bit is opening the sluice-gates,' he said. 'But thank God we've Mr. Fabian here who did it before.'

Fabian nervously looking at his boots now all this was on him.

Frau Dieter coming to his rescue, Frau Dieter seeing in her head all the plans she and Fabian had conjured up for both the mill-workings and the mud-baths, factioning in all that would need to be done.

'Let me see if I've got this straight,' she said. 'Sluice-gates get opened, water floods down the lett and into the graduation towers. They've got water-wheels, I presume, to push the water up and over?'

Piet quick to agree.

'That's it exactly. Wheels push the water into the tubes that go up the primary tower, creates a vacuum that draws it on, helped by the pressure behind that will push it into the aqueducts.' Piet scratching his chin. 'But there's valves in both towers to contend with, and I've no firm idea when to open them or how long it will take. And timing's real important. Water's to go out over the hedges at precisely nine o'clock, and then there's the other sluice-gates to open afterwards for the mud-baths.'

'All right then. We've got just over an hour to get this figured out,' Frau Dieter marshalling her troops, putting them to best use, General of a small army glad to have her at their helm. 'First off, Piet. How are the pyrotechnics set up?'

Piet smiling, glad to give a bit of good news.

'They're primed and ready. Just need a flame adding at one end and the rest will go up on their own.'

'Well, that's in our favour. Your Holger Stoss certainly knows how to schedule a performance,' Frau Dieter said, *or rather knew how to, if what I've gathered is true.* Genuinely sorrowful for a man like Holger Stoss to be facing the prospect of his mind disintegrating between his ears.

'Very well,' she commanded. 'Here's what we do. Piet and Caro to the bonfire; Ruan to the lett, his duty to open the sluice-gates first to the towers and next the mud-baths. Myself and Fabian will go to the first graduation tower where we'll ascertain the rate of flow when the water hits the wheel. Piet to come to us soon as possible to aid Ruan with the opening of the sluice-gates. Ruan and Caro next to the second tower. And I need a pocket watch. Does anyone have a pocket watch?'

'Got one here,' Ruan obliged. 'Can check its local accuracy when the church clock starts striking out its hours.'

Right on cue the bells of St Peter's began to chime out eight o'clock, Ruan adjusting the minute-hand of his time-piece to match the last strike.

'One hour, then,' he stated. 'Think we can do it?'

Frau Dieter replying with a short and merry laugh that was so out of character her cheeks ached with the strain.

'We can,' she assured, despite her heart beating out a tattoo she couldn't stop. 'Lucky for us water is a very predictable medium in controlled circumstances, and more lucky for us it's controlled in this case by gates and valves. Given enough parameters I have no doubt myself and Fabian can figure it out.'

Quick nod at Fabian, who answered with the same. Fabian hearing in his head the song the Polovtsy brothers used to sing:

*Homeland is all. Do or die, but never be taken captive.*

Some irony then that they'd been taken captive, and Fabian more captivated than he'd ever been in his life. Fabian not a man who'd fought for homeland or glory. Fabian one more hapless conscript thrown into battles not his own. But everything worth it, for this moment, for the chance of meeting a woman like her.

HOLGER HEARD THE CLOCK strike eight, feet and hands twitching, knowing he should be up and doing but could not remember what. Stayed instead upon his bed, curled like a snail inside its shell. Mind twisting into tight and tighter tangles; displaced memories conflating the past with what was happening now, making him bat at shadows, uncertain what was real and what was not.

'Mathilde!' he called, she his only anchor, the only person who could keep him right in this desert where the dunes kept shifting: a vast landscape of memories he could no longer keep tally of or in order. Aware he'd pissed himself in his panic; sudden desperation then for Mathilde, what she would have to deal with when he truly lost his mind. Wished he was dead. Wished he'd chucked himself off the salty hedges when he'd had the chance...and then could no longer remember what the salty hedges were, nor what they meant, although knew they meant something. Heart leaping as Mathilde came and sat by him, took his hand, stroked it gently.

'It'll pass, Holger. You merely need to rest,' she spoke softly, bringing his hand up to her cheek, him feeling the wetness of her tears.

'I think I've soiled the bed,' he whimpered, shameful and anxious as when he'd been a child. Mathilde closing her eyes.

'It's nothing to worry about, my love,' blinking back the tears. 'You've had a long hard day, so try to rest. We'll clean up in the morning. I'll bring in the bath trough; fill it with piping hot water. Would you like that?'

Holger sighing, taking in her care, the sound of her voice, the touch of her cheek against his hand, rolling his body away from the wet patch towards Mathilde, folding his body about her own as she released his hand and laid it gently on the coverlet, began instead to stroke his hair, the side of his face, rubbing her fingers against his chin.

'Go to sleep now, my dear,' she murmured, kissing Holger's forehead, straightening her back, half whispering, half singing a verse from a cradle song her mother had sung to her when Mathilde had woken to childhood nightmares of trolls truly terrible.

*Be still, my dearest, be still and still and still, for sleep will surely come.*

*When you've gone into the darkest woods, when the night is falling,*

*Never doubt that dreams of beauty, flowers and meadows will soon come calling.*

*So be still, be calm, be silent, and soon will come your sleep.*

*So be still, and still and still...*

Holger soon sleeping softly. Mathilde rising from the bed, gazing at the outline of her husband in the darkness, the gentle lift of shoulders and chest as he was still and still and still. Mathilde afraid to light a lamp for fear of waking him;

afraid of what was happening to him, of how it would go if he couldn't find a way out.

The words of that cradle song running through her head from amongst the many she could have chosen, because they were so apt.

*Be still and still and still.*

*The woods are dark, the paths are hidden, but beauty will come your way if only you are still, and still and still.*

Privately she doubted it. Couldn't see where she and Holger might be headed, although had to be a place bad and dark, no beauty there, no meadows.

And sleep no remedy at all.

PROFESSOR JORN WAS in his stride, standing erect at his lectern, shoulders squared, suit brushed and polished, lapels and shoulders shining in the dim light.

'It's my utmost pleasure to have so many of you here,' he began, 'and I'm indebted to two men in particular for making this very special spectacle possible.'

Not one glance in Piet's direction although Piet was gratified for the mention, thinking maybe all was not lost for Holger Stoss, that Professor Jorn had come to regret his rash words and would reconsider Holger's position. Piet soon disabused of that generous notion.

'I mean of course my father,' Jorn pontificated, 'whose genius it was to erect the mazes and the hedges and design the graduation towers back in 1780. My father, who made this place what it is today. Secondly my thanks must go to Herr Bomberg, our mayor, who has done so much to raise the profile of our town. Without him we would not have the mills providing our flour, making us independent of importing it from elsewhere. A great boon in these troubled times.'

Enthusiastic applause from the crowds, for the mill-workings had indeed been immensely beneficial, lowering the price of flour so even the poorest citizen could afford it, and if you had flour you had bread, and if you had bread you had the barest minimum needed for subsistence living. No bread riots here in Bad Salzbaum, as there'd been in many cities across Europe these last few years.

Fabian and Frau Dieter walking briskly away, if not out of earshot.

Frau Dieter outraged.

'That man has some nerve,' she nipped. 'I practically had to go down on bended knee to gain Bomberg's permission to go ahead with the mill-workings. He'd never have agreed if we hadn't already secured Napoleon's backing. Not to mention you POWs. It's a travesty, is what it is.'

Professor Jorn hearing none of this, waving his hands to quell the applause before going on at length about the benefits of spa, hedges, and now mud-baths – as if they were his own special achievement.

Ruan oblivious, off on his way to the lett. Ruan thinking on the books he and Caro had been moments away from breaking into. It might be dark, it might be night, but once done with this hedge malarkey he was going to get straight back at it.

He'd a love for books that simultaneously gnawed and nourished him. Couldn't imagine a life without them. A book-trader he'd known back in Holland, Hippolyte Gerhard, had had a stroke one day out of the blue. No warning. No telling headaches or feelings of ill-ease. Fine one minute, devastated the next. One of those mysterious bleeds in the brain that destroys one area, leaves the rest intact. Gerhard left with a weakness down one side and a palsy that made his left hand shake. The worst of it being he'd lost his ability to read or write, to speak in sentences. Language, in those respects, entirely gone from him.

He understood what was being said to him but could not answer with any coherence. Jumbles of words coming out that meant nothing to his interlocutor. The loss incalculable. Gerhard spending his days reverting to what had been a mere hobby previously: Gerhard painstakingly painting city-scapes of Deventer and in every one - every single one - there would be one corner, one shady nook, in which he painted books. No writing, of course not, on covers, spines, nor splayed-open pages. Instead Gerhard scribed intricate clues to the titles of the books he most missed, the ones he knew in his head yet could no more articulate than a barnacle can tell you why it hooks onto one rock rather than another.

Something niggling at Ruan to have these thoughts in his head of Gerhard, something sparked off by his brief look through the breathing holes beneath the strops. That glimpse jiggling on in him, seeking its direction, as he went from hotel to bonfire and from bonfire to the sluice-gates he was to open when Piet gave the word.

*When Piet gave the word;*

*Gerhard, who could no longer read nor write, who conveyed meaning through ideograms and pictures.*

*The hedge-man curling himself around his books.*

Snatch of words coming to him, snatch of conversation with Gerhard before his stroke, and before Ruan's haring off to Dortmund to do the inconsequential which, at the time, had been Ruan's bread and butter.

*Look at this,* Gerhard had said, *for you'll not see its like again. And you're the only one I trust to research its provenance and get it placed.*

Ruan seeing Gerhard taking a manuscript from a dusty folder, after undoing the faded frayed ribbon that kept it tight.

'One of Tsarina Katerina's men found it 1792.'

Ruan raising his eyebrows, such finds being ten a penny, a view Gerhard freely admitted to.

'I know, I know. And yes, there's the usual folk tales and religious tracts like always. But there's something else in this. Something unique.'

Ruan struggling to recall the details.

Unexcited by the find at the time, Russian not one of his skills. Brought up in English, Dutch and Latin, and latterly acquiring enough German and the Romance languages to make his way along the tracks of the books he'd been asked to travel. Early days in Ruan's career as a book-finder. Ruan returning a couple of months later to find Gerhard had had his stroke and gone out of business. His small shop of manuscripts and books sold off by Gerhard's sister to pay for the care he would need until the day he died.

Ruan distraught on Gerhard's behalf when he'd visited; Gerhard a man he'd always liked and trusted, as Gerhard did him. Gerhard on that visit laboriously picking out one of his paintings, stressing that Ruan look into its shadows by an exaggerated nod of his head, pointing out with his painting stick the particular volume he'd chosen to depict in one unenticing dusky corner: usual city-scape of Deventer, small stall to one side, book-seller parading his wares on a barrow. A single manuscript opened to the viewer: squiggles scrawled in minute script across its pages that looked, at first glance, like nothing meaningful at all. Until Ruan bent down, looked closer. Saw the Cyrillic letters for what they were. Gerhard robbed of language, robbed of the ability to form proper sentences, if not of the ability to communicate in another that was pictorial, at least to Gerhard's damaged brain. Ruan leaning in. Ruan seeing clearly what Gerhard had written; sluice-gates of Ruan's memories opening as he thought on it: the Russian letters - Слово о полку игореве.

'The Song of Igor's Campaign?' he'd asked Gerhard. 'The manuscript you wanted me to research?'

Hippolyte Gerhard nodding vigorously.

'Where is the manuscript now?' the question useless, Gerhard unable to reply in words that made any sense. Gerhard's words not entirely random, if anyone had spent enough time with him to figure it out – which they had not. Gerhard's mind groping through his vast internal archives, snatching up any that lay nearby what he actually meant. Gerhard trying to tell Ruan: *It's one of a kind. It's secular, for starters, which is very unusual. And, like I already told you, it's about Prince Igor's defeat by the Polovtsy tribe who were*

*later assimilated into Hungarian society, although they took
centuries to do so and would not do so now if they could get out
of it. They need a spur, and this document could be exactly that.
A basis for national identity and revolt. You've got to find out
more about it. You've got to!*

What came out was not any of this.

What Hippolyte Gerhard's side-drooped mouth
managed to tell Ruan was a struggled string of words that
had made no sense at all, all connectors lost; no *ands* or *buts*
or *becauses*. Only nouns and the odd verb or adjective to
work with.

*Alone pen, garden kuman...*

Spittle aggregating at the sides of Gerhard's mouth as he
fought on.

*Slovo bottom booming...furrows furrows...*

Gerhard clenching his fists as he tried to make Ruan
understand.

*Kuman,* he repeated. *Kuman feet-sky. Opals rubies
diamonds. Red-feet. Kuman red-feet. Kuman feet-sky.*

Ruan wrote down the words, nodded at Hippolyte
Gerhard and smiled, made out he knew what he'd been
talking about.

'Well,' he'd said, 'at least I've a place to start, and for that
I thank you.'

The lie easy on his lips as he saw Hippolyte Gerhard
breathing deeply, believing Ruan, believing Ruan had made
the connections and understood the importance of what
he'd tried to convey.

Hippolyte Gerhard not lasting many weeks longer.

Hippolyte doing what Ruan assumed he himself would do in the same circumstance.

Hippolyte Gerhard - having relieved himself of his burden, bequeathing it all to Ruan Peat and believing in Ruan Peat implicitly – tottering his way on his sticks through the night streets of Deventer to the lagoon and toppling himself in on the skirl of midnight, when no one would be abroad to fish him out.

FABIAN AND FRAU DIETER reached the first graduation tower and lit the lanterns placed in niches inside its walls, taking several minutes to look over the mechanism needed to bring the water up. Fabian not daring to look at Frau Dieter, for she seemed brighter somehow, a lamp without a shade. She'd stripped off her gloves, lifted her mud-stained skirts, clambered to the first platform to inspect the valves. Fabian an agitation by her side.

'Each pipe is five centimeters in diameter,' Frau Dieter announced, without need of measuring tape, 'so a working width of four centimeters, assuming a five mil thickness of the metal.'

Proud of her adoption of the French system of measurement – a requirement attached to their funding for the mills – that seemed so eminently sensible, based on the decimal rather than the cumbersome Rule of Twelve. She rubbed her nose, chewed her bottom lip, spoke more to herself than Fabian.

'So given the median speed of the water in the lett and its temperature, which have to be the same as ours as they both come from the same spring, coupled with the pressure dictated by the width of the pipes...'

A few more calculations going on in her head as she looked into the gloom of the tower above her.

'And given there's valves on each of the five platforms, I should say eight minutes to get the water up the tower until we throw our lever to release it into the channels up top. Two minutes for it to get from one side to the other while the second wheel catches up. So ten all in all.'

Fabian clearing his throat.

'Best give it a few more minutes. Holger told me it takes that long to get both wheels turning at maximum speed.'

No rancour in Frau Dieter for this correction, instead swift to agree.

'Quite right. Thank you, Fabian.'

Allowing Fabian to take her hand, guide her back down the steps, feeling his thumb brush, oh so softly, oh so casually, at that sensitive stretch of skin between thumb and index finger before releasing her.

'I'll open the first valve,' she said, 'while you do the second, and meanwhile I'll get up to the third platform and so on, and we'll get Ruan and Piet to do the same in the second tower.'

Fabian nodding. Thinking how odd all this was.

'I'd best go check all the valves are workable, haven't seized,' he said and was off, grabbing one of the lanterns from the niches and heading up. Frau Dieter watching him take the steps two by two, heard his boots hitting the second platform and then the next and the next, Frau Dieter waiting down below, Frau Dieter wondering about Fabian Guichot and that slight stroke of his fingers on her skin. Embarrassed to find herself wondering what else those fingers might be capable of.

'Oh shush yourself, woman,' she whispered to herself, but didn't move, didn't shift. Kept her eyes fixed on the bobbing lantern as Fabian took himself to the very top of the tower, fittled around with his valves, crossed from one tower to the other and repeated the performance before returning.

'All fine?' she asked.

'All fine,' Fabian agreed.

The two of them suspended at the bottom of the tower, the moment broken by Piet hauling open the door.

'Bonfire's only minutes away, fireworks next. How long have we got? When do we need to open the sluice-gates?'

Frau Dieter briefing him, Fabian getting himself up to the second platform.

Time to get doing.

# 17

# And Up Goes The Bonfire

PROFESSOR JORN ENDED his second speech, parenthesizing those given by the other great men of Bad Salzbaum. A lengthy business, during which most folk melted away to the stalls, stall-holders doing a roaring trade: gingerbread-maker completely sold out; barrows of nuts and fruit down to their last; tool-trader left with a few spare handles for hoes and rakes; knife-grinder hot with all the sharpening; ribbon-and-button purveyor regarding her empty boxes with satisfaction. Folk returning for the main event, sitting on the makeshift seats scattered about the bonfire.

Professor Jorn holding up his hands.

'Mayor Bomberg will now set the bonfire going!'

Piet handing Bomberg the lighted firebrand as Bomberg came down the steps.

'Just do the first one,' Piet whispered. 'I'll do the rest.'

Bomberg nodding, doing as Piet directed: first branch quickly catching, primed tinder springing to life in gleeful crackle, huge plumes of leaping carefree flames snaking with ease through Holger's carefully laid bundles as Piet lit the rest. Crowds whooping as branch after branch, bundle after bundle, caught to flame, colours flying up from the precipitate: reds and greens, blues and oranges, bright as pheasants' plumage in Spring.

Bomberg taking a smart step backwards as a couple of cinders leapt and sizzled through the outer layer of his trousers; Jorn aghast, batting at Bomberg's leg with his hat. Bomberg not caring. Bomberg finding the situation so glorious, so unexpected, he actually laughed out loud and couldn't remember when he'd last done that, when he'd last felt so playful, so childlike in his wonderment to be so close to the roaring inferno he'd set burning with his own hand.

'Oh my! What a sight!' he called out, taking another few steps back as the heat intensified, small boys running around the circle of the bonfire flinging loose branches into the conflagration, throwing on anything they could find: dropped gloves, twigs, empty food wrappers; all laughing and laughing. Smoke curling up into the night, away over the unsalted salt hedges and the mud-bath enclosure and the town and all the way up to the mill-workings where the night watchmen sat, guarding the milled flour from pilferers, noses twitching as they got to their feet, placed their hands above their eyes, looked towards the small bright speck of the bonfire away on the other side of the valley.

Light jumping in everyone's eyes; stall-holders glad Holger Stoss had moved them so far back. Only a few minutes before the entire heap took hold. Golden light spilling up into the evening, rainbowed jumps of colours as the various precipitates spat and burned, visitors and citizens of Bad Salzbaum sharing delight.

Mayor Bomberg led back up the steps to the dais by Professor Jorn, the towns-men drawing their chairs together, talking animatedly, puffing grandly on cigars and supping from glasses constantly refilled the moment they were emptied, until the lot of them - bar Professor Jorn, who never drank to excess – were tight as corks. Mayor Bomberg included.

'Such as spectacle! Such a night!'

'And there's more,' Professor Jorn reminded, raising his hand, letting it drop, telling Piet to get the pyrotechnics going.

Caro at the ready, grabbing the lit branch Piet thrust at him.

'This here's where you need to light the first touch-paper,' Piet had explained, pointing out to Caro the mechanics of the display: five rows carefully spaced. 'There's fuse-lines running from the first row to the next and so on, and from each firework to the other.'

Caro whistling, taking a deep breath.

'What if it goes wrong? What if the fuse-lines don't work?'

Piet had worried about the same, but Holger hadn't left anything to chance, as Piet now told Caro.

'It'll work. On the faintest chance it doesn't then there's back-up fuse-lines at the end of each row so you can set each going individually if they don't go up on their own. But,' he warned, 'what you mustn't do, what you absolutely mustn't do, is go between the lines.' Telling Caro what Holger had told him. 'If one particular row fizzles out halfway through then let it fizzle. Start the next instead. Are you ready? Professor's just given the sign.'

Caro nervous.

'Shouldn't you be doing this?' he asked, Piet smiling, revealing crooked teeth that glinted in the light of the bonfire.

'Ever opened a sluice-gate before?'

Caro shaking his head.

'Didn't think so. You'll be fine. Do as I've told you and come join us at the towers when the last line of fireworks is going up.'

And oh my, did they go up!

Coruscating lines of fire arcing through the sky that had the crowds oohing and aahing, craning their necks to breaking point. Scents of saltpeter and cordite in the air, pops and bangs as one or other of Holger's fireworks gained ascendance and exploded as if the world itself was about to end; burning rosettes and rainbows in the sky no one had ever seen before that had dogs and cats cowering under tables and chairs, mice and rats skittering beneath floor-boards. The citizens of Bad Salzbaum out there to a man, witnessing the greatest spectacle they'd see in their lifetimes.

Professor Jorn agog at what the mind-empty Holger Stoss had achieved. Not that he was counting his blessings yet. Greatest spectacle yet to come. And only twenty minutes left. Quick glance at his pocket watch. Nerves in him like he didn't know he'd ever had. Or maybe only the once.

Fireworks done, everyone chattering as the bonfire burned, glad for its warmth. Big men of the town belly-filled with fine food and drink. Professor Jorn taking out his pocket-watch again, flipping it open, counting down the minutes.

And then the bells of St Peter's began ringing out nine hours and he'd new worries overtaking the last. Eyes fixed on the hedges, seeing them as he'd never done before: so still and stark a backdrop to the hustle and bustle of townsfolk and stall-holders whose bright faces glowed in the roaring rumble of the fire; hedges stern and steadfast like a guardian, or an enemy now that he thought on it, with that dark hollow at their core. Caught a wink of light coming from the nearest graduation tower – undoubtedly Piet getting ready to do whatever he needed to do. Thought occurring, too late, that he should have offered help now Holger Stoss was out of the picture. Although if Piet botched the job he'd skin the lad alive.

Five strikes of the bell, and Professor Jorn blinked behind his glasses; this his first self-organized hedge dressing, as impressed as everyone else by the wonderment of bonfire and fireworks, the gala so bright and busy it might have been born of the fire itself.

Seven strikes of the bell.

A shiver going up his spine, heart racing.

Professor Jorn getting to his feet, hands gripping the side of his lectern.

Eight strikes... Jorn's nerves jangling, eyes flicking spasmodically from tower to hedges and back again, aware that several of his fellows had tottered to their feet behind him.

The ninth and final strike.

Jorn's throat gone dry, someone beating him to the punch, making his pronouncement for him.

'Here it comes!' Mayor Bomberg yelled, right in Professor Jorn's ear, others down by the fire taking on the call, all standing in unison, producing a sound like bees swarming from a hive.

'ALL SET?' PIET CALLED.

'All set,' Ruan agreed.

Sluice-gates opened, water rushing down the lett to the water-wheels.

At the first graduation tower Frau Dieter saw the wheel begin to spin.

'Are we ready?' she asked Fabian, her call merry as a lark in spring.

'Ready,' Fabian answered, blinking at this newness to her, this lightness so contrary to her usual formality. A few minutes of worry before Ruan, Piet and Caro arrived to man the second tower, but come they did – in the very nick of time.

'Listen for my shout,' Frau Dieter commanded. Frau Dieter taking up Ruan's pocket-watch. Frau Dieter waiting until the second hand hit the mark.

'Go!' Frau Dieter yelled to Fabian.

'Go!' Ruan commanded Piet.

Piet, Caro and Fabian scrambling up the towers, Ruan and Frau Dieter coming on behind them, all loosening their allotted valves, the water shooting up the tubes of its own volition, up the graduation towers and out over the hedges.

And on the dot of the ninth strike it began: moonlit slips of water sliding along the runnels like molten silver; silent ribbons seeming to ripple and hover above the great dark shoulders of the hedges; a communal catching of breath as people watched the water race and settle; a rustling as folk rose from the environs of stalls and bonfire, running for the hedges, pouring into the dark space between. Jorn, caught up in the moment, leaping from the dais to do the same, hustled and jostled as he went, hat knocked off and forgotten and, once inside, caught fast between the hidden space between the hedges, he stilled, as did the rest, listening to the water dripping its way through the blackthorn bundles; saw the glitter of stars up above and the silvered drops of water cascading from the tops of the hedges, a faint mizzle pattering down on the crowd crammed inside who held out hands and tongues, eager for its blessing.

As did Jorn, who'd never felt anything like it.

Never a religious man, not after what he'd been through.

Yet here, in the confines of the hedges, with the sound of water running across the boards above and droplets hanging like diamonds in the moonlit air and everyone about him calm, eyes closed, eager for their touch, he understood what it was to feel part of a greater whole; why people gathered together in church, mosque and synagogue, or knelt before their shrines, for here he was doing the same: partaking in the numinous, sharing the secrets of the hedges which perhaps held the healing power he'd espoused if not truly believed.

More things in heaven and earth than you could shake a stick at.

Stick of Professor Jorn unbending in the moment.

Piet about to get a bonus, be declared Head Groundsman for providing the enormity of the night the empty-headed shell of Holger Stoss had put in jeopardy.

ONE MAN, NEWLY ARRIVED, detached himself from the celebrations, going in the opposite direction to the general hubbub, heading towards the spa hotel; pushing open its ornate glass doors, slipping inside, uncertain which way to go. On impulse he turned to the left where he'd spied a bolted door, unlocked it, caught the sweet dank smell of a cellar and edged his way forward to the head of the stone stairs. Feeling around him for a candle niche, finding a short stub inside, taking out his tinderbox and getting the stub lit before descending into gloom.

Once at the bottom he held up the paucity of his candle, peering into darkness.

Others might have found the cellar daunting, shivered with its chill, seen ghostly shapes moving with menace in every shadowed corner. Not him. This man having spent his early life buried in the calc-tuff of the Szépasszonyvölgye – the Valley of the Pretty Lady – honeycombed with wine cellars burrowed into the rock. Troglodytic dwellings too for those who couldn't afford better, as his family had not. Home back then a long dark tunnel hacked out inch by inch, yard by yard; small chambers to left and right making kitchen and sleeping quarters. Big stack of potatoes and sacks of grain at its farthest end. No fear here for him, although intook a sharp breath when his eyes flitted over the curled up body on its bales.

And it was a body; the head, for no reason he could think of, missing.

'So here you are,' he murmured, 'after all these years.'

*What a bloody waste. And what a way to go.*

A boy nestled in needles, his pursuers a breath away.

Mystery solved of how he'd been there one minute, gone the next. They'd always assumed he'd got himself into the hotel, hidden himself and his prize away; had maybe been heading for this cellar, now he thought on it.

A shock to learn, the previous night, of the corpse found buried in the hedges. Making perfect sense of the abandoned dray, the disappeared boy, the non-appearance of what they'd stolen seven years back.

*That little shit! If he hadn't already buried himself alive I'd gladly have done it for him.*

Zsolt always so good with his words, expressing the moment.

*Buggaring well here all along, after all our head-bashing. Mokush, go check it out. Our crate has to be in the hotel and we need to get at it before those blasted book-finders.*

Crate most likely removed from corpse and cellar to somewhere more convivial. Suspicion confirmed as Mokush looked but did not find. Lick of sympathy in him for the buried boy as he retreated, but time running on: small candle soon self-extinguished. Mokush going back up the steps, closing the cellar door, pushing home the bolt, thinking he might shift himself into the hotel proper and have a gander. Interrupted by two of the bonfire gawpers returning early, pushing open the glass doors, passing him by, climbing the grandiose stairs. Snatch of conversation on their lips.

'Surely this can wait until morning?' the younger man chivvied. 'It's been such an exciting night, and I'm pretty much pooped.'

The older man smiling. Rook black hair. Stubble evident on chin and cheeks.

'Get yourself back to our quarters,' he said. 'Nothing here but me bashing my way into a load of old books.'

'I don't know what you think we'll find,' the younger man said, halting briefly on the landing, the two of them standing statue still for a moment, their doubles in the mirror clear as day to the man at the bottom of the stairs. Mokush listening closely. Mind shifting. Breath halting. For these had to be the book-finders. Mokush taking note of them, swallowing them in, fixing them in his memory, as too their words.

'We'll not know until we look,' the older parried. 'And by the way, you're filthy as a miner.'

'Might well be,' said the younger. 'But there's no way on heaven or earth you're going to open that crate without me.'

'All right then. Let's have at it.'

Last words Mokush heard as the two gained the upper corridor and disappeared from view.

Mokush gazing after them, staring into the blank expanse of the vast mirror, nothing to be seen from his perspective but a dark cowl of sky hovered over with thin clouds and the bright circle of a moon pushing against them.

Mokush standing inanimate as the doors to the spa were pushed wide to usher in a twittering crowd.

'Restaurant's still open!' Professor Jorn loudly informed his guests. 'As of course are all the lounge rooms. Eat well, ladies and gents, drink your fill. This has truly been a memorable evening and I hope you will consider coming back to visit us soon.'

And away the tide of folk went, chittering and chattering, quaff-time upon them, restaurant beckoning.

No one noticing Mokush as he stole back into the night, made his way along the grass by the hedges, touching his fingers to the place where the lad had apparently been found, passed the clickety-clack of stall-holders breaking down their tents and trestles, passed the small cott in which Holger Stoss was lying on his bed.

Mokush taking long strides over the small bridge above the lett.

His guts in a roil to think of all that must come and all that must next be done. What his brother would dictate to be their next course of action, which had to be the re-stealing of what they'd already stolen before.

And Hela.

Mokush thinking of Hela most of all, because he coveted her. Love too romantic a word for what he felt: a deep avaricious longing for the woman who'd chosen his idiot brother over himself. Bitterness in every bone to accede, but accede he'd done because that was how it was in his family, his tribe: patriarchy and hierarchy taking precedence as they'd always done back home. Thought only occurring now that Hela was not from home.

Hela from somewhere else entirely.

Hela from the home of Håkon Tryggvason.

Hela knowing all about the hedges, taking such an interest.

*My mother's childhood friend is the wife of the man who does all this.*

She'd mentioned it several times, been proud, had wanted to contact the woman.

Contact Zsolt insistently forbade.

*Hiding is all we have, and we will carry on doing it until the day we arise victorious.*

His brother always so pompous. Not a trait Mokush admired.

Mokush weighing up what he was going to say to Zsolt when he got back.

Mokush thinking that maybe he should hang around for a while until the spa guests had retired to their beds, see if he could get back inside the hotel, see what the coal-miner and Mr. Rook-Black had found in their crate. No time like the present.

Mokush teasing through threads of thoughts, pulling at one in particular: which was why the boy had run at all. Seeing another hand, another agency behind that running. A slim hand, pale and delicious as it held the knife to cut their meat, their bread, the apples she bought in the market. A woman who could move freely, as he and his brother could not; a woman who knew more than they about hedges and spa; a woman well able to direct Constantine directly towards the hedges.

Why she might have engineered Constantine's larceny and escape he couldn't comprehend. Mokush standing in this dark night on this tiny bridge before going back over it, looking at what Constantine must have looked at as he'd run, panting, pulling his dray through that other dark night. Didn't seem so mad a theory now, for there was another place he might have been heading other than the spa hotel; a place - given the night and the panic - he might have missed.

A place which, with Hela's name upon his lips, would have given him sanctuary, relief, and the help he needed.

Boots on wood as the water brooked and ran on unconcerned beneath the bridge. Boots on grass as he walked slowly back towards the hedges.

Eyes fixed on the glimmering groaning remnants of the bonfire, the last of its bundles resembling men rolled side by side, burning right down to their bones. Eyes flicking left and right in its dying light, espying the small square of a work-shed a hundred odd yards to the right.

Eyes drifting from work-shed to a copse of ash trees that reveled in these lime-rich soils, latching onto the cottage built in the copse's shadow, protecting it from prevailing winds, providing all the wood needed for its fire.

Windows closed and dark, not dissimilar to the hard black buds the ash trees held tight throughout the Winter months.

No light inside those windows. No movement in that tiny house. Only a curlicue of smoke coming from its chimney, as if summoned by the night.

# 18

## Jokers And Jackanapes

———⟡———

'THAT'S SOME BRASS NECK you've got,' Mick said, clapping Ivor on the back. 'Bit doolally, am I? That the best you could come up with?'

Ivor blustering, feeling hot, hoping that hefty hand wasn't about to shove a knife into his gullet.

'Bit short on time,' he answered, bracing himself for the strike, unnerved by the growling coming from Mick's throat – Mick's only concession to laughter - Greta coming alongside and shoving an elbow into Ivor's ribs.

'He's only joking you. That was real quick thinking!'

Ivor blushing at the compliment, unable to articulate an answer, looking instead towards Zeebrugge. Feeling it a beautiful morning, mostly because they hadn't been shot on the spot a few hundred yards down the sands. Also because it really was a beautiful morning. Marram grass scribbled on one side with frost, moon a visible disc in the sky, sea a calm blue expanse welcoming the several fishing vessels plying from the port.

'Did he take much? That soldier?' Ivor asked. 'Has he left us enough?'

Mick snorted.

'That man's no solider. He's a marauder, pure and simple. Seen enough of them. French army's filled to bursting with the bastards. But have to hand it to his Commanding Officer. One of the good guys he is, and no mistake, and there's still plenty left. Had some real class leaders in the Legion. Just because you're fighting them,' Mick cast a glance at Ivor, 'don't make `em all bad.'

Ivor creased his brows.

'*Liberté, Égalité, Fraternité* and all that,' Mick added.

Ivor, amateur philosopher, acceding Mick the point. Liberty, Equality and Fraternity grand ideals. More suited to the English side, as he saw it, than the French. Ivor stepping up for the defence.

'That was the Revolution,' he argued. 'Napoleon's a despot. Has his *Maison de l'Empereur* run like a state within a state. Three thousand staff, grand paintings by grand painters, chests of coin and precious stones that would feed his entire army twice over if he sold them off.' Ivor on a rant that wasn't at its end. 'And you of all people should know that everywhere Napoleon goes also goes sixty odd coaches of luxuries to keep him and his favourites well provisioned.'

Mick scratched his ear with dirty fingernails.

'Aye well. Heard about it,' he agreed, for it was common knowledge and a common gripe amongst the men. 'But your lot ain't exactly short on palaces and hordes of servants running up and down their stairs like rats through sewers.'

'My lot?' Ivor jerked his head in annoyance. 'Who do you mean, *my lot?*'

Mick sighed, staring up the sand towards their goal.

'Don't mean no insult by it, man, but you ain't exactly no ragamuffin from the back streets. And nobs is nobs, wherever you find 'em; and nobs is nobbity. Not much equality doing on that front. Kinda why you're with us, if you haven't forgot.'

'Think your lot came over to Ireland to spread a bit of happiness?' Greta weighed in. 'You've been stamping over our land for a cupla centuries and nothing good's come of it, least not for us.'

Ivor under siege. An ill-equipped lawyer tasked with pleading for a client he knew was guilty, gritting his teeth when Mick once again came to his aid.

'Now that ain't fair, Greta. Can't shove the entire criminality of a nation onto one man's shoulders.'

Ivor screwing up his eyes. The notion of England as a criminal entity unpalatable, and yet – as he was beginning to discover – not without foundation. His beautiful morning no longer beautiful. But no going back for Ivor. The last of the English army decamping from Walcheren at this very moment, the French amassed to take it the second they were gone.

Nothing for Ivor Merrill to do but go on.

———— ❧ ————

'WE DID IT,' PIET SAID as he emerged from his tower, Ruan already off with Caro to open the sluice-gate to the mud-baths. An easy task with no complications, Fabian's engine already on the go, and the mud-baths nothing to do with Piet. Piet glancing towards Holger's cottage, seeing no light there. His delight at his achievements tempered by Holger not being here, by Holger not being able to face it.

Frau Dieter and Fabian Guichot emerging from their own tower, Frau Dieter glowing like a glimmer from the bonfire had set her alight inside.

'We did it!' she cried exuberantly. 'We really did it!'

*Just because we're not what everyone expects us to be doesn't mean we're not capable of greatness.*

Words she'd spoken to Fabian after fishing him from the mire of the mill-workings. Words meant and acted upon, for both mills and mud-baths.

'Piet,' she called. 'There's something I need to speak to you about. And Fabian too. It occurring to me earlier...'

Speech arrested by the reappearance of Caro running across the grass towards her, thin face pinched with anxiety. Ruan a few yards behind.

'I hope we've done it right,' Caro worried. 'The mud-bath pump kind of hiccupped after we opened the sluice-gate. We've no idea if that's good or bad.'

Fabian regarding this young scrap with indulgence.

'It's fine,' he said. 'Just the water heating up.'

Relief evident on Caro's face.

'Oh thank the Lord. I thought we'd mucked it all up.'

'You've mucked up nothing, my fine young friend,' Frau Dieter assured. 'And we couldn't have done any of this without you.'

Frau Dieter alarmed when Caro flung his skinny arms about her waist. Frau Dieter looking at Ruan for direction,

Ruan shrugging his shoulders. Ruan always perplexed by Caro's easy allegiance to people he hardly knew, envying him that stalwart belief in the goodness of others which surely hadn't been earned and should have been knocked out of Caro early doors. If Ruan had undergone what Caro had, he'd have been as sour as an under-ripe lemon and never trusted another person again.

But that was him, and this was Caro.

'Why don't you and Frau Dieter go check all is right with the mud-baths?' Ruan advised, Caro releasing Frau Dieter, Frau Dieter agreeing to the diversion, taking Caro's hand in her own, never feeling quite as alive as she was now.

'And why not?' she said. 'Just take a breath, and then let's go see.'

Frau Dieter walking over the moonlit grass thinking how grand life was. Reaching the baths to find all in order. Caro running off to take a closer look, fascinated by the gurgling of the warming mud-water creeping through the tiled channels. Several visitors arriving to do the same, check out this new addition to the spa. Visitors impressed by the murals Fabian had painted inside the atrium and the warmth of the mud when they dipped in their fingers to test it.

'I need to talk to you about Holger Stoss,' Frau Dieter said, as she and Fabian hovered on the outer edges.

'I kind of thought you would,' Fabian replied easily, Fabian pre-empting her. 'Why don't we set the Stoss's up here? Holger can see to all the towels and whatnot, Mathilde can do the rest. I'd be happy to build an extension. It won't be grandiose, but will be enough.'

Frau Dieter lost for words. Frau Dieter grasping Fabian's hand as Caro had grasped his about her waist. A lifeline here, she knew. A lifeline most weren't given the chance of. A man who understood her, anticipated her, and got it right.

'How did you know?' she asked. Fabian looking at his boots, unable to meet her eyes or acknowledge her small fingers on his own. Feeling gruff and large and clumsy.

'Can I show you something?' he said in answer. Frau Dieter releasing him, hating she'd made him feel uncomfortable.

'Show me,' she said. Fabian leading her a few yards up the lett. Fabian kneeling down, lifting from the grass an odd contraption: an apparently empty box, a tube running into an upright set of pipes above which hung a pegged cylinder attached to a small water-wheel, a miniature of those they'd set going below the towers.

'Whatever is it?' Frau Dieter asked, mystified.

Fabian nervously putting the wheel to the water so it began to turn.

'Bit of a toy, really,' he explained. 'But thought, if you liked it, we could build a bigger one...'

Frau Dieter watching as the wheel splashed and paddled in the watcr, pegged cylinder turning, pipes beginning to play, the sound soft and reedy like wind blowing over hollow posts: utterly unpredictable, unworldly, a ghost of a melody, such as the moon might make if given voice.

'It's...entrancing,' Frau Dieter whispered, looking down at Fabian on his knees in the wet grass, one hand keeping the wheel in the watcr, the other holding the instrument steady as the cylinder turned and the pegs caught the tiny levers that opened the tops of the pipes, released the air compressed by the weight of the water, allowing the miniscule organ to play.

'Thought we might ask Professor Jorn if we could build a full scale model for...'

'Professor Jorn nothing!' Frau Dieter interrupted with contempt. 'We'll build one all right, we'll build it right here. It'll add perfect ambience to the mud-baths and it will be astonishing,' said the astonishing Frau Dieter. Fabian so surprised he brought the wheel out of the water, dropped it on the grass. Frau Dieter quickly kneeling beside him, the wetness of the grass creeping up the silk of her skirts the moment it touched, darkening its silver sheen.

'Do let me try,' she said. 'It's the most marvelous gift anyone has ever given me. Thank you, Fabian.'

Fabian Guichot embarrassed, unable to reply. Would happily have stayed on his knees, in the wetness of the grass, watching the wonder on Frau Dieter's face as she got the little toy working, for the remainder of his life.

'HOW'S HOLGER DOING?' Piet asked, Mathilde opening the door, closing it behind him. She looked exhausted, had obviously been crying. Piet sorry to have come, to have disturbed the two of them. No whist going on tonight. No lanterns. The mere flicker of stove-fire to see by. Holger on the bed with his back to them, an acrid waft of urine sour in the air.

'Not too good,' she said. 'But he's asleep now, for the while at least. I'm sorry you had to take the brunt. You've always been a good lad, to both me and Holger. It's probably time you knew the reason. And there is a reason, Piet. No matter what anyone thinks.'

*No matter what bloody Professor Jorn thinks,* was in Piet's mind.

'I wish you'd tell me,' he said. 'I'd help if I could.'

Mathilde spinning out the time putting pancakes on the fire-pan, boiling the kettle, tucking a tea-cloth into her belt.

'There was a bad fire a long time ago,' she said, telling Piet of the burning man, how the sights and smells of that night had burrowed deep into Holger's marrow. How of late it had clawed its way right out again so it was with him day and night, filling the holes in his memory until he could think of nothing else. How because of it Holger had begun to realise what Mathilde already knew: that his mind and memories were on a lease, become a debt he would have to keep on paying until there was nothing left.

Words like coarse hairs sticking in her throat. Words she didn't want to speak. But it was night, and it was dark, and only Piet here to hear them and she finally got them said. That no amount of rest was going to put Holger right. Only a dark and empty road opening up before him and Mathilde since the Professor had ordered them from their home.

Piet twiddling with the empty cup, trying to find a solution despite knowing none was to be had.

'Is there anything at all I can do?' he asked. The question hanging in the air between them. Mathilde flipping the pancakes, the kettle thrumbling as it boiled. Mathilde making tea, pouring it out. Putting the pancakes on a plate, adding a lash of butter, placing the plate on the small table between them.

'It's the oddest thing,' she said, as she handed tea to Piet, 'and it's going to sound a little mad, but there is one thing.'

She coughed, cleared her throat. Piet taking the cup, sipping, closed his hands about its warmth.

'You can say anything to me, Mathilde,' Piet said.

Mathilde creasing her brows, pulling in her lips, rubbed a hand about her chin.

'You'll not know this,' she began, 'but I wasn't born here. I was born in a place called Torghatten in Norway. Where I first met my Holger.'

*My Holger.*

Piet had tears incipient, blinked to hold them back. Took another sip of his tea. Waited for Mathilde to go on.

'We were a small community, cut off, so to speak, from the rest of the world. The merest chance Holger's ship got caught in the ice off our shores back when we were young.'

Mathilde pushing a pancake about the plate, couldn't bring herself to fold it and put it to her mouth.

'The thing is,' she went on. 'I saw someone in the market a couple of weeks back. A young woman buying a bag of apples. I'd no idea who she was, but I knew that I knew her. It sounds contradictory, but in Torghatten, in Vettie's Giel, we were so close knit. Every family having its own peculiarities, and I would swear, absolutely swear, she was one of our own.'

Mathilde seeing the young woman prevaricating over the apple barrels: *I'll have two of these and three of those, thank you very much.* The exact same accent Mathilde had, and the exact same profile of Mathilde's childhood friend Ussi. Ussi, who'd been maid-of-honour at Mathilde's wedding; Ussi, who had led Mathilde down the crooks of the bird's-leg path to Bergenstift to tie the knot. Ussi, who had wobbled over the bridge because she was a little drunk – because they were both a little drunk, if truth be told. And why not? First outside wedding Torghatten had seen for as long as anyone remembered. Mathilde marrying Holger a happening extraordinary, to be celebrated.

And oh my, how they'd celebrated! Bergenstift folk up in arms about how long the Torghatten folk had sung into the night, how long their fiddles had been playing. And how Ussi had slid away with Torgi Erikksson, a man no one liked, least of all Mathilde who'd known how vile a man he would become since they were children: a bully, an aggravation to boys and girls alike.

Ussi returning to Vettie's Giel with tight lips, bruised arms, ripped skirts. Everyone knowing what must have happened, but if Ussi was so foolish drunk she'd allowed herself to be alone with Torgi Erikksson then what could she expect? Ussi two months pregnant when Mathilde and Holger left on his rescue boat, not that Torgi was going to step up and do what might have been considered right, and Ussi thanking God for it every day. One night with him bad enough, so much she'd confided to Mathilde. A lifetime with him not bearing contemplation. But Ussi loving her little girl when she came. Someone to care for, to cherish, tell tales to, especially after Mathilde had gone.

'What are you asking of me?' Piet unsure where this was going.

Mathilde poking at the fire, shoving in a few more sticks.

'I want you to find her,' she said, oh so very quietly. 'I need to know if she is who I think she is.' Words coming fast now she was voicing what had only been vague notions before. 'And if she is from home, I want her to talk to Holger. I want her to tell him about the ice, the scree, the hills. About the people there and what became of them. I know he doesn't recall much about recent yesterdays, but he remembers distant ones well enough and I want them to oust the burning man, go further back, to the happy times when we first met.'

'He doesn't remember them?' Piet asked quietly.

Mathilde fiddling with her apron, fiddling with her cup.

Pretended to pour more out more tea where it wasn't needed.

'I don't know,' she replied truthfully, unable to lift her eyes from the kindling in the stove. 'But I do know that bad bonfire is burning away in him, burning away all the other doors in there that might be able to take him to better places. And this woman I saw, if she is Ussi's daughter, well. Maybe she can open one of them at least.'

Piet nodding.

Doors and gate-ways seemingly the theme of the night.

Open them rightly and all goes to plan.

Open them wrongly, or the wrong one at the wrong time, and there was no putting the water back into the stream when it's already run into the lake, as the old saying went. Or the old saying where he'd come from. Him and Mathilde not dissimilar, both from faraway places cut off from the rest of the world, both ending up in Bad Salzbaum.

As too, perhaps, had this daughter of Mathilde's childhood friend.

'Have I ever told you about my family?' he asked, although knew he had not, and neither more to Holger. Mathilde looking up at Piet, frounce and frumple about her eyes deepened by the shadows of the night, by this shared intimacy in this darkened room.

'You never have,' she said, unconcerned by this swerve in the conversation, seeing it like that bird-leg lane creasing down the cliff back home: bends and twists, turns and curves. Frail bridges over fast-flowing rivers. Everyone getting where they were going in their own time.

'It's kind of an in-between place,' Piet began. 'A nowhere place. A place invented.'

Seeing timber forests; orchards of apple, peach and pear, scraggly banks of quince rippling with petals in Spring-time; bees and flies bumbling about, ecstatic with scent and glut.

'A place folk went who didn't fit elsewhere,' Piet went on. 'Germans, Dutch, Poles, Lithuanians, Jews. All settling for different reasons, but we were a community. Like your Torghatten. Lots of Arminians and Remonstrants not overly liked by the mainstream church back home, my parents included.'

Mathilde having no idea what an Arminian was, nor a Remonstrant; said nothing as Piet paused, regarded the butter congealing about the pancakes. Piet seeing in them some faint figuration of his homeland that had been divvied up in 1772, not long after his parents moved there. One part to Russia, another to Prussia. His own community's little piece delivered to Austrian rule.

Telling Mathilde all this.

'They rechristened us. Named us Galicia, after the ancient kingdom of that place.' Piet feeling his way forward. 'What I'm trying to say is this: I came back. Was late-born, my folks in their forties when I came along. Both dying when I was young.'

A spasm of movement as Mathilde put her hand to his knee.

'Oh Piet, I'm so sorry. Why have you never said?'

Piet shaking his head.

'Because I was never a part of them, not really. Nor of their religion, which was stern, strict and spare.'

Mathilde understanding this much. Nothing about Piet neither stern, strict, nor spare.

'My point is,' he explained, 'I understand how complicated close-knit communities can be, how they work. I came here because this is where my father came from. From Bad Salzbaum. Only a name back then, but I was curious. And it strikes me that maybe this apple-buying woman is not here by chance. Have you never thought she maybe came here to find someone, and specifically you?'

RUAN HEADED BACK TO the hedge-man's crate, his itch to get at the books unrelieved by bonfires, pyrotechnics and sluice-gates. Caro a reluctant adjunct as they opened the doors to the hotel and went inside.

'Surely this can wait until morning?' he queried, as they took the stairs to Professor Jorn's private rooms where the crate had been stowed. 'It's been such an exciting night, and I'm pretty much pooped.'

Ruan softened. Ruan delegated. Ruan allowing Caro his perfect night.

'Get yourself back to our quarters,' he commanded. 'Nothing here but me bashing my way into a load of old books.'

Caro yawned, but was not about to let Ruan bash his way into that load of old books without Caro being present.

'I don't know what you think we'll find,' he argued as they got to the landing, saw themselves in the great glass mirror, Caro realising he'd smudges from the bonfire all over face and clothes.

'We'll not know until we look,' Ruan said. 'And by the way, you're filthy as a miner.'

Caro rubbing his face with his sleeve, making the smudges worse.

'Might well be, but there's no way on heaven or earth you're going open that crate without me.'

Ruan grinning at Caro, Caro grinning back.

'All right then,' Ruan said. 'Let's have at it.'

BEHIND THE STOSS'S tiny cottage, Mokush Polovtsy havered and hawed beneath the ash trees. Habit engrained in him to be secretive. Seven years hanging around Bad Salzbaum without being discovered to be an escaped POW not lost on him, never mind they'd not been POWs in the first place, had merely tagged the Prussians down country because they were heading the same way. Zsolt's idea to infiltrate themselves into the loose ranks of POWs when they heard where they were to be dumped, which was Bad Salzbaum itself.

'It's perfect!' Zsolt had enthused. 'It gives us cover of entry. We'll merely be more of the Hannover men who didn't want anything to do with the Prussians or their Northern Convention.'

'It's not perfect,' Mokush had protested. 'It's insane. We'll be prisoners, for God's sake.'

'Ah but,' Zsolt undeterred. 'They'll not be anything like that. They'll be nothing but a rag-tag work force. There's not going to be gun-towers at every corner, just a load of laggards who've no idea where they are or what else to do. Unlike us, who'll know exactly what we've got to do.'

Mokush had shaken his head. If he'd had his way he'd have knocked Zsolt down, trampled him into the dust, had he not his mother's piteous pleas ringing in his ears: *It's for Hungary, Mokush, and for us. For the Polovtsy bloodline. I want to see it flourish in my lifetime. I know you're the cleverer of you two but you're also the youngest, so you've to do as your older brother tells you.*

Always so hung up on bloodlines, who was in charge: grandfather first, father next, older brother following, younger brothers getting in line. Not much doing for the female members, although his mother had her ways. She the reason Zsolt had been allowed to fritter away what little money the family had left on book-finders of every shady and unreliable kind, ostensibly to track down the origins of the ancient story of when the Kumans had bested the Russians. For if they'd bested them once, they could do so again. Oral history as alive on their mother's lips as if the saga had happened the previous week instead of centuries before.

She the reason he'd gone on under Zsolt's shambolic command, and why he'd submitted and become a putative POW, working all those back-breaking months until Zsolt finally had in his pocket the letter he'd been waiting for. Zsolt not wrong about the situation of the POWs: the men allowed to go about their business much as free men might, so long as they kept within the confines of their labour camp. Permitted to write letters home, if they could write, receive missives and packages of clothes and food in return.

'Tryggvason's come through!' Zsolt had exclaimed that Christmas night of 1801, taking Mokush to one side. Zsolt's eyes sparkling, cracked lips licked wet with anticipation. 'It's here in Bad Salzbaum, just like he said it would be. And now he finally has a name!'

Mokush not so filled with fervour, Mokush suspicious from the off. Mokush never trusting the man they'd met in that dark and smoky tavern in Moscow as Zsolt had done: yet another book-finder, this time claiming discovery of a book having relevance to their cause and, more startlingly, having knowledge of the original cache of manuscripts on which that book had been based.

Mokush sighing.

'He's a crackpot,' Mokush advised. 'He's religion leaking out of him like water from a rusty sieve. What makes you think he wants to help us? Why would he? I don't know what the hell you were thinking, putting your trust in the likes of a man like him.'

Smart punch in the face from his brother. Zsolt's teeth glinting in the meagre light.

Mokush undeterred, rubbing his split lip with his fingers.

'He's offering you what you want. He's seeing an easy pay off.'

Zsolt smiling, taking the upper hand as usual. Looking on his spineless brother with contempt.

'He doesn't want money,' Zsolt stated. 'He's never wanted money. He wants what we want, to see that right is done, like he did the first time we met him.'

Mokush spitting away the blood bubbling in his mouth, for that wasn't his recollection at all: seeing the Norwegian hunch-backed at their table supping copiously at their drink and everything Zsolt could tell him about their clan's glorious past.

'He's a conman,' Mokush persisted, his lip smarting and bleeding all over again as he spoke. 'He'll have forged it. He knows we've finally got to the place he told us it ended up and now we're here he's to find a solution to that problem. Let me guess: it's somewhere impregnable. Somewhere hard to get at.'

Zsolt not replying, and Mokush not finished.

'Maybe some third party we need to meet up with?'

Zsolt hesitating, because his brother was right.

*It's going to need some planning and wherewithal to get at, but I've just the person to help you.*

Zsolt taking his time, re-opening the letter from Håkon Tryggvason and reading it one more time. Zsolt watching his brother wipe the trickle of blood from beneath lip and nose, seeing a thin line of it missed, drying on his beard. Seeing that insufferable half-smile on his brother's face and was not going to be beaten.

'We're doing it anyway,' he declared, 'but we're taking insurance with us.'

Insurance being the fellow POWs with whom they shared their quarters: two notorious grumblers, slackers and thieves. Friedrich and Ricard quick to agree. Easily convinced money might come their way if they did what they were told.

The fifth escapee not going easy. Constantine snatched up from his bed in dead of night with Zsolt's large hand over his mouth to stop his screaming, Auslander and Gericault holding arms and legs that were kicking and thrashing in protest.

Mokush uneasy as they brought the boy out bound and gagged.

'What the hell are you doing?' he'd whispered at his brother. 'This wasn't part of the plan.'

Not part of Mokush's, but apparently part of Zsolt's.

'Need an eel to slip through the trap, brother. And you're no eel, as no more am I.'

# 19

## The Wrong Kind Of Owl

THEY CARRIED ON UP the sands, conversation lapsed following their previous brief harangue; Ivor and Greta keeping their thoughts to themselves, both reconsidering, both coming to the conclusion there might be right on both sides.

Mick undented, everything forgotten. Only object now being the mission. Mick a man who'd been thinking around corners for years, couldn't think any other way. All focus on the next corner and what might be beyond it. Feet tramping on, noting how the water was creeping up the beach, forcing them to veer left towards the dunes.

'We need to get our story straight for when we reach the port,' he said. 'It's almost high tide, when the biggest boats will leave and we need to be on board.'

'Why would it matter?' Ivor asked. No problem he could see. Just three people looking for passage from one place to another.

'Think it might,' Mick said. 'Thinking on why those soldiers were in Knokke in the first place. Thinking it might be to do with us. I'm wondering on the frigate that almost had us in the water. If they saw us coming down the Schelde they must've at least suspected we'd come from Walcheren. That most likely we were heading to Ternauzen, and not a great reach from there to wonder if we weren't a group of English spies heading into Ghent.'

Ivor couldn't see why Mick was so concerned.

'How would that connect to us? What does it matter if they go on to Ghent, or even to Ternauzen?'

Mick coming to a stop, casting his eyes back down the sands stretching along the way from Zeebrugge to Knokke. They looked so benign, those yellow ribbons, which didn't mean bad things couldn't happen at either end, or at any point in between.

'Because,' he said, 'when they get to Ternauzen and start pointing guns at the locals someone will likely squeal, and Ternauzen's where those soldiers were heading, I'd lay bets on it. Won't take much for someone to put two and two together when they tell their tale.'

Ivor finally getting it, looking down the sands as Mick was doing. Ivor seeing several black points emerging from the horizon, could almost hear the faint jingling of harnesses, the thudding of hooves on soft sand.

'They're on their way,' Ivor said, sweat prickling on his palms. 'What do we do?'

Mick's face setting into that hard rigidity Greta knew so well which meant he was shuffling options, looking ahead, figuring how to avoid the obstacles about to trample them into the sands of Knokke if they didn't shift it and shift it fast.

'We run,' Mick said, turning his face towards Zeebrugge, which was maybe a quarter mile away. A fit battle-trained horse at full gallop able to cover a mile in two minutes; a fit battle-trained person running at full tilt averaging the same in eight, maybe seven at a push.

Greta, Mick and Ivor turning as one and running for their lives.

'CAREFUL THERE,' RUAN advised Caro. 'We don't want to damage the locks. There's a lot they can tell us.'

Leaning in closer, flicking open a small knife. Placing the point of its blade beneath the first loosened plate. 'If we can...just...'

Gently wiggling the blade until he had it against one of the screws, wiggled some more, repeated the operation several times before adding in a chisel, giving it a gentle hit with the mallet.

A plinking sound as the lock-plate came away from the wood, its four fixing screws coming with it, the lock itself perfectly intact. Caro following the method, having the second one off exactly as Ruan had the first.

'We'll study these later,' Ruan said, 'but now,' he announced, 'do you want to do the honours?'

Knowing Caro would; recalling the first Christmas spent with Caro and how excited Caro had been, how he'd kept blinking and blinking when Ruan handed over his gift. Caro rubbing thumbs against fingertips, trying to intuit what lay inside the wrapping, prolonging the moment, savouring the anticipation.

'Oh for heaven's sake,' Ruan had chided. 'Just get it done!'

Caro untying the pretty bow fashioned by the girl who'd wrapped the present. Caro removing the paper, opening the box, revealed the thumb-sized piece of scrimshaw: a section of walrus tusk, a wild sea battle finely incised and inked. Caro turning it this way and that.

'Oh but this is...' Caro had stopped, eyes brimming with tears. Ruan embarrassed, had put no thought into the gift, merely snatched it up in the market the night before because he'd been told he had to get the lad something. The back-then Ruan completely unprepared for the effect the gift would have.

'It's wonderful!' Caro finally got out, going over to Ruan, giving him a clumsy hug Ruan tried his hardest to avoid.

'I'll keep it with me always,' Caro had whispered. 'My first ever Christmas present.'

*My first ever Christmas present.*

Words unexpected, words that had made Ruan blush and wonder. Made him realise he'd had a blessed upbringing, and not everyone as lucky as him.

A turning point for the arrogant young man he'd been back then. And a delight ever since to go into the Christmas markets and choose a gift for Caro, knowing how much Caro would anticipate its giving and treasure it once received. As had been that little piece of scrimshaw: set in silver, put on a thong about his neck.

'Are you sure?' Caro asked of the crate of books, Ruan seeing the same signs of excited anticipation.

'I'm sure.' Ruan said. 'Lift the lid. Let's see what we've got.'

'Thank you,' Caro said, smiling his wide Christmas smile, fingertips going to the lid, gentle creaking as the precipitate in the crevasse between lid and chest protested and then gave, showers of chalky dust ploofing onto the rich red-gold threads of the luscious carpet beneath.

Lid raised, small sigh as Caro lifted it and the secrets of centuries yawned and came back into the light.

IN HOLGER STOSS'S TINY cottage Piet was holding Mathilde's hand, about to bid her farewell, when came footsteps over the grass. He cocked his head, certain they'd originated behind the cottage and not the fore. Put a finger to his lips as he listened.

'Are you expecting anyone?' he whispered, although *surely not* had to be the answer to that, for who would call on anyone at this time of night, and this night in particular.

Mathilde shook her head.

Brief mad thought of Professor Jorn relenting, coming back to apologise.

But no. The likes of Professor Jorn did not relent, nor did they apologise. Two weeks they'd been given, and two weeks all they would get. Creep of worry in her that he'd sent men to turf them out right here, right now. Mathilde gripping at Piet's arm, Piet unpeeling her fingers as he stood.

'Stay here,' he said, as if Mathilde would do anything else. 'Let me go see.'

Two strides and he was at the door. Stood for a moment, hand on latch, heard those footsteps turn a corner, come around the front, the single window of the cottage darkening as someone passed before it. Piet lifting the latch, pushing the wood open, put out his hand and grabbed at another already raised, about to knock.

'What can I do for you?' Piet asked, stepping outside, pushing the door closed behind him with his heel. Hearing Mathilde slide home the bolt, her soft breathing behind the wood, wondering if she was pressing her cheek against it to hear what was being said. Leading the man away; the man, caught off-guard by Piet's sudden appearance, going with him without protest or murmur.

'Who are you? What do you want?' Piet demanded, once they were ten yards distant.

Hedges hiding the low moon from them.

Two dark men standing in the hedges' shadow.

Two dark pillars standing, legs akimbo, as they faced one another, wondering what was what, and who was who. Piet releasing the stranger's wrist, small jitter of light from the dying bonfire revealing a stocky man, square-shouldered, square-jawed, dark eyed. A strong man, strong-faced, cheek bones of a Slav.

'What are you doing here?' Piet repeated, muscles tensed, ready for a fight. His opponent shifting his feet, taking a conciliatory step backwards.

'No harm,' he said, holding up his hands. 'Don't mean no harm. Just came to introduce myself to...' struggling for the name, a few beats before he had it. 'Mathilde Stoss. I've news of an old friend of hers.'

Hesitation not lost on Piet, nor the invocation of that conversation just had with Mathilde and how odd the timing was. Thought occurring that maybe it wasn't just Mathilde who'd held her cheek to the wood to hear what was being said, that maybe this man had been at the back of the cottage for that specific purpose. Walls thin and treacherous. Piet hooking thumbs into his work belt figuring what he had to hand: two short-bladed chisels for levering up machine-parts, putting marks into trees needing to be felled; small bill-hook for scything errant stems off the topiary; couple of serrated knives used for anything and everything; some loops of twine that always came in handy; small-headed hammer for knocking the life out of the moles Professor Jorn hated for churning up the grassed walkways leading from hotel to hedges.

A small armoury at his fingertips.

'Who do you mean?' he asked. 'What old friend?'

He could have used a name. Chose not to.

The man making to move away.

'I've made a mistake,' he said.

Shadows shifting.

Moon rising above the hedges as they spoke.

Soft yolk of it glancing light off their two faces.

'I'll come back in the morning,' the man tried, Piet thrusting out an arm and catching him by the throat, taking out one of his knives with the other. Metal glinting. Threat given. Piet knowing this was no ordinary encounter, even if he didn't know the why.

'You'll do no such thing,' Piet stated. 'You'll tell me now why you're here to see Mathilde or I'll stuff you into that hedge, let you linger there like the man we just found dead and blasted in it. And don't think I don't know how to do it because I'm the man who laid that hedge, and by hook or crook I'll have you in there before you can say lickety split.'

Mokush caught.

Mokush unable to take another breath while those calloused fingers were gripped about his Adam's apple, never mind the knife pricking his neck.

God's sake, Zsolt was going to be more angry than he'd ever been in his life. Mokush seeing the streak of a stoat tearing across the grass two yards distant, black tip of tail held aloft like the sail of a pirate ship. One wriggle and it was gone. Mokush closing his eyes, fighting for air.

'Hela,' he wheezed. 'Hela, from Torghatten.'

Pressure released.

Mokush falling to his knees.

Hedges looking like they were regarding him with pity, or despair, as Mokush was dragged up again, hands bound at his back, twine tied tightly about his wrists.

'Come with me,' Piet said, pulling Mokush on. 'Someone I need you to see.'

CARO DELVED AND CARO dug. Ruan quick to snatch up the faded folder Caro ignored: an unassuming piece of tattered cardboard tied loosely with fraying ribbon not catching Caro's fancy. Ruan recognising it immediately; lump in his throat to see the small stamp Hippolyte Gerhard put on each item passing through his hands, as libraries and traders always did. Hippolyte's neat writing on the front listing the contents in Cyrillic and translation, including the one he'd asked Ruan to follow up - Слово о полку игореве - *The Song of Igor's Campaign.*

Ruan struggling to recall the meagre research he'd carried out while he'd been a month in Dortmund, substantiating what Gerhard already knew: Russian, secular, rare. In fact unique, as far as Ruan had discovered. Not that unique and rare necessarily implied important or valuable, particularly as the text of the manuscript had been published in book form, along with others from the same cache. What Gerhard had never known was the information gleaned from that book's publishers in Moscow, to whom Ruan had written. Reply arriving four or five months later giving Ruan the results of their enquiries, which had established that the original documents on which they'd based their book had disappeared from the Moscow archives in which they'd afterwards been stored. Presumed stolen by one of the few people who knew they were there and how to access them. Top suspect being the Norwegian assistant of the man who'd unearthed the documents in the first place. Håkon Tryggvason the name of the suspected thief, who had melted away like the ice floes on the Moskva River dividing the city's heart in two. Assumption being he'd stolen the manuscripts, sold them, scarpered back to Norway on the proceeds. Neither man nor manuscripts heard of since.

*If you've knowledge of them, or him, we'd dearly like to know it,* the letter had politely ended. Ruan not writing back. Gerhard's shop by then dispersed and Gerhard dead.

Ruan reassessing, bringing back the salient points of that reply: theft occurring at some point after the Autumn of

1799, when the manuscripts were returned by the publishers to the archives. Small window thereafter during which *The Song* and its companion pieces must have travelled from Moscow – or possibly Norway – to land on Hippolyte Gerhard's desk in Holland. Sold on from there by Gerhard's sister, ending up in the hedges of Bad Salzbaum in the late Summer of 1802.

Ruan cursing himself for not pursuing it at the time. Gerhard's sister having no interest in books unless they contained recipes or advice on how to keep a good and tidy house. But a good and tidy house she'd prided herself upon, kept records of every sale, had even offered them to Ruan to look over in case there was one volume or another he had particular interest in, seeing as he was Gerhard's friend.

*You bloody fool,* went the conversation in Ruan's head. *You knew how much it meant to Hippolyte. You should have taken the time to do him one last favour.*

*In my defence,* came the other side, *I couldn't possibly have known it might turn up here, of all places, and in such circumstance.*

*But if you had,* his internal logic dictated, *then you'd know in which particular batch they had been dispatched, presumably to here, to Bad Salzbaum, and to whom they'd been sold.*

Recriminations rattling about his head.

Ruan murmuring the words Hippolyte had fought so hard to get out, on Ruan's last visit, about the Igor document. Seeming nonsense at the time, yet Gerhard so desperate to get them out they had to mean something.

*Alone pen, garden kuman...*

*Slovo bottom booming...furrows furrows...*
*Kuman.*
*Kuman feet-sky.*
*Opals rubies diamonds.*
*Red-feet.*
*Kuman red-feet.*
*Kuman feet-sky.*
*Kuman feet-sky.*

Ruan regarding those words ever since as a poem whose every line you couldn't quite grasp the meaning of yet, once you'd got to the poem's end, you sort of understood the whole. Insistence there, a definite building from beginning to reiterated end. He'd good recall when it came to books, could see their pages lying before him when he conjured them up. No need to untie the ribbon and open the folder to see *Igor's Song* dance and jitter before his eyes in the Cyrillic script he couldn't read.

Hippolyte, before his stroke, giving Ruan a brief rendition of its contents, smattered through with names and places meaning nothing to Ruan. Igor's Song documenting a three-day battle in the 1100s resulting in the catastrophic and humiliating defeat on the Donets River of a famous Russian prince by some nomadic tribe he couldn't remember the name of. Ruan picking up one of the two lock-plates, finding the indented marks meaning it had been manufactured in Deventer. Deventer famed throughout the Western world as a centre for learning and book craft. Hippolyte Gerhard well known for dealing in the esoteric and exotic. Hippolyte one of the few book-men in the west who understood and traded in the languages of the east, including Russian.

Ruan summing up what he thought he knew: this crate of books undoubtedly come from Hippolyte Gerhard's store in Deventer, packed up with some erraticism by Gerhard's sister. Gerhard's sister telling Ruan she'd laded Gerhard's books into crates in the order her brother had left them on shelves and desk. Filled one crate, moved on to another, an approximation of their contents distributed to the contacts found in Gerhard's business ledgers. All going at auction to the highest bidder.

A travesty of book-selling Ruan could have stopped had he been there at the time, which he had not. And no more had he been afterwards. Ruan and Caro off on yet another book-hunt whilst Hippolyte Gerhard rotted and turned to dust within his grave.

Ruan needing to know more.

Needed to find out who had bought this particular chest at Gerhard's sister's auction, for it seemed to him that whomever had made that purchase had never got around to unpacking it, as Caro was doing now. Not unusual, collectors buying pigs in pokes all the time in hope of uncovering something wild and rare. Buying them, leaving them with a pile of others for later opening and possible discovery.

And this particular lot contained the wild and rare: contained the original and - as far Ruan knew - singular manuscript of *The Song of Igor's Campaign* stolen from Moscow's archives, from the Empress Katerina's archives, eight or nine years previously. Possibly there was another rarity in the mix, two jewels haphazardly thrown together by

Gerhard's sister from whatever other volumes Gerhard had had lying on his desk, a coincidence of jewels Ruan couldn't yet dismiss. Yet came those words again:

*Opals rubies diamonds.*

Ruan looking up as rain slammed against the windows, creating rivulets of liquid silver reflecting the light from his side of the glass. Sudden revelation about water, the many forms it could take: ice, rain, hail or snow; slow-flowing glaciers, fast flowing rivers. Silver trickles slipping haphazardly down a pane of glass. And how like language it was, how one word could have several meanings, each one approached from differing avenues.

Gerhard not talking nonsense at all.

Gerhard approximating lost words, substituting them with those nearby where they sat.

*Opals, rubies, diamonds.*

Gerhard maybe literally meaning treasure.

*And it also means I've been looking at Gerhard's poetic litany all wrong.*

Ruan rubbing his eyes, needing to think as Gerhard might have done.

Gerhard groping blindly in a closet trying to pull out a scarf, ending up instead with a pair of gloves.

Ruan reconsidering the words Gerhard had bequeathed him.

*Alone pen, garden kuman...*
*Slovo bottom booming...furrows furrows...*
*Kuman.*
*Kuman feet-sky.*
*Opals rubies diamonds.*

*Red-feet.*

*Kuman red-feet.*

*Kuman feet-sky.*

*Kuman feet-sky.*

Ruan bringing to mind all he could of the afternoons they'd spent together. All Gerhard's esoteric and unusual interests. All his paintings. The way he spoke. The way he thought.

Opals rubies diamonds: *Song of Igor* a treasure to someone, maybe a threat to someone else, given how it had resurfaced.

Of *garden kuman* he could make no deduction, nor of the rest, no matter how many times he swirled the phrases around in his head. The sift and sort of his new way of looking bringing one notion clearly to the fore: the meaning of *kuman* key, the most repeated word in the puzzle.

Solve that, and he might be on his way.

*Rain down windows.*

*Rain evaporating from seas and rivers into the clouds, falling into other rivers, other seas.*

*Rain falling hundreds, maybe thousands, of years ago, bubbling up in the springs about Bad Salzbaum.*

*Like the Igor document has bubbled up.*

*Lying hidden in some unknown cellar or loft of the Russian Empire until Katerina's men came asking, hawking for histories, songs and prayers from the old days, all to make Katerina proud.*

Ruan abruptly diverted from his meanderings by a hesitant knocking at the door, Caro springing up like a cricket to answer it.

Bells of St Peter's beginning their chime of ten.

Faint scrum heard, as Caro opened the door, of people heading from dining rooms to upper floors and beds; skirts rustling, silk coats bustling along beside them, talk loud and exuberant, folk pushing up the staircase, admiring themselves in the panorama of the mirror before moving on.

Ruan taking Hippolyte's folder, secreting it beneath his coat. No need for Professor Jorn to see it, if it was he at the door.

Strong chance this chest of books had been stolen from whomever had bought it blindly from Gerhard's sister's auction, from someone right here in Bad Salzbaum. Ruan smiling as he got ready to deliver the bad news; smile faltering as he saw Piet Hoost on the threshold, cap in hand, round face trammeled with stress.

'I need you to come down to the cellar,' he said. 'There's someone I want you to see.'

Unconsciously repeating the words he'd said to the stranger who'd been skulking around the Stoss's cottage, wanting him to view the hedge-man, gauge his reaction. Piet pushing his captive to the bottom of the cellar steps to find the hedge-man not entirely whole. Found him decapitated. Piet having to turn quickly to one side, disgorging the tea he'd shared with Mathilde, throat strafing with the aftermath. Couldn't understand why this had been done, only that the book-finders must have done it.

And knew how to find those book-finders.

Ruan off to see the crate, and the crate in Jorn's study.

Book-finders immediately up and out on Piet's heels, locking the door behind them. Piet mutely taking the lead, thinking on the name squeezed from the throat of the man apprehended outside the cottage.

*Hela,* he'd said. *Hela, from Torghatten.*

Daughter of Mathilde's childhood friend.

The woman Mathilde had wanted Piet to find.

A woman who, as Piet had surmised, might need no finding; who instead had come to Bad Salzbaum expressly to find Mathilde Stoss.

Only hiccup in his theory being that Hela hadn't apparently found – or at least not yet approached - her mother's old friend, despite being here at least a couple of weeks, given when Mathilde had seen her in the market. The whereabouts of the Stoss's homestead easy to discover: a few questions here and there about Holger Stoss would have provided the answer in the space of a day.

Piet standing at the top of the ornate stairway with shoulders heavy.

He couldn't figure any of this out.

Regarded by his parents and their church as a turnip-head who wouldn't follow their rules; Piet regarding his parents and their church moribund as corn-fed geese who could no longer waddle nor move forward, bound into their worshipful book, become part of the pages they'd no desire to escape.

Piet pitying them.

Piet escaping. Every new day away from such constriction a blessing. Loved his journey, his job, loved Holger and Mathilde. Loved the books he'd bought with saved-up coins, Piet reading from them while Mathilde saw to her bread and Holger picked at his teeth with a thorn, before all three set to with a game of cards and then off to bed. A simple life of satisfactory repetition doing them all well. A simple life of satisfactory repetition coming to an abrupt halt this afternoon.

Piet stumbling down the stairs as the book-finders overtook him. Piet seeing in the mirror his own round face, the reflection of the spa's glass entrance doors, the darkness beyond. Another round face bashing suddenly into the glass: a short-eared owl, small-bodied, long-winged, yellow-eyed. Yellow eyes able to move only if the head moved with them. An owl diurnal, never hunting at night and certainly not in Winter. An aberration to the norm. For who knew what had winkled it out.

Foreboding there, felt Piet, hearing the scrape of the bolt as the book-finders reached the cellar door. Something terribly wrong.

*Hela from Torghatten.*

*Book-finders from who knew where.*

*Arminians, Anabaptists, Remonstrants, Russian Orthodox and Jews, in no particular order. Different books, same kinds of people folded into their pages.*

*Hedge-man burying himself alive to protect whatever lay inside his crate.*

Piet shivering inside his skin to know how far die-hards would go to unbury what might best be left alone.

# 20

## Books Bought By The Yard

OVER THE SANDS WENT Greta, Mick and Ivor; beach fast diminishing, tide pulling in on their right, boots splashing in the soft breakers sweeping up the bay, damp sand easier to run on than dry. Mick powering ahead, eyes fixed on the hugger mugger of people forging up piers, over gangways; large sails hoisted, bellies filled, wind risen with the tide, canvases blooming and billowing: meaning big ships, no mere fishing boats these.

Greta gasping for breath, a bitch of a stich in her side as she forged on. Ivor behind her, panicky as a lamb with a dog on its tail. Ivor looking over his shoulder to check their pursuers' progress: black dots no more, horses straining at the bit, men high in stirrup and saddle as they whipped their charges on, already halfway up the sands towards them. Ivor distracted, tripping on a few strands of kelp. Ivor face down in the shallow water, gurgling and gasping. Ivor's arms pushing himself to his knees, spitting out sea water, compelled to make the grand gesture his training demanded.

'Go!' he yelled. 'Go on!'

Ivor's grand gesture dismissed as the folly it was by Greta skidding to a stop, returning to scoop him up - no time for words - Ivor squelching to the vertical, Greta punching him in the small of his back to urge him on. Mick lost to sight as he reached the environs of Zeebrugge before them, elbowing his way through the crowds, garbling a few questions, garnering his direction, spying the ship they needed to be on. Mick turning back, grabbing at Greta's elbow as she stuck to the edge of the crowd as he knew she would. Ivor heavy and clumsy beside her, clothes soaked, face glistening with salt and shine.

Quick gruff commands from Mick as he thrust his purse of coins into Ivor's hands and the Abbott's letter into Greta's.

'Get yourself on that ship there,' he pointed. 'Don't care how you do it. Shove everyone else aside if you have to, just get yourselves on.'

'What about...' Ivor started to ask through panted breaths, Greta pulling at him, shushing him.

'He knows what he's doing and we've to do as he says.'

The two of them barging through the crowds and up the pier, up the gangplank that was already being lifted, work paused to allow Greta and Ivor time to run up the slippery wood, get on board, smartly shoved aside by the men hauling the gangplank in.

'Always bloody someone cuts it too fine,' one of them grumbled, the other winking at Greta as she nodded her thanks for their brief delay before slipping away with Ivor into the crowds.

Horses thundering up the sands of Knokke.

Horses splashing through the shallow breakers.

Horses pulled up short as they reached the port.

French soldiers in their tattered uniforms scanning the crowds.

'Hold up! Hold up citizens!' came the shout. 'We're looking for a threesome of spies: young woman, young man, older man with them. Hold up, hold up!'

Folk of Zeebrugge bemused, until a rallying cry went up from somewhere amongst their ranks.

'We'll not hold up for anyone, and certainly not you French!'

Mick Malloy shouting out his protest in ragged words and moving on, shouting out again as if another man entirely.

'Quite right! What are they to us? They're invaders! They shouldn't even be here!'

Murmuring in the crowds as Mick popped up again.

'And who even knows if they're spies? We're under siege, people. Are we really going to let these foreign soldiers tell us our business? Do we no longer belong to ourselves?'

Outrage then, on both sides.

Zeebrugge folk crowding in on the soldiers, barring path and passage.

Soldiers striking out with whips, making the situation worse.

'We can't let them get away with this!' that lone out-crier cried out again, Mick ducking down quickly, not so fast he wasn't spotted.

'There!' Alfonse spat. 'It's that mad one! The one from the sands!'

Alfonse dismounting, thrashing his whip, bringing out his pistol, holding it up high.

'Out of my way! Get out of my way!'

Mick filtering himself off, dodging between the stalls of fishmongers. Mick aided by a group of gutting women who parted ranks and allowed him through.

'It's wicked what those French are doing, so good on you,' said one, knife raised, knife lowered, knife-point splitting fish-belly stem to stern, ripping out its guts, tipping them into the bucket she had by her work station, gulls a squalling cloud above their heads.

'Think they goddamn rule the world,' another added, as Mick disappeared behind their skirts, back bowed, head low, could see the top sails of the ship for Amsterdam weighing anchor and was off. Diversion achieved: Greta and Ivor away with the rest of the passengers, the diamond merchants, the cargos of salt, sulphur and wool.

Mission on target.

Rumpus and ruction continuing as the soldiers stamped their way up and down the ginnels of the port-side. Alfonse red-faced and huffing, looking for one madman amongst the many, for these folk had to be mad to be assisting spies. Alfonse would never have put his life on the line to aid someone he didn't know, unless there was something in it for him. His few stolen coins deep-held within deep pockets. And some satisfaction in that. Satisfaction too on seeing the look on his Captain's face in Ternauzen when he realised he'd been duped by a tale skinnier than the whores of Antwerp with whom soldiers took respite and relief. Or with whom Alfonse took respite and relief, doubting his Captain ever had. His Captain as soft and vulnerable as the bellies of the fish the women were splitting and gutting on the several stalls he was closing in on. Would have done the same to his Captain in a blink if no one was looking. Such did army life engender: the brave made braver, the complainers more complainant, the violent more violent. Men like Alfonse finding grim joy in the fighting, leaping off the cliffs of restraint into waters deep and dark where anything went, kicking away anyone who afforded no use.

Alfonse kicking now towards the fisherwomen.

Mick leaping up, jinking and diving through the narrow vennels between fishers and mongers. Alfonse spotting the movement and raising a loud *Hie! He's here! Come on, men!*

Alfonse unsheathing his sword, brandishing it at every side, raising his pistol, firing a shot that had the women ducking and the seagulls rising and screeching as one of their number dropped in a whirl of bloodied feathers at Alfonse's feet. Those feet trampling monochrome wings shivering and fluttering, virulent trickles of blood in coverts and secondaries as the bird, that long-winged screamer cursed by fish-gutting women the world over, laid itself down and died.

'HE SHOULD HAVE BEEN back by now. What the hell is keeping him?' Zsolt Polovtsy worried, draining his glass of beer. Hela moving swiftly to pour him another, brushing the tips of her fingers against his neck as she did so. This man like a child, needing only the gentlest touch to abate or arouse him, whichever she chose. So unlike the men of Vettie's Giel who had always outnumbered the women, expected women to service not only husbands but their single brothers and widowed fathers too. Excitement and variety for some women, if not for most. And not for Hela. Hela getting out in the nick of time and finding a new way, a new cause.

'Always so impatient, Zsolt,' she reprimanded. 'He'll be back when he's back. He's probably enamored of the festivities. We didn't exactly get the opportunity last time.'

Zsolt huffed, caught at Hela's wrist, swung her around, pushed away the table with his foot and pulled her onto his lap, placed his chin on her head.

'You don't know what you do to me,' he whispered, closing his eyes, fingers stroking the bare skin above her breasts, pushing at the edges of her dress. 'I don't know what I'd have done if I'd never found you.'

Hela laughing, restraining him, hard push of him against her leg as she sat and moved, teased and then released him.

'God's sake, woman,' he murmured as she got up, his fingertips touching hers as she moved away. Zsolt always so desperate for her ministrations, so eager, so unlike any man Hela had experienced. A hard journey taken from Vettie's Giel to Holland: *you'll not pass by here, woman, you'll not find passage down this road, you'll not get berth on this boat. Not unless I get something in return.*

No warning from Håkon how bad those roads would be. Håkon enduring no such obstacles. Håkon's travels studded through with moments of glory, fellowship, meeting like minds on the fringes of Finnish lakes or out on the Steppes or in deep dark taverns. Håkon leaving Norway a robust young man looking for enlightenment and adventure, returning home with both achieved. And with his treasure locked away until the day he trusted someone enough to do his bidding, set the wheels of his Big Plan turning. Håkon imbued with the power he'd discovered by chance, thrilled with how big his Big Plan might turn out to be; setting one part of a nation against another, of maybe setting one entire nation against another. The greatest of actions any revolutionary, such as Håkon considered himself to be, could be proud of. And action at a distance, no need to get his own hands dirty. Which was as he liked it.

'Couldn't squander it in Russia,' Håkon had explained to Hela. 'Too dangerous, too many questions, too much risk of someone discovering where I got it from. But get it to Holland and get it authenticated by a respected trader, and we've a chance.'

Research done, route planned.

Hela his chosen emissary because Hela was so desperate to escape from Vettie's Giel, from the desolate years of hard labour, bad marriage and misery awaiting her if she stayed. Håkon had seen it in her the first time he'd met her: that fitful fever in her eyes, the bitterness burning away in her heart, the all-consuming need to make of her life something other than toil and dread.

Every master needing a fervent acolyte, and she was his. Trusting her with his treasure, giving her his itinerary.

*Bergenstift*
*Trondheim*
*Bergen*
*Ship from Bergen to Holland*
*Amsterdam*

*Deventer*

Hela, against the odds, doing as he'd tasked her. Delivering Håkon's manuscripts to the book-seller Håkon had specified. Hela giving him her instructions.

'There'll be a lot of interest in some of what I'm giving you,' she'd said, 'particularly in Hungary. A clan there, the Polovtsy.'

The old book-seller looking over his glasses at her. Hela hoping he wasn't one more man about to force her into one more bed-shaking, bone-juddering hoop.

Which he was not. Hippolyte Gerhard a gentleman, who lived for books and books alone.

'It's going to take a while,' he said, flicking through the folder. 'I'll need to research authentication, find the specific buyers you're needing. It will be at least a few months.'

Hela agreeing, Håkon warning her it might take as long.

'Do you have friends here?' Hippolyte had asked.

'I don't,' she'd answered.

Hippolyte writing a name on the back of the chit of paper serving as his guarantee he'd received her cache of manuscripts and would duly act as agent in their sale.

'Take this then,' he'd said. 'They'll see you well, and won't charge you the earth. And it means I can contact you if I find anything out sooner.'

The boarding room clean and cheap.

Hela biding her time in Deventer. Hela walking about its streets, over its bridges, dallying in the market which overtook the main square in day-time, deserted it at night.

Hela thrifty with the money Håkon had given her, eking it out, finding a part-time job in a bread shop. The days fair racing by as she got to grips with the Dutch that wasn't so different from the German she'd learned in Vettie's Giel from several members of Holger's crew who'd never left. Hela hardly registering how many days had passed. Hela waiting yet another month before returning to Hippolyte's shop to discover the man dead: body fished out of Deventer's lazy lagoon – eyes, toes and nose nibbled away by hungry crabs and fish - the entirety of his possessions sold at auction, dispersed and gone.

Hela disquieted but undeterred, a different person to the one she'd left behind in Vettie's Giel. Hela a woman honed and hardened, demanding to know where her manuscripts had gone. Producing her chitty of ownership to Gerhard's sister, threatening lawsuits if her property wasn't returned to her. Gerhard's sister quavering under this brash woman's loud insistence. Gerhard's sister flustering and fluttering. Gerhard's sister searching through her records, narrowing down the possibilities.

'I think it's in Bad Salzbaum,' she told Hela. 'No, I'm sure that's where it went. And I can give you the name of the buyer.'

Hoping the information would be enough, which it was. Hela nodding, taking the name and address of said buyer.

Hela sending off a letter to Håkon, early Autumn of 1801, gist being:

*Complications. Can't do this on my own. I need help. Will stay in Deventer until I hear from you.*

Håkon's reply equally brief.

*Time to shift yourself to Bad Salzbaum. Help arranged. All not lost. You're a hero, Hela. Your name will be sung in songs long after we both are gone.*

Hela as thrilled by the prospect of her part in Håkon's Big Plan as Håkon was himself. *Your name will be sung in songs!* A wondrous promise, a wondrous future bequeathed to her, to Hela from Vettie's Giel who would otherwise have amounted to nothing. Would have ended up exhausted and disappointed, dead and buried with nothing to show for a life lived, had it not been for Håkon.

Hela duly uprooting herself from Deventer and getting to Bad Salzbaum a few miles over the border, finding lodgings, wangling a job in a bakery, spending her days pummeling dough, learning the arts of patisserie, how to make twenty different kinds of pastry for twenty different kinds of desserts.

Hela on hold, until she received a letter from Håkon when Christmas was just around the corner.

*These are the brothers I told you about before. The ones I met in Moscow who will do anything and everything to see our manuscript comes to its proper light.*

Our manuscript. Hela's and Håkon's. Hela as invested in its importance as was he. Hela's life swerved from the norm into the extraordinary, into a woman who would be remembered and written about, have songs glorying her name.

*And now we have it coming from a respected Deventer dealer we've covered our tracks. This is it, little sister. Triumph is not far off. Soon our beloved Norway will no longer have a ravening lion, a treacherous wolf, as its neighbour. Soon enough*

*we'll have that lion's pelt as our bed-cover, and the fur of that*
*Slovak wolf wrapped about our feet to keep us warm.*

Heady words, and heady times when Håkon had first preached of his mission when everyone in Vettie's Giel – and the rest of Norway - feared the Russians might at any moment come crashing over their borders, take Finland in its maw, spit it out, move on to others whose borders were as badly defended as their own. Russia's war with Sweden in the 1790s neither forgotten nor forgiven.

Heady words, then as now.

Hela still Håkon's most fervent acolyte.

Håkon choosing well.

Håkon never a man to take decisions lightly.

Håkon not forgetting the loose-lipped Polovtsy brothers he'd engineered a meet with in some Moscow dive. Brothers overly enthused by the publication he'd presented them with; brothers – one of them at least - banging on non-stop about Hungarian nationalism and the great defeat their clan had inflicted on the Russians hundreds of years before. Time well-nigh to do it all over again in their opinion; and in Håkon's, and in Hela's.

Håkon checking out their tale, checking back through the history books, finding nothing more. The entire episode of that campaign wiped from Russian consciousness. Russians wanting to remember victories, not defeats. Only one book he'd found making mention of it, making his skin fizz when he'd learned of the Polovtsy connection. Håkon intimate with the single document he'd ever come across mentioning the Campaign of Igor, and Håkon one of the few men alive who knew where that document was: buried in the mausoleum of the Moscow archives, where the Empress Katerina wanted it to stay.

Katerina valuing knowledge; Katerina corresponding with intellectuals the world over, her particular favourite being Voltaire in France. Katerina expecting every courtier she graced with a visit to have an extensive library. Håkon laughing his socks off with one particular Moscow bookseller, Klostermann, who made a grand living furnishing faux libraries, selling those hopeful courtiers books by the yard: 50 to 100 roubles depending on the quality of their bindings, books stamped with impressive titles, eminent names. Books containing dross cut from cheap editions having nothing to do with their titles, many of which - fittingly, given Katerina's love of Voltaire – Klostermann imported from France.

Such was the power of books in Katerina's court.

And Katerina all about power: partitioning Poland in 1772, war with the Turks a couple of years later and next with the Swedes; followed by another war with the Turks in 1792 - the same year Håkon and his colleague recovered the Igor document amongst a stash of others.

Song of Igor all about the Turkic Kumans obliterating the might of Russia by the River Donets outside Karkov. Kumans taking prisoner Prince Igor, Igor's son, his brother and his nephew. Not what Katerina wanted to hear at any time, especially not when at war with those very same people. And certainly not when France was in tumult, executing their aristocracy every chance they got.

No murmurings of dissent needed in the wings.

Katerina dealing with dissent with swift and harsh decision.

Prince Ivan murdered in the castle of Schlüsselburg, for heaven's sake, after the disaffected Russians had pinned their hopes on him instead of her.

Song of Igor quietly filed away.

More wars following: incorporation of Courland extending Katerina's reach to the Baltic Sea.

Had Katerina not died, the Igor document would never have been allowed to surface in any form whatsoever. But died she had, in 1796, and Håkon's colleague and superior laboured for several years, managed a surreptitious publication of all those documents he and Håkon had uncovered in Kupyansk, just up country from the Donets River; documents conjured up by some old woman who'd dragged them out of a moldering chest in her moldering home and given them up for inspection; sold them off for a couple of coins that would keep her in funds for a month, maybe two if she was thrifty.

Håkon's colleague having no idea of the uniqueness of that one document amongst the many, as no more had Håkon until Håkon had met the Polovtsy brothers.

Random moments being what life was all about.

Random moments, and someone able to put them together to make meaning - as Håkon had done. Håkon Tryggvason the only man in the world with knowledge enough to recognize the true worth of that document to the Kumans – the Polovtsy clan – who'd defeated the Russians with such definitive spectacle. Folk labouring under yokes ever since: Russians one side of their history,

Hungaro-Austrian Empire the other. Both intent on strangling the life out of their language and culture.

Not anymore. Not once the Igor document was released into Kuman hands.

*Kuman red-feet.* Kumans wanting blood, as did Håkon and Hela.

*Kuman feet-sky.* Kumans looking for a way out of servitude, as Hippolyte Gerhard might have explained had he still been around.

# 21

# Cryptographics

RUAN AND CARO WENT down the stone steps into the cellar to meet Piet's captive, who had curled himself up and was busily trying to release himself from his ropes by use of his teeth. Ruan reminded of hagfish, who tied their boneless bodies into knots slithered up from slimy tail to slimy head to give their jaws heft and heave enough to rip a mouthful of flesh from whatever they were predating.

Nifty trick in hagfish. Nifty trick not going so well for Mokush.

'Found him skulking outside Holger's cottage,' Piet explained, as he came down and stood by Ruan's side. 'And neither rhyme nor reason he had to be there. Certainly not so late.'

'The timing is rather suspicious,' Ruan agreed, 'but there had to be a reason.'

Piet chewing his lip.

'He was asking about Mathilde. About her friend from back home. About the woman Mathilde saw in the market a couple weeks back.'

Ruan pulling at his ear, looking at the captive who had stilled.

'And where is Mathilde's home?' he asked.

'Torghatten, Vettie's Giel, in Norway,' Piet supplied. 'That's where she met Holger after his ship got frozen up in the ice there.'

No great leap for Ruan to see how that could have come about. Ruan tasked, a few years back, with locating a particular volume about Baffin and Bylot's expeditions in the area for a scholar who was meticulously drafting a Mercator map that had, at its very centre, the North Pole. His map moving out from that single point to 66° 33' so the Arctic Circle appeared as exactly that: a circle covered in perennial ice, water turgid most of the year, sweeping in slow gyres to the north of Norway, trapped by Siberia, Alaska and Greenland. Greenland an island larger than the whole of Continental Europe, frozen through with permafrost to depths no one had yet devised instruments capable of measuring. A map of the world that had startled Ruan, made him view it from a different angle, as if he'd been standing on the moon.

'You'll not have heard of my colleague, Heinrich Von Kleist,' had said the map-maker, 'but he's given me a quote to put at the start of my book that's precisely right.'

*Paradise is now shut and locked, barred by angels; so we must go forward, go around the world, see if somehow, somewhere, there is a back way in.*

A quote oddly apt, now Ruan was down in the cellar, for a back way in was exactly what was needed to this hedge-man mystery.

Back door opening right there and then.

'You chopped off his head,' Piet stated. 'Why would you do that?'

Caro leaping into the limelight of their meagre lanterns, scooping the man's head from the bucket of tannin with a pair of tongs, holding it up by a clutch of hair, laying it quickly down beside the rest of him.

'We thought someone would be able to make out his features more clearly,' Caro explained. 'And I think it's worked.'

Mokush coughing, trying to pull his shirt over his mouth, bile coursing up his throat to see the young features of Constantine so clearly delineated, the dark liquor from his head spreading across the lines of straw.

A lot of things in life Mokush could never comprehend: first off being his family's gripping to a tale long past and placing so much on it, turning his life to mud and mire; second off being Hela's attraction to his brother and his insane cause; third being how anyone could chop off the head of a boy, stick it in a bucket of tannin, take it out again as if it was of no more worth than a spoonful of coleslaw.

The plot, as Mokush saw it, rapidly getting out of hand.

Constantine in two pieces in this cellar below the spa hotel not the worst. The worst being he'd solved the problem of where Constantine and their crate of books had gone, yet was a prisoner no closer to getting his hands on those books than he'd been before. Someone had to be made responsible for all this mess.

Dolt Zsolt top of his list on that score.

Hela the Jezebel not far below.

Mind wandering back to the man who'd got the two starry-eyed idiots churning up history like there was no tomorrow, who by proxy had stirred up the entire clan back home with what he could provide.

Kumans red-feet.

Kumans feet-sky.

The Song the spur to goad their revolution: proof that Russia could be weak and Hungary, and the Turkic Kumans exiled there, could be stronger.

Revolutions started by far less.

Martin Luther's ninety-five theses nailed to a church door in 1517. Not a book, not a song, only words that had nevertheless sliced European Christianity down the middle, birthing the wars of the Reformation, of the Counter Reformation, and too many deaths to be tallied.

*Oh Igor. Where are your men now?*

Gone and buried was the answer to that.

Not so the descendants of the enemies who had crushed them.

Mokush heart-rent.

Mokush needing to salvage himself and the Song.

Mokush fixing his gaze on the man with eyes like a rook, black and dark as his hair, same shine in both from the lanterns.

'I know who that boy is,' Mokush croaked, bones creaking as he fought to straighten himself within his bonds, 'and I was at the Stoss's house because I needed to talk to Mathilde about Vettie's Giel, about someone she knew there...'

Mokush's attempt at bargaining hampered by the rook-man pulling Mokush unceremoniously to his feet.

'Let me guess,' Ruan said, 'he's called Håkon. Håkon Tryggvason. A Norwegian who travelled to Russia and then returned. Brought back with him opals, rubies, diamonds.'

Mokush frowning, not understanding. Pulse of blood ticking through the vein bisecting his forehead. Ruan pushing him onto a sack of cabbages that looked uncommonly like a jumble of human heads.

'And by opals, rubies, diamonds,' Ruan went on regardless, 'I mean this.'

Taking from beneath his jacket a folder tied up in its tattered ribbon, holding it aloft for the small cellar-crowd to see.

'And for the love of God,' he added. 'I've just worked it out!'

*Alone pen, garden kuman.*

*Slovo bottom booming… furrows furrows…*

*Pen,* as in writing, *alone* as in rare and unique.

*Grad* the Russian suffix for city, same root as garden: a place where best to grow your citizens, keep invaders out.

*Slovo,* the Song – as of Igor.

*Bottom booming* – not so precise, although Ruan presumed the defeat of Igor had set warning tocsins going off across Russia and, most of all, in the palaces where Tsars and Tsarinas made their nests. A defeat completely unforeseen in a battle no one believed could have been won by a minority they'd never considered a threat.

Bottom booming indeed.

No words more apt.

And *furrows furrows.*

Ruan shaking his head not to have thought of it sooner, a smile on his lips as he thought on Hippolyte and how wondrous were the workings of his mind, even after that mind had been so devastated. Hippolyte of the opinion that every book ever written - no matter how insubstantial, how little read or ignored when put abroad - would leave its mark, as a plough-share does through a field. History strewn with furrows pushed up by what the many had regarded as insignificant, like the defeat of Igor hundreds of years ago and the Song that had been made of it.

Hippolyte telling Ruan how furrows started could not be unmade. Furrows begun by the Song of Igor still extant. Young Constantine proof of it, if proof was needed – which apparently it was.

Caro the first to ask what the blazes Ruan was on about.

'What have you worked out? And where do rubies and diamonds come in?'

Opals apparently not making the grade.

Ruan pointing to the folder.

'Because this here,' he announced, 'is a stash of documents stolen from Moscow at the turn of the century. Name of suspected thief being Håkon Tryggvason. And one of these documents is the *Slovo o polku Igoreve.* The Song of Igor's Campaign. An account of a battle between the Russians and a nomadic Turkish people, the...and oh of course! Now I have it! Hippolyte told me. Nomadic Turkic clan as they were back then, the Kumans.'

Last piece of the riddle falling into place.

*Slovo* an account of that battle by a man who'd taken part in it.

Very rare. Possibly unique. Not necessarily valuable.

Which no longer seemed the case, given how and where it had been found.

Mokush feeling like he'd been hit by a sledgehammer.

*He knows.*

*He knows of the Slovo.*

*He knows of Håkon and Hippolyte.*

*He knows our clan's ancient name.*

Mokush slipping to one side under the loose grip Ruan had kept upon his shoulder, as if he'd been physically kicked off his seat of cabbages.

Thoughts racing swift as sprites through his head as he went down, cracked his skull on one of the cobbles jutting from the uneven cellar floor.

'Oh for heaven's sake,' Ruan muttered.

'You should have got his name before you did the dramatics,' Caro observed, going down on his knees beside Mokush, pushing his small hands beneath Mokush's head. Mokush's limbs going into spasm as he looked into the face looking into his, saw the disembodied ghost of the boy he might as well have murdered with his own two hands.

# 22

## Into The Drink

GRETA AND IVOR ON THEIR way from Zeebrugge to Amsterdam, thanks to Mick's diversionary tactics. Luck on their side to have arrived the same day the Amsterdam ship departed which, under sail and favourable winds, could cover four or five knots an hour. Greta estimating they'd hit port within twenty four hours. Mick, hopefully, following as soon as he could manage it. If he hadn't been caught. If he hadn't already been tied to a post and shot.

Had to believe that was not the case, that he would get out of Zeebrugge and get his way back on track. Had to believe it.

Absolutely had to.

Greta pushing herself against the rails as she watched the coast of Holland slipping by, contemplating the trickiest part of their plan. Getting through Holland would be easy now they were going by sail and not by foot. What would happen when they got to Apeldoorn was another matter, resting entirely on this blasted Ivor who'd been thrust into her company. A man she couldn't quite make out. A man who seemed angry at everything and anyone – herself included - and yet appallingly, and perhaps appealingly, utterly helpless in other regards. A man who could trip over his own boot-strings and demand she go on, despite knowing that if she left him behind their mission would be entirely lost. A man who reminded her of Ruan Peat, of whom she didn't want reminding. Ruan on the surface insufferable, who'd nevertheless turned into a hero. A man who'd wanted to marry her. An offer refused because there were more important things to be doing at the time than considering personal happiness.

Saving Ireland the cause back then.

Saving Holland and the Servants the cause now.

Sacrifices needing to be made, not least by Greta. Greta sacrificing the good life she might have spent with Ruan, and now maybe Mick thrown onto the burnt altar too.

*Will they sacrifice?* The neigh-sayers had asked Nehemiah as he began rebuilding the walls of a Jerusalem destroyed. *Will they recover the stones from the heaps of rubbish, including those that have been burned?*

Nehemiah stout and strong: *Of course they will, as should you, because we're fighting for our brethren, our sons and daughters, our wives and homes.*

No idea when those words had first been spoken and later written down. Vague memory of a Sunday School teacher telling her it was well over two millennia ago.

*And still relevant to our cause,* she'd said, *because we too will soon be called upon to fight for our own families and homes.*

A fight Greta had joined and jubilated in, had carried on with even when all appeared lost.

A fight she now knew Mick Malloy had never lost sight of in his exile, enlisting in the Irish Legion in the hope the French would help the Irish retake Ireland at some point in the future, as they had promised – and dismally failed to carry out – back in 1798.

Hard to comprehend how some fights just went on and on with no resolution in sight, and yet the fighters kept on fighting. Like Nehemiah and his Israelites. Like her and Mick, and all the other countless Irish who would never give up the hope of having Ireland free and clear and all their own. Like maybe Holland felt now, and the Flemish, as the French began assaulting the border towns between the two. Peoples besieged and bewildered, but not giving up.

As no more would she.

One more day until they got to Amsterdam, followed by a two day tramp – if they went full speed – to cover the fifty odd miles between Amsterdam and Apeldoorn. And, once there, all up to Ivor and the letter Mick had thrust at her, written by the Abbott of the Servants of the Sick, the goal of both to bring the English on side to protect the trade routes Napoleon was seeking to sunder.

Not much resting on it then.

Big thoughts, noble thoughts, thoughts brought to a crashing halt by Ivor elbowing his way into her solitude. Elbows large and swollen, now she looked on, as he placed them next to her own. Elbows large and swollen by bad nutrition, by the mosquito bites that had caused so many of his fellows to be shoveled into the shallowest of graves on

Walcheren. New respect for him he'd not chosen to decamp with the rest, had instead chosen to be one of the fighters despite the possibility of success being slim to non-existent.

New respect ditched the moment he opened his mouth.

'I can't believe these people are so primitive,' Ivor quarreled, the angry scowl ugly on a face that might otherwise have been tolerably handsome. 'You'll not believe it,' Ivor up in arms. 'They've no proper sanitation on board! We're expected to piss and poop right over the edge of the ship. It's disgusting, is what it is. Disgusting.'

*Oh Ivor, if only you knew.*

Greta dismissing his complaint for what it was: petulance come from a man who'd never been in the ranks, pushed high above them solely because he had the right name, came from the right family, came from money.

Greta despising him. Greta despising all his class and their beggaring pretentions. Greta thinking on all the times she'd peed behind hedges, evacuated herself in holes scraped by blunted fingernails, using handfuls of moss and leaves to clean herself up, like everyone normal did.

Greta reminding herself Ivor was not normal, Ivor not in the usual run of life, which was precisely why he'd been suborned into this particular escapade.

*Think anyone high up is going to listen to the likes of you or me?*

Absolutely not, was the answer.

Although maybe they'd listen to Ivor Merrill, who could so casually refer to the leader of the pitiful Walcheren campaign by his first name. God damn and blast him. Greta gritting her teeth, glad of the sting of salt on her cheeks as the ship ploughed on and a mizzle blew down upon them, hiding him from her.

'And when we get to Amsterdam we're to stay put,' Ivor went on, as if Greta was one of his lowly soldiers. 'We batten down and wait for your Mick Malloy to catch us up before we go on.'

Greta looking down at the water, watching the mizzle soodling upon its surface, touching and pulling back like it knew it was kin. Greta sympathizing, feeling not dissimilar. Ivor kin of a kind, both soldiers of sorts, although she suspected she'd seen more battles than he had ever done, battles experienced from the bad end – down in the mud and blood with all the rest – and not from some well-constructed tent stocked floor to ceiling with good food and wine, serviced by separate tents concealing latrines emptied and cleaned by their underlings.

Greta no underling, never had been and never would.

Greta no neigh-sayer either.

*Will they sacrifice? Will they recover the stones from the heaps of rubbish, including those that have been burned?*

Of course they would, and of course she would too because that's what people like her did. If the citadel was destroyed, they and she would rebuild it. If it was destroyed a second time they would do it all over again. Sacrifice what needed sacrificing. Scratch the stones, including those burnt, out of rubbish and rubble and put them back to use.

Ivor rubbish and rubble to her, yet the only stone she had to work with.

She would not let the Servants down. Nor Mick, if he had survived this latest battle and, if he hadn't, would not let his sacrifice go to waste.

Didn't bother to turn her head.

Didn't shift her stance.

Kept her gaze on the mute surface of the sea.

Snaked her hand along the railings, got her fingers gripped about Ivor's wrist. Nails digging into his skin.

'You don't seem to understand what's going on here,' she said, as Ivor yipped and yawed, tried to pull away from her grasp without success. 'You're not in charge, Ivor,' Greta continued. 'And I doubt you ever have been.'

Greta loosening her body from the rails, turning to face him through the shifting veils of mist as they came and went, thickened and thinned, like the low-down clouds they were. Greta not releasing her grip on Ivor's wrist for a second, twisting it as she pulled him around so they stood body to body, face to face, so close any onlooker, had there been anyone on-looking, might have taken them for lovers. A pretty notion, which would have been promptly dismissed by Greta's next pronouncement and Ivor's sharp intake of breath as she twisted his wrist once more.

'So let me enlighten you,' words spoken through tight lips, tight heart, tight intention. 'We get to Amsterdam and go up country, exactly as planned. You're nobody to me, Mister high and bloody mighty,' Greta pausing to take breath, Greta's nails drawing blood as she pulled Ivor's arm behind his back. 'You'll piss and poop over the sides of this boat until we get there and, once we get there, we go on.

Understand? And please tell me you do, or I'll pitch you into the water and not be sad about it.'

Ivor blenched, Ivor quailed, his wrist burning like hell-fire beneath her grip, his shoulder complaining in its socket. He squirmed, but could not get free. The mist was down upon them and he was finding it hard to see, but not so blind he couldn't interpret that look upon her face: a face set and determined, hedgehog spikes of red hair glistening with the water droplets condensed there. He'd never been so frightened, nor so enchanted. He didn't doubt she would twist him up and chuck him over if she had the mind to. Came to the sudden epiphany that here was a woman like no other he'd ever met. Saw himself through her eyes: a weak, pathetic man who needed others to lead him into the places he was feared to go. A man who had been given this one chance to prove himself and had fallen – quite literally - at the first hurdle, when he'd gone arse over tit on the sands and told her to go on without him.

Realisation that she was giving him a choice: *take my lead or be done with it.*

Realisation too that never had any woman he knew taken charge as she was doing now.

'I need an answer, Mister high and mighty Ivor Merrill,' words harshly spoken, spat from Greta's lips right into his face. 'You either do what I'm asking or you're over the side and into the drink. We've other people to think of, people who - unlike you - don't spend their lives dancing around in swan feathers and ermine. Take a choice. Man up, or you're gone.'

Tickle of laughter in Ivor's throat at the swan feathers and ermine, a humour undermined by the fact that one of his sisters had worn a swan-feather cape at her wedding, and her highly illustrious Lord having ermine lapels on his morning suit. The two of them waltzing elegantly around the sprung wooden dance-floor in fowl and fur, exactly as Greta had surmised.

*Foolish,* Ivor thought, *to have tried to take charge.*

As foolish as he'd always been.

*Get yerseln out while the going's good, lad. No one'll hold it agin you.*

That kind-worded man conjured up in the screels and skeins of mist as a ghostly presence behind Greta's shoulder; a blunt-featured soldier who'd barely an inch of skin that hadn't been punctured and pocked, slashed and scarred, from repeated assaults by sword, gunpowder, flying shrapnel. Bluff Yorkshire accent, bluff Yorkshire farmer pushed out of his tenancy, as far as Ivor could recall, joining the army so as to have a few meals beneath his belt come the end of every week. Ivor distressed he couldn't remember the man's name.

That he'd maybe never asked it.

Ivor a foolish man through and through, and an utter failure.

Swan feathers and ermine.

Privilege giving him a command he'd never earned.

His own view of himself dovetailing with Greta's.

All this hammering through his head in the few moments since Greta had laid out his choices, no doubt in him she'd carry out her threat, had probably chucked other men over other rails before. Maybe figurative rails in their case, if not in his. And oh, by all that he held dear, he didn't want to go over.

He wanted this chance more than ever. Wanted to prove himself to that Yorkshire farmer, to all the men who'd had the misfortune to come under his pitiful command; wanted to prove himself most of all to this spikey-haired woman who'd lain down the gauntlet, challenged him to step up, stop being the ninny she so obviously believed him to be, and which he was at core. Ivor wanting to vanquish that ninny, command it to be gone, evaporate itself along with this mist so, when it lifted, Ivor Snivels Merrill – the unappealing nickname he'd accrued in Spain – would be replaced by plain Captain Ivor Merrill.

Real soldier, real man.

No sniveling for him this time around.

No complaining about the poop deck.

Yorkshireman philosopher dissolving into the mist.

Only Greta here and now.

Only Greta needing to be convinced.

Ivor Merrill swallowing down the very last of the pride he'd hung onto, saying what she needed to hear. What he needed to believe.

'I'll do whatever you ask,' he said. 'You lead, and I will follow.'

Greta looking at him, Greta pulling down his arm, releasing him, regarding the blood her nails had caused to flow.

'Very well then,' was all she said. 'Might want to get a bandage on that wrist. As luck has it, I've one with me if you want it.'

'Nothing you can offer me that I'll not take,' Ivor replied, and immediately regretted it, the implications Greta might find in those words. Greta ignoring any subtext. Greta taking out a screel of bandage and a pot of ointment from her back-pack. Greta seeing to him as any sister might a brother who had fallen in the yard and scraped his knees to the bone.

'Got to learn to take what you're given,' she advised, as she slavered on the ointment, rubbed it in, wrapped the bandage about the wounds. 'And you have to be doing this because you want to,' she added, as she tied the bandage off. 'It has to be as important to you as it is to us, else when we get to Apeldoorn you're going to sound like a bleating sheep.'

Ivor sitting down, leaning his back against the rails, newly bandaged wrist cradled between his knees. Ivor breathing long and hard. Ivor Snivels Merrill trying not to snivel.

'It is important to me,' Ivor said, as the mizzle wraithed and reeled like a swan-feathered cloak being spun about a dance-floor. Ivor shaking his head, pinching the bridge of his nose between thumb and the one extant finger of his left hand, sinuses throbbing with damp and stress. 'It'll probably be the only thing I'll ever do that is important.'

'Oh for the Love of Mary,' Greta muttered, squatting down beside him, Greta regarding self-pity as the most useless emotion ever invented. Greta batting his hand from his face with one swift movement, which had the effect of making his thumb bash his sinuses, making them throb all the more.

'You can't go on like this,' she advised. 'Yes, it's important, but it isn't the only important thing you'll ever do. You helped Peter get to the truth of what was going on in Walcheren when everyone else kept their lips sealed tight as cockles. At least cockles that haven't been put on a peat fire when, let me tell you, they open up in seconds.'

Small smile from Ivor, as intended.

Greta not finished.

'You've to start thinking right,' she informed him. 'You've to remember you're not the only wheel on the cart, and that we're not the only cart. That there's a whole load more out there trying to do exactly what we're doing.'

Ivor rallying.

It might have been the most obscure analogy anyone had ever tried to embolden her troops with, but was having effect. No balderdash about crying *God for Harry, England and St George!* No *Once more unto the breach, dear friends, or close up the walls with our English dead.*

Greta very likely happy to stop up myriad walls with as many English dead as she could lay hands on. The English Greta's enemy, not without reason. Ivor having a sudden stab what this mission must be costing Greta by associating with the likes of him: consorting with one foe in order to out-do another, that by going to Apeldoorn, by Ivor delivering their message, they would be inviting more enemies into the battle in the form of the Duke of Brunswick's troops who at present were kicking their heels on English soil. If not the Duke himself, if the gossip of the officers in the camp on Walcheren was to be believed. Tattle being the Duke had returned to Holland to discuss tactics. Apeldoorn the obvious place for him to go.

If he really had left England.

Could be vital if their mission was to succeed.

Ivor realising that he cared.

That he wanted Mick to have survived, that he wanted this mission to succeed.

That its success hung on him.

Greta's only part to get Ivor where they needed him to go.

All resting on the shoulders of Ivor Snivels Merrill, and one shoulder not feeling so great since Greta had almost ripped it from its socket. But needs must, and only now did Ivor get to grips with the fact that there truly was a need; that the French embargo of Lowland ports needed to be stopped. And he'd try his damndest to make it so. Whether he halted it by a year, a month – even a day – it would be worth it.

# 23

# Lies That Grow Like Lichen

---⟨∾⟩---

'I'M GOING TO HAVE HIS bloody guts for garters.'

Zsolt was not happy.

Kept looking at the clock on the mantel above the small ingle-nook where Hela lit a fire every morning before she went to work in the bakery, strung a pot of water for the brothers' coffee, or a pot of soup for their lunch. Hela always rolling out of the bed she shared with Zsolt whilst it was still dark, unspooling herself from about him.

Zsolt hairy as a goat, front and back, and Hela loving it.

Hela smooth and sinuous, flat-bellied; no children in the offing in all this time, although whether she had her own body or Zsolt's to thank for it she didn't know. Twenty three years old when she'd left Norway. Older when she'd first lain with Zsolt, dread in her every month whether she would have her menses. Yet come it had, every time, every month, or every five weeks in her case.

Hela's life safe.

No squalling children to interrupt the intervening happy years spent with her getting up each dark morning to go to the bakery and pummel dough, or dip her hands in ice-cold water before setting to at the pastries. Hela's job to provide their strange little household with enough money to see them through.

Zsolt's job to lounge around at home writing tracts imbued with revolutionary fervor sent back to his homeland to keep the fires burning, writing letters off here and there to compatriots who believed, as he and Hela did, that Russian expansionism had to be stopped before it swallowed up the whole of Eastern Europe and Scandinavia too. Hela's zealous and patriotic fires, first stoked by Håkon and her involvement in his Big Plan, augmented by Russia going to war once more with Sweden the previous year, and still at it now. Finland already fallen. Finland no longer an independent country, a mere Royal Duchy. The Russian Tsar – or Tsarina - its Grand Duke. Lions and wolves around every corner. Lions and wolves needing to be stopped.

Zsolt writing too to Håkon on occasion. Håkon's replies stuttering and stilling over the years, and finally ceased. Håkon sick or dead for all they knew, or had simply lost interest since the Song had disappeared and he'd figured the campaign lost, knowing as well as they that it was fine and dandy to have the text of the Song in published format but, without the original for learned men and scholars to pore over and declare its authenticity, no one was going to bat an eyelid over it. Only when they had the actual manuscript would the discovery cause a storm: a document the Russians – and Empress Katerina in particular - had conspired to suppress; a document liberated heroically from the Moscow archives and spirited away, lost and since re-found.

Which would be revolution in the making in Hungarian circles if nowhere else, and amongst the Polovtsy clan most of all. Fire up one revolution and others would surely follow. Finland enabled to rise up too, once Russian weakness had been detected and exploited. Hela more certain of it than ever, despite the lack of communication from Håkon.

Whilst Zsolt wrote his fiery epistles and Hela worked at her bakery, it was Mokush's job to scour every street, every book-seller in Bad Salzbaum and beyond, make connections, add himself to catalogue and auction lists, all in expectation of the news that one day the cache of books they'd liberated from the Bad Salzbaum dealer Gerhard's sister had named – stolen from under their noses by Constantine - would resurface, for it surely had to turn up somewhere down the line. Mokush to be ready and waiting when it did. At which time they would try playing Hela's chitty of ownership, demand their property's return. Or retrieve their stash of hard-saved coins and buy the Song legally. If neither plan worked, which they assumed would be the likely outcome, their final plan was to steal the cache all over again.

Previous to that liberation they'd tried the direct approach, Hela going to the dealer's door with her chitty for that one particular lot within his crate. Hela and her chitty rudely dismissed by the dealer's wife. Hela told to go boil her head for all the use her chitty would do. Only option afterwards being to steal the crate, achieved with rare ease thanks to the lithe form of Constantine acting under orders.

Constantine performing his own small act of liberation, snatching it away from beneath the noses of the Polovtsy brothers. Let himself out of the dealer's house as planned, loading the crate onto the cart left discreetly outside, as planned. Brothers lurking at the corner of the street, waiting greedily for Constantine to deliver to them their birthright.

Well past three in the morning.

Fifteen minutes since Mokush had unlatched the small pantry window through which he'd funneled Constantine. Mokush knowing, from a bit of tittle-tattling with the dealer's housemaid, aided by several tongue-loosening libations and liberal doses of flattery and flirtation, that the crate they needed was in a small cupboard in the lobby next to the front door. Shoed in there unopened, the dealer having gone out of town on other book-business. The plan falling fully formed into Polovtsy laps, as if dictated by destiny.

Zsolt right to have taken Constantine with them. Auslander and Gericault of no use, once the brothers had scouted out the dealer's house and Mokush had gained his information from the house-maid. Auslander and Gericault cut loose, for which they were grateful. No skin off their noses. Melting away from Bad Salzbaum the very next day.

Polovtsy boots stamping quietly and impatiently on the cobbles of their dark corner on the night of the destiny-blessed theft, until Zsolt held up a hand.

'Listen,' squeaky wheel of a laden cart coming from the opposite end of the street as Constantine heaved it around a different corner.

'He's bloody well gone the wrong way,' Zsolt fumed. Cursing the nitwit boy who couldn't tell left from right.

Brothers after him on a run to intercept. At the junction, no sign of him. Zsolt going one way, Mokush the other.

Mokush the one to spy the shadowy outline of Constantine steering his cart onto the smooth-grassed edges of the spa grounds five hundred yards ahead. Mokush realizing the truth of it. The boy not the nitwit Zsolt had painted him. Constantine knowing full well he'd gone the wrong direction from the brothers. Treachery abounding.

Neither brothers nor Hela fully understanding why.

Assuming it was spite.

Tit for tat.

Constantine removed from the camp against his will, returning the favour the only way he knew how.

Constantine a small and quiet creature since they'd liberated him, and never a word of thanks for that liberation. Never a word at all.

Sat in the corner of the cottage in the space they'd allotted him. Took food and water as it came. Relieved himself in the bucket provided.

Guarded over by Zsolt as Hela went to her work and Mokush ferreted out the particulars of the dealer who had their crate.

No notion how many of Zsolt's ravings Constantine had listened to during his sequestration in the cottage Hela had secured for them.

No notion Constantine had been press-ganged from village into army, what he'd witnessed and seen perpetrated because of it. How deep ran the furrows of protestation in him, young as he was. How greatly he detested fighting in all its forms. How avidly he admired Fabian Guichot and Frau Dieter for all they'd achieved despite it. How extreme the innocent can be in not wanting to be held responsible for any more of what they despised. Namely more cruelty, more war and the forcing into such a war of yet more young folk like himself who'd never wanted anything to do with it.

How obvious it had been to Constantine in the cottage that Hela and the Polovtsy brothers were intending to do exactly that. Constantine not wanting any part of it. Could not, would not, bear the burden of blame of another revolution, another war, being dropped upon his small young shoulders. Nations against nations all they'd spoken about. Meaning blood and blood and more of it.

Constantine feet-sky.

Constantine attempting escape.

Constantine needing to get back to Fabian and Frau Dieter, however he could.

The night of the theft of the crate of books the single time, the only time, since he'd been abducted from the mill-workings, to be allowed any agency, out of physical reach of one or other of the brothers' strong arms. Meaning this might be his only ever chance of escape from them.

Constantine knowing one of his pursuers was not far behind him in that black emptiness of the night. Hearing heavy boots stamping quickly down first one street and another, and onto the soft grass behind him. Constantine frantic for a place to hide, and a place to hide the crate of books with him. Desperate determination making him haul his cart onwards all the quicker. Seeing the huge pyramid of blackthorn bundles piled up for the burning. Decision in him to shove the crate in amongst the heap where it would go up in flames on the morrow and be lost to the Polovtsy clan forever. Not foreseeing how stiff the blackthorn bundles

would be with precipitate, how vicious and spiky, how sharp
the calcified thorns would be. A few moments of tearing his
arms from fingertips to shoulders before giving up the task,
casting about him, trying to breathe deeply, calm himself,
think as logically as Fabian or Frau Dieter would have.

Mokush closing upon him.

Constantine hauling the cart away from the impregnable
slouch of the bonfire and on towards the hedges. Saw a slim
chance of salvation: nearest hedge only partway packed. No
knowledge of Holger's helper taking sunstroke, hence the
delay, nor that Fabian had been brought in as back-up.
Constantine seeing only that here might be sanctuary, here
a way to divert a revolution he could not contemplate being
responsible for starting, and for him returning to Fabian and
Frau Dieter's care.

Constantine heaving the crate up with the last of his
strength and pushing it into the hedge, running back a few
yards to deposit the cart before returning, launching himself
in beside the crate. Curling himself about it, making himself
as small as he could be. Had not pulled any of the fresh
blackthorn bundles about him as Fabian has surmised, had
merely gone in and lain, such urgency in him he felt no more
pain than sting and smart as he burrowed in. Heard Mokush
close upon him. Mokush striding by mere yards from his
hidey-hole. Mokush finding the cart, kicking at it, cursing it
and Constantine in equal measure.

Constantine sighing softly, concealed within his
spike-studded prison.

Constantine bleeding from arms and wrists from his
previous wrestle with the bonfire; bleeding from back and

calves with the new assault of his hidey-hole, without conscious note of it. Constantine sticking to his station, strong and stalwart as any soldier. As constant as his name implied.

Braver than you or I might have been under such circumstances.

Brave as the bravest men the world over during their own battles.

Far braver – had he only known it - than Prince Igor, Igor's son, his brother and his nephew, after their own capture by the Kumans following the battle by the Donets River where all this had begun.

Constantine certain that come the morning he would be found and salvaged, be able to stagger out alive, be cosseted and welcomed back by all those he had previously been snatched from. Not in so much pain as Fabian had imagined; didn't realised how much of his life-blood was trickling away into the bales; had instead been oddly peaceful, knowing the righteousness of what he'd done and the nearness of returning back to what he considered his home at the mill-workings. Had laid his head upon the crate and slipped into a sleep as deep as it had been a long time coming. Constantine on constant alert in the cottage with Hela and the brothers, seeking a chance, a chink, a possibility of escape. None ever forthcoming, until now. And oh how sweet it was to Constantine to know that come the morning he would be rescued and be freed, the burden of possible revolutions taken from him.

*Frau Dieter will know what to do about it all,* being his last thought as he drifted away. *And Fabian will always see me right.*

Constantine peaceful the whole night through, until he woke early morning feeling weak and dizzy. No notion how much blood he'd lost during that peaceful sleep. Heard someone out there in the darkness and tried to claw his way towards the noise. Tried to shout, tried to push himself out of the hedge. Found himself caught up in spike and spine, coat and trousers securing him as if by ropes and binds.

Awful irony in Fabian being so close at hand, for he would have clawed away the entirety of the hedges had he known Constantine was cossetted so cruelly within.

That faint bleat in the morning, when Fabian had gone out to relieve himself, ignored.

That faint bleat in the morning the last sound Constantine would ever make.

Blood by then leaking from him like juice from blackberries pushed through a sieve to remove all their pips before making of it a fine jelly. Constantine so weak he couldn't shout out to the one man who would have done anything to save him.

*Oh you Slovo, what have you done to our fine young men?*

Not saving Constantine, for one.

Constantine secured fast and tight in his hedge as any netsuke night in Vettie's Giel.

Constantine too depleted and disoriented to engender his own escape before Fabian and Holger's bundles piled down upon him.

The heft of them collapsing Constantine in on himself, concertinaing his leaking body about the crate. The going of him as bad as Fabian had imagined. An agony of slow suffocation as each successive air pocket was snuffed out one by one and the spikes kept on digging and the heft kept on coming, until the final puff of breath was forced from the punctured lungs of young Constantine and he could draw in no more.

And so unnecessary.

Constantine so near to his survival.

Instead, Constantine secreted within his hedge.

Fabian going back to his work with Holger, and next to Frau Dieter.

The years ticking by.

In the cottage Hela shared with Zsolt and Mokush the clock on the mantel reminding them of it every month, every day. Hela content. Hela happy. Hela dallying in the markets of Bad Salzbaum before her work, as she'd done in Deventer, picking out onions, potatoes, apples...

Not so this morning. And it was morning. The clock on the mantel had just struck one after midnight. Hela fretting. She was on late shift at the bakery, meaning she'd to be there by eight at the latest. She'd said before to Zsolt not to worry, that Mokush was most likely merely enjoying the festive mood.

Hela not sure now. Plenty of time for Mokush to have returned, and more.

Hela delivering her bakery gossip the previous evening: a body found in the hedges along with a mysterious crate.

Book-finders brought in not long after, so obvious what must be in the crate.

Hela's face at the time bright and exuberant as she'd given the brothers the news.

Zsolt yelling *This is it! It has to be!*

Mokush advising caution, saying he would check it out. Plenty of folk milling about later that night for the bonfire celebrations, and he would be among them.

All three having quickening pulses, hopes rekindled like sunflower seeds shoved into warmed earth springing into plants practically before their eyes.

'Something's gone wrong,' Zsolt said, eyes and body feverish with frustration, fingertips alternately fidgeting and then drumming at the table top.

Clock on the mantel striking out the half hour.

'I've always hated that clock,' Zsolt said. Part of the sparse furniture in the cottage they rented and not theirs to dispense with; clock Hela's only means of getting to her work on time and even Zsolt recognized the need in that. Nevertheless Zsolt suddenly standing, looking for the nearest cupboard into which he could hide the blasted thing, did not want to see the jerky movements of its ancient hands or listen to its incessant ticking for another minute, nor hear its judgmental chimes telling him what he already knew: that the longer Mokush was away the more likely it was that everything had gone to hell. Seven long years he'd been listening to that beggaring clock, and it was quite long enough.

'There is one thing we could do.'

Zsolt halted by Hela's voice, as musical and beguiling as the clock's was emphatically not. Zsolt turning back, looking at her, Hela's exquisite hands wrapped together on her lap.

'I'm not sure you're going to like it,' she went on. 'But it's the only thing I can think of.'

MATHILDE STOSS WAS too worried to sleep, had stayed in her chair by the fire after Piet had left. She'd slid the bolt and waited, but Piet hadn't yet come back.

She didn't want to go to her bed. Holger still sleeping, and didn't need disturbing. Nor did she want to lie on the sheets he had soiled, sheets she was going to have to boil up come the day. And only two short weeks to sort out the rest of her and Holger's lives. What she could take, what she would have to leave. Where they would go.

Didn't know how everything had got so difficult with such ease and speed.

One morning she'd woken up fearing the hedges had turned into trolls, and now it appeared they had. Not literally. Of course not. All that sort of nonsense she'd left behind in Vettie's Giel where the men were as much trolls as actual trolls might have been. Thinking back to Ussi and her child. Ussi, who'd conceived after a single night with the insufferable Torgi Eriksson. Mathilde without progeny. Always the way with Vettie's Giel. A place where normal didn't apply, where there were always more men than there were women to go around and too many women infertile because of some back-behind trait carrying on down the generations.

Thinking on the woman she'd asked Piet to find. An impossible task. She hadn't even given him a description. A ridiculous idea.

The bells of St Peter's chiming out the hour of seven in the morning. What had happened to the night?

Mathilde sighing, putting more wood into the stove.

Mathilde catching a faint noise as of a curtain being drawn, or maybe the sweep of skirts across frosted grass. She stood, moved about the bed, looked out of the tiny window. Saw the hedges tall and dark, and a woman making her way down one side of them. Saw her coming directly towards Mathilde's cottage. Mathilde's breath catching in her throat as the woman paused, looked up into the sky as if begging the moon to tell her right. And in that movement, the lifting of her head, she presented her profile as perfectly as if she'd meant to do so.

And in that moment Mathilde was certain.

This was Ussi's child, making her way to Mathilde's door.

Piet right. No accident she was here in Bad Salzbaum, instead come to find one person and one person only. To find Mathilde.

Mathilde's throat tightening as she slipped through all the reasons why that might be: maybe Ussi ill or dying and had one last message for her old friend; or Ussi already dead, Hela coming to tell her in person. Or, more likely, Hela trapped in some god-awful marriage and here to ask for help. Mathilde tripping over her skirts as she went the two yards to her door and drew back the bolt. Mathilde opening the door onto the raw braw early morning and calling out.

'Hela, oh my dear Hela! Is that really you?'

The startlement of the opened door and the voice halted the woman, her face pale, blanched by the moonlight, and then brightening into a smile as she swept swiftly onwards, Mathilde opening wide her arms and welcoming Hela in.

'HE'S NOT COME AROUND yet,' Caro said, tapping lightly at Mokush's cheeks.

'There's an awful lot of blood,' Piet worried.

'It's a head wound,' Caro assured. 'They always bleed like buggery. No need for alarm.'

'How would you know such a thing?' Piet asked, watching the young man wrapping the stranger's head gently in a compress swiftly whipped up from an empty flour sack soaked with the contents of a couple of jars he'd found on the shelves.

'Spent a lot of time on boats and ships when I was young,' Caro replied without looking up. 'Really got to watch yourself when they're running or tacking or heaving-to, else those jibs and booms will have you every time. Even luffing will do it if you're not careful.'

Caro speaking a foreign language as far as Piet was concerned.

Ruan interpreting.

'You get whacked in the head by those bits of wood the sails are attached to when they swing around in the wind. Guess it pays to be a short-sprat if you're a sailor.'

Piet frowning, finding the attempted humour inappropriate.

Ruan paying him no mind.

'Give him a slap, Caro. We've been here practically the whole night.'

Ruan yawning loudly. Church bells chiming out another hour.

Piet about to protest.

He might have found the man suspicious and therefore had him constrained; and those suspicions might have been proven to be well-founded, given what the man had started to say before he'd toppled off his cabbages, but he didn't want to be responsible for a death and, despite Caro's assurances, the man did not look well.

'Can't we just let him be?' Piet pleaded. 'Give him time to rest?'

Ruan stamping his feet to get the blood moving, for it was cursed cold down here.

'No, Piet, we can't. Last thing we want is for Professor Jorn to come barging in on us before we've figured out what we're dealing with.'

Piet having to admit the truth of it.

Last person he wanted to see being Professor blasted Jorn. Piet incandescent about his treatment of Holger and Mathilde. Piet trying to work a way out of it, although what that could be he'd not a single notion.

'How about we move him, then?' Piet offered. 'Take him somewhere the Professor's not likely to go.'

Ruan stopped his stamping, looking at Caro, Caro looking back.

'Now that's not a bad idea,' Ruan said. 'It'll need to be somewhere close. The Stoss's maybe?'

Piet shaking his head.

'You saw the place. There's not enough room to swing a cat. And I don't want Holger disturbed.'

Ruan seeing it again: the tiny cottage, the single room with its tiny table, several chairs, a stove, a bed. Hard to believe those two had lived in it cheek by jowl for several decades without murdering one another.

'We'll take him to the mud-baths,' Caro decided for them all. 'And, before you say it, yes I know it's opening day today, and yes, Professor Jorn will probably go there to see how it's doing and it'll be overrun by visitors, but it isn't his place. It's Frau Dieter's. And there was a room out back, and Frau Dieter's a good person. She'll not deny us, not once we explain.'

'Won't it be locked up?' Piet quick to see the downside. Caro putting him right.

'You have to be joking! Mr. Guichot will be there. He's probably been nursing his steam engine the whole night through, making sure it'll run right. And he's another good person.'

The thought once more in Ruan's head how Caro could sum people up so succinctly and with such accuracy. Caro rarely wrong, not since a long time.

'Then that's what we'll do,' he agreed with Caro's plan of action. 'There's a load of empty sacks at the back of the cellar. Piet and me will make up a sling or stretcher of some kind. Find something we can transport our prisoner in, insensible or not. In fact insensible would be preferable. Let's pour a bit of brandy down his neck to make certain.'

Ruan snatching up a bottle of the good stuff and uncorking it with his teeth.

'Caro, you go ahead to warn Mr. Guichot. And, while we're at it, let's take everything else with us too. Hedge-man, crate and books.'

'We can't do that,' Caro protested. 'Professor Jorn will have a fit! They're his property, as far as he'll see it. The books at least, if not the body.'

Ruan swerved out an expression halfway between grin and grimace.

'He will,' he agreed. 'But we've already established he doesn't give a curse about the hedge-man, will probably have him dropped into the first unmarked grave he can get dug. As for the books, well. I've still the key to his office. We'll do exactly as he's asked. We'll find out if any are of value, find out everything we can about them. Mainly because I can't help thinking there's a tale here, like our knock-headed friend began to tell us. And Professor Jorn, I fear, is not a man for tales.'

Ruan paused, felt the folder once more tucked into the back of his belt, the corners of it against his skin.

One of the lamps spluttering out.

Caro speaking into the quiet darkness as it extinguished.

'Has he paid us anything? Given us a deposit or a contract? Anything of the like?'

Soft sound of Ruan snorting, because of course a man like Professor Jorn would never have done such a thing, which now rather played to their advantage. Their right entirely to remove the books until the Professor coughed up at least a portion of their fee.

MATHILDE HELD HER FINGERS to her lips as she led Hela in, nodding over at Holger sleeping soundly in their bed.

'He's not well,' she whispered, motioning Hela to one of the chairs, lighting a lamp, placing it on the table between them where last night's pancakes lay untouched.

'What's wrong with him?' Hela asked, no pussy-footing for the women of Vettie's Giel where secrets never lasted long. Mathilde sighing, studying her husband, assuring herself he was actually asleep.

'We've had rather a night of it, I'm afraid. Holger had a bit of a wobble up top the hedges,' the scene running through her head like a magic lantern show. 'If truth be told,' she went on, 'he's got a bit lost in his mind this past while. And. Well. I'm afraid the long and short of it is that he got the sack. We've been here nearly thirty years, Hela. But in two weeks' time we've to be up and out.'

Hela drew in her brows and studied her mother's old friend, saw the stress lines etched across her face like birds' feet leave tracks in damp sand, the grey streaks running through her hair. Cast her eyes about the dingy cottage, which was smaller than her own front room.

'What will you do?' she asked, this not at all how she'd imagined it going, which had been joyous reunion followed by general chatter into which Hela would interpose her questions about the man found in the hedge and all that had gone on afterwards. Main objective being to find out what had happened to the crate, and Mokush. Questions she meant to find answers to, but plainly it was going to take longer than she'd anticipated.

'I don't know,' Mathilde answered honestly, shrugging her shoulders then squaring them, smiling over at Hela. 'Let's not dwell on that now. What I want to know, my girl, is what on earth you're doing here. I knew I'd seen you in the market a while back, buying apples. Ussi used to love apples. How is she? Is she well?'

Such entreaty on Mathilde's face that Hela hated to tell her the news, although no need. Mathilde seeing what was there, unspoken.

'So that's it,' Mathilde said. 'She's dead, then. Is that why you've come all this way, to tell me?'

Hela's heart juddering at the easy in she'd been given, lies lining up on her lips. Lies she'd been practicing all the way into Bad Salzbaum about how she'd ended up at Mathilde's door. Lies she was quickly adjusting to the situation. Mathilde seeing her in the market giving her a bit of a jolt. No reason Mathilde shouldn't have seen her there, but for Mathilde to have recognized her for who she was seemed unlikely in the extreme. She'd never clapped eyes on Mathilde as Mathilde had never clapped eyes on her. Mathilde sailing over the ocean to a new life before Hela had been born. But this new Hela, who had travelled alone from Vettie's Giel, was not about to be put off. This new Hela understood such wild coincidences could happen, and if she could wind a man around her little finger there was surely room about another finger for one person more.

'She spoke of you often,' Hela began, 'as of course did everyone, or the women at least. You were a hero to us girls when we were growing up. It was all so romantic, how you got out with Holger. You know how it was back then, and it's no better now.'

Mathilde nodding sadly. Mathilde smiling too. Mathilde a hero! She liked the sound of that, despite how everything had gone lately.

'And your mother, did she ever get married? Have you brothers or sisters? We corresponded for a few years after I left, if not for long. It didn't seem right. Not to either of us.'

Hela knowing as much, and more her mother's decision than Mathilde's. Ussi regarding Mathilde's missives as barbed thorns digging into soul and flesh to know Mathilde was making a go of things as she never could. One illegitimate child followed by another. Ussi fair game in Vettie's Giel once everyone knew she'd been despoiled. Hela not about to mention her lame-armed brother to anyone, for he was hers and hers alone. The cape fringed with hares' ears too decrepit to be worn these days, stowed beneath her bed. Deep regret in her she'd never fixed that last ear to its edge to make it complete, there being no more hares in Deventer than there were in Bad Salzbaum.

Hela weighing up her words.

'She didn't,' Hela replied. Honesty one side. Deception another. 'Mostly because she didn't want to. You know how they are back there, and they haven't changed. But she loved me, raised me right. And she loved you too. I think that was why she stopped writing, because she wanted you to go on and not look back.'

Not the truth, but it was enough.

Silence between these two women as they contemplated the old times and what had come from them. Mathilde wishing to God she'd kept a wiser eye on Ussi during her wedding celebrations, despite it being the one time she could never have kept watch, and Ussi regretting it so sorely afterwards and then not so sorely once she'd discovered she was pregnant. A rare gift back then, and Mathilde horribly jealous Ussi had managed it on her first time.

Hela regarding how mean was the shack into which her hero Mathilde had been cossetted all these years – and she had been a hero. She'd not lied about that. Some pity in her Mathilde was about to be turfed out of this same shack because her man was losing his mind - if she'd got that part right, about which she wasn't sure.

'Have you been happy?' Hela asked, the question out of her mouth before she'd time to think it through. Mathilde's fingers going to the locket about her neck as she regarded her friend's daughter, this miracle materialized out of the frosted night. Mathilde contemplating her life as she'd not done before. Mathilde coming to the conclusion that no matter how things went, no matter what was about to befall them, that yes. She'd been happy on more occasions than she could count. And was happy still, because here in her house had come the one person she believed might be able to help her Holger.

A man who had lit fires beneath her feet and made her dance; a man who'd surprised her at every turn, and she him. And oh, how good their life had been together, no matter children had never arrived. And now here was Hela, at the right place, the right time.

'Oh my dear,' Mathilde said, leaning over, taking Hela's hands in her own, seeing the bright fjords pass her by as

Holger's ship took them away from Vettie's Giel: the blue-green snubs of glaciers, the waterfalls tipping from the sheerest of cliffs; sea water bright, clear as crystal, whales and narwhals surging through the gaps opening up in the ice; the joyous nights spent with stars spread above them thick as daisies in grass and all the more spectacular.

'Yes,' she said to Hela, 'we've been happy. More happy than I can say. But what about you? How has it been for you?'

And how had it been for Hela?

Hela not sure how to answer.

Absolute bloody purgatory for a long time after Ussi had died and the folk of Vettie's Giel tried to force her into one marriage or another.

Absolute hell, until Håkon Tryggvason had returned to provide a different path to follow.

Absolute hell from Norway to Holland.

Absolute hell no longer, since she'd met the Polovtsy brothers, met Zsolt who worshipped her. The art of keeping men satisfied hammered into her all her long journey until she had it to perfection. Not so great men's needs, as it turned out. Nothing she couldn't deal with. And with Zsolt she truly had a connection: shared goals, shared philosophies and convictions.

Break the back of Russia and we set Europe free.

Song of Igor the heart of their rebellion. The stepping stone across their river. The way out for her and everyone like her. Maybe even Mathilde who, on this moonlit soulless morning, was so obviously in distress. Circumstances overtaking Mathilde when they had - up to this point in time - ladled out happiness to her for free.

Yet nothing was ever free, Hela knew well.

Everything had its price.

Freedom no different from anything else.

*Opals, rubies, diamonds.*

Hela needing to find the terms on which the Song of Igor could be released back into the world. Hela no stranger to haggling.

'There's something I need to ask of you,' Mathilde said, her eyes shifting over to her husband and back to Hela.

'Anything,' Hela replied, haggle thereby beginning.

'I want you to talk to Holger,' Mathilde spoke earnestly. 'I want you to remind him of Vettie's Giel, of the people he met when he was there. Of the place, the hills, the fjords, of Torghatten, of Ussi.'

Hela surprised her task would be nothing more onerous than to talk of home. Mathilde seeing that surprise, squeezing Hela's hands in her own.

'You don't know how much it would mean to him, to me,' she went on quickly. 'Holger's stuck in a bad place, and I need him to go back in order for him to go forwards. I need him to recall the good times, the start of it, the start of our good times. And all of that began in Vettie's Giel. And you're so new from there it will be far fresher coming from you than me.'

Hela suppressing a laugh, for this was a joke indeed. Hela long gone from home, about as fresh as a hen's egg evading the capturing house-wife's hand and left to rot beneath the hedge it had been born under. The irony of the image not unamusing, given where she was and why she was here.

'I will do it day and night if it will help,' she said easily, 'but I can't do it now. I've work to get to. Did it not occur to you why I'm so early at your door?'

Hela wishing back the words too late. Mathilde frowning, for it had not occurred to her. All she'd seen was her miracle stepping out of the night.

'I've got work in a bakery,' Hela added swiftly, 'and I daren't be late. Not so quickly after I've been hired.' The best lies always containing a germ of truth. 'It was only yesterday I found out where you were, and it was only as I was coming into work this morning and had a few minutes to spare that I thought I'd come by, fix the place in my memory so I could come back later. I didn't expect anyone to be awake.'

Hela fighting back a grimace, knowing she'd said too much. Had deviated from the script she'd set herself, provided personal information. Seeing the doubt on Mathilde's face, Mathilde's lips opening slightly as she thought this information through. Mathilde about to ask the question Hela knew must come. Hela's mind a spider swiftly spinning out its web in order to catch the on-coming fly.

'I know you and mother corresponded in the early years, like you said,' she span her tale, 'but after she died all was lost with her.'

Hela wanting to kick herself. Another gaff. Riffling through their conversation and finding her way out. Miraculous. Everything about Hela apparently miraculous in this hellish morning.

'She died a while back,' Hela explained. 'Several years. First thought in my mind was that you should know of it, but no way to reach you. You know the way of Vettie's Giel, how the men barge in and take over. They took all her papers, burned them before I had a chance to look them through. And you know too how tight-lipped men can be when they want to keep you in the dark.'

She lowered her head, willed tears to drip from her lashes, tears not long coming. Think on bad experiences and tears will follow, and Hela had so many bad experiences stored up in her she had a plethora to choose from. Odd thing being, to her at least, that it was the memory of her unfinished cape managing it this time around.

'It took me ages to find out where you went. Those old Germans who stayed on simply wouldn't tell me and, God forgive me, I gave up after a while. I tried and tried to scour my memories for where it was Holger came from, asked my old friends from school. But, well. By then they were all married off and were either told to keep their mouths shut or didn't remember. I'm so sorry. Can you ever forgive me?'

The tears so real Mathilde couldn't see past them. Couldn't see the myriad holes in Hela's story. Saw only what she wanted, which was her friend's daughter crying in shame and self-recrimination that she'd not got to Mathilde's door before she had. Mathilde folding her hands about Hela's.

'This is not your fault,' she said, needing to excuse, to comfort. 'None of this is your fault, so hush yourself. We'll sort this out. You get off to your bakery. Come see me after your shift is done. Oh please don't cry, Hela. Please don't. I can't tell you what a boon it's been to see you, to meet you. And you come all this way.'

Home and heroine reconciled.

Mathilde helping Hela up, wiping both Hela's eyes and her own with her soiled apron.

'Thank you for coming to me,' she said, as she ushered Hela out the opened door. 'I know the way must have been hard. I can't tell you how grateful I am you chose to take it, that you thought of me, came here despite it all. Such a strange night it's been. You haven't been my only visitor, and that one. Well. Thank goodness the book-finders took him away, because I don't think he meant well. Not like you.'

Hela's heart buzzing with these last words.

Hela heading off into the coming morning.

Hela still wiping her eyes until she was out of sight.

Mathilde – infuriatingly – standing at her cottage door to watch her progress across the grass. Hela bowing her shoulders as if she was the lost girl Mathilde presumed her to be.

Bells of St Peter's ringing out the half of seven as she went on her way, got around the hedges, lost to Mathilde's sight.

Hela going the wrong way precisely so that would be the case, not wanting to add to her slips by pointing Mathilde in the direction of her bakery. More than one in Bad Salzbaum, Hela hoping the ruse had worked. Hela extraordinarily relieved, rolling her shoulders, brushing at her eyes with her fingertips, annoyed she had butter on her lashes from Mathilde's filthy apron, and could smell it too. Hela pausing as she saw someone else abroad on this dark morning: two men toting a cart across the frost-strewn dew-dimpled grass. Two men toting a cart laden with an odd load: a square wooden crate, and what appeared to be two rolls of sacking – one small and short, the other longer – the latter having feet and face sticking out at either end. She couldn't tell if its cargo was dead or alive, although would have recognized those boots anywhere - she'd blackened and buffed them often enough - even had she not recognized the abundantly bearded and side-whiskered face of Zsolt's brother.

Bloody blasted Mokush.

No need to entertain further the blessed Mathilde Stoss, of whom she'd had her fill. Holger's lost mind could wander away all it wanted as far as she was concerned. Hela watching. Hela waiting in the shadow of the hedges until she was certain of their direction.

Zsolt was going to blow a gasket.

Not so Hela.

Hela seeing this as deliverance.

Hela seeing where they were heading, which had to be the newly built mud-baths that the entire population of Bad Salzbaum had been gabbing on about these last few months.

*Oh you spiders who spin out silk, you're never going to spin out more webs than Hela from Vettie's Giel can do.*

Hela waiting until the coast was clear before hitching up her skirts and sprinting over the grass towards the town. She was going to be late for her shift, no matter how fast she ran. Lies already forming on her lips, as easy on them as lichen grows on a sun-warmed boulder.

*Lies and haggling.*

*When did they become my métier?*

Thoughts short-lived as she rubbed hard at her eyes to make them red and swollen - the rancid butter helping - to aid whatever story she could conjure up before she bowled up at the bakery door and hauled herself in as a miserable wretched woman in need of succour, bravely going at her work despite the sorrows she had yet to invent.

# 24

## Along The Winding Shore

CARO FOUND FABIAN GUICHOT standing station by his steam machine, treble-checking valves, tightening tubes, face a flurry of worry, hoiked-up hare-lip purpled with the effort.

'Need any help?' Caro asked, Fabian so concentrated on his tasks he barely noticed the intrusion, nor the early hour.

'All running well,' he murmured. 'All going to plan. Fuel ready, stocked and stored. Valves clear and free. Water accurately diverted, going where it needs to go. All tip-top for the opening.'

'We need to ask you a favour,' Caro went on, undeterred. 'Your backroom? The one in the mud-baths. Can we borrow it for a few hours? Maybe a day?'

Fabian straightening, taking a few moments to focus on Caro, remember who he was. Fabian frowning, looking up into a sky furrowed over with clouds like a field newly harrowed, moonlight glinting at their edges, hint of dawn a way over in the east.

'You're asking me what?' Fabian replied, abstracted.

'Your back room,' Caro repeated. 'Can we have the loan of it? It's important.'

Piet and Ruan hoving into view, having roughly sewn together a few abandoned sacks into serviceable use and stowing within them their serviceable goods – namely Mokush, hedge-man and crate of books – Piet quick to fetch a cart from the work-shed in which to transport them all to their destination.

Fabian uncertain, Fabian not so wound up he couldn't see this was unusual.

'Please,' Caro said again. 'We wouldn't ask if we had anywhere else to go. But we need to stow these...things...get them away from Professor Jorn. Please, Mr. Guichot. I wouldn't ask if wasn't needed.'

Mention of Professor Jorn enough for Fabian who couldn't stick the man, given the way he treated Frau Dieter on a regular basis and everyone else Jorn regarded to be within his service. The earlier episode with Holger Stoss making his blood boil. High-handed a generous misnomer. Ruthlessly dictatorial more the order of the day. A delight to both him and Frau Dieter that this place, these mud-baths, would be run by themselves alone. Franchise granted, legalities underwritten. Frau Dieter making certain of that before they'd proposed the venture in the first place.

'What are you wanting?' he therefore asked in his stilted dictum that this lad Caro appeared to have no trouble interpreting. 'Tell me and we will help.'

Small blush to have included himself and Frau Dieter in a *we,* but no fuss once he understood.

'Bring them in,' Fabian said, 'and let's see what will follow.'

'There is one other thing,' Caro forewarned Fabian. 'The man in the hedge. We've isolated his head, enhanced his features.'

Fabian stopping short, trying to grasp what was being told him. Brows drawn. Caro speaking again.

'You thought you recognized him before. Now it will be much more obvious if it is who you suspect.'

Fabian having to swallow away the obstruction in his throat, the constriction to his airways that made him take an involuntary gasp. One thing to have suspicions. Another to be certain.

'If it is your friend,' Caro was solicitous, 'at least you'll be able to give him a proper burial.'

Caro remembering other friends lost. Burial small comfort, a way to close one life's book, place it upon a shelf inside your head where you could revisit it at will. Open it at the good parts, ignore the bad if bad there were.

Piet and Ruan drawing level.

Ruan looking at Caro, Caro giving a small nod. All heading, without another word, along the line of the lett towards a place they'd be free of Professor Jorn's pomp and pernickety interference. Fabian leading the way, Fabian pushing open the gate into the enclosure and next the door by the ticket booth and into the farther room. The room he and Frau Dieter had already designated as the Stoss's new place of work. Not that the Stoss's knew it, nor whether they would accept the offer.

*First duty of the morning*, Frau Dieter had said. Frau Dieter meaning to get it done at first light, long before the mud-baths' official opening, which would be at ten o'clock precisely, the folk attendant at the Spa Hotel not notoriously early risers. Fabian thinking, as he strode along, how indiscriminately the world had placed its citizens: some wealthy, most not. Poorer folk, like himself, getting it in the neck every time. All these wars they'd no interest in making it worse: taxes and tithes raised beyond tolerance forcing tenants from their lands, fathers into armies, women into servitude, orphaned children left to fend for themselves. Constantine of the latter, a boy abandoned; Constantine, who'd needed help, and not the kind provided by the army. Help Fabian had singularly failed to provide once Constantine was taken from him; and no help in the world to save him now that he'd returned.

If he had returned.

The matter soon resolved as they gained the room and from the cart was fetched first Mokush in his sacking-stretcher, pungent with spilled brandy, laid out on the table; next the crate. Hedge-man last. Caro making Fabian sit in case his legs went from under him as Ruan unwrapped the sacking. Fabian involuntarily remembering the small Christmas present from all those years ago, Constantine's bright face and merry eyes as Fabian took his medallion wrapped in a piece of hessian. Their barracks liberally adorned with flour sacks from the mills that had seen better days; sacks used for shadowy curtains letting in zig-zags of light through rip and tear; or turned into extra blankets during Winter, their several layers providing more warmth than you would suppose from their thinness, their covered sleepers arising dusted with a smattering of the flour trapped in twisted corners the mice hadn't been able to get at; sacks torn into squares for handkerchiefs, wrapping lunchtime pieces, or used as washing cloths and bum-wipers; sacking strips wrapped about lower limbs as makeshift gaiters to keep clegs and ticks from getting into their trouser-legs during the hotter Summers.

Fabian going through this list to distract himself from what he was about to see, which was so much more terrible than he'd anticipated.

*We've isolated his head, enhanced his features.*

And so they had.

Hedge-man's body obstinately curled and grey, slightly sparkling from the remaining precipitate as Ruan lifted it from the cart in its sacking sling. The head left in the cart, a horrid lump with a few strands of hair poking from its top-knot roughly tied with string. String now loosened, sacking falling away, protective layer of precipitate dissolved and gone. Fabian seeing the peaty brown skin stretched out upon its bones, the lines of cheek, brow and chin easily demarcated, as were the paper-thin eye-lids partially closed, eye-lashes clear and free, hair the same peaty hue as the skin.

Fabian hanging his head. Taking deep breaths to calm himself.

'It's him,' he croaked out. 'It's Constantine.'

The shred of doubt he'd harboured, nurtured, since his first sighting extinguished.

Book closed. Shelf awaiting.

Caro's earlier words coming back to him.

*At least you'll be able to give him a proper burial.*

The very least he could do for Constantine, and the very last.

FRAU DIETER ROSE AND washed, dressed in a grey silk dress exactly like the one she'd worn the previous day. Another two exactly like them in her closet, Frau Dieter liking order and similitude. That previous-day dress regarded with quiet elation: muddied and torn, spattered and soaked. A dress that had done its duty well and had one more to perform. Washed in soapy-water and dried by the fire the previous evening. The culmination and proof of a strange night, an exhilarating night: feeling the thrum of it in her veins, that slight vibration spiders must detect when their webs are butted into by a fly.

The coming day promising to provide more of the same.

Frau Dieter leaving her home not long past dawn, the streets criss-crossed with draggles of yawning men and women heading to their places of work. Frau Dieter nodding to one here, another there: the fruit-sellers in the market who'd dragged their wares in darkness along the pocked lanes towards Bad Salzbaum; the ostlers just around the corner; the elderly woman who sold pins and ribbons; the late-shift bakery workers smelling of flour and yeast, their gentle wholesome scents overwhelmed by the vile stench of dried tripe as a girl came around the corner pulling her loaded cart. The girl nodding wearily at Frau Dieter, unable to raise a morning smile, her life too hard and arduous. Frau Dieter always purchasing a bag of the dreadful stuff whenever she saw the girl, specifically to make her life less hard and arduous. Stuff given gratis to her two-doors down neighbour who had a liking for ferrets, and ferrets apparently having a liking for dried tripe.

The brown paper of her parcel crinkling beneath her elbow.

Frau Dieter totting up in her head who had the most need of the spoiled dress Frau Dieter could no longer wear. Choice quickly made.

Tripe-girl the winner. Handing it over.

'Still got life in it,' she said, as she did so. 'Hope you can make use of it.'

After which Frau Dieter left the streets and stepped onto the neatly clipped grounds of the Spa Hotel, hesitating as she approached the Stoss's cottage.

It was hardly light, just enough to see by, and possibly too early to be calling on anyone, let alone the Stoss's who must be in great distress. Frau Dieter surprised when the cottage door opened and Mathilde came out to greet her as if she'd been waiting, as if she'd seen her coming, a beatific smile on Mathilde's face Frau Dieter could not interpret.

The bells of St Peter's ringing out their eight as Frau Dieter stood on the grass and Mathilde Stoss welcomed Frau Dieter in, the strange and exhilarating day Frau Dieter had anticipated thereby officially begun.

OVER THE AMSTEL RIVER, in the 13th Century, a dam was built; and around that dam a compact city of commerce grew. No need for cathedrals or palaces. Need here for canals, bridges, narrow streets, tall houses, all radiating from the singular point of that ancient dam like spokes about a cart-wheel's axle. A city as much water as it was brick and wood. Vast sprawls of docks and harbours posted with paint-peeled signs indicating destinations the world over. The Dutch East India Company might have officially collapsed in 1798, which wasn't going to stop the merchants of Amsterdam who sent off their fleet vessels and welcomed them home with all the spices, silks and exotics they could carry.

Ivor disembarking into the vertiginous bustle and business of the port: stevedores swinging massive bundles of goods right over his head from emptying holds, straining ropes hooked about bollards and winches; livestock bleating and bellowing; barrels piled on one another haphazardly, seeming ready to roll and tip at any moment; black-gowned merchants calling out, making tallies, jotting notes and numbers in their books; smells of sweat and dung; prickling scents of pepper, rose-petals, cardamom. Cornucopia of languages in Ivor's ears as Greta grabbed his elbow and pulled him through the thronging streets: Dutch and German, French and Spanish, Poles and Turks.

Greta guiding him through the crowds who alternately conglomerated or divided in no discernable pattern. Greta sure-footed, leading him along noisy streets, houses narrow at the front because they were taxed by width and therefore grew up tall and thin, topped by winches and cables so front doors could be opened from the upstairs rooms and furniture brought in which wouldn't fit up narrow staircases. Ivor brought over bridges that were everywhere to be seen and must number in their thousands, bright stripes of water beneath them rippling with boats and barges passing to or from the docks; great rafts of birds complaining, rising at the disturbance, settling back once boat or barge had passed.

Easier walking, easier breathing, once they reached the main thoroughfares of Weesperstraat and Wibautstraat which took them out of the city directly parallel to the River Amstel. On and on they went, the morning cold, clear and crisp, unafflicted by snow, for which Ivor was grateful. By late afternoon they were over the other side of the river, walking the main lane to Utrecht. Greta diverting them off track, keeping them close to the river before calling a halt, the short day done.

Night quickly down. Greta telling Ivor they'd covered twenty, maybe twenty five miles, with approximately the same distance to go before they reached their destination.

'How do you know this stuff? How far we've walked?' Ivor asked her, as they settled themselves into one of the small hostelries dotted along the wayside every few miles to service people like themselves tramping from one place to another.

'I just do,' Greta said. 'Spent a lot of time walking back in the day, and you gets to know your pace pretty accurately. You've got to. A lot can depend on it.'

Ivor not pursuing this curious statement, mainly because he was too damned tired and because their dinner had just arrived. Ivor surprised how complicated the fare on offer was, a knock-on effect from this being the main route from the docks to Het Loo, the palace at Apeldoorn to which they were inexorably heading. Greta opting for the basics, the *broodje* she'd got used to in Deventer: small breads stuffed with meat and cheese served with scrambled eggs and pickles, a pot of boiled potatoes drenched in butter.

'You're a bit of an enigma,' Ivor stated between mouthfuls, food more delicious than he'd tasted in a long while.

'How so?' Greta asked, no more curiosity in the question than in the food she took in like a workman who needed to get it done. Ivor looking over at her, adding up in his head exactly what he knew about her. Which wasn't much. Only that she'd taken an active part in the doomed Irish Uprising back in the late 1790s; Greta the cousin of Peter Finnerty who'd since established himself in the London Press, invited by the English Army to accompany them to Walcheren, which seemed to Ivor a misguided plan at best, a foolish one at worst.

John bloody Earl of Chatham.

'Like how you know Dutch,' Ivor went on. 'How you know Joachim and the Abbott of the Servants so well, and how you know your way around Amsterdam.'

All easily explained, of course, if she'd been to those places before, spent time here learning the language. Which had been when? And how? A girl growing up in Ireland who apparently had no other family than Peter, and moving with him to London where both had been living this last while.

Greta finished the last of her *broodje.* Didn't answer his question, instead changed the subject.

'What do you think will happen when Peter publishes?'

Ivor answering without thinking.

'I expect poor Castlereagh will get it in the neck again.'

Ivor looking up, seeing Greta's face twitch and change. Greta staring over at him with the silent hostility of a heron about to stab its victim through the belly, haul it out of the water and gulp it down in one.

'Poor Castlereagh,' words drawn thin from her lips as wool is from a bobbin.

Ivor realising he'd made a blunder, if not the nature of it.

Greta skewering the blunder home.

'Another of the aristocracy you're on first name terms with?'

Ivor's heart shriveling, fearing what might come. For yes he'd met the man and even worse – apparently - liked him. Or maybe pitied might have been more apt. Robert Stewart Castlereagh thrust into a political life he was ill-suited to, a man despised by his peers more than admired. Firm friends with Arthur Wellesley since they were lads, a friendship tattled about in high society circles: those two Anglo-Irish boys born in Dublin within weeks of each other who'd become respectively the Secretary of War and The Iron Duke.

'I didn't exactly know him,' came Ivor's weak reply, a simmering beginning in him as Greta leaned forward, tapped a finger hard on the table.

'Your poor Castlereagh,' Greta explained, 'was a man of so poor stock his family had to transplant some of their own from their huge estate in Scotland to another huge estate in Ireland they couldn't even be bothered to buy. Does that sound poor to you?'

Ivor opened his mouth. Greta not finished.

'And shall I tell you what was said when the law was decreed in your parliament that made such things possible? The law that gave those estates to your poor Castlereagh for absolutely bloody nothing? Well I shall tell you, whether you want to hear it or no.' Greta's years with Peter in London finally yielding dividends. Greta having at her fingertips the words of Sir John Davies about the Plantation of Ulster way back in 1610 that still held sway, quoted several times in Peter's articles and pamphlets. Greta reciting those words verbatim for Ivor's benefit.

'*The natives must remove themselves from the precincts allotted to the Britons, whereupon a clear plantation is to be made of English and Scottish without the Irish. And the land assigned to those natives being in different quantities and portions, according to their different qualities and deserts.*'

Greta looking over at Ivor. Greta not giving him breathing space.

'And guess what, Ivor,' she said. 'There weren't very many natives accorded quality or desert, not in Ulster, nor anywhere. And even when those quantities and portions were granted to the deserving few they were about as useless as a spanner when you've no nuts to turn.'

Ivor by then viewing the buttons on his coat, his emptied plate, with undeserved interest, unable to meet Greta's eyes. Up and up this Irish question kept coming, and Ivor ill-prepared.

'You and your lot have no idea what goes on on the ground,' she simply couldn't stop herself. 'What it's like for us little folk. You don't give a cuss about anyone but yourselves, and your Castlereagh is one of the worst.'

Greta clattering her plate to one side to emphasize her point.

Ivor dismayed to see her eyes and cheeks were wet and darkened like slate in rain. His throwing that one name into their conversation making Greta like a person who'd opened her front door to find someone looming unexplained and unexpected, setting her heart racing, feet stumbling backwards, hands gripping out for support.

'I don't even know why we're doing this.'

Greta getting up, hating that she was crying in front of this man who represented all that was wrong with her world, and hating too that she was blaming him for it. 'I'm tired. I've got to sleep.'

Swiping at her eyes with bunched fists, stepping backwards, bumping into the neighboring table whose inhabitants had perked up at the disturbance and looked with disapproval at Ivor, who was obviously culpable of upsetting this strange young woman who turned tail, retreated up the steps of the small hostelry into the tiny bedrooms above.

Folk tutting at Ivor, Ivor trying to shrug them off. The waitress returning with a small chocolate galette, placing it before her paying customer who'd gone all green about the gills, who shook his head and waved at her a hand missing its middle three fingers, which had the effect to this young girl of negating the gesture. Her leaving the dessert on the table. Ivor nauseous to look on it, seeing in the dark mirror of its perfectly tempered chocolate his own wan and ineffectual face.

Ivor Snivels Merrill weary and defeated, feeling of as much use as that piece of stranded kelp drying on the sands of Knokke that he'd tripped over.

And where he might as well have stayed.

THE HEDGES OUTSIDE the Stoss's cottage kept vigil, stood tall, new and strong as dawn uprose and swept its pale arms about the environs of Bad Salzbaum, came swift and sudden down the hills housing the mill-workings in the west, and crept across the grass leading to the hedges.

Inside the Stoss's cottage Mathilde was quiet and vigorous as the dawn, had formed her own conclusions about the new day, made decisions, heart-happy there was someone here she could tell them to.

'How good to see you again, Frau Dieter,' she exclaimed. 'Do come in, please do.'

Frau Dieter obeying; Frau Dieter ushered into the chair Hela had recently vacated. Hela, who had got out of this place quick as she could and almost knocked shoulders with Frau Dieter in the street in her rush to get away: the source of that scent of yeast and flour Frau Dieter had so keenly smelled.

'I'm going to take Holger home,' Mathilde prattled, fussing with her kettle, got it filled and on the fire. 'You'll not believe it, but there's someone here in Bad Salzbaum from that very same place. She came to give me sad news, and instead provided me with the opposite. We'll take our last two weeks' wages and we'll put them to good use, take ourselves back home.'

Frau Dieter stiff and upright in her chair, Mathilde not the broken wreck she'd believed she'd find. Mathilde instead lithe of foot and hope despite the paucity of this cottage she was about to be turfed out of.

Frau Dieter stretching her jaw muscles before she spoke.

'I'm so pleased you have plans, that you have a way out.'

Mathilde sitting on a chair that ricked and rocked before its feet settled. Mathilde leaning in, casting a quick glance at her husband who was rolled up in a thin lumpy eiderdown on their bed like a log caught against the banks of a slow-flowing stream.

'He doesn't know it yet,' she whispered, 'but he soon will. And I hope, oh how I hope, it will make him better.'

Mathilde thrusting her gaunt face before Frau Dieter's, hands laced together on her lap. Frau Dieter seeing in the eyes of that gaunt face an unearthly kind of light, one she'd seen before, that came from ungrounded belief and faith. Same light seen in the eyes of the proselytizers at the turn of the millennia who had confidently predicted the end of the world, burning piles of books in the streets and squares of Bad Salzbaum to make their point. A point badly thought out and badly made. Those same people slinking out of Bad Salzbaum like slurry to a cess-pool once the year turned and the millennium proved no more harmful than the flutter of a fly, the buzzing of a bee.

Everything going on as normal. Time not, after all, at their indiscriminate whim and beck. No end of the world for anyone. Except it was the end of the world, as far as Mathilde Stoss was concerned.

Frau Dieter thinking how illogical Mathilde's plan of escape was: taking an arduous journey with an ailing husband to a place she'd not set foot in for thirty years. Returning exiles more often greeted with disregard and disgust than with respect. Frau Dieter schooled in the classics, and this plan of Mathilde's prompting thoughts of Odysseus's return to Ithaca to find his palace besieged by The Suitors – men who'd been eating and drinking their way through his wealth whilst his wife barricaded herself in the upstairs rooms for all the ten long years he'd been off on his grand adventures. Odysseus returning in the guise of a beggar, belittled and humiliated by the gorging Suitors, until he took up his weapons and wrought his revenge, killing the lot of them, leaving them – as Homer had it - *like fishes hauled up by fishermen from the iron grey sea onto the winding shore.*

'There might be another way,' Frau Dieter spoke with hesitance, seeing the flicker of accusation in Mathilde's eyes. 'Or rather not another way,' she corrected. 'Maybe more of a hiatus. A time to draw breath, plan properly, make sure all is as it should be.'

Leave the fish in the iron grey water a little longer, and the fishermen in their boats.

At least until Mathilde had sounded out the winding shore, and whether there was anything waiting for her and Holger at its other end.

# 25

## Several Hammerings At Several Doors

HELA WAS FEVERISH AT her work, her apologies for her late appearance accepted without question for plainly she was in distress and turmoil. Eyes red and swollen, her usual banter with her co-workers subdued and non-committal. Hela routinely chattering about this and that, eager to improve her German, chip the edges off it, for it seemed to those who worked with her that she'd learned the language in isolation and had no knowledge of recent idiom. Hela freely informing them this was the case, telling them of her Norwegian origins, the romance of the shipwrecked sailors who'd ended up in Torghatten by the merest chance.

Hela feverish because she'd been too free with her words in telling Mathilde she'd not long arrived in Bad Salzbaum, had started working in a bakery, that it had taken several weeks to find her. Lies needing keeping track of. Hela wishing back those slips, but done was done. Hela feverish too because Mathilde had mentioned the stranger accosted at her door, taken away by who knew who and to who knew where. It had to be Mokush, for she'd seen him a few minutes later in that cart. What he'd been doing sniffing around the Stoss's cottage she didn't know, although had to mean they were closing on their goal.

She was desperate to get away, tell Zsolt all she'd learned. Hela incredibly relieved when her boss let her go two hours before end of shift, mostly because she was hammering the pastry so hard it was going to turn out tough as the bottom of his boots.

'Get yourself off home,' he advised. 'And take a day off. Only one, mind. And let me see you back when you're on a more even keel.'

Hela could not have been more grateful, the words she used in reply designed to elicit a favourable response.

'I'm sorry I've been badly today, only I've just learned that my mother back in Norway has died. And I'm so far away, and anyway it's too late. They've already buried her.'

Hum of concern from the women in the bakery.

*Oh my dear, you should have said.*

*Oh but this is awful.*

And, more stridently, from an old maid Hela couldn't abide:

*I'm telling you this, Johann,* words spoken to their supervising baker, *and I'm telling you now. You'll give this woman two days off from her work – paid, mind – so that she can do some proper mourning. Ain't every day a woman loses her mother.*

That woman old enough to be a great grandmother three times over, great grandchildren about whom she never shut up. Johann obeyed, and Hela gave the irritating old biddy a quick kiss on the cheek before she left.

'May Heaven bless you and yours,' Hela said, taking off her apron, Hela not wishing that blessing in the slightest. Hela wishing merely to be gone and preferably never to have to come back.

'We're on the cusp,' she said to Zsolt, once she'd got back to their home, interrupted him taking the blasted clock back out of the cupboard where he'd stored it the day through. 'I think we're nearly there. Mokush has been discovered, but so too has the crate and with it has to be the Song. All we need do is take it.'

She couldn't be entirely sure where those shadowy figures with their shadowy cart had been going, although certainly couldn't have been going far. Not easy pushing a heavily laden cart across wet and frosty grass with the dead weight of Mokush on it. Constantine had got a fair way with his, late Summer and dry and only the crate to contend with. Mud-baths her conclusion earlier, another tripping on its tail while she'd been at work: Mokush and crate in such proximity meant it had to be their crate. Mokush had found it, been caught during his no doubt kack-handed attempt at its liberation. Mokush always dead weight, the hairs on Hela's arms shivering to attention at the possibility he was really dead. For if so, no matter. She and Zsolt were equal to the task. And the main task was to retrieve the Song. Mokush never so resolute as they; Mokush always bitter to be the younger, jealous of his brother's status in the family, of Hela's cleaving to Zsolt instead of him. Hela never in any doubt about to whom she should cleave: always go for the leader, for the strongest, and the rest will leave you be.

Mathilde's simpering words back at the cottage about how happy she'd been with her Holger a dull reverberation in her ears.

Well good on Mathilde.

It was Hela's turn now.

She and Zsolt would return to the Polovtsy clan with something of far more worth than meaningless tales of matrimonial bliss.

She and Zsolt would return to Hungary with something really worth crowing about.

And nothing meaningless about that.

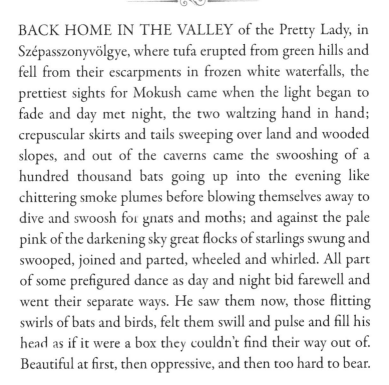

BACK HOME IN THE VALLEY of the Pretty Lady, in Szépasszonyvölgye, where tufa erupted from green hills and fell from their escarpments in frozen white waterfalls, the prettiest sights for Mokush came when the light began to fade and day met night, the two waltzing hand in hand; crepuscular skirts and tails sweeping over land and wooded slopes, and out of the caverns came the swooshing of a hundred thousand bats going up into the evening like chittering smoke plumes before blowing themselves away to dive and swoosh for gnats and moths; and against the pale pink of the darkening sky great flocks of starlings swung and swooped, joined and parted, wheeled and whirled. All part of some prefigured dance as day and night bid farewell and went their separate ways. He saw them now, those flitting swirls of bats and birds, felt them swill and pulse and fill his head as if it were a box they couldn't find their way out of. Beautiful at first, then oppressive, and then too hard to bear.

Those beating wings battering at him for release. Heard a
sound, a low rumbling grumble as of river ice in thaw, broken
floes piling up against themselves within the bounds of their
banks. The pain breaking over him, head clamped inside a
tightening vice.

'I think he's coming around.'

Small light voice somewhere at the edges. Small light
voice leaking in like dew dripping from mares' tails when
they were in their second disguise, when they flowered and
flowed instead of budded and spored. Another memory.

'His eyelids are fluttering. Fetch me some water.'

Dampness at his lips, and oh the joy of it and the
sweetness. Mokush sucking it quickly down and spluttering
the most of it back out as Caro put his arm beneath his neck
and drew him up.

'Take it slow, mister,' Caro advised, putting the cup back
to Mokush's lips.

Mokush obeying, sipping gingerly. Opened his eyes and
swiftly closed them again because everything was spinning.
Brief perception of unknown faces, unknown surroundings.
Slow gathering of wit and sense as birds and bats departed
through chink and crack, left him feeling like he'd been
broken open, a stolen egg dropped from the sky, from sharp
claw and greedy beak, to break and rot.

'What's going on?'

Words thick from this throat. Someone leaning over
him. Someone else speaking.

'Hungarian. He's talking Hungarian.'

Another voice entirely. One he kind of recognized. One he vaguely understood he feared hearing. Harsh and guttural, like a water rail. A voice that had once given orders.

'Which kind of validates our theory, thin as it is.'

The first voice. The bright light mares' tail voice.

'What did he say?'

'I don't give a traveller's cuss what he's saying, but I know fine well who he is.'

Fabian Guichot could have gone on, could have quickly constructed a Juggler's Box used by lawmen to punish thieves; put it to direct and deserved usage to burn and brand the hands of the thief who had stolen Constantine from him. Might not have been stopped, had not Frau Dieter tapped on the door at that moment and come in.

'I've Mathilde Stoss with me,' said Frau Dieter, 'and she's given me some rather startling news.'

'We've news too,' Fabian Guichot replied, looking hotly up from the captive man, meeting Frau Dieter's eyes. 'We've Mokush Polovtsy. The boar has returned to the vinyard and fallen fair and square into the pit.'

The idiom from his homeland translated badly, although everyone seemed to get the meaning.

Including Mokush, inside whose head those bats and birds began again to swirl and fly and beat the air with their wings in recriminatory excitement, for Mokush Polovtsy had been discovered, unmasked, unmanned and named.

*So much the younger brother.*

Hela's words burrowing into his bones as shipworms into timber these past seven years.

*Is it any wonder I chose your brother over you?*

Hela salting his ragged wounds every chance she got, wounds she herself had ripped in him by her rebuffal and scorn, his love of her curdling, become brittle and harsh. Mokush once a beautiful pool until she'd turned her sun upon him, drained him dry, leaving only bitter weeds, stones and dust. Mokush hearing her voice as if she were standing at his shoulder, pointing her beautiful finger right into his face. Anguish in him that he still found every part of her beautiful.

*Look at you, Mokush. You're a joke, and a bad one at that. An imbecile who has allowed himself to be caught in the net of our enemies, and we so close. You should be ashamed of yourself. You're a Polovtsy unworthy of the name.*

What will come now, Mokush?

What will you do?

'I think he's gone again,' the owner of the mare's tail voice declared and laid him down, Mokush allowing himself to go. Closing his eyes. Mokush thinking he would hear what he would hear, garner what he could garner, all the meanwhile planning some spectacular escape that would impress Hela, bring her to her knees in admiration, god damn her.

*Kuman red-feet.*

*Kuman feet-sky.*

Mokush as much a Kuman Polovtsy as his brother, or so he told himself in this hour of darkest need, swearing to himself he would not go down without a fight.

Mokush's mind sauntering off down its own avenues, coming to junctions and cross-roads having no signposts, no direction given him. A few words filtering into his blanched landscape as Frau Dieter unburdened herself of Mathilde's startling news.

*Market.*

*Apples.*

*Hela.*

*Ussi's child.*

*Vettie's Giel.*

GRETA LAY ON HER BED in the early morning light, odd thoughts slipping through her head. Like how elegant it was the Dutch had two words for day: *Dag* for daylight proper, *Etmaal* for the twenty-four hours marking one day off from another, including the night. No notion why such had occurred to her until she heard Ivor Merrill moving about in the next room. Heard the creaky complaint of cheap and rusty bedsprings as he arose, heard him unlatch and push back the shutters to let in the cold dawn of the outside world. Heard him splash water from the bowl provided upon the ill-built dresser by his bed.

The walls between these upper rooms thin, mere skeletons of wood filled with paste masked either side by skins of paper furling from the edges at floor and ceiling. Heard him sit back upon his bed to another chorus of decrepit springs. Imagined him doing up his boots in the silence that followed; imagined him tightening belt and braces, straightening his Servants' shirt and jacket. Thought mostly of what he must think of her, and what he must think she thought of him, following their argument the previous night. If argument it had been. More diatribe on her part, she knew, and she entirely to blame.

A visceral habit to hate the Other, those who chose to call her own folk vermin, accused them of bringing the land to ruination by their slovenly habits. A specious argument designed to provide those Others with the self-righteous duty of taking that land for their own in order to improve it for the good of all. Except the all never got the good of it, the most driven to the margins, to the poorest, stoniest places where they lived the poorest most stoniest of lives.

If only Ivor would quit aligning himself with those Others she wouldn't have to kick her heels so hard against him. An involuntary response she needed to curb because she needed Ivor, and could not afford to alienate him. She'd erred in her path, she knew. Allowed prejudice to dictate action, which made her as bad as the people she despised. The difference between *Dag* and *Etmaal* both qualitative and quantitive, as should be her regard of Ivor. He might have been born into enemy ranks but was of the day and not the night, and deserved to be treated as such. At core a man of good intention, worthy of her respect. Very few in his position would have risked that position to do what he'd done. Certainly none of the other officers on Walcheren. And, because of it, a man, she realised, she could learn to like.

Deep thoughts for so early in the morning galvanizing her, clarifying her objectivity, putting her feet in the right direction for the tasks to come.

She rose and put on her boots, sluiced hands, face and mouth with water and went to Ivor's door, tapped softly at its wood.

'Will you let me in?' she asked.

The door opening immediately, Ivor standing there looking like he'd spent the night chewing on wasps.

'I need to apologize,' Ivor speaking quickly, pre-empting Greta's own about-to-be proffered apologies. 'I'm such an arse sometimes,' he went on. 'The men under my command thought so, and I know it to be true. If I'd a bigger mouth you can be certain I'd shove in not one boot but two.'

Greta raising her eyebrows, amused and belittled he'd taken her blame as his own.

'It's me who should be apologizing, not you.'

Ivor regarding her solemnly.

'So all is not lost?' he asked.

'It is not,' Greta replied, smiling with relief that her impetuous accusations had been forgiven.

Greta radiant to Ivor in the moment of her smile.

Greta shifting their enjoined embarrassment and apologies on.

'Yesterday is done,' she decided. 'Today there are carts to be rolled, and we can do it, you and me, if you're still up for it.'

Ivor needing nothing more.

'Let roll the carts!' he announced – away with those wasps! - giving her a short bow, as became her. Would have dragged those carts to Het Loo palace in Apeldoorn all by himself, shoulders bound to the wood, an ox in harness, to experience another moment like this: all forgiven, slate wiped clean. Starting over with someone who had hope in him, and need.

Ivor's stomach grumbling, making mockery of the moment. Ivor reddening about ears and neck as Greta looked him up and down.

'Best get you fed and watered then,' she advised, as if he really were that ox and she switching her cane, readying themselves for the off.

PROFESSOR JORN WAS not a happy man. Professor Jorn not a happy man at the best of times, and particularly not when he knocked on the book-finders' door and got no answer, assumed they were already up and abroad so went to his study to find no book-finders, and no crate of books either. Professor Jorn cursing under his breath as he took his way down the staircase, stopping to check himself briefly in the mirror. All satisfactory. All smoothed, pressed and suave. The cravat a little garish for his tastes, assured by his tailor it was the height of fashion and so he would endure it through the grand day about to begin.

Opening of the mud-baths due at ten o'clock. Another boon for his Spa Hotel, certain to attract more visitors. A boon, he was beginning to realise, he had no control over after re-reading the contract Frau Dieter had laid before him and had him sign when, fool that he was, he'd put his signature on the line. Had not foreseen how tight she'd made it, had not had the wit to study it word by word, nor had a lawyer look it over before putting his name to it. In short, she'd tricked him into a franchise that might be on his grounds but was, in its entirety, under her control. He would get ground rent and a small cut of the takings. Nothing more. And he'd signed a ten year lease, for God's sake. What had he been thinking?

Knowing what he'd been thinking: that Frau Dieter was a woman, and therefore a simpleton who could no more draw up a tidy contract than she could have added up to ten. No need to read the small print, he'd assumed, despite knowing the small print was all. She'd duped him. A mistake he meant to rectify as soon as he found out what had happened to the blasted Ruan Peat and his irritating sidekick.

He got to the cellar door and found it unbolted.

Another annoyance, for he presumed on finding it so that this was where Ruan Peat must be – and where he'd taken the crate of books – but absolutely didn't want to go down there. All that damp and mildew made him shudder, and none of the hotel staff close at hand to do his bidding, stand at his back – all gearing up in the kitchens and restaurant for the onslaught of guests due any minute, the first already on their way down the stairs to breakfast.

He opened the door. Called out.

'Are you down there, Mr. Peat? I need a word.'

A polite way of saying: *What the hell do you think you're doing spiriting my books away in the depths of night?*

No answer.

Nothing but a faint echo of his own voice bouncing back up the dark steps. He pushed the door full back, took the two paces needed to bring him to the top of the steps leading into utter darkness.

No hint of light down there, no sounds of movement nor of people.

'Mr. Peat?' he called again.

Only emptiness replied.

He couldn't understand where the man had gone, nor where had gone the books. Possibly down there, although Professor Jorn was not going to take those treacherous steps without a strong light to see him through and a companion who could dispel his dread of being alone in the dark, especially when he knew the homunculus they'd taken from the hedge was down there too. Professor Jorn unable to see that article as the man he'd once been. Ruan right to believe Jorn would throw him into the nearest grave-pit he could cause the soonest to be dug. A duty Jorn meant to perform later this very day, once he was assured his guests were happy in the newly laid hedges, or up to their necks in mud.

The morning proving as galling as he'd assumed it would be victorious. Professor Jorn closing the cellar door and bolting it. Small victory if Ruan Peat really was down there refusing to answer, giggling over his pilfered books.

*Let him stew,* thought Professor Jorn, striding across the grass towards the mud-baths meaning to deal with Frau Dieter first - see if he could wangle better terms - and the others afterwards. Professor Jorn entirely unsatisfied with Ruan Peat and his skinny little helper, finding them both as common and unprofessional as he'd been assured they would be the opposite.

*Best book-finders this side of Berlin,* he'd been informed, thinking himself lucky to discover they were just down the road from Bad Salzbaum when all this fandangle had begun. But fandangle it still was, and time to put an end to it.

Professor Jorn marching across his self-fiated kingdom, believing himself in charge.

Professor Jorn casting a slight despising glance at the Stoss's cottage as he walked it by. Small mercies being small mercies: no bungling groundsmen for him. Holger Stoss patently at the tail-end of his competency and of no more use.

Professor Jorn taking the small bridge over the new lett to the mud-baths with measured and important stride, annoyed all over again – and a little anxious, if he was truthful – to see the magnificence of the board giving legend to the beneficial properties of the baths and the grand edifices in which they had recently been encased. If he wasn't careful the maddening Frau Dieter was going to steal his livelihood right out from beneath his feet. One thing to have his hotel stuffed full of monied guests, quite another for them to come to his hotel to ignore his hedges and find their cures in her beggaring mud-baths.

Nothing good fomenting in the Professor's head as he gained the other side of the pretty bridge and strode past the ominous sign, pushed open the gate to the mud-bath enclosures and chapped his cane hard at the door of the ancillary building where the robes, tickets and towels would be kept and cleaned, above which read a new sign:

*Welcome to our wondrous mud-baths! They will be an experience you'll not forget!*

ON THE OTHER SIDE OF that door there was somewhat of a commotion.

Fabian's clear recognition of Mokush backed up by Frau Dieter, as too had been the identification of the hedge-man as the lad Constantine, both Fabian and Frau Dieter severely distressed to find it irrevocably so.

'I don't understand what any of this this means,' Frau Dieter was saying. 'I can't understand how Constantine got caught up in this, whatever this is. What are you telling me?'

Ruan shifting his weight from one foot to another, not entirely sure himself. He had the bones of it, if not the flesh. They'd established the man in the hedge was not a man at all, but a boy barely shy of sixteen. They'd established their captive was Mokush Polovtsy, a POW who'd scarpered with the entirety of his small cadre following the Christmas of 1801, taking Constantine with them – presumably under duress. They'd established too that Constantine, for unknown reasons, had chosen to hide himself in the part-laid hedge with a crate of books stolen from a Bad Salzbaum trader, presumably by the Polovtsy brothers and their companions, Constantine dying there, possibly to give that crate protection or maybe to evade the men who'd stolen him from the camp.

Given all that, Ruan wasn't certain how to go.

He'd one thread to follow, namely Frau Dieter's introduction of Mathilde and the news of her recent visitor.

'Before I venture to answer your question, Frau Dieter,' Ruan began, 'can I first ask a few of Mathilde?'

Mathilde colouring under his scrutiny. She'd only left Holger to come to the mud-baths because Frau Dieter had said she might have the solution to their problems – and

Lord knew, Mathilde needed that - but all Mathilde had found was a roomful of strangers, and a very odd situation.

Ruan either didn't note her disquiet or didn't care.

'This woman who visited you,' he began.

'Hela,' Mathilde volunteered, voice thin as a reed and about as quick to break. Mathilde coughing quietly, hiding her mouth with her hand, horribly embarrassed to have become the centre of attention in this strange room with all these strange people she hardly knew. The young blonde lad bringing forward a chair and ushering her onto it.

'There's no need to worry, not at all,' Caro assured, placing a comforting hand at her back, proffering her a glass of water. Ruan waiting until Mathilde was settled.

'Frau Dieter said she was from your homeland. From Norway?'

Mathilde nodding.

'From Torghatten. Yes. The daughter of an old friend of mine. Come all the way here to tell me her mother Ussi had died.'

'I'm sorry about your friend,' Ruan treading lightly, 'but let me ask you this: do you know anyone called Håkon Tryggvason?'

Mathilde looking up in surprise.

'Well yes, of course. He was a youngster when I knew him.'

The one who'd ferried himself over to the island in the bay on his home-made raft, stayed in the hill punched through with a hole as if an angry troll had got there before him. Mathilde unpleasantly reminded of her fancy about trolls and hedges that had her so discombobulated a mere few days before: a warning, she now saw, of all the bad things to come.

'And did he go away, this Håkon Tryggvason? Perhaps to Russia?' asked the man with the black hair whose name Mathilde had forgotten, their previous meeting brief and having so much more to worry about since. She creased her brows. Threw her mind back to that time.

'He went,' she said uncertainly. 'Although where he went no one knew. And I've no idea if he ever came back.'

Ruan not so uncertain, Ruan having as many of the pieces as he needed for the time being: Håkon leaving Torghatten and at some point reaching Russia, become part of the many teams sent over its wild wastes to wrest from the populace all the ancient manuscripts, books and pamphlets Katerina had ordered her minions to uncover. Håkon a book-finder, just as Ruan was. Håkon finding something exceptional, although hadn't realized it at the time. Had allowed it to be stowed in the archives from where he'd later stolen it and retreated with it back to Norway and his home, from where he'd sent it to Hippolyte Gerhard. A little bit of research about book-traders would have told him Deventer was the crossroads of Europe as far as book-trading went, and Hippolyte an expert in the field of Eastern and Cyrillic scripts. And both Hippolyte and Deventer far from Russia where the theft might still be tattled about, if not actively pursued. And from Gerhard to Gerhard's sister after Gerhard had died so unhappily, and from her to the book-seller in Bad Salzbaum, and from him to the Polovtsy brothers, and from them to Constantine and into the hedge. This last aspect of the whole saga the most perplexing. For what could the youngster Constantine have found so disturbing in this second or third theft, as you chose to see it, which would have made him sacrifice his life for it? If he had chosen it, which was not established.

Ruan about to put his thoughts into words when Professor's Jorn's cane came hammering at their door and all looked up, wondering whatever else could be about to fall.

# 26

## Kaspar Larriscarri Turns His Tricks

HOLGER STOSS LAY ON his bed, lips moving in mussitation, words forming, never reaching their soundful end. Breaths coming harsh and uneven as he fought to get himself up, needing to remove himself from the damp of trousers and sheet where he'd soiled himself the previous night. The morning light, wiltering through the glass of the single window, seeming to empty itself of energy so the room was in gloom and despondence. A mere flicker coming from the stove, a mere flicker in Holger as he sought to calm himself from the panic that was surging through him to find Mathilde gone, even though he knew it for she had leaned over him and kissed his forehead mere minutes before.

*I'll not be long, my dearest. I'll be back soon, get us both clean and fresh. Start our day properly, and it might be a good day yet.*

How it might be a good day had to be to do with their early morning visitor. He'd not been entirely awake, neither more entirely asleep. Someone had been here, talking softly to Mathilde and she to her, although who and why he didn't

308

know. Obscurely, he'd woken with thoughts of Torghatten in his head, of those dark netsuke nights closed and tight: a place perceiving its universe as a nut in its shell might have done, if only it had sentience. And the sea, the glory and fear of those freezing waves closing in about them, catching them fast, the creaking cribble of wood as the waters hardened and pulled about them, splintering the boards one by one until they'd no choice but to abandon their ship, crawl out over the ice, grasp the ropes being thrown to them by Mathilde's folk on shore, fingers so numb they'd seemed to belong to someone other than themselves. Landed like so many fish rolling onto land and backs and couldn't stop laughing at the desperateness of their plight and the unquelled joy of rescue. The up-there sky going on forever, seeming at first representative of infinite release, and then become oppressive as progressively, day by day, it grew meaner and darker, the wrecked sailors looking with longing at the ruination of their ship which had become a squat black shadow out there in the rucked-up ice that gleamed and grinned blue, green and white. A sky looming low and thick and accusatory.

*Whatever did you expect? You came unbidden to our land and didn't bother to learn our rules, you fools. You've only yourselves to blame.*

The Winter bearing down on them, heavy and heavier, bowing their shoulders, blocking off the single path out of Vettie's Giel, making grown men weep. Villagers taking them in with begrudgement to be divvying up their meagre food supplies, until someone pointed out that the ship, although crushed and snapped in two about the waist, might yet have salvageable supplies, if the ice was hard enough to bear their weight, when everything changed. Men gathering themselves into gaggles about their fires, puffing at their noxious pipes as they made their plans in criss-crossed languages: how to get safely out and back again, how to transport whatever they might find. Men slapping shoulders, rubbing determined hands together, dredging sheds and out-houses for ropes, snow-shoes, skis and sleds, galvanized by common intent.

It had felt to Holger and his fellow stranded sailors that the stone had been rolled from their tomb and Emmaus beckoning them out; natives and incomers burrowing into the belly of their abandoned ship, knocking through the remaining deck boards, dismantling all they could. Bringing back vast amounts of timber for the burning; uncovering two pens of livestock whose inhabitants had frozen solid, dying too quickly to rot, animals needing to be taken apart with axes and ice-saws. Uncovered also were several barrels of limes and oranges that had escaped the salt, soon transformed into marmalades and puddings making the whole of Vettie's Giel zing and smart as women stirred and chattered and threw in all the sugar from the heaps of beets in the barns they could spare. Stacks of weevil biscuits and mealy-ridden flour dissolved into the sea, for which every sailor was thankful. And, on the very last day of salvage – for meanwhile the ice had hindered, continued collaring and closing, and a storm was grumbling on the horizon and would soon be hard upon them – a cry came up from some bleak cranny already in-bubbling with sluggish sea-water halfway to ice

'There's rum down here! There's twelve full barrels of rum!'

Norwegians and Germans shoulder to shoulder regarding the complication of ropes and pulleys with one eye and, with the other, saw and cursed the heavy bellied clouds rolling in from the north that threatened and glowered and sent first the wind to buffet and holler at them, and next the snow tippy-tappying out of the dusky sky in dribs and drabs. First three barrels out, the wind rising and screaming about their ears; the snow thickening, slapping at their faces, flurried and scurried, as out came the fourth barrel and the fifth. Further hardship to fetch the rest. The last barrel, and the last man, hauled out, bashed against the boards as they went, him whooping and singing some old drinking song whipped away by the wind the second he was out of the hold and onto the splintered deck. Everyone off, heads down, caps slammed over ears, scarves over faces, sleds tied and secured, and off victorious over the ice and up the cleft in the cliffs to Vettie's Giel.

That salvaging the making of them, all firm friends as the first barrel was tapped, drained and drunk in a wild week of celebration.

No dread of anyone starving over the Winter, not with the animals they'd found on board, no matter how bad the storms got, and this first the worst. Heaping snow six foot deep over everything left out in the open. Folk locked down in their houses with their portions of meat, marmalade and rum. Norwegians and Germans bunked up together, telling tales, swapping jokes and yarns. All thrown into the same situation, all able to access the frozen livestock that had been hacked into usable pieces and buried in the snow outside everyone's doors to be brought up and cooked when needed. Limes and oranges stored in every available jar and pot equally apportioned, so always something sweet to look forward to when bannocks and porridge got too unbearable on their own.

The start of something good and new, despite the heave-down of Winter upon them. A Winter so harsh and careless Vettie's Giel would not have survived as well as it did if not for their unasked-for visitors.

And the start of Holger and Mathilde, neither of whom had any appetite for rum, who spent their nights otherwise, playing chess or cards, reading to each other from tattered books, teaching each other their songs: Holger in his execrable German croak that couldn't seem to hit a right note and yet made Mathilde laugh; Mathilde in her sweet voice that had no volume and cracked if she tried to make it carry. Holger having to lean in to hear the words, found his hands one evening snaking across the table and taking her own in his whilst her parents glugged down strong drink at the other end of the room.

'You saved us,' he said.

'As you have us,' Mathilde replied.

And that was all it took.

Seven short words, and four months later – when all was clear of ice and snow - they took the bird's leg path zig-zagging down the cliff to Bergenstift to take their vows, the folk of Vettie's Giel singing and dancing the whole night through, much to the irritation of the locals. Holger Stoss almost brought to his knees every time he thought on the whims of the world that had brought him to Vettie's Giel and the greatest joy of his life.

Thoughts of that time tumbling through him as he gained the edge of his bed and sat there, wondering what next to do. Thoughts and words he couldn't make head nor tail of once he'd left those early days of ship and ice and rum. Had to leave them behind, glorious as they were, when a knock came at his door.

He didn't move. He couldn't stand. Was sitting on the side of his bed. Mathilde was no longer here. Didn't know what to do.

'Who is it?' he asked, voice tremulous, unwilling to admit anyone he didn't know.

'It's me. Hela, Ussi's daughter,' came the reply. 'I came back soon as I could.'

Holger had no knowledge of anyone named Hela, but Ussi he recognized. Of course he did. He'd only just been thinking on his wedding day, and Ussi had been Mathilde's greatest friend, her Maid of Honour. Had a vague memory she'd not been so very honourable, but present trumped past. And presently he didn't want any visitors.

He kept quiet, didn't move, stayed perched on the side of his bed in his piss-stained pants hoping Mathilde would come back to intervene.

Holger appalled when the door was pushed open and the face of Ussi herself was revealed to him, and Ussi not only opened the door but came in, came up and sat beside him, apparently unaware of the stink.

'Well Holger Stoss, as I live and breathe,' said Ussi, brushing her fingers through the sparseness of his hair. 'And so well you look, sir. But it's your wife I'm needing. Can you tell me where Mathilde went?'

Holger gripping at the side of the bed with his fingers until the knuckles were white as the ice of Torghatten. Holger not quite with it, Holger wondering how Ussi could be here when he'd just been thinking of her.

Which of course she couldn't. Nothing more than a phantom conjured up by his dreams, so no harm answering.

'She went to the mud-baths,' Holger said. 'I think that's where she said.'

And up went Ussi's ghost, quick as that.

Not another word to Holger Stoss.

Not a *thank you* or a *how do you do.*

Then again, hadn't that always been the way with Ussi?

Mathilde saying the same after they'd got back from Bergenstift to Vettie's Giel, everyone tutting and tattling about Ussi's disgrace. Ussi refusing to notice, refusing to worry.

*It's just Ussi,* Mathilde had said. *She'll not change. She's not been given the chance I have, and if you'd not come along then who knows? I might be the same.*

They both knew it was a lie, that Mathilde could never be like Ussi, the two as dissimilar as a rock was to a cloud. That Mathilde would always be a loyal friend to Ussi whether Ussi returned the favour or no. Mathilde writing to the woman for several years, worrying about the way Ussi's life might be going, it niggling at her like a mouse at a floorboard, a dog trying to break free from a fence.

'Don't judge her,' Mathilde had tried to persuade him. 'You don't understand what it's like in Vettie's Giel.'

Years later, when she'd finally spelled out to him how things were for women there. Holger almost weeping, Holger thanking the Lord every day since that he'd been the source of Mathilde's rescue from such a life.

Not so odd then, for Ussi to come calling on her old and loyal friend.

Not so odd, Holger thought, until Holger forgot whatever it was that had been odd, or why he'd been thinking on it.

Forgot that anyone had been here at all. Knew only the absence of Mathilde.

Holger Stoss sitting on the side of his bed waiting for her return as the morning rolled on without him.

Holger Stoss sitting on the side of his bed, trying to recall the name of that strange hill he'd once seen that had day-light and star-light in its belly.

Holger Stoss sitting on the side of his bed, watching dust motes float in the strata of light falling from the single window splaying their lines across the tiny space of the room.

Holger seeing in them a strange narrow path cricking down a cliff like a bird's leg towards a valley, and the thin strip of a bridge, made from moss and bark swaying beneath his feet, all that was keeping him from the tumbling rocks and rumbling water a hundred yards below.

*Got to get your own bones down to Bergenstift, Holger. Can't remember the why of it, only that it has to be done. Bones to Bergenstift. Everyone knows it. You should have learned the rules, you fool! Whatever else did you expect, you strangers, coming to a place like this?*

FRAU DIETER OPENED the door to find Professor Jorn, silver-headed cane held high in his hand ready to knock again. Professor Jorn looking as if he would gladly have knocked his cane right into her head. Professor Jorn catching himself, bringing his displeasure under control. Forcing out a smile which did not sit well on his long and dour face.

'Frau Dieter,' he managed, words pressed out between overly lengthy and faintly feral teeth. 'What a pleasure. I've been meaning to speak to you. I wonder if we could have a word about...but what's all this?'

Frau Dieter having stepped back and opened the panorama of the room to him. Professor Jorn's eyes flitting from left to right and back again, taking in that not only here were the cursed book-finders, his missing crate of books, but also an unknown man trussed up like a turkey on the table; and, in disparate dribs and drabs about the central scene, were Mathilde Stoss, Piet, and Frau Dieter's overseer from the mines. A penumbra of complicity and conspiracy dropping over him, sending his skin pale, his teeth to grind and grit.

'What it all is, Professor Jorn,' Frau Dieter said smoothly, 'I believe we were about to find out. Will you join us?'

The cordial invitation taking Professor Jorn on the hop. He came in, one hand gripping hard at his cane, fingers of the other fidgeting with his fashionable cravat, feeling out of place surrounded by this shabby crew and distinctly out-numbered. Not the time to be talking contracts, no more the time to be toyed with.

'What, by all that's holy, is going on?' Querulous words meant to convey command. 'Why are you all gathered here? And who gave you permission to remove from my purview my rightful property?'

Meaning the books, not the man.

Glances jittering around the room because everyone knew it, and despised him for the same.

Ruan stepping into the breach.

'If you're meaning the crate,' he said, 'well there, Professor, you might have a problem.'

'How so?' Professor Jorn barked sharply. 'It was found on my land and therefore is my property. You'd no right to remove it, sir. No right at all.'

'If we're talking rights,' Ruan unfazed, 'then perhaps you ought to consider restoring the property to its actual owner. He's right here in Bad Salzbaum. I don't know his name, but it won't take much to find it out, and I'm sure he'll be glad to know that what was stolen from him seven years ago has finally turned up.'

The silver-topped cane tapping twice upon the floor in quick succession as Professor Jorn regarded Ruan Peat with undisguised contempt.

'You will not argue with me about the law, sir, for I know it well.'

'As do I,' Frau Dieter put in. 'And the law states quite clearly that if restitution of stolen property can be made to the original owner then there is a legal obligation to make it so.'

Professor Jorn turned his neck towards her with the swiftness of an orca about to rip a seal from the sands.

'I hardly think, dear lady, you have the law at your fingertips, nor the mayor's ear to bend.'

'And you hardly suppose I can draw up contracts either?' the seal politely side-stepped, the orca sent reeling back into the waves clearing his throat preparatory to giving his reply. Frau Dieter faster.

'And while we're talking contracts,' she added, 'I should like very much to view the original one your father drew up with Holger Stoss. Isn't that so, Mathilde?'

Mathilde's fingers knitting together in consternation as she took the cue, gave a small nod, having nothing left to lose.

'Very well then,' Frau Dieter concluded the matter with a small decisive nod of her own. 'I will attend your study this afternoon, Professor, if that is convenient. The matter is, after all, rather pressing.'

Professor Jorn squaring his shoulders, stretching his spine, raising his chin, giving a further two inches to his impressive height, or so he thought. All the others saw was a grey, stringy runner-bean trying to climb up its pole.

*Or up its own backside,* Fabian Guichot was thinking. *Good on you, Frau Dieter, you marvellous woman.* Twisting his twisted lip in an unsuppressed smile as the Professor sniffed in acquiescence. The Professor's first thought being that he would find the blessed contract and destroy it; second thought being that this woman wouldn't stop, would lodge a request with the Jorn family lawyer if need be and, if that came out, and if the contract was discovered to be favourable to the Stoss's, then his name would be muddier than Frau Dieter's wretched baths. His irritable dismissal of

Holger Stoss – and the stringent terms of that dismissal – well known to the various witnesses to it, all of whom were in this room. Shadow of a memory in his mind of his father taking him to see a puppet show of the popular character Kaspar Larriscarri.

*He presents as an idiot. He seems to act on errant impulse, without logic or reason. He always endangers his family, puts in peril his own life, usually ends up in the hangman's noose. But learn this lesson well, son. He will always come out on top and Kaspar Larriscarri is the representation of folk like him, folk who, like Kaspar, would rise up against their masters, against the likes of you and me, if only they had the gumption.*

The boy Ottelius learning his lesson at that puppet show as the crowds clapped for Kaspar, jeered at the mayor and the hangman. The man Ottelius seeing the reality and brutality of it twenty odd years later whilst spending several years at the University of Champagne-Ardennes in Reims when Revolution broke out in Paris. No worry for him in Reims, closeted within his university, everything going on as normal. Bravado amongst his colleagues, exhilaration to be witnessing history in the making – if at eighty miles removed - when the new Constitution adopted Thomas Paine's Rights for Man declaring all citizens equal. Mocking laughter when King Louis XVI was made to don the *bonnet rouge* of the revolutionaries, make a declaration to the Revolutionary Assembly that they should go to war with Prussia in order to preserve the advances of their revolution.

Merest ripple of concern when, in riposte, the Duke of Brunswick delivered his own manifesto on the 25th of July threatening all Frenchmen with dire retribution if Louis and his wife were harmed, that the anarchy at the heart of France was not to be tolerated, the intention being – gladly cheered on by Jorn and his fellows – for the revolutionaries to stop behaving like idiot children and submit to the general order. All, up to that point, seeming a dander and a gander to Ottelius Jorn. A lively episode of education, the clooping of unstoppered corks garnishing evenings of debates with fine French wines.

Everything changing with the speed of a lightning bolt once the Brunswick Manifesto hit Paris: outrage amongst the revolutionaries, proof the king had been plotting with foreigners intent on invasion and overturning all they'd accomplished for ordinary citizens' rights. The King's palace stormed, his Swiss Army Guards slaughtered, the King – the King, for God's sake! – imprisoned, as was everyone suspected of supporting him. The First Terror of the Revolution begun.

And the very next day the Duke of Brunswick invading Lorraine, taking Longwy, Verdun capitulating a couple of weeks later. The Royalists welcoming them in, clearing the road to Paris. Paris learning of it on September 2nd 1792; Paris panicked, outraged, and out for blood. A four day rampage ensuing, during which émigrés, royalists, imprisoned aristocracy and their families were murdered without mercy or trial in their prisons cells.

Violence catapulting out to Versailles, Meaux and – worst of all for Jorn – to Reims. Coming on them without any warning. One minute they'd been a group of sauntering young students, the next they were dragged from college premises out onto the street, beaten with hammers, stones, whatever other weapons were at hand, for being foreign and wealthy and obviously therefore in sympathy with Brunswick and the coming Prussians.

The younger Jorn almost scoured up with the rest.

Jorn getting out by the merest chance, arriving at the university twenty minutes late because he'd forgotten to wind his pocket watch the previous night. Jorn seeing his erstwhile colleagues' corpses pulped and pulverised, chewed at by growling dogs with haunches and hackles raised. Jorn not waiting to see if any were still alive and needing help. Jorn, pulling his coat over his mouth to stop the retching, slipping into the back streets, heading away from the mob and the sounds of splintering wood, the shattering of glass, as they moved on to the houses of the wealthy.

Jorn getting himself out of Reims without returning to his lodgings; deliberately ripping and muddying his clothes so he looked like the worst kind of vagabond, shifting stoop-shouldered through forty miles of countryside and sporadic villages until he reached the Belgian border several days later when he took stock, took a breath. Plucked a professorship out of the air to return home with, which no one could equivocate about, the whole of France by then burning.

Became a man scared and terrified of what men could do to one another and how swift could be the turning; built about himself a carapace not to be broached under any circumstance. Never married, never had liaisons of commitment with men or women because he understood nothing in life was guaranteed. That all could be ripped away in moments. And that kind of ripping away he never wanted to experience again. No self-realisation that was exactly what he was doing to Holger and Mathilde Stoss.

Memory instead strong in him of a phrase quoted by a friend back in those wine-fuelled debates he'd so enjoyed: words of George Herbert – poet priest, dead of consumption as he turned forty – *we paint the devil foul, yet he has some good in him, all agree.*

No one agreeing. Arguments going on long into the night, Ottelius's friend laughing at the mayhem he'd caused by proposing it. That friend no longer able to laugh, one of those colleagues dragged off and executed by the mob on the bloody streets of Reims. Jorn's own philosophy, since his escape, being to keep out that devil as long as he could. Did as his father had done: settled himself, took charge of his surroundings, became king in his own kingdom, however meagre that kingdom might be.

And here, in this stifled room, he smelled the devil foul leaking from every corner; sensed his kingdom about to topple like France had done. Shifting from amusing revolution into outright terror.

He took off his glasses – didn't need to wear them, merely a part of his disguise, his posturing as a Professor – and folded the temples, slid them carefully into his top pocket.

Old habits never dying easy. Old habits old habits precisely because they were reinforced each time they were performed. Old habits performing now.

Professor Jorn not about to throw himself into the chaos going on all about him.

Professor Jorn as terrified as he'd been back in the old days.

Professor Jorn narrowing his eyes, casting a mean stare at every person in the room, avoiding the trussed-up turkey on the table. Curiosity and pity not for him. Professor Jorn rigid and unbending as a fence post, as unforgiving as a wire tautened from one post to the next to keep out all the badness the world had to offer.

Professor Jorn banging his cane hard on the flagstones at the end of each clipped sentence in the little speech that followed.

'I don't know what you're all plotting here,' said he, 'but I want no part of it. No part, do you hear? I have a business to run. I cannot have cockroaches scurrying under my feet at every turn. Frau Dieter, I will see you this afternoon as agreed,' as if he was the one who had specified the meeting, 'and you book-finders will be there also. And you will do your duties, sirs. You will have with you my books, and you will have them itemised and valued. Good day to you all.'

Professor Jorn marching out of the room, without the courtesy of closing the door behind him.

Professor Jorn not closing it because he feared his hand would shake and miss if he tried.

Professor Jorn leaving his erstwhile companions gawping at his discare.

Cockroaches indeed.

Cockroach Caro breaking the silence.

'I wonder if he goes to sleep with that top hat still on his head,' he commented, 'because if he does, he must have a really, really long bed.'

# 27

## Sand And Stone

———

MICK MALLOY STAYED hunkered down amongst the fish-wives' skirts, the latter reconvening after that impetuous pistol shot, immediate danger over. Gob-spitter and pistol-firer Alfonse admonished for his impetuosity, sent to pier's end on the look-out for the spy who had slipped the net. Enquires made, knowledge gained: the two others most likely off on the ship to Amsterdam, which was no doubt where the escapee would be attempting to go. Cordon flung around the port: no one in or out without rigorous interrogation and inspection.

Mick caught fast. Mick ushered beneath the stall on which the women carried on with the last of their gutting and splitting, the stink vile, vaguely bearable after twenty minutes of smelling nothing else. Early morning market about to pack up shop, buyers of early morning fish already dragging their carts to Bruges to sell their wares.

Fisher-women sympathetic to his plight.

Fisher-women trying to figure his way out of it, without that way being dragged off in irons.

'It's not exactly Amsterdam I've to get to,' Mick explained. 'All I'm needing is into Holland any way I can. I've a duty to carry out for the Servants over the water on Walcheren. Do any of you know of them?'

As indeed they did.

Blessed folk. Doctoring folk. Folk who'd cared for members of their own community when no one else would help. And if Mick was aiding them then they would aid him.

'There is one possibility,' a woman offered as she stuck in her knife, sliced it neatly down the belly of a cod longer than her arm, pulled out its slippery guts and drained them into the barrel next to Mick's head. 'If we can get him into Bruges by midday he could take the coach that goes from there to Antwerp, and from Antwerp to Arnhem. That's in Holland, isn't it?'

*Yes, by hell's teeth, yes it is. And only a clip from Arnhem to Apeldoorn,* Mick was thinking.

Subterfuge thereby forged, the women taking charge. They couldn't hide Mick's formidable mono-brow or squint although came up with an adequate disguise, kicking a few ragged clothes under the stall into which he wriggled; Mick donning over his forehead a monstrous hat clarted with seagull excreta; Mick wangled onto a fish-cart heading to Bruges, the stinkiest one they knew of, one of the last to leave: a cart pulled by straggled donkeys, manned by an ancient couple who took the barrels of fish-guts into town to sell as fertiliser.

'Ain't no smell on earth as bad as that,' one of the women warned, 'so keep a scarf across your nose else you'll be heaving up your insides before you've gone five minutes.'

The couple briefed to take their passenger direct to the square in Bruges and deposit him onto the midday coach, to delay their journey if necessary so they got there minutes before the coach was due to leave.

'Look sharp, and don't tarry,' was the fisherwomen's advice to Mick. 'There's not too many French in Bruges, but Antwerp is seething with them.'

'And try not to speak,' another advised, 'your French is dithery as a duck's.'

Her companions laughing raucously, echoed by the gulls screeching overhead who dipped and dived for stray wriggles of innards that had missed the barrels.

'Don't care who you are,' said a last, 'but them Servants gave my mother an easeful end and a decent burial, so go with God.'

And go with God he did, curled up on the cart of the ancient couple between the stinking barrels, scarf pressed to his face to shield him from scrutiny and because the stink was as noxious and noisome as the women had predicted. Twenty minutes not long enough. A life-time not long enough to get used to that particular stench. Soldiers holding their noses as the donkeys pulled up to their check-point; soldiers retching and coughing, clamping hands about mouths and noses as the couple presented their cart for inspection; soldiers' stomachs turning themselves inside out, soldiers waving them quickly through the cordon, and off was Mick Malloy and away.

Mick stinking like the cargo he'd shared quarters with and, when he reached Bruges square, told to take the out-back seat on the midday coach, which suited him. No one to start up awkward conversations. The routine repeated once arrived in Antwerp. A little shakier there, a small wobble when the coach-runner claimed his vehicle was full, demanded extra payment, and soldiers roaming if not seething. Most down at Antwerp docks requisitioning the last serviceable boats, getting ready to follow their fellows to Flushing, take Walcheren now the English had scarpered with their tails between their legs.

Mick having kept enough funds to pay the extra.

Mick soon underway to Arnhem.

Mick calculating he wouldn't be so far behind Ivor and Greta, might even be ahead of them if they took their way on foot from Amsterdam to Apeldoorn, which had to be their amended plan.

Mick discarding his disguise and poop-hat at the first place the carriage changed horses. If anyone noticed they didn't say, nor had reason to. Old woman getting off, middle-aged man getting on, taking her ticket and her place. And at least the stench had diminished now the old woman had left, and everyone thankful for that.

Everything for Mick going swimmingly.

Mick having the time, as the coach went on, to reassess the situation. Mick concluding Ivor might not be their only advantage; maybe another way to crack open the formidable doors of Het Loo Palace, strengthen their hand.

Greta wasn't going to like it, which wasn't Mick's concern.

She would have to deal with it like the soldier she was.

───── ⟲∾⟳ ─────

GRETA AND IVOR STARTED from the door of their
lodgings in chill beauty, their path sheathed in hoar frost
crick-cracking beneath their feet, lined by bowed-over
grasses; the twisted remnants of frozen curly dock set to
plink and clink by the slight breeze like miniscule
chandeliers. On the broad wind-ruffled waters of the rolling
river, columns of ducks swept down the lines of ribboned
currents dictated by the lay of the rocky bed beneath. Ducks
taking no mind, spending their time lifting one wing or
another, getting themselves primped and preened for the
coming day.

The travellers pressing themselves along the skinny path
in silence. A few miles on they left the river, gained a wider
track, Greta assuring Ivor it would lead them soon enough to
Apeldoorn.

'We'll reach the environs of Het Loo by nightfall. Our
wisest move is to rest ourselves over, approach the main
mission in the morning.'

A statement not needing Ivor's input.

A statement Ivor was glad to abide by, for the closer he
got to Het Loo the more he worried that no one would let
them through the outer gates, let alone the inner. He might
be as high-born and well-connected as Greta and Mick
assumed him to be, and Greta had folded up in her pack
the smart doublet and hose she'd caused him to buy in
Amsterdam, and soon he would have the Abbott's letter too.
None of it guarantee enough. He had a few well-placed
names to bandy about, first and foremost being his erstwhile
commander John, Earl of Chatham. Which had to his best
approach, pretend he had an urgent message from John

direct to the Duke of Brunswick himself, assuming the Duke was at Het Loo.

Everyone there surely knowing by now the English had abandoned Dutch soil, retreated across the channel with the remnants of their disease-riddled men. Even a dullard like John would have sent messages out once he knew the departure was scheduled, and if one messenger could get inside Het Loo then Ivor might get in too. Get the ear of the Duke and it might be substantial enough to persuade Louis to fetch those other English troops back across the channel to ward off his brother's rulings - at the very least from Rotterdam, Amsterdam and the Northern end of Holland.

Greta he would have to leave behind. Her presence would only serve to sow confusion; cause him to confabulate complicated explanations, which was the last thing they needed. No more was he going to mention the possibility of the Duke being there, it being speculation at best, misplaced gossip at worst.

'What's this place like?' Greta asked, opening the first conversation they'd had since they'd shared a sparse breakfast. Ivor hesitating, wondering how to get it said. He'd never been to Het Loo although knew about it, as presumably Greta did not. Ivor's mind flitting through all he could say and all he must not, given their recent truce. Ivor recalling history lessons given by his tutor – for yes, Ivor had had tutors, which was definitely on the *no* list – how the back story of England, Holland and France, let alone the rest of Europe, was akin to the mess made by a hedgehog rolling itself up in several balls of wool: *it's a right royal tangle, lad, of spine and twine. You could spend a lifetime trying to separate all the threads and you'd still never get to the end of them.*

Het Loo intrinsic to that tangle of spine and twine, and the on-going tangle of spine and twine between himself and Greta. Ivor ticking off in his head all that was permissible to mention.

Het Loo beginning life as a Royal hunting lodge.

So much so good.

Before being turned into a palace when the Dutch stadholder William of Orange, or William the Silent – depending on how you knew him - became William III of England, Scotland and Ireland by virtue of his marriage to the English princess Mary Stuart.

*Please don't mention Ireland in that sentence, Ivor!*

Het Loo a place famed and fabulous, on a par with Versailles once William and Mary ascended the English throne and erected their new grand palace surrounded by acres of landscaped parterred gardens, mazes, fountains and pavilions, all hemmed in by the Royal hunting forests.

How William had died after he'd fallen off his horse when it tripped over a mole hill.

*Mention that, Ivor. Greta will love it!*

Het Loo the growing-up place of the Dutch Royal family, Summer residence of governance back in the day, and now the favoured abode of Louis.

On the *no* list was how stadholder William had made insistent incursions into Scotland and Ireland to beat back the rabid hordes of Catholics who still clung to the previous King, James II, before William himself took over the job.

And what he absolutely must not mention was that William was responsible for the defeat of the Jacobites at the Battle of the Boyne in 1690. A victory so decisive James was forced into French exile, the Catholics humiliated, the Protestants sent on their Ascendancy. Ireland in turmoil ever since.

Never mind that William the Protestant had married his English cousin Mary whose uncle was the most rabid Catholic anyone could find on English soil.

Neither more should he tell Greta that Mary, the true holder of the English crown after the ousting of James, had insisted she and her husband rule jointly, with William taking the upper hand.

No.

None of that could he say.

'Where's the cat?' Greta asked over her shoulder, Ivor unaware he'd fallen a couple of steps behind as he over-thought what should have been a simple reply.

Ivor perplexed.

'Cat? What cat?'

'The one what's got your tongue,' Greta replied smoothly, 'unless your mouth is already occupied by your boots.'

A fine riposte to his silence, Ivor needing to fill the gap, gabbling out the first fact he could come up with, which was on neither of his lists.

'It was the Het Loo maze that inspired the creation of the one at Hampton Court.'

*Oh for God's sake, Ivor two-boots Merrill. Did you really just say that? How is anyone supposed to be impressed by such a snippet, except for nobbity nobs like you?*

Oddly, Great did not react.

Greta did not say anything.

Greta's attention fixed on several words in that sentence and what they conjured up.

*I'm heading to a place I've never been before, called Bad Salzbaum. It's a stone's throw from Deventer - and from Gronau, where I am now - and right on the border, if we can still talk of borders as having any meaning. It's said of the place, Bad Salzbaum, a health resort, that it has a maze planted on the same plans as those at Het Loo and Hampton, although I suspect it will be rather a shabby copy.*

Ruan's latest letter to Joachim, received the day before they'd fled Walcheren. Joachim giving her the letter because he was all for Greta and Ruan meeting up again, pointing out a path across the desert of wasted years separating him from her for all this time.

Joachim so certain it would go well, if it happened.

Greta not so sure.

Greta unable to say anything.

Ivor gabbling on about Williams and Marys she'd never heard of, about Royal this and Royal that.

Ivor foot-in-the-mouth Merrill crushing the glory from Greta's day, making her stamp on regardless, wondering if Ivor knew how pompous and vainglorious he sounded to the likes of her who'd been brought up on turnips and potatoes instead of – well, on that point she wasn't sure. Maybe coddled eggs and roasted partridge, so far as she knew, although doubted either could taste as good as potatoes newly pulled from the ground: peeled and boiled within the hour, slathered in butter, wild mint and ramsons. Which was just about the best thing anyone could ever eat.

Ivor Merrill's experience of the world leagues away from her own.

Greta tramping her way onwards, wanting only to get to where she was going and hand Ivor over to do what he'd been trialled to do.

Greta wanting to forget there had ever been a man named Ruan Peat, despite the memory of him stalking her down the long years since she'd parted from him, when she'd told him there were better things to be getting on with than love and marriage.

*And still better things to be getting on with now*, she told herself.

Although it didn't feel like it, not at the moment. Not when Ivor Merrill kept shoving his floppy hair off his forehead with his de-fingered hand.

*Just get it cut!* she wanted to shout at him, wanted to get out her knife and do it for him, there and then.

The Ruan-shaped hole in her being gouged out further with every step she took.

*Goddamn,* she whispered as she went on her way, head lowered, boots hammering on the track, negotiating without conscious thought the potholes, ruts and stones, the mounds of horse-ordure that had frozen solid and tripped up better people than she.

*He died when his horse tripped over a mole-hill,* Ivor was saying, although who in hell he was talking about Greta didn't know.

Ivor not getting the laugh he'd expected.

Ivor keeping a few reverential steps behind Greta, aware his ridiculous attempts to teach her the history of Het Loo had failed dismally, pretty sure she hadn't even been listening.

Greta's heart beating too fast. Greta feeling like her morning's repast was forcing its way back up her throat.

Greta's hands clinging to the edges of the back-pack holding her bedding role, her cup, her water bottle, her emergency supplies, just like in Ireland. Along with new additions: Ivor's smart doublet and hose so he wouldn't look like a beggar when they reached Het Loo. The Abbott's letter she would give Ivor at the end of this journey.

Journey and mission on the cusp of being enacted, and yet no gladness for it. Everything seeming to Greta hollow and without substance.

*Goddamn. Goddamn. Goddamn.*

Life sometimes so hard and obdurate it made you want to weep.

ZSOLT HUNG ABOUT THE edges of the hedges like a last gasp of the precipitate mist, unable to keep still. Zsolt moving first into the hedges' interior and then out again, keeping apart from the first hotel guests who wandered its lengths, admired its heft and height, the marvellous construction, cocking their heads to catch the faint dripping of health-giving water coming from the aqueducts above.

Normally, at this hour, Holger Stoss – or more latterly Piet - would be on hand to take them into one of the graduation towers, give budding civil engineers a short tour pointing out the mechanics, take them onto the viewing platform to see the layout of the aqueducts up above. Neither Piet nor Holger present on this particular morning, which left one or two of the guests a little piqued, prompted them to take out pocket watches and tut, before suggesting they went instead to the new mud-baths, the opening of which promised to be invigorating and entertaining, if not the spectacle of the bonfire the night before.

Zsolt chewing at a hung fingernail, regaling in the pain of ripping it from its side-bed with his teeth. He'd such fine nails as a lad, nails long and strong. Nails long and strong a thing of the past: half his lower calf sculpted away by a psoriasis that had bloomed and burned like acid, when he might happily have chopped off his leg to stop the pain; a psoriasis eventually abating, but still a source of burning itch when Summer days were long and the sun too bright and hard.

Gone too had been the viability of his nails, on fingers if not on toes.

'We don't know why it happens,' the doctor informed him. 'Only that it does. I've seen it a hundred times, and you're no different from the rest.'

Zsolt back then in no position to tell the doctor he was different, would one day be the man who would deliver his entire clan from servitude.

Zsolt still suffering those weak nails that broke and split and had white striations running through them from bed to tip.

Hela – once they'd become intimate – regarding his disfigurement with nonchalance; never mentioning her lame-armed brother who had died because of it, going over a ledge whilst chasing hares, unable to pull himself out. Vettie's Giel a vicious, cracked-open landscape littered by many such ledges and overhangs; months until they'd found him, and not much to be found when they did. No point dragging up his rags and bones.

'Best off where he is,' the elders decided for Hela. 'Still with us someway and somewise. And Jule always thought Vettie's Giel the best place on earth.'

Hela having to concede that it was so, not that Jule had seen any more of the earth than Vettie's Giel. Hela hoping he'd found another Vettie's Giel in heaven, for maybe that was what heaven was: being allowed to bide for perpetuity in the place you'd loved best. Which must make it a paradoxical place, enchanting and bemusing its inhabitants as they visited their neighbours' favoured terrains. Hela imbibing such notions from Håkon Tryggvason, who did not hold with organized religions of any kind. Håkon Tryggvason viewing them as different facets cut from the same stone, differing segments of the same fruit.

Håkon Tryggvason always so clear with his words, so convincing in his arguments. Håkon teaching his acolytes that one religion was no better than another. Håkon having to explain that yes, there were other religions, other mythologies of creation.

'Meaning that if there really is a God who has created us all then why would he, she or it,' a construction of the Godhead never come across before by the inhabitants of Vettie's Giel, and one that had enchanted Hela, 'why would he, she or it allow us such division and plurality? Why not impose One Rule, One Truth, if he, she or it was not of the mind to wind us all up, set us going, see what we would make of this world we have been put in? He, she or it has probably been laughing their socks off for millennia – if God wears socks – to see the mess we've created by our varied constructions of our creator.'

A valid point, Hela agreed.

'Which makes whoever it might be a capricious kind of God who, perhaps, is not deserving of our faith when we've no certain notion what the Godhead actually values. Logic instead dictating we live according to our own principles, make our lives matter, be remembered by our deeds, our words; for this can be the only worthy way into heaven if heaven exists, and if heaven is worthy of having us.'

Making perfect sense to Hela who, unlike her brother, found Vettie's Giel a stiflement, a hell that had clapped her in irons, forced her to live as others there had always done. The utter relief of realizing it might not be so, that there might be other avenues to travel, had been the making of Hela.

Her first awakening coming from the tales of Mathilde and Holger who'd met, wedded, and got away. Hela not lying when she'd said Mathilde had been a hero.

Second awakening coming with the return of Håkon Tryggvason, right when Hela was finding her life impossible. Vettie's Giel closing its fist around her. When she'd been considering throwing herself off the ledge to join her brother as the only means of escape.

Håkon Tryggvason Hela's saviour.

Håkon telling Hela of the footprints he'd seen of gigantic animals no longer extant: footprints first made in mud, the following millennia compressing that mud into stone.

Like Constantine in his hedge, Hela thought as she emerged from Mathilde Stoss's cottage, her brief exchange with Holger unsettling. Dragging up all those memories of home, of Jule, of Håkon's diatribes about the Godhead and the sort of life every man – every he, she or it – should aim to lead.

Hela seeing Zsolt nervous and jittery by the tower, chewing at his damaged nails.

'There you are!' Zsolt exclaimed as she came to him, grasped her arm, kissed her forehead. 'What have you learned? Does she know anything about Mokush? Or anything about the books?'

'She wasn't there,' Hela said shortly. 'But I know where she's gone. Please don't,' she remonstrated, as Zsolt wrapped his arm about her waist and pulled her to him. 'It's too public.'

Hela repulsed by the affection now they were so close to their goal.

Song of Igor her banner. Song of Igor her aim. Pelts of wolves and lions ready to be laid about her feet. Nothing more important to her at this moment than the Song.

Find the Song, and they could set the whole of Hungary on fire with an insurrection that would bring Russia crashing to its knees or, at the very least, recall Russian manpower from the Finnish borders in the north – and therefore also from Norway beyond it - and send them all to deal with the troubles at the other end of their empire.

She'd not much care for Mokush. Him she would sacrifice in a heartbeat, and Zsolt too if he put up any fight.

Hela emboldened.

Hela not about to foozle away her time on earth.

Hela red-feet, Hela feet-sky.

Hela aiming not for sand nor mud, but stone. Footprints left that would not only be seen in her lifetime but for millennium to come.

# 28

## Mangles And Mysteries

THE BELLS OF ST PETER'S rang out the half of nine a few minutes after Professor Jorn had left his scurrying cockroaches to their own business and bad jokes. Fabian taking a quick look out the open door as he moved to close it, put a hand to his chest and gasped.

'There's quite a crowd out there,' he said. 'What do you want me to do?'

Looking with entreaty at Frau Dieter, who was quick to get the situation under control.

'Very well,' she replied. 'I'm afraid, book-finders, whatever you were about to explicate will have to remain unexplicated for the moment. But I for one am very keen to hear how all unfolds. Would you do me the courtesy of remaining while we sort the opening of the mud-baths?'

Caro jumping up and offering his services.

'Whatever you need. Tell us what you want us to do. I'd be glad to give aid to Mr. Guichot if he needs it.'

Frau Dieter looking from Caro to Ruan, who raised his eyebrows and smiled.

'Like Caro said, whatever you need. It will give me time to have a proper look through the Professor's crate, get it itemised and so forth, as I've been commanded.'

Frau Dieter not fooled for a moment. Frau Dieter smiling back.

'Very well. That's decided then. Use these premises as you will. It's off-limits to the paying public. Speaking of which, Mathilde. Would you consent to stay a while too?'

Mathilde not so eager. She'd already left Holger far longer than she'd have liked.

Frau Dieter seeing the hesitation and alleviating it.

'I have a little plan,' she explained. 'It seems to me you and your husband are needing alternative occupation and I can offer it. You and Holger here, issuing tickets, taking payment, handing out the necessaries, towels and whatnot. Getting them cleaned afterwards and so on. Of course once I've studied your husband's contract it might all be moot, but still...'

Mathilde unable to respond to such evident and unearned kindness.

'You'd be doing me a favour,' Frau Dieter went on, as she too took a glance out of the door. 'There really are far more people here for the opening than I'd anticipated. I'm sure Caro would nip over and fetch Holger here to aid you.'

'I will,' Caro agreed, and was off out the door before Mathilde could say yeah or nay.

'Well then, here we are,' Frau Dieter concluded. Took Mathilde to the booth, where visitors would hand over their money before gaining entry to the mud-baths proper. Frau Dieter quickly explaining procedure.

'You'll need to keep tally of time,' she warned, showing Mathilde the ledger she had ready next to the till. 'One hour per paying customer, or twice that if they pay double – a small discount if customers choose the latter option. We've to keep a tight rein on it or the entire system will go out of the window.'

A comment meant to be light and frivolous, not that Mathilde took it that way. Mathilde's mind a maelstrom. Mathilde given a life-line. Håkon Tryggvason's capricious God might have been notching up tallies in Frau Dieter's favour had he, she or it been bothered enough to look down on this drama of mismatched people brought together because a man – a boy – had been found in a calcified hedge.

Mathilde nodding uncertainly, hand shaking as she got sat on her pew and the blind of the booth was pulled up.

'I'll do my utmost best,' Mathilde quavered, worry further etched on her already worried face.

'Yes you will,' Frau Dieter assured. 'And you'll do more, my dear. We're not the cockroaches certain people assume us to be, and we are not on this earth simply to be trodden underfoot. We're women and we're strong. We're resilient and we help our own, and don't you ever forget it.'

Mathilde proving a choice well made, more than equal to the task. Mathilde quick with times and coins, nothing different to how she divvied up her husband's meagre earnings and made them stretch and bend. Mathilde a little shaky the first few hours, Frau Dieter by her side lending strength and organisation. Mathilde soon finding a calling here, a liking of the small-talk expected of her as she sorted out tickets, towels and sandals. Mathilde delighting in being able to say *that one in number two has been overstaying his welcome,* and *that couple in number four I think might be being...a little unseemly. Several people have commented on the noise.* Caro nipping out at her bidding to cough quietly outside the offenders' enclosures, to hurry them up or quieten them down.

Holger too proving useful: strong hands and shoulders finding easy work in drubbing towels in the washing tub endlessly supplied with warm water from Fabian's steam engine; squeezing them through the mangles, putting them to dry on the pulleys hanging in neat rows from the ceiling. Holger bemused by this new work, finding rhythm and sense in its non-complication. Tasks he was equal to when he'd believed his working life at an end.

All the guests enjoying themselves immensely. Everyone admiring Fabian's frescoes and the unusual Roman ambience; exhilarated by the warmth of the mud on this cold and frosty morning; leaving feeling happier, healthier, and somewhat liberated. Gaggles of women prattling like peacocks as they re-donned their finery. Spas become quite the fashion all over Europe. The better-off visitors to Bad Salzbaum spending several weeks, even months, of their year visiting one spa or another. Bad Salzbaum leaping to the top of the list of those they would choose to return to again and again: hedges, mazes, topiary gardens, and now mud-baths too. Not many places having so much to offer.

The morning a coup. The afternoon drawing nearer.

Neither Professor Jorn nor Frau Dieter had specified a time for their meeting, both tacitly assuming it would be on the dot of four when the lunch detail at the hotel came to an end and the short day began its swift inclination towards night, and the visitations to the mud-baths might be presumed to cease. Except cease they did not, indeed increased as folk realised there would soon be cressets set to flame to light their late afternoon and early evening immersions.

The perfect place for quiet chats, business meetings, other meetings more illicit. The quiet lick of firebrands refreshing the frescoes, giving brightly coloured figures shadow and shape. More than a few of those who had attended early doors returning to see them. Happy to pay to sit and gaze instead of bathe once the shadows had gathered on the eastern side of the hedges, and the sun in the west began to fall, and the slow chug of Fabian's steam engine went on late into the night, far later than he'd anticipated. But paying customers were paying customers and this their first day, so he kept it going as long as was needed.

Later on – once he and Frau Dieter had installed their water organ – that steam engine would carry on chugging until midnight, particularly when the moon was full and folk took a sojourn through the gardens and hedges and lastly to the moon-viewing platform Fabian would build onto the side of the enclosure, gasping as they raised to their eyes the provided telescopes, saw the flat moon become a new white world of depth and height, craters, hills and shadows.

But that was later.

For now, we've had the first luxuriant morning of the mud-baths opening, when all went better than planned.

And for now we've Mokush strapped up on a table while everyone went about their business as if he wasn't there. Only Ruan left with Mokush, and Ruan completely ignoring the bound captive as he got on with unlading the books from the crate, laying them out in various piles about him, separating those that might have value from those having no value at all. Ruan nonchalant, not giving a hint that he had another ribbon-tied folder tucked under his belt. Ruan merely murmuring as he sorted his heaps, *well this is nothing. Yet another version of the Eikon Basilke, and oh for heaven's sake! No one needs another copy of that.*

Ruan coming to a stop after hours of all this havering, taking a brief lunch of the fare offered to the guests for a few extra coins. Ruan returning, looking over at his turkey who was by now groaning piteously as he strained his neck to see what Ruan had taken out of the crate. Ruan going over to his captive, adjusting the ropes about ankles and wrists.

Mokush able to lift himself. Get himself to sitting. Started squaring his shoulders, fearing what would come. Ruan giving him water and a small portion of buttered bread and sausage that got stuck halfway down and had to be eased on with more water so Mokush didn't choke. Ruan starting to speak.

'I have to ask myself,' he opened with, 'why you Polovtsy brothers have chosen to reveal yourselves after all these years.'

Mokush rubbing his lips together, lifting his hands to stay an errant drip of water spilling from his beard, unable to remove his eyes from the books and folios Ruan had laid out on the floor, assuming one had to be the document Ruan had flashed before his eyes in the cellar.

'Unusual name, Polovtsy,' Ruan went on, 'presumably Hungarian.'

Mokush saying nothing, trying to piece together all the fuzziness that had gone on in the cellar, knowing this man knew too much, if not exactly what. Mokush electing silence, fixing his eyes upon the little stack of unbound folios, looking for pink ribbons, which was all the detail he could recall of Ruan's opals, rubies, diamonds.

'It's an odd thing,' Ruan continued conversationally, 'that Hungarian originated in the Ob valley of western Siberia, more closely related to Finnish and Estonian than any other language on earth. A good friend of mine told me that.'

Meaning Hippolyte Gerhard, from whose vast knowledge of the languages of the east he had culled this particular snippet.

No reaction from the sat-up turkey. Mokush staying still as he could. Not the interrogation he'd expected, finding this casual approach menacing, coming at him from angles he could not anticipate.

'Its earliest linguistic relatives are the Ob-Ugric languages of Khantsy and Mansi. And please don't ask me about them,' Ruan apologised, 'for all I know are their names, and that the people who spoke them roamed the Russian steppes and plains of Europe on horse-back. And oh, now this might be worth the mention as far as you Polovtsys are concerned,' as if he'd just thought of it, instead of having racked his brains every minute of the morning to bring this information to the surface.

'Some of those ancient Ob-Ugrics split themselves off from the main branch to become the tribe of Kuman, scourge of the Russians way back when. Big battle, my good friend Hippolyte told me, near the Donets River, where the Kumans – you Polovtsys as you later became – well and truly drubbed a Russian prince from Novgorod. Igor, I think, was his name.'

Mokush well and truly rattled.

Mokush sifting back through his cellar memories, adding them in with Ruan's linguistic ramblings that boded ill: *Hippolyte, Kuman, Igor*. Vague memory he'd thought all this before, and couldn't comprehend how this stranger knew so much about their business. Dread compounded by Ruan throwing his next dagger with an accuracy that had Mokush's heart skipping a beat.

'Makes me wonder how it could possibly be that you and your brother became French POWs under Prussian control. Makes me wonder if you were ever POWs at all.'

A shocking statement of truth bringing those errant thoughts Mokush had had, before his knock on the head, resurfacing with the vigour of dolphins launching themselves from the surface of the sea.

*He knows.*

*How does he know?*

*He knows of the Slovo.*

*He knows of Håkon and Hippolyte.*

*He knows our clan's ancient name.*

*He knows what we want, and he has it.*

*And I don't even know if it's in this room, nor where this room is.*

*But he has it, and I have to get it back.*

Throat sore and scratchy from the trussing and straining, trickles of understanding running down and away like rain on ground so hard-baked it cannot drink it in, despite its desperate need.

'We need it,' Mokush said, with the cracked timbre of a Summer toad. 'We need the Slovo. You don't understand what it means to me and mine.'

Mokush's words not as impassioned nor articulate as he would have liked, but out those words were. He twisted about on his table, looked directly at the man with the rook-black hair and saw in his face not the belligerence he'd been expecting. Something else entirely. Regret maybe, or sympathy. Certainly curiosity. Weighing all up as if he was a judge of ancient times.

'It's our destiny,' Mokush laid his case out into the following silence, voice recovering, getting stronger. 'It's the fight of the few against the many, of the downtrodden who've suffered tyranny for centuries.' He'd actually read a few of his brother's tracts and was quoting from them now, his own words not up to the task. 'It means a metaphorical recreation of that earlier battle that will make our land and our people great again, sever us from the yoke of...from the yoke of...'

He stopped.

Couldn't quite recall the end of the sentence.

Ruan offering possibilities.

'Imperialism, maybe? Or perhaps foreign domination? They've both got a bit of a ring. Scourging usually comes into it somewhere. Scourging and yokes often go together, I find. Have you noticed?'

Ruan raising his eyebrows, inviting Mokush's opinion. Mokush having no answer. Mokush coughing in protest, humiliated by this inscrutable scrutiny as Ruan went on.

'I suspect it's because a scourge is a whip used to shift on livestock who would rather spend their days chewing grass at the wayside than pull a plough. Which seems to me an entirely reasonable position for the livestock to take.'

*What the hell was this man talking about?*

Mokush completely lost the thread; Ruan kindly holding it back out to him.

'And if scourge and yolk come from Russia on the one hand, and the Austrians on the other, well. That kind of makes you Hungarian Kumans the lazy livestock in between the two, don't you think?'

Enough for Mokush.

Humiliation one thing – he was a captive, when all was said and done, so humiliation the order of the day - outright insult to his family and his name quite another.

'You've no idea what you're talking about!' Mokush hot under the collar. 'Our people have been marginalised and dehumanised for centuries. Shunted here and there like the blasted cattle in your blasted story. Batted about as if we have no worth at all. As if we're a people to be tolerated at best, crushed at worst. Scourges and yokes is exactly right. But the Song will change all that! Will lift yoke and scourge and make us free once more.'

*Oh thank you, Zsolt, for your fine words, and thank you, Håkon, for putting most of them into your mouth and encouraging you to crow them out loud and long.*

Ruan impressed.

Ruan not unsympathetic to the plight of any folk below any yoke. The Scots as ambivalent about the pressed-upon-them Union with the English as any self-regarding Kuman must be about being tossed out of Russia into Hungary and told there they would remain; Hungarians hardly over-joyed about accommodating in their roost people regarded as incipiently Russian, and therefore the enemy. Scots feeling the same about the English, and the English about the Scots.

A world in turmoil.

Maybe the world always in turmoil.

Maybe that was just the way the world was supposed to be, as far as humans were concerned. Other animals got on well enough, their orderly predation of one another preserving an orderly balance never getting out of hand. Unlike humans, who seemed designed and destined to argue and fight, divide themselves off from one another to all their detriment.

A lot to think about. A lot yet to be done.

Time racing on.

His meeting with Professor Jorn almost due.

Ruan therefore scooping up the books, putting them back into the crate in the order he'd divided them into, calling out for Caro who appeared as if waiting for his summons.

'We've to go,' Ruan informed the trussed-up Mokush, who was hanging his legs over the side of the table and beginning to wriggle and test his bounds. 'Holger!' Ruan called. Holger turning his head, looking over, had been entirely absorbed by his new duties to give these two yabberers any mind.

'This man is to remain here until I get back,' Ruan commanded. 'If he tries escape then break his neck, or put his hand through the mangle. Anything you like, just keep him here.'

Holger nodding grimly. A straightforward command he could easily understand and act upon. A trussed-up man an obvious enemy, and Mathilde not far away. Enemies and Mathilde needing to be kept far apart. Holger's mind not so decimated he couldn't anticipate what might happen if the two collided.

Ruan returning his attention to Mokush.

'And before you ask, yes. I have your manuscript. And no, you will not find it. But let me think, because it seems to me we both have a great deal to think about.'

Mokush settling on his table, picking up a piece of sausage and getting it down with another swallow from the jug of water Ruan had left by his side.

Mokush remembering the man in the garish cravat calling this man a book-finder. A man, therefore, perhaps more attuned to profit than scruples, so maybe deals here yet to be done.

Mokush watching intently as Ruan and his young helper heaved up the crate of books and went with it through the door. Mokush given a brief glimpse - between the opening of the door and its re-closing - of the fidgety queue of chatterers waiting to enter the mud-baths. Pulse quickening as he recognized the one amongst the many who was neither fidgeting nor chattering, was instead standing tall in graceful isolation, neck as pure and white as any swan's.

Hela.

Somehow Hela knew he was here.

Another mystery piled upon all the others he'd so recently had to cope with.

No matter, for Hela was coming to his aid.

Mokush heartened.

Mokush thinking he'd put his own hand through that blasted mangle if only Hela could get him out of this mess.

# 29

## Dark Nights Of The Soul

PROFESSOR JORN STOOD at his window, hands clutched together behind his back.

The hedges standing strong as forts, graduation towers attentive sentries at their ends, inner cathedral all but deserted. Beyond the hedges could be discerned a gay group gossiping about the mud-baths' entry-gate. Only one woman detaching herself from the crowd, a woman alone, which was unusual. A woman oddly serene, who'd presumably decided it was not worth the wait. Professor Jorn silently applauding her.

He supposed he should be pleased the mud-baths had proved such a popular attraction. Undoubtedly they would add to the spa's prestige. Nevertheless he was irked by its usurpage of his hedges the very day after the laying ceremony. Only himself to blame, having agreed with Frau Dieter it seemed the right and natural time for the opening. How she and her tongue-twisted foreman had got all erected and completed on time, and to such evidently high and entertaining standards, he was still coming to grips with.

Privately he'd thought the whole project would be shambolic; in all probability would collapse halfway through, at which point he would have stepped in magnanimously and taken over. Instead, the mechanics and building work had raced on ahead of schedule, as aesthetic and unobtrusive as he had insisted it be in his part of the contract. A tic pulsing in his right temple, a heavy ache growing from the base of his neck up the back of his skull.

What was it with that blasted woman and her blasted contracts?

He'd unearthed the one made between his father and Holger Stoss. It hadn't taken long, all employees having to sign their chit of paper before receiving their first wage, ensure they wouldn't tittle-tattle about the guests at the hotel - important and high-up people as liable as their poorer counterparts to take their holidaying a tad too far.

His father's contractual obligations less stringent and more generous to his employees than his son's; Holger Stoss's stating that if he reached thirty years of employment he would be entitled to retire with a small pension from the estate to keep him ticking along for the rest of his days. Holger two years short, which was going to look like petty vindication – given his apparent collapse of mind – if Jorn refused to honour the spirit of the agreement. And undoubtedly both his father and Holger Stoss had assumed he would carry on in post as long after his thirty years as he could.

What grated most was how Frau Dieter had intuited this to be the case.

Women were supposed to be prettily attired, empty-headed ornaments, sitting gracefully on chaise-longues whilst their menfolk talked about important things. Or else drudged in kitchens, laundry rooms and dairies.

A bewilderment to Professor Jorn how Frau Dieter had escaped her gender's calling, become instead the pike in the reeds who took the bait without swallowing the hook, finished its victory by biting through the line. His headache worsening as he saw Frau Dieter break away from the gaggle hanging at her gate; the book-finders following, carrying the hedge-man's crate between them until they located their cart and deposited it on the boards.

More problems presenting.

He'd assumed a quick sale of its contents, a profit turned to pay off the book-finders, send them packing – and he dearly wanted to send them packing - him pocketing the remainder of the cash. Professor Jorn no sluggard when it came to business logic, and business logic dictated there had to be value in the crate for it to have been so hidden.

He'd previously not given a fig about how or why it had got into his hedge. Was reconsidering that position, as he was reconsidering his harsh treatment of Holger Stoss. The recent treacherously vivid memories of his experiences in France unsettling and unseating him.

The revelation of the crate belonging to someone right here in Bad Salzbaum a bad blow, unless it wasn't so. Unless it had merely been a ruse to rattle him. For how could the book-finders know such a thing to be absolute? Professor

Jorn regretting his earlier outburst at the mud-baths when explication had been in the offing.

Kaspar Larriscarri coming back to mind.

Kaspar Larriscarri: idiot entertainer of the masses whom the masses applauded because, completely without reason or cogent plot, he always came out on top.

He could hardly bear it.

No uprising peasants for Professor Ottelius Jorn, who knew what happened when uprising peasants were allowed their way.

France his touch-point and his proof.

Friends hauled off and bludgeoned to death in the streets.

France left to dangle its feet in blood, until the militaristic upstart from Corsica wrested the reins of governance from the hands of the revolutionaries. France once more organised and unified, if no less boltered in blood. The entirety of Europe in uproar, unsettlement and war because of it. Bad Salzbaum, and places like it, a retreat, a haven, where people didn't have to consider what was going on outside. Bad Salzbaum Ottelius Jorn's haven from the brutality he knew the world could descend into in a breath.

Never, since Reims, had he felt so soul-shaken, his self-constructed world-order teetering upon the lip of a chasm, fearing a hand in the small of his back might, at any moment, push him over.

And approaching him now came more unrest and insurrection in the forms of Frau Dieter and the book-finders toting their way towards him. Jorn nauseous, skin contracting, eyes focussing on the source of his panic as they traipsed across the grass. He wanted to vomit. Had to put his hand to his throat to stop it. Had to spit. Had to cough. Couldn't articulate, even to himself, why he was having such strong physical reactions to a vague anticipation of conflict.

His guts knowing it, even if his head did not.

Here he'd made himself a home, a safe place, where manifestos and politics could have no cause nor effect. Had once been mere minutes away from being pummelled into nonexistence for no other reason than being a foreigner at a backwater university. A situation that must never happen again, and certainly not here.

Every day since then darkened by the shadows of how close he'd come to an excruciating, needless and entirely undeserved death. Shadows taunting him, following him, become absorbed into him. So much a part of him he'd forgotten they were there. Except shadows like that never left, had their own way of living. Chose their own time to rise up and out and heave their hosts into darkness when they least expected it.

And that time, for Professor Jorn, was nigh and he was ill-equipped to deal with it.

He made a decision.

He would capitulate.

He would save himself at any cost, as he'd done before.

He would bring out the contract his father had drawn up with Holger Stoss, agree to the terms and the pension, given Holger Stoss was falling to bits at the seams.

He would accept whatever the book-finders advised him to do. Return the crate to whomever it belonged, pay Ruan Peat a pittance and be rid of him.

He would not quibble with Frau Dieter about the mud-baths. He would instead be full of praise. After all, the first day might have been stupendous but novelty was exactly that: it was novel and would wear off.

He and his spa would be safe.

Ottelius Jorn would be safe.

Nothing like the dread of being hacked to death in the streets to make you value safety.

Ottelius Jorn never speaking to anyone about such things. Ottelius Jorn spending his life, since he'd got back to Bad Salzbaum, making certain he never did. Not even to his father. The older Jorn questioning his son's return, bemused by Ottelius's unexpected enthusiasm to learn the family business.

*What's happened to your high ideals? All that guff about learning?*

*It's gone, father. You were right all along. My place is here. I should never have left.*

Sent by his father to study safer subjects than philosophy, spend a few years learning the rudimentaries of the business world. Missing the hedge-laying that time around, as he'd missed the previous one, the first one, when everything had gone so wrong.

*Safe then, safe now.*

All he could think about.

Jorn dealing swift and business-like with both Frau Dieter and Ruan Peat, agreeing without preamble to their terms before dismissing them. Informing Ruan he should take the crate of books to whomever Ruan believed it belonged, and to Frau Dieter that the Stoss's would get their pension, if not their cottage - which was tied to the job of Head Groundsman, and would go inevitably to Piet.

'What about Constantine?' was Frau Dieter's only question, Professor Jorn keeping his eyes on the space above her head.

'I don't know who that is,' he said. 'But whomever he is, I'm sure you'll deal with him as you see fit.'

And with that he washed his hands of the lot of them, turned back to the window, eyes prickling with tears to see the long reflection of himself stranded alone in the glass.

Frau Dieter about to remonstrate; Caro putting his hand softly on her arm and pulling her back with him to the door, closing it gently behind them as they gained the hallway.

'That was too easy,' Frau Dieter said hotly. 'He's planning something. How dare he not care about Constantine!'

Frau Dieter not beyond barging back in and giving the insufferable Professor Jorn a piece of her formidable mind.

All three arrested as they heard the unmistakeable sound of a sob, a hand-stifled wail beyond the wood dividing them from the man with the too-long face who had turned from the glass, unable anymore to look himself in the eye.

All three gazing at one another in puzzlement, unable to reconcile what they'd heard with all they knew of Professor Jorn which, they realised simultaneously, was next to nothing.

'Everyone has a past,' Caro sighed, 'and can tell you right now that some of his has just caught him up.'

Wise old man sheathed in Caro's young body, which had a past less good than most.

'Come on,' Ruan advised quietly, one of the few people who knew how bad Caro's past had been. 'Let's get everything done as he said, in case he changes his mind.'

'He won't,' said Caro. 'Dark nights of the soul and all that.'

'Dark nights of the soul, indeed,' Frau Dieter put in. 'I can't think what you'd know about those, young man.'

Despite her attempt at humour she was unsettled, and didn't miss the glance passing between the two book-finders which spoke of nights so dark they had spilled into days for one or other of them, or maybe both.

Frau Dieter shivering as she descended the palatial staircase, studiously avoiding looking into the vast mirror on the landing for fear of what she might see of her own dark nights. For everyone has them. Even, apparently, a one-dimensional irritation of a man she'd previously believed to have been knocked together out of pieces of wood and blocks of ice.

Everyone has a past, and she had to admit she was mighty curious about Professor Jorn's.

BOOKS BACK IN THE BASEMENT cellar.

Constantine reassembled and placed in a coffin Fabian had constructed from scraps of planking left over from the mud-baths' erection. Coffin-ensconced Constantine taken to the church of St Peter's, Frau Dieter electing to sit vigil the night through, and Caro with her. Caro knowing he might have ended up as young and dead as Constantine, had Ruan Peat not intervened in his life.

Mathilde, spilling over with gratitude, joining them once she'd finished at the mud-baths, settled the sticks of furniture Piet had brought from their cottage into the room assigned them, and settled Holger too. Rent to be paid in kind, by their work at the mud-baths, supplemented by a small wage and the pension from the spa. Mathilde and Holger catapulted from one life into another inside twenty-four hours. The previous morning all that lay ahead of them had been a grinding track. A track Mathilde had briefly believed would take them back to Vettie's Giel. A track she'd come to realise would have taken them nowhere of the sort. Only one place that kind of track went: shallow paupers' graves, husband and wife separated at the last, unless they fortuitously popped their clogs on the exact same day, at the exact same time.

Such awful prospect averted by the alert and vociferous intervention of a woman who hardly knew them. Mathilde, no scholar of the flow of history, recognising – as her childhood familiar Håkon had preached to Hela - that certain individuals could change history's course by their singular actions. Some reviled as monsters, others regaled as saints, dependant on the outcome of those actions. Frau Dieter in the latter camp, as far as Mathilde was concerned. Owing the women a debt she could never fully repay.

Mathilde therefore sitting vigil in a cold grey church throughout the dreary hours of a cold grey night for a boy she'd never met. A place pitiful when Mathilde got there: the coffin on its bier too short for any normal boy, and far too wide. The petrified curl of Constantine undisturbed. No point cracking his joints to make him as he'd been in life. Head placed adjacent to the neck from which it had been severed.

An open coffin, and a gristly sight.

Mathilde shocked to see the grey stone of the body, the face with its grimaced lips and emaciated features delineated in shades of peaty brown.

Mathilde nevertheless genuflecting and kissing her fingers before touching them to his forehead.

'They've to see him,' Frau Dieter murmured in explanation, as Mathilde lit her candle and took her place beside her saviour and the blonde-haired book-finder whose face was so shadowed and serious it seemed like he might have suffered three lives through.

'They've to understand how he lived and why he died,' Frau Dieter added.

Mathilde fidgeting as she took her seat, tried to splay her apron right to spin out the time. Then got it said.

'I'm sorry to say I've no idea who this boy is. How he lived, nor why he died. But if he's important to you then he's important to me. We owe you our lives, me and Holger.'

Frau Dieter drawing in a breath, swallowing down her tears, overwhelmed to have two strangers sitting next to her keeping company with a corpse they barely knew the name of.

Mathilde hoping she'd not offended.

'To be completely honest, Mathilde,' said the magnificent Frau Dieter, 'I don't know that either. I know how Constantine lived, and I can tell you he was a joy. An absolute joy. A boy who did kind things without thinking about them. Did them merely because it seemed the right thing to do. But why he died, I simply don't know.'

Mathilde understanding.

Constantine Frau Dieter's joy, Frau Dieter Mathilde's.

A short silence, until Caro spoke up.

'I think Ruan knows the most of it,' he said. 'And I'm guessing that by the time we've buried Constantine he'll have it all worked out. He's really good at finding traces and, if there are any, Ruan will find them.'

Frau Dieter's heart jumping at the words she desperately needed to hear.

*He'll work it out.*

*He'll find the traces.*

*We'll find out how and why Constantine died, and it will not have been for nothing.*

# 30

## Close And Closer Come They

MOKUSH HAD NOT HAD such a good afternoon.

Mokush taken from the mud-baths, brought back to the cellar.

If the spa guests had been curious about a bound man being escorted across the grass and past the hedges not a one commented on it; assumed him to be a common thief, a pick-pocket who'd chosen to plague the wondrous ceremonies of hedge-laying, bonfire-burning and mud-bath opening. Tapping at their pockets, wrists and necks to check for valuables. All safe and sound, so of no more concern.

Barely half past four when the book-finders returned from their meeting with Professor Jorn and fetched Mokush up again, took him to his billet for the night. Courage in him when he'd crossed eyes with Hela melting away from the queue as if she could no longer bear to wait another minute. Quick flash there telling him he'd not been forgotten, that she had a plan of action. And it would be hers, not Zsolt's. Zsolt being so full of words and ideals he couldn't plan his way out of a sack of peas.

Great gift to Mokush being reunited with the cache of books, no matter what the book-finder had said about the Song not being there. Book-finders lying all the time, as Mokush knew first hand.

Great consternation in Mokush when the book-finder, after the blonde lad had left, casually informed him the crate was about to be returned to its legal owner.

'I'll bet you didn't expect that,' the book-finder stated, lifting the lid, looking earnestly at his previously predetermined piles. 'Feeling your revolution slipping away from your fingers?'

Hells bells, the man was insufferable, if playing right into Mokush's hands.

Deliver everything back to the original owner, and all he, Zsolt and Hela had to do was steal it all over again, this time without any piss-arsed little whiner deciding their loot should not be allowed to escape into the wider world. And, now Hela knew where he was, would surely have waited and watched, they maybe wouldn't have to wait that long.

Right on cue, the cellar door broke open and down the steps thundered his brother bearing a barrage of arms: a vicious elm-wood knout hard as stone at its working end; a bill-hook purloined from the work-shed outside which it had been fortuitously left; several stout sticks stolen up on their way into town and sharpened into points. Hela a couple of steps behind.

'Release the captive!' Zsolt demanded theatrically, giving the book-finder a whack in the head with the knout, having Ruan on the ground before he could open his mouth. Zsolt and Hela getting Mokush free. The book-finder soon tied up in the same ropes he'd held Mokush captive with.

'Who's the turkey now!' Mokush laughed, as he spat on Ruan Peat who was groaning and throwing up all at the same time. Mokush brave and strong now Hela was in the room. Zsolt quickly down on his knees pawing through the contents of the crate, strewing them without care about him.

'Where is it? Where is it?' he kept repeating, in between a choice string of Hungarian curses.

'He told me it isn't here,' Mokush informed his brother. 'That he's hidden it. And he knows, brother. Or most of it at least.'

*Hippolyte, Håkon, Kuman.*

Hela stepped in closer.

'How is that possible? What did you tell him?'

Poking Mokush hard in the chest with her whittled stick, sharpened end going with ease through the loose worsted of his jacket and inner shirt, pricking his skin. The light going out of her eyes as she cast them at Mokush with hatred and dark suspicion.

'I told him nothing,' Mokush protested, holding up his hands. 'He's a bloody book-finder. That's what he does for a living! And he's a friend of that book trader in Deventer Håkon sent you to.'

Hela turning away from Mokush, fixing her eyes on Ruan who was coughing up blood and spluttering on the ground, trying to right himself, mind a bright mess of splintered images and sharp-edged thoughts he couldn't seem to put into any kind of order.

'The Song can't be far,' Hela stated. 'It's got to be on the grounds, for he's not stepped a foot out of it as far as I know. And I've been watching.'

Hela sweeping down and up in one graceful movement, bringing with her the bill-hook Zsolt had abandoned in his febrile search. Zsolt unaware of whatever else was going on about him, Zsolt scrabbling, ripping apart folios and folders, scattering their contents like feathers from a plucked bird all about the cellar until he was surrounded by useless purge and page.

Mokush seeing Hela standing like some ancient goddess: a single spot of red at the base of her throat, the rest of her stretched neck pure and white as the egrets he remembered from back home; Hela holding the bill-hook high in her strong, bread-pummelling fingers, looking like she might slice the head off the book-finder as the book-finder had done to Constantine.

'Search him,' she ordered Mokush, remembering only then that straight line bisecting the book-finder's jacket when he'd passed her on the grass. A small sign she should have pounced on before. 'I'll wager it's tucked into his belt at his back.'

Ruan might have appreciated her acuity had he not been so confused, having starlight sparking through his brain throwing out images of disparate objects without context: opals, rubies, diamonds. Boys in hedges. City-scapes of Deventer. Manuscripts bound with faded ribbons.

Mokush's fingers hauling at Ruan's jacket and shirt, until at last, at last, after seven long years, after centuries - there it was.

The Song of their Revolution.

Manuscript in its folder tied up with pink ribbon, exactly as Håkon had given it to Hela who'd handed it on to Hippolyte Gerhard.

Mokush breathless, too exuberant to speak, too slow to stop Zsolt tearing it from his hands, snatching up his prize, his treasure, his Kuman heritage. Hugged it to his chest, his Kuman heart beginning to beat against the manuscript that was about to set them free.

Hela's marble white face shining in victory and perspiration in the jittering light of their single lamp. Closing her eyes, savouring the moment, before getting back to the job in hand.

'How much does he know?' she asked, jutting her chin at Ruan, Mokush scrambling to put together what Ruan had said since he'd the misfortune to cross paths with the man. Or maybe the fortune, as it turned out.

'He's a friend of Hippolyte Gerhard,' Mokush repeated quickly, eager to impress. 'And he knows about the provenance of the Song; where it was discovered, where it was stored, that it was Håkon who liberated it, that it's one of a kind. And I think he...' Mokush faltered, went on. 'I think he knows about you.'

Hela's expression unchanged, as those of marble goddesses rarely do.

'Now that, my two brothers Polovtsy, is very interesting,' said she. 'We have here a book-finder; friend and colleague of Hippolyte Gerhard who is respected by the best in his profession. A book-finder, therefore, whose words will go far.'

Hela moving forward, going down on her haunches, studying the man's face, the blood bubbling from his mouth. Mokush a few paces behind, studying Hela's bared neck as she leant forward, her collar bones sliding beneath her dress as it shifted a few inches with the momentum of her crouch. Mokush excited by the movement, the erstwhile threats of violence, this rare view of Hela, the sheen of white skin never before glimpsed.

'What's his name?' Hela asked. 'His name!' she demanded again, when neither of the brothers replied. Hela sighing with exasperation. These brothers both such blockheads, cut from the same tawdry cloth. Hela standing, regarding them with despisement. 'Do I have to spell it out to you?'

Which patently she did. Mokush looking at Zsolt and Zsolt looking back at his brother, slight shrug of both their shoulders because what was the what with that? They had the Song. Surely that was enough.

'Have you forgotten everything Håkon told us?' Hela a taut bow-string, flitch at her back filled with all the barbed arrows she was ready to spit out into the world the moment she got the chance. 'Has all this been for nothing?' she hissed. 'All my travels and travails? We need his name. Without his name we have nothing!'

Mokush and Zsolt bewildered, for how could they possibly know it? And what did it matter anyway?

'You idiots,' Hela stared them down. 'How can you not understand? The Song is worth nothing unless someone can tell us where it came from, authenticate its age, in what manner it was written, how it can give up its history. And this is the man to do it.'

*Alone pen, garden Kuman.*

*Furrows furrows.*

'Just get him awake,' Hela sighed, swinging her bill-hook in her hand, glad for its substance, its weight, its ability to deal out more than cutting through a slice of air. 'And get him in a position so he can write, and get something he can write with.'

Mokush and Zsolt looking about them, seeing nothing able to fulfil her demands.

'Oh for love of God,' Hela muttered, for the love of he, she or it; snatching up the lantern, marching off across the cellar's floor, regarding all the bottles and jars lined up upon the myriad shelves.

'Here,' she said. 'This one's filled to the brim with maturing ink.'

Heading off into the darkest coolest recesses where meat was hanging from hooks, plucking several quills from the geese, some fine stiff bristles from the hogs.

Returning with the makings.

'Find the blank back of one of those pages Zsolt has made such a pig-sty of,' she commanded. Zsolt and Mokush doing as bid, the brothers belittled, awed by Hela's imperious grasp of the situation that had completely passed them by.

'And get him conscious,' Hela went on. 'There's ammonium salts on that shelf above the brandy that'll do the trick. Get him to write down all he knows about the Song, about what Hippolyte Gerhard confided. Get him to sign it and date it. After that, we'll get rid.'

'Get rid?' Mokush asked. 'What do you mean?'

Hela turning her withering gaze on Mokush.

'Exactly what I said. Once he's contributed to our cause in the provision of a sound and signed provenance then we despatch him. He's seen us, he knows us. You don't think he'll cry down the rafters within ten minutes of us leaving?'

Ruan could no more have cried the rafters down than could a dried-up mat of moss. His jaw fractured in two places by Zsolt's knout.

'But the others?' Mokush objected quietly. 'He'll have told others, and we can't despatch them all.'

Hela tutting.

'We don't need to, you imbecile. No one knows we're here. They'll come and they'll find him dead and they won't know a blessed thing. They might suspect, but they won't know. And suspecting and knowing, Mokush, are two very different things. Which is why we need his stamp on the Song. His, and his avowal of Hippolyte Gerhard's worthy opinions. Save us a lot of shillying and shallying when we get it where it needs to be.'

Mokush not so sure. Mokush understanding she meant to get the Song to Hungary however she could. Mokush no longer harbouring the vague notion of her aiding Constantine in his escape. Would instead have put her hands around Constantine's throat and throttled the life out of him if she'd caught him up on that long ago night.

Hela as obsessed by the task as his brother was. Maybe more so.

Hela come from grind and dirt, restriction and exploitation.

Hela more wedded to the notion of the Song saving the Kumans, and thereby saving herself, than Mokush had ever been.

Mokush also realising how the scenario she had presented him might go: Mokush the only obvious suspect for the murder of the book-finder. Certainly Hela had visited the Stoss's, but only in the guise of the daughter of an old friend. No link from her to Mokush and Zsolt anyone would be able to find. Himself, by contrast, had been intimately connected by the book-finder and his acquaintants to the crate of books, the death of Constantine, and the original theft of his purloined crate.

Mokush, like Ottelius Jorn before him, seeing the executioner's yard only steps ahead. Mokush viewing Hela as he'd not done before: a woman ruthless, as hard and honed by circumstance as Zsolt's elm-wood knout; the woman who had selected Zsolt above himself solely because Zsolt was the older brother, the representative of their clan. And a woman who had denied her own homeland, elected theirs in its stead, who would not hesitate to throw him to the dogs if it meant she and Zsolt could get away free and clear, Song and respected book-finder-signed provenance secreted, the two off to Hungary and heroism as Zsolt had always promised her.

But only the two.

Mokush absolutely certain as Zsolt looked at Hela and Hela looked back at Zsolt.

Mokush wondering if this had always been their strategy. Mokush marked out from the beginning to be the first martyr on their march to revolution, everyone knowing revolutions needed martyrs to get them properly fired up and going. The Polovtsy clan back home would lap it up like overheated dogs shoving their tongues into a puddle on a hot Summer's day.

'Our son! Our lost son!' they would wail, throwing their hands above their heads in outrage.

The spark to the fire.

Mokush the blockheaded piece of wood designated to feed its flames.

UP TOP THE CELLAR ANOTHER man brinked his way through the left-open door, stepped in and stopped. Stood statue still. A man who didn't like the dark, and didn't like the sounds he was hearing, voices he didn't know. One of them a woman's, and an angry woman at that. A situation obviously occurring that couldn't be good. Angry women never part of anything good. The man taking a breath, retracing his way from the short corridor leading from steps to door and getting himself out.

Closing the door quiet as he could.

Slowly, slowly, pushing home the bolt.

Locking the door between himself and trouble.

Old habits dying hard.

Getting out of there fast of breath and quick of step, and not looking back.

Sweat at collar and cuff.

The past, so recently resuscitated, come stalking him. Threat seen in every corner, every shadow. A past never spoken about to anyone; the fear of it entombed deep inside him rising revenant from its grave.

Hedges tall and straight, dark arms reaching out to him in this darkest of dark nights.

His hollowed-out heart drawn to the hedges' own. Going in, gaining their emptied centre, leaning his back against their solidity, their certainty, wishing their characteristics to be his own.

Breathing deeply once inside and hidden. This darkness nothing to be feared.

Breathing deeply to be safe and alone, spreading his fingers against the wooden skeleton keeping the blackthorn bales in place.

Raising his taut face, gazing up through the extremities of the hedges. No glimpse of stars tonight. Sky raddled over with long clouds rizzled top to bottom by the light of the moon they were trying to hide.

Panic abating.

Peace here, succour and solace.

No one here but him.

Any late-goers neglecting the hedges for the mud-baths, for which he was thankful.

Until he saw the devil at the opposite end of the hedges.

The devil moving directly towards him.

The devil broad and strong of limb and foul of breath, the faint aroma of rotten fish an invisible cloak about his shoulders as he bore inexorably down the nave of the hedges towards Professor Jorn who quailed, as petrified as the homunculus found in these very hedges, the devil gaining speed and substance.

Ottelius Jorn no Kaspar Larriscarri who could twist the plot, the devil, the hangman or the mayor at the last moment of the play. Jorn's chest tightening, couldn't breathe, thought on Reims, couldn't move, could not turn and run. And oh Lord, the stench had him retching as the ghastly figure drew level, black face heavy browed, features scant in the scribbled light allowed by the clouds. The devil putting out a gnarled hand with evident evil intent.

Professor Jorn crumpling in on himself, slumping to the ground, certain his heart was about to implode inside his cowardly chest. Sending up a brief prayer, as cowardly men always do when they believe they are about to take their last gasp.

*Only save me, and I swear, I swear, I will be a better man.*

# 31

## Kaspar Larriscarri And The Devil

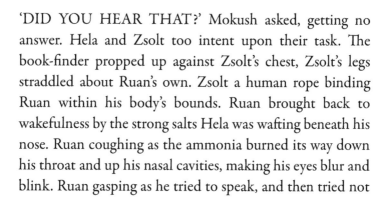

'DID YOU HEAR THAT?' Mokush asked, getting no answer. Hela and Zsolt too intent upon their task. The book-finder propped up against Zsolt's chest, Zsolt's legs straddled about Ruan's own. Zsolt a human rope binding Ruan within his body's bounds. Ruan brought back to wakefulness by the strong salts Hela was wafting beneath his nose. Ruan coughing as the ammonia burned its way down his throat and up his nasal cavities, making his eyes blur and blink. Ruan gasping as he tried to speak, and then tried not to.

'Write, book-finder,' the woman commanded, thrusting into his hand a quill quickly fashioned by her knife, her hand about his as she dipped it into the bottle of oak-gall ink. 'Write down everything you and Hippolyte Gerhard know about the Song and where it came from and maybe we'll go easy on you.'

'I really think I heard something,' Mokush said again, Hela tutting in irritation.

'Well go look then,' she commanded, Mokush's heart fluttering to be given such easy escape. Mokush up in a moment, taking the cellar steps two by two. Mokush thinking *This is it! Get up and out! No martyrdom for me. No merry burning of Mokush, no matter all your plans.* Mokush grabbing at the door, elated. Mokush pulling its knobbed handle, pulling and pulling, desperate for escape. Tears of frustration coursing down his cheeks when nothing happened. The door stuck and fast. Heard the rattle of the bolt on the other side as he braced his foot against the wood and pulled again.

And let it go. Had to give it up. No way out for him, nor for any of them. Mokush snuffling into his beard, shaky fingers wiping at his eyes. Would not be seen to be weeping, not by the likes of Hela and his blasted brother.

The Song at its end.

The jig up because some passing kitchen maid or boot-boy had noticed the cellar door open when it should have been shut.

At least they'd all go down together, and some comfort in that. Mokush no longer the scapegoat to be chucked alone and wretched into the flames.

'It's been bolted,' words hard to get out as he lumbered back down the steps, tears hot in his eyes, throat closing in defeat. 'Someone's bolted the door.'

'HOW ARE YOU? ARE YOU feeling better?'

Mick Malloy crouching down beside the fallen figure in the hedges. He didn't have much time to waste but a fallen man was a fallen man, and help the fallen man and maybe the fallen man would help him. Mick strategizing as always. Five minutes neither here nor there. He'd gained a good few hours on the Arnhem coach and, once alighted there, had taken the few miles to Bad Salzbaum on foot. Idea being to grab up Ruan Peat, whom he knew from Joachim to be in that town, add him to the quiver already armed by Ivor Merrill and the letter from the Abbott of the Servants. Great advantage, a bit of intelligence, and he'd learned from Joachim how Ruan had had dealings with someone significant in the Duke of Brunswick's entourage, tracking down several documents that proved him great and grand enough to inveigle himself into the English Court when he got over the water.

Mick's other way into Het Loo.

A way that might prove more promising than Ivor Merrill, who had the backbone of a cuttlefish – which meant no backbone at all. Cuttlefish marvellous creatures in their own environment, who could change colour at will, blend into any background. Not so Ivor Merrill. Mick fearing how he and Greta had got on. Mick fearing Ivor might already have cut and run, this duty proving too onerous a burden. Not so Greta, his faith in her absolute and unyielding. Doing now as he'd always done, as Greta would expect him to do if he had the means: providing a second strategy in case the first fell through, as first strategies often do. Mick having the means and the time, slim as it was, given his precipitate fleeing from Zeebrugge, thanks to the fisherwomen there.

And give them thanks he did.

Giving thanks too to the girl in the market place who had been about to shut up shop when he'd approached her. A young girl selling the most godawful stink of dried tripe, but in a rather fine silk dress; a dress a little torn about its hem that had to have been given her by someone better placed. The girl eager to be stopped at her packing up and being asked about the woman who had given her the dress that very day, which seemed a natural way for Mick to start the conversation.

'Oh she's so lovely, and always so very kind,' had said the girl. 'She always smiles at me. Always buys my wares, although I doubt she really needs them. She's to do with the spa hotel, I think, and told me all about the man they found in hedges there. So awful. Such a tragedy.'

Mick alert, Mick asking more questions, the girl eager to supply answers for her day had been the best she could remember. Grey silk skirts rustling about her ankles. Grey silk skirts that would last her the rest of her short life.

Grey silk skirt girl telling Mick all that had been recently going on in Bad Salzbaum. And Mick, once apprised of what had been found in the hedges, in no doubt about where Ruan Peat was to be found.

Hedges no miracle for him.

Mick too prosaic for that.

Hedges meaning only great cover, hidden passage to bring him nearer the spa hotel where he suspected Ruan Peat was berthed. Mick finding at its middle a man so shocked and traumatised he'd slid down the side of the hedge and collapsed at its base. Mick so used to shocked and traumatised men he'd acted on impulse, held out a hand to aid him. Down that man had gone nonetheless, and down had gone Mick beside him.

Five minutes not much.

Five minutes he could afford.

Five minutes proving themselves worth the wait ten times over.

'THERE'LL BE ANOTHER way out,' Hela decided. 'There's got to be some other door so the trades-folk don't have to interact with the guests.'

Hela snatching up the lamp and setting off to find it. Hela leaving Zsolt behind to do the clean-up, despatch the book-finder now he'd served his purpose. His letters scrawled but legible, his sworn deposition about the Song as valuable as the paper it had been written on had previously been worthless. Hela guiding the words, making mention of herself as the person who had delivered the Song to Hippolyte - Hela still having Hippolyte's chitty in her possession to prove the claim - provenance of where the Song had been found and when. Its liberation from the Moscow archives, its deliverance to Deventer. Done and dusted. Ruan's deposition carefully placed between two other sheets so the ink didn't run; deposition placed within the Song's folder and tied neatly up.

Hela going to the farthest reaches of the cellar, pushing past the hanging carcasses of geese and hogs and coming out the other side. Small ice-house slotted into the farthest wall and, right next to it, a tall hatched door bolted top and bottom from the inside instead of the out.

*I knew it,* she murmured, hanging the lamp on the hook provided, bending down to shift the bottom bolt, about to reach up to undo the topmost when she heard the most god almighty tumult and Zsolt screaming out her name.

*You dolt, Zsolt,* she muttered under her breath, putting the flat of her hand to the base of the door and pushing it open, unhooked the lantern, ducked down and went out.

# 32

## Hela Feet-Sky

GEORGE HERBERT PROVED right: the devil foul, but not all bad; the devil foul solicitously proffering Professor Jorn a canister of water and politely asking after his health. Professor Jorn grateful, and dreadfully embarrassed. To be degraded by his past in the solitude of his study one thing, to have it publicly witnessed, even by a single man, quite another.

'I'm so sorry,' he apologised. 'I don't know what came over me.'

Professor Jorn struggling to gain his legs, weakness in every joint, cartilage turned to wet sponge. The devil who was no devil, despite the stench, helping him to his feet.

'We calls it Satan's Vapours,' commented his aide, making Jorn choke as he took a sip at the canister, halfway laugh, halfway groan.

'Battle veterans get it all the time,' the man explained. 'One minute you're fine and dandy, the next you see something or hear something,' – *or smell something,* thought Professor Jorn – 'and it's like the whole world has exploded,

382

taken you back to the one place, the one time, you never wanted to be again.'

And now Professor Jorn did laugh: a weird scritchety sound squeezed from a throat whose muscles have forgotten what laughter is.

'Reims,' he said, after a few deep breaths. '1792.'

Hardly believing he'd said it out loud. First time he'd said it out loud to anyone.

'That'd do it,' his companion agreed. 'Bad times.'

As if he'd been there, as if he knew.

Communion here, private confession, words unable to escape the hedges, absorbed by them, taken in as one with the scrimshaw-scratch of newly emerged moonlight on the jag of blackthorn spikes.

'Got to remember you got out,' the man went on. 'You were the lucky one. Trick is to make that luck count. Come on,' he said, completely ignorant of the fact he'd just imparted the most deep and meaningful piece of advice Professor Jorn had ever heard, taking hold of Jorn's arm. 'Let's get you home. And, while we're at it, I could do with some information. If you're up to it.'

Professor Jorn up to it.

Professor Jorn indebted and enheartened by the easy understanding of this unknown companion, by his certainty and bulk, as if he were the incarnation not of the devil but of the hedges themselves. Small worry in Professor Jorn that he was imagining all this, that he was still a slumped mess disgracing himself at the hedges' base, until his companion broached the subject of the information he required.

'I'm here to find a man named Ruan Peat,' Mick stated. 'I don't suppose you know of him?'

HELA HAD DISAPPEARED with their only light source, leaving Mokush and Zsolt in utter darkness. Neither concerned. Early years spent in caves drilled into the hills, well used to finding their way around without light of any kind. Blindness without being blind. Hands not groping, instead swift and certain. Zsolt getting to his feet bringing his prisoner with him, taking him to the straw bales and throwing Ruan onto the unseen spills and leakage of Constantine's lopped-off head.

'Get the knout, Mokush,' Zsolt commanded, Mokush grabbing it up from the floor after one brief miss.

Zsolt's hand held to Ruan's head, keeping it immobile, keeping track of his target. No fight from Ruan. The pressure and pain of that hand as his face was shoved into the straw excruciating. Body choosing its best option, and shutting down.

Ruan helpless and unconscious.

No deep thoughts about mortality or the desirability of putting it off.

No wandering memories of Greta or Loch Eck.

Ruan's mind a barren place about to be flung into the blankness of nonexistence.

Only hope for Ruan – if Ruan had been capable of hope, which he was not – being Mokush hesitating as he picked up the knout, thinking he should maybe bash it at his brother's head instead of Ruan's, save himself, get out with Hela, take

Hela for his own, take the two of them back to Hungary. Assuming she'd found a way out.

'Get on with it!' Zsolt said sharply. 'You heard what Hela said to do. Oh, give it here.'

Jolting Mokush back to obedient brotherhood. Mokush always the weak one, Mokush meekly handing over the knout.

Zsolt taking hold, taking aim, taking swing, hammer set to hit the nail when, from up above, came the metallic screech of the bolt within its housing and the scraping of wood upon stone as the door crashed open and down the steps came the dark bulk of a man who swiftly barged first into Mokush and next his brother, knout missing Ruan's head by a hair's breadth.

'Hela!' Zsolt hollered as he hit the floor. Mokush tumbling down beside him, oomphs of air going from their lungs as they hit, gleam of light catching them in tableau as a lantern was held high, giving Mick a brief second of advantage. Two against one, Polovtsy brothers scrambling and scuffling, kicking out, swearing, grabbing for weapons beyond their reach. Mick landing punches with accuracy, calculated to do most damage. Years of hand-to-hand combat at his command. Scrum and scrimmage, fight and fists. Mick keeping the brothers down, if not for long. Zsolt shoving his brother away, hand scrambling along the base of the bales for the fallen knout, the light jittering and jinking as someone got there before him, grabbed it up, slammed it against Zsolt's skull and laid him out.

Mokush ceasing his struggles as Zsolt collapsed beside him.

Zsolt gurgling Hela's name on bloodied lips.

Mokush holding up his hands.

'Enough,' he called out to the heavens, to Mick Malloy, to Ottelius Jorn who had – at the last – done as Kaspar Larriscarri might have done: picked up a weapon and fought the inevitable back.

'Please,' Mokush pleaded, Mokush collapsed, Mokush panted. 'Please. It's done. It's all done. I'm done.'

# 33

## Spine And Twine

A HARD DAY FOR GRETA, if a hard day done.

Brief conversation with Ivor about how the morrow would go before they joined the other travellers at a long table. Women one side, men the other. A communal repast laid out between them. Large pottery platters and bowls filled with butter-glistened potatoes, salted beef shredded in an ample gravy enriched with beer and dried mushrooms, mounds of crusty bread, several choices of cheese. All washed down with a hearty wine brewed by the hosteller's wife from last year's cherries and damsons. The various dishes passed up and down the table until all had had their fill. Lively conversations flitting to and fro, in which Greta did not partake. Most folk here seeming to know one another, many of them traders returning from some festivity which had apparently gone better than expected. Greta about to excuse herself and retire when a man somewhere down the table began a strange tale that had her leaning forward, rooted to her seat.

'I'm of the opinion the Bad Salzbaum bonfire went better than the last time, despite what they found in the hedges when they stripped them bare.'

General hubbub of agreement.

'When was the last time? 1801? 1802?'

'Definitely 1802,' another added. 'They did it in August, if you recall, because of Napoleon's birthday. Caught us all out. Really mucked up my schedule that year, but Bad Salzbaum bonfire not to be missed.'

'You're right. And it was an absolute winner this year. Those colours in the flames, and those fireworks! And what did everyone think about the mud-baths?'

'Think the rich are pigs enough to think them real grand!'

A couple of back-slaps at this remark, hearty laughter. None of these folk rich, nor ever would be.

'Found what?' someone asked more saliently. 'What did they find in the hedges?'

'Ah now,' the first man held up a finger, lowering his voice, enjoining them all in the conspiracy of a hidden tale he'd been saving for precisely this moment. 'Spa folk tried to keep it quiet but I heard, from one of the kitchen maids – that pretty one with the ringlets...'

A few guffaws, if not by the men who had wives with them.

'Heard from her,' the man went on, 'that when the bales were stripped out they found a man in the hedges. Petrified he was. And not petrified as in frightened. Petrified as in turned to stone.'

Greta also turned to stone in that instant.

Greta sitting straight-backed and strong.

Greta re-reading in her head all the lines of Ruan's last missive to Joachim.

*Bad Salzbaum, hedges, mazes.*

Greta looking over at Ivor Merrill on the other side of the bench and finding him insipid at best, insubstantial at worst. Ruan Peat once more the centre of her world. Greta as eager to hear what might next be said as the rest of them.

'They took him out of the hedge and put him in the cellar of the spa hotel,' the tale-teller informed his rapt audience. 'Him and some crate of books.'

*A crate of books.*

Greta hearing the booms of bitterns in the marshes, the fluted kleeps of slim white avocets with their upturned beaks as they studded through the sands of Walcheren on the first day she and Ruan had returned there from Deventer.

'And I also heard – and this, folks, you're not going to believe, but I have it on very good authority, namely from the ringlet girl's brother who has ears keener than a bat's - that they chopped off his head. Chopped it off and put it in a bucket of tannin to bring out his features. Couldn't have done it meself, oh no. Couldn't have done that.'

*Ruan could have*, Greta thought, *and Ruan would have if it would bring results.*

Greta knowing it as certainly as she knew she wanted to see him again.

*Bad Salzbaum. Body in a hedge. Box of books. Chopped off head.*

Had to be Ruan. Just had to be.

Ivor none the wiser.

Ivor finding the conversation about the table diverting, nothing more. No care in him about the supposed body found in the hedges of some place he'd never heard of. No noting how keenly Greta was listening. Ivor dog-tired and needing his bed.

'They reckon he was one of those POWs they kept on to do the mill-workings.'

'Ah now,' another man interrupted, 'there's something tremendous. Flour for all, and all the year round. Wish someone would build one of those for us back home.'

The woman to Greta's left ignoring this last comment.

'Why would he have gone into the hedge, and how did he get in there? And what was he doing with a crate of books?'

There indeed was the mystery, speculations rife and luridly imaginative.

'Well obviously he pinched them. Bad Salzbaum folk always said those POWs weren't to be trusted.'

'Who would? They're French, and no one trusts the French, not these days.'

'Not back then neither,' a reasoned thinker in their midst. 'Must have got in during the last laying, no other explanation. And we were all there, mind. And my guess is he didn't go in willingly.'

Greta's neighbour shivering as she thought on it. Shivering, not with fear nor pity, rather because she'd been so close to the action.

'My money's on Hals Werther,' Greta's other neighbour opined. 'Explains why he stayed home this year. Couldn't handle returning to the scene of the crime.'

A few chuckles at this remark, someone saying what all were thinking.

'If it was Hals, there was a woman involved.'

'But he was young, said my sources,' the tale-teller announced.

'The young liable to do foolish things,' the philosopher added, 'especially when it comes to love.'

Oh, and so right there. Greta's heart contracting at the foolish things she'd done when she'd been young and in love with both Ruan and the Cause, choosing the latter over the former. Impossible to start a marriage bedded on the betrayal of her country. She would never have been able to square that circle, could never have been happy. Not truly. And therefore could never have made Ruan happy either. Greta right to leave him behind when he'd chosen not to follow.

Greta pushing away the anger she'd felt for him back then because it was an anger irrational and undeserved. Greta having no right whatsoever to demand Ruan throw himself onto the sacrificial altar of her choosing. Ireland's debasement by the English nothing to do with him. Not his fight. As no more was it Ivor's now. Ivor, sudden revelation coming to Greta, thereby achieving a heroism Ruan had been unable to match. Meaning Ivor not so insipid a man as she'd previously thought him. A man with backbone and honour at his core, no matter how out of his way he'd gone to obscure those virtues. And tolerably handsome, undoubtedly a man with prospects who could offer her more than retreating back to the London she hated when all this was done. Ivor reconsidered. Ivor maybe the man to whom she could cleave and grow old with if a reunion with Ruan went badly, or never happened at all.

Greta no longer listening to her fellows' conversation as she looked over the table, her face bright, a smile ready on her lips, to find Ivor gone.

Ivor up to his tiny room with his stomach in knots, worrying for the morrow.

Ivor doubting himself, doubting his meagre abilities.

Ivor regarding the fine clothes he'd bought in Amsterdam. Nothing new; he could live with that, most folk not monied enough to buy new. Most folk buying pass-me-downs, two-times, three-times over, getting them re-tailored. Ivor having no time for the retailoring part, Ivor taking what was given him: an emerald green doublet barely reaching his thighs, a rather dull pair of breeches that would sit above a startlement of purple stockings going from foot to knee. Ivor regretting he'd not spent more time in the shop, had not taken what the tailor first thrust at him that appeared to be in his size.

'You'll look like a gentleman at court,' the tailor was delighted.

And a gentleman at court had been the general idea. Although a tailor who put purple and green together with such a pallid complexion as Ivor's should really find a new job. Ivor anticipating what he would say to Greta to allay it, concocting a humorous anecdote in his head about the Sumptuary Laws England held way back in Medieval and Tudor times dictating what colours and materials each stratum of society was allowed to purchase and wear.

Ivor wondering why he cared so much what Greta thought of him.

*Because she's twice the man you are.*

The thought so sudden and shocking Ivor Snivels Merrill packed away his fine doublet, put breeches and stockings beneath his hard hummock of a pillow so they would press right and at least look their best.

Ivor besieged by self-doubt, and by the certainty that if Greta was in his place she'd do a better job.

Ivor laying down upon his pillow a lesser man than he'd started off that morning, when all had been a new beginning, a slate wiped clean.

GRETA TOO THINKING of new beginnings.

Greta gazing out of the small window of her bedchamber, thankful not to be bedded down below with the traders who couldn't afford the luxury of a room of their own. Greta trying to breathe slow and deep, listening to the wind playing through the dried beech leaves gathered in deep heaps about the back wall of the hostelry; leaves resisting decay as others did not. Beech leaves like Ireland, in that respect. The Cause as deep in dead bodies as those dead sweeps of leaves, yet refusing to rot away as if they had never been. Would never entirely go under. Would rise again. Maybe not in her lifetime, and for once she hoped that would be so. She and hers having given up too much to go through it all again so soon after.

And if the Cause was slumbering, if not dead, she would be free, for the time at least.

And knew what she would do with that time.

Once Het Loo was done – whether it went badly or, against the odds, succeeded – she would plant her feet on the road to Bad Salzbaum and seek out Ruan Peat. Ask him the end of the tale about the boy in the hedge and his crate of books. A tale that might be all they had left between them, and might not be enough; the desert stretching from past to present too arduous and arid to afford anything more endearing than stiff politeness. But dear Lord, she was going to give it a try.

And if Ruan would not have her, if there was nothing left on which they could build, she had other options. She had Ivor. Hadn't missed the way he sometimes looked at her. Mightn't be the worse way she could go. Bravery always top of the list of attractions for a woman like Greta. Maybe swan feathers and ermine her way to go after all. Also the added fact he would be able to help Peter, if things went as badly back in England as both she and Peter had assumed.

Had to be a time when she could lay down her sword, lay down her head and rest. Let others carry on what she had spent so long doing, lost so much because of. Had not enough fingers or toes to tally up the people she'd known and liked who had died for the same.

Had to be an end to the reckoning. To spend the rest of her days with a man like Ivor, English as he was, not an option to be dismissed. Remembered those swollen elbows on the railings, the feel of his de-fingered hand upon her arm at Ellewoutsdjik Point when she'd feared they'd been lost and he'd encouraged otherwise. Ivor a good man, with a good heart, and Lord knew, Greta knew, as Hela might have agreed, they were mighty thin on the ground.

Greta didn't close the shutters on the window. Greta lay on her bed, on its over-washed sheets yellowed and frayed at their edges and slightly damp, fixed her eyes on the small square of window. Tried to breathe deep and slow, put herself in step with the wind as it soughed about the corners of the hostelry and nudged through the beech leaves. Tried to sleep, and could not. Spent the night entire imagining what Ruan Peat might look like now, what she might look like to him. Whether he would be able to look on her at all, or meet her eye to eye. Mind drifting off towards early morning, seeing black-backed boulders strewn across dark and raging rivers, as she'd dreamed of before.

This time it was different.

This time there was, on the other side, Ivor Merrill; straight and stalwart, smart and crisp, hair clipped short, holding out his hand.

*Only come, my love, and I will save you.*

IVOR UP AND AWAKE NOT long past dawn, body honed to the light, attuned to the coming of the day. He'd been scrubbed clean of the lice plaguing the camps when he'd been at the Servants during his dying days, and blessed the Servants for their ministrations. Never sleeping so well as he had these past few nights, despite all the desperate worry he would be found inadequate and ill-equipped for the task he was being put to.

Now the time was upon him he felt otherwise, was filled with a fervour akin to jubilance. Everything hanging on a moment, a chance, the serendipity of occupying one particular place on earth or another, to slaughter or be slaughtered.

Not that Ivor ran the risk of slaughter.

Either Ivor inside the gates of Het Loo Palace at Apeldoorn or those gates barred to him.

Success dependant on his plea, on the Abbot's letter, on his own family connection to the Duke of Brunswick, on the vaguer relationship Mick Malloy had with one of the Duke's low-down men, on how well Ivor could convince the gate-holders he was errand boy for John, Earl of Chatham.

He'd been rehearsing the conversation he would have with Greta as they took the last few miles to Het Loo, his light and possibly humorous subject of English Sumptuary laws skewing her attention away from him once he'd donned his finery. Encouraged by the light in Greta's face as she descended the staircase to join everyone else at the breakfast table, and the smile she shone at him.

Greta apparently having no need nor appetite for breakfast, packing away bread, cheese and ham into a square of linen, declaring it time to be off. Het Loo three or four miles away, an hour's tramp. Best time for them to arrive being when all the traders did, which was around the hour of nine. Greta apparently doing her intelligence-gathering the previous night, of which Ivor had been ignorant. Ivor feeling like Chaucer's Chanticleer in his get-up, smart doublet and hose belied by filthy boots and sweat-lined shirt.

Greta's only comment on his new look being:

'You'll do. I've another shirt in my back-pack. We can swap it out with yours when we're almost there so you don't get it all stinked up beforehand. And we'll clean and shine your boots with beeswax blacking.'

Greta sounding remarkably optimistic.

'There is just one other thing,' Greta said, taking from her belt a knife far too sharp and vicious for the mere cutting of bread and cheese. 'Got to say it, Ivor Merrill, but that hair of yours. It's really been getting on my nerves.'

Ivor flinching, and a little thrilled, as Greta came about the table, grabbed his forelock in one hand and slashed it through with her knife before moving on to his pony-tail, sides and back, nicking one of his ears in the process. A lobe that began to bleed down his neck and into his bad shirt.

Some life coming back into Ivor as Greta pinched the wound shut between her fingers, got it slavered with her ointment so the blood didn't disfigure his new doublet.

'Green and purple?' she asked, as she pinched the lobe, waited for the blood to stop. 'Are they really supposed to go together?'

'All the fashion at court,' Ivor answered, encouraged, 'or so the tailor in Amsterdam told me.'

'Think he was just selling off his worst lines,' Greta commented. 'Trust you to have bought them up.'

No despisement in those words, instead a whiff of amusement. Ivor glad for her enjoyment, to see the dimples in her freckly cheeks as she raised a small smile at his obvious ignorance.

'Back in the day, in England, they had these things called Sumptuary Laws,' he started, about to regale her with the idiocy of those laws, make her smile again.

'I don't doubt it,' Greta cut him off. 'But we've a lot more to contend with today than whatever they are.'

Greta casting an anxious glance towards the door of the tavern.

Ivor intuiting of a sudden what she was waiting for, who she was hoping for: Mick Malloy arriving to save the day because he, idiot-headed Merrill, was not up the task. Ivor boiling over with humiliation. Ivor clad in the garb of a botched dragonfly who'd been told his shirt was too dirty, his hair annoying, that even his boots needed smartening up.

He swung round on Greta, recriminatory words bubbling out without forethought, spoken softly so others would not hear, but with a harshness that brought Greta up short.

'You think I don't know that? It's me doing you the favour, not the other way around. So you will not denigrate me, and you will not chide me like a blasted child. You will take me to Het Loo as planned, and I'll do as I've been tasked to do. I'll get in and make my case. Make your blasted case. Because, if you've forgotten it, little Miss Perfect, I'm the only bloody chance you've got.'

Greta putting the last of Ivor's shorn hair into a linen bag, regarding him with admiration for the unexpected outburst and the swearing. Looking him up and down. This the Ivor she'd been musing about the night before. All standing and falling with him, and if he could blag his way into Het Loo.

Servants to save.

Continental System to be avoided at all costs.

Possible recompense to the Irish Cause if he succeeded.

Ivor a possible life-partner if other avenues failed.

Ivor correct to be angry. Greta saying so.

'You're right,' she said, holding up a hand in apology. 'I've a tongue tarter than unripe gooseberries. My mother said it, my brother said it, and Peter has said it more times than I can count. Here, take this as a peace offering.'

Greta handing over the small bag of Ivor's hair.

Ivor angry all over again, feeling as denigrated and chided as he'd ever been.

'Why are you giving me this? What am I supposed to do with it?'

Small frown on Greta's face, puzzled Ivor didn't understand the gift.

'Well it's obvious,' she said. 'You can sell it to a wig-maker. They're always glad of hair, and yours is particularly fine. It'll be a start, maybe give you money enough to get yourself back home, dead as you're supposed to be. Isn't that what you want?'

Oh god, and how Ivor Merrill wanted to laugh. If there was anything in the world she could have done to stymy his rage at her he couldn't think of it. And if there was anything in the world that demarcated his place in it from hers he'd no idea what it could be. That his hair might be a commodity had never crossed his mind. Greta giving it him as a peace-offering and a possible way back home the most ludicrous, the most tender gift ever given him.

'And for the record,' Greta said, as Ivor took his bag of hair with due deference, 'I'm most definitely not perfect.'

*Oh but you are,* Ivor wanted to say. *You're the most perfect person I've ever met.*

Words thought, unsaid. Ivor too ebullient to say anything.

'I know how hard this has been for you,' Greta was not to be stopped in her extended apology. 'So what I'll tell you is this: you, Ivor Merrill, are grand. And grand is what you're doing. What you are about to do.'

Greta coming closer.

Greta taking out the letter from the Abbot, slipping it into the top pocket of his garish doublet. Patting at it once, twice, brushing a hand across his chest, Ivor thrilling at her touch.

'We're in your hands, Captain Ivor Merrill,' said Greta. 'And we're in your debt. I know you'll try your damndest, and that's all we ask of you. No more tellings off, no more lecturing. From here on in, it's all up to you.' Ivor thought his heart might stop. 'And I'll tell you more. See it through and I, Greta Finnerty, will be standing here, right here mark you, to salute you because you're a fine man and a good one, one I'm proud and privileged to call my friend.'

Chanticleer could go flutter about his coop. Ivor Merrill braced his legs, straightened his shoulders, feeling like the most important man in the world.

UNKNOWN TO GRETA OR Ivor, Mick Malloy really was on his way.

Mick not giving a cuss about what had been going on in Bad Salzbaum.

Mick having, by lucky chance, met Professor Ottelius Jorn in the hedges, and Professor Ottelius Jorn telling Mick about the surreptitious goings on in his cellar, of which he assumed Ruan Peat to be a part. That Ruan Peat had been a part in no doubt once Mick and Jorn barged down the steps. Two men about to do in a third being the obvious conclusion. Mick knowing none of them. Mick responding as his battle-boltered body told him to: two against one never being right.

Ruan saved by Mick's intervention and Professor Jorn's timely dealing out of the knout.

Ruan muted, like Hippolyte Gerhard before him, unable to get out a single word of thanks due to the two hairline fractures in his lower mandible.

Mick quick and able at the diagnosis and what should be done. Splint swiftly knocked together from the liberal scatterings of paper on the cellar floor and gutta-percha from one of the pots on the cellar shelves pointed out by Professor Jorn, who knew every canister, every bottle. Of course he did. Professor Jorn distrusting anyone except himself to do a proper inventory at the start of each month, knowing his employees would likely filch something or other. Most probably wine or brandy. A bottle here and there all adding up.

Ruan's jaw held tight, splint tied in place by a leather strop fixed at the back of head and neck.

'No talking, no movement of the jaw, no eating solids,' Mick commanded, having seen these kinds of injuries more times than he'd have liked and knew the way to get them healed. 'It'll take five or six weeks for the fractures to re-bond, and a few more after that before they'll be stable enough for you to chew and speak.'

Ruan hammering impotent fists on the bales.

Ruan needing to say all that needed to be said.

*She's gone! The woman Hela has gone! She's got the Song, and she's got my provenance. She's got to be stopped!*

Alone pen, garden. Kuman feet-sky.

No one listening, no one understanding.

Ruan no artist, as Hippolyte had been.

Ruan trying to demand paper and writing materials. Getting none, until Caro reappeared. Early morning burial of Constantine carried out with haste so it wouldn't interfere with church schedule. Caro afterwards going straight to the cellar, as Ruan had presumed he would and so had stayed there the whole night through, refusing Professor's Jorn's offer to take him to his room in the hotel. Professor Jorn unnaturally solicitous. Professor Jorn parting from the company, shaking the stranger's hand with both his own and giving him his utmost thanks.

*And who on God's earth was this man? This burly squint-eyed rescuer who had arrived so fortuitously? And what had he done with the real Professor Jorn?*

Ruan having a hard time of it. His jaw hurting like the devil despite the splint and the laudanum this doppelganger Professor Jorn had administered with unaccustomed liberality. The squint-eyed man staying the night through, leaving at first hint of dawn.

No point Mick staying on, now Ruan was obviously out of action.

No word of explanation from Mick about who he was or what he was doing here.

Ruan unable to ask questions.

Ruan never more glad to see Caro as Caro first sauntered down the steps and then almost tripped in his rush to get to Ruan as he saw all was not well. Ruan wobbling on his bales of straw, half his face hidden by a leather strop and Ruan obviously frustrated. Caro might only be able to see Ruan's nose and eyes but he'd know that look anywhere; and two men – one of them their prisoner of the previous day – tied up back to back.

Caro quick to Ruan's side.

'What on earth's been going on?' he asked. 'What's happened to you?'

Ruan pointing to his jaw before miming out his need to write, to explain.

Caro quick to understand. Caro soon finding the bottle of ink that had been upturned in the turmoil yet had a few slicks left, enough for a couple of sentences. Found the quill Hela had thrown aside once Ruan had written and signed what she'd needed. Caro scratching up from the cellar's floor a few pages and bringing all to Ruan, along with a hard-backed volume on which he could lean his writing.

*Jaw injured. Hela escaped,* Ruan scribbled furiously. *Ask Mathilde Stoss. Gone with the Song. Has to be stopped.*

Caro reading as Ruan wrote, filling in the blanks left by the less than perfect quill, and immediately departing. Quick dithering on the cellar's steps as several of Mayor Bomberg's men came down to take charge of the prisoners by request of Professor Jorn, hauling the Polovtsy brothers up.

'You are hereby arrested under several charges. Namely that you are escaped POWs. That you perpetrated the theft of valuable books from a citizen of Bad Salzbaum,' Ruan not the only one able to make deductions. Jorn, after he'd left the cellar, totting up all he'd been told in jigs and jags and making his own. 'It is also suspected you are implicated in the death of a fellow POW and were about to perpetrate another murder, had a third party not intervened.'

Third party nowhere to be found.

Mick Malloy off and away, as was Caro.

Caro straight to the mud-baths and Mathilde Stoss.

Mathilde offering Caro two points of salient information: certain she'd seen Hela in the market two weeks previous to her visit to Mathilde, certain too Hela had said she'd found work in a nearby bakery.

Caro narrowing down the options with the perspicuity Ruan had taught him.

Caro finding the relevant market and next the bakery within an hour of Mathilde giving him the information.

Caro told, on arrival at the bakery, that yes, a woman named Hela was employed here, had been for years, maybe six or seven. But no, she wasn't here today because her mother had not long died. Had been given two days leave because of it. And no, no one knew where she lived. Only that she wasn't from here, was Norwegian, learned her German from some sailors who'd once been stranded near her home.

So, Hela lying to Mathilde.

Hela here all the time, probably with the Polovtsy brothers who'd been on the run since their escape from the POW camp seven years before.

Spines and tangles.

No one ever finding her house, nor that of the brothers – assuming they were one and the same. Polovtsy brothers never giving the information up.

The home-owner, once the monthly rent-day was well over-due, going to investigate. Finding the small cottage dusty and abandoned, littered with dictates declaring the need for Hungarian Independence, which she immediately consigned to the flames. Finding too – rather oddly, in her opinion – an old cape in a chest sequestered beneath the main bed; a cape thin and mouldy, fringed about its edges by the ears of what might have been rabbits. Who was she was to know? Either way, she found it disgusting and it went swiftly onto the flames fired up by all that revolutionary claptrap she had no truck with.

No interest in town news; no knowledge of the discovery of the body in the hedge, nor the arrest of the Hungarian POWs in connection to it.

Most puzzling for her was why her beloved grandfather's clock was closed up inside a cupboard.

Lifting it out.

Setting it again on the mantle above the fire roaring below with Hela's cape.

Not that Hela would ever know it.

Nor would anyone.

Hela far away by the time anyone came looking for her.

Hela feet sky.

Hela Kuman feet sky.

Hela as free as she'd ever been, mission not forgotten.

Hela heading to Hungary and the Polovtsy homeland.

Hela finding the way not so hard now she was so much older and so much better at avoiding the avoiding the traps the men she passed tried to shove her into. Hela having a number of 50 stuiver silver coins, bearing the portrait of Louis/Lodewijk, sewn into the seams of her skirts. Hela, throughout these years spent in Bad Salzbaum, always keeping a small portion of her wages for herself, amassing and saving, knowing no man was ever to be fully trusted, might need the means one day to take her own path. And that day was now.

Hela, aided by her scrimped-for stuivers, reaching the Polovtsy strongholds in the Valley of the Pretty Lady in late Spring of 1810, welcomed in once her story had been told. Hand-wringing and keening as the capture of Zsolt and Mokush was learned of. Two martyrs to the cause instead of the one she and Zsolt had assumed might be needed. No matter to her. Such was the way of the world. The bad world she'd escaped in Norway, and the better one she'd found since Håkon had set her feet on a new path, given her purpose, assured her she would be a hero, have songs sung about her. A woman who held the liberation of the Polovtsy clan in her hands, and who might, because of it, be able to divert the Russian wolf from the doors of Norway.

A mission mighty and magisterial.

A mission making of her a woman admired and fêted, feasts held in her honour as she went from one Polovtsy household to another where the Song was reverentially read out loud by the best of their story tellers. Song of Igor disseminated and celebrated wherever it went. Seeds sewn, plants slow to grow, nevertheless getting stronger throughout the passing years.

Hela aged and old by 1847 when the Kumans - when Hungary - finally roused themselves in anger, united under Lajos Kossuth who headed their need and will for independence from Russian hold. Hela still alive in March 1848 when the poet Sándor Petőfi read his Twelve Points for Liberal Reform from the steps of the National Museum, and next ran through the crowds shouting out his newly composed National Song:

*On your feet, Magyar, our homeland calls!*
*The time is here – now or never!*
*Is it to be slavery or freedom?*
*Make your choice.*
*Take the oath to be slaves no more!*

A single man, a single song, sparking off the Hungarian Uprising: the gathered masses surging from the square on his heels, pouring through the streets and across the river to Buda, rallying before the Imperial Council who cowered in the face of this foot-stamping, song-singing rebellion, and conceded. Signed the Twelve Points, abolished censorship, freed political prisoners. Poured fire onto the cause.

Polovtsy clan Petőfi's staunchest supporters, for they knew the power of a song; Polovtsy clan standing in line behind one old poet and one new, behind the author of their Song and now of Sándor Petőfi's too for if his could unleash a rebellion of this magnitude then so too could theirs.

Magyars first, Polovtsy clan's sure to follow.

*Alone pen, garden Kuman.*

1848 a year of uproar all over Europe.

Hela dying happy in the lap of the Polovtsys that Autumn. Hela a hero, as Mathilde Stoss had been before her, believing their rebellion won. And songs already sung about her and her part in their rebellion.

Hela not alive to see that rebellion spilling over into 1849, when the last battle of their uprising would be enacted.

The date: 31$^{st}$ July 1849.

The place: Segesvár.

The players: Hungarian Revolutionary Army, men of the Polovtsy clan amongst them, augmented by Polish volunteers, coming up against the Russian V Corps and the Austrians. Emperor Franz Joseph in alliance with Tsar Alexander II, the latter offering 200,000 soldiers in support, from one Emperor to another.

Outcome: Russians proving the worst of enemies – as Hela, Håkon and the Polovtsys had always known them to be - driving the Hungarian Revolutionary Army back to Fehéregyháza in defeat.

Kuman red feet all over again.

Sándor Petőfi presumed dead, his body never found. Rumours abounding that he was one of the two thousand Hungarian POWs marched off to Siberia by the hated Russians.

Polovtsy clan vociferous in that hope, eagerly promulgating Sándor Petőfi's new style of nationalistic poetry that turned Hungarian literature on its head and far outlived its author, as their Song had far outlived its own.

Song of Igor not lost.

Song of Igor like the beech leaves outside Greta's dark-night window: dried and fallen, apparently dead, yet refusing to rot back into the ground from whence it came.

*Slovo bottom booming.*

*Furrows furrows.*

Quite.

Well done Hippolyte.

You got it exactly right.

Although it took a long time coming.

# 34

## Het Loo Staggers, Amazes And Disgusts

ONE HOUR'S WALK FROM their hostelry to the outer edges of Het Loo.

One hour, during which neither Greta nor Ivor spoke.

Greta no longer looking out for Mick, confidence instead in this new Ivor Merrill who had finally boiled over, shouted out, complained and sworn. Her kind of man. Greta's morning turning on its heel from shallow dawn to full blown day as they approached Het Loo. Discovered it to be entirely other than she'd expected: a palace enormous, stubbily squared artful buildings an intimidating monster in the distance, fortified on every side by vast hedges, soldiers bristling at every turn.

Stomach turning over.

Stomach lurching.

'Seem to recall you telling me this was some kind of hunting lodge,' she said to Ivor. Ivor buoyed up. Ivor knowing it to be so. Greta obviously never having listened to his history of the place, as he'd thought at the time.

'Hunting Lodge originally, palace now,' he explained succinctly. 'Point me to the tradesman's entrance and I swear to you, Greta, I'll get myself in.'

Greta not needing to point it out for it was obvious: a stream of carts and their incumbents coming in from another track to their right. Traders arriving not only from their direction but from Deventer and the border towns, including Bad Salzbaum from where the palace of Het Loo got all their flour. Bad Salzbaum a prayer on all their lips. Bad Salzbaum their imposed King Louis's favourite place: hedges, mazes, topiary, mills, spas, and now mud-baths too. His courtiers couldn't shut up about the place they'd so recently returned from.

Ivor astonished when Greta quickly kissed him on the lips before he parted from her.

'You'll do grand,' she said. 'I believe it, I know it.'

Words he couldn't stop repeating in his head as he jiggled himself into the mix of traders.

Ivor listening and absorbing.

Ivor's missing fingers tingling, tapping out their own tunes.

Ivor letting them do what those phantom fingers had been doing ever since they'd been blown off and dispersed on the battlefields of Spain.

*Here's the way,* they told Ivor. *Follow and we'll take you with us, and you'll do grand. She believes in you, and so do we.*

Ivor knowing it was all in his head, his missing fingers not rational beings independent of himself, and yet Ivor following their orders. *This way on, and here's the way. You'll do grand.*

Ivor reaching the gate, piling up with all the other folk wanting into Het Loo.

Ivor squaring himself, Ivor on the cusp. Ivor getting the words lined up his head.

Do or die.

Missing fingers fidgeting as they waited in line, listening to each of the preceding petitions before they had their turn.

'We're here with the broadsheets from Deventer.'

'I've a load of sweet chestnuts your cooks will be mighty interested in.'

On and on. Ivor and his fingers finally getting to the head of the queue.

Ivor ready, straight-backed and imposing. *Come on Ivor, I believe in you.*

'I'm here by order of John, Earl of Chatham, and the English army,' he stated, 'who have recently departed Dutch soil. I've an urgent message for the Duke of Brunswick and King Louis. And God help you, and all of England and Holland, if you do not let me pass.'

Ivor in, after the merest twitch.

Greta watching from her standpoint, eye-glass pinned on the queue, seeing a dead man passing through the outer gates. Greta tracking the mismatch of green and purple as Ivor gained too the inner gate, and then another and not the tradesman's door. Ivor escorted through a far grander entrance, after which he was lost from her view.

*He did it,* she whispered. *He really did it.*

So concentrated on Ivor Merrill's progress into the disgustingly luxurious palace that was Het Loo she let down her guard, neglected to inspect her environs with any regularity, allowed someone to creep up on her without her knowledge. Large hand falling on her shoulder so unexpectedly she barely had time to whip out her knife to confront her assailant.

'Well hello to you too!' Mick Malloy grabbing her wrist, knife blade a wisp from his throat.

'Mick!' Greta laughed with relief. 'You made it! You're alive!'

Arms about his waist, swift brush of her lips at a painfully bristly cheek in her palpable relief.

'Seems rising from the dead is what I do,' he commented, as Greta released him. 'And our other resurrectionist?'

Motioning to Het Loo. A little nervous, but Greta being here a good sign. And Greta's dimpled smile an even better one.

'He's in,' she said. 'He's in, Mick. He really did it.'

IN BAD SALZBAUM, THERE were a lot of explanations on the go.

Hela hadn't been found and the Polovtsy brothers wouldn't talk of her. Certainly not Zsolt, who'd fared far worse than Ruan at the application of his own knout in the lilied hands of Professor Jorn. Nose bones thoroughly splintered, as were those of his left cheek; nose swelling, closing itself up so he could only breathe through his mouth; cheek bones refusing to bond. Still shifting, a week later, as he lay on his paltry and filthy prison pallet, lips begging for help, for Hela and for Hungary. None of which came his way. One or two nose splinters drifting from their moorings by his laborious mouth-breathing, slipping into his gullet, and no hope for Zsolt from there on in. Zsolt coughing and choking. Mokush streaming a river by his side, holding his brother's hand as Zsolt spasmed and fought, kicked and struggled, raged against an opponent he could not best. Splinters digging deeper into his lungs, airways bleeding and swelling, closing down.

Not much hope for Mokush either.

POW charges not dropped, despite Mokush freely admitting they'd filtered into their ranks for convenience, as Ruan had surmised; for why would anyone believe him?

Rest of the story coming first from Ruan, later acknowledged by Mokush who fine-tuned it here and there. Mokush acquiescent now his brother had died so dismally. Only piece of information he refused to give up being where the three of them had been holed up these past seven years. Mokush protecting the Song to the last, owing his brother and his clan that much at least.

Bitter admiration for Hela, who'd had the foresight to take with her both Song and provenance when she realised the cellar had been broached. Bitter admiration too that she'd obviously found a way out, choosing to abandon both himself and Zsolt in favour of saving her own skin. And saving too the Song. And absolutely certain she would not abandon it as she had abandoned them, that she would get it to their homeland however she could.

Last thing she needed was for their cottage to be discovered, not with all Zsolt's patriotic literature littering its every surface, detailing where she was heading, where the heartland of the Polovtsy clan lay. Wouldn't take much to pinpoint then where she was heading, and wouldn't take too much thereafter to stop her in her tracks.

No.

A source of frustration to his interrogators who couldn't understand his reticence, not as Mokush did. For who knew what Hela and the Song might achieve once they hit home. Maybe everything Håkon had foretold.

Had to be a chance of it.

Had to be.

Mokush convicted without much thought: escaped POW; attempted homicide of one Ruan Peat – book-finder from Deventer; Mokush a man who, by his larceny, greed and indifference, had indirectly caused the death of young Constantine Honoré.

Constantine Honoré a scrap of a boy snatched up by General Moreau's forces as Moreau led the French Army over the Rhine in 1801 in need of extra bodies. Constantine in service to Moreau until the Prussians overran Hanover and captured the small French unit encamped there, which had included Constantine.

Everything changing thereafter, as the Prussians shifted allegiance.

All this discovered by Ruan and Caro, who would not let lie the fact of an unknown boy dying within a hedge. Did for the boy as they did for books, finding out all they could.

Thomas Campbell, take a bow.

*Silence deep as death, as the oldest held their breath.*

Battle of Copenhagen in 1801 the heart of what had happened to Constantine Honoré.

Prussians all against the French until the English attacked the Danish Fleet in Copenhagen's harbour and forced Denmark's retreat from the Northern Convention, thereby forcing Prussia's hand to uprise against the English, realign themselves, consort with the French against a common enemy.

French POWs therefore needing ditching. Bad Salzbaum deemed as good a place as any to drop the lot of them off, Bad Salzbaum being partway German, partway Dutch, and not so far from French borders. Let Bad Salzbaum do with them what they would.

History heave-hoing onwards as always, without regard for those snatched up here and deposited there. Wherever was handy.

A salt hedge not so handy – everyone agreed on that point.

A salt hedge partially laid an awful place to hide, dismal and dumose - everyone agreed on that point too.

Some difficulty understanding the why of it, why Constantine Honoré would have seen it as his only way out of a situation he'd been forced into. Ruan doing his best to explain the circumstances, would have shouted them out to the judiciary if he'd been able.

*Furrows furrows!*

*Slovo bottom booming!*

*A single book, a single song, able to change the course of history!*

Wrote down all he knew, all that Mokush had agreed to be the case: everything from the discovery of the manuscript in Kupyansk, up country from the Donets River; how it had been suppressed and later stolen. Made its way from Russia to Norway and from Norway to Deventer, and from Deventer to Bad Salzbaum, and was probably at this very moment on its way to Hungary in the hands of the mysterious woman named Hela.

Ruan's reasoned arguments treated with derision.

*For the sake of a book?*

Everyone found it ridiculous.

*And not even a proper book, merely some old song written about some old battle no one has ever heard of?*

Constantine, if he'd truly died to stop it getting into the wrong hands, which Ruan, Fabian and Frau Dieter certainly believed, cast as a fool.

Ruan a fantasist.

Hela a nobody who'd worked in a bakery, unmissed and unmourned when she'd disappeared.

Mokush, when asked, shrugging his shoulders.

*We just escaped and thieved a load of books,* was all he would admit to, *and it got a bit out of hand.*

Which was all Bad Salzbaum needed to hear.

No complicated back-stories for them.

Everything to go on as normal.

Mokush Polovtsy forgotten, sentenced to twenty years hard labour he might or might not see the end of.

Constantine too forgotten by most, except as a salacious foot-note brought up at every subsequent hedge laying. Never forgotten by Frau Dieter or Fabian. Frau Dieter bringing out his amulet from her Christmas box and threading it on a silver chain worn every day. Might have worn it every night had those nights not soon become shared with Fabian Guichot.

Bad Salzbaum scandalised by this acquaintance, her accountancy firm taking a nose-dive. Not that she cared, turnover from the mud-baths enough to see her through.

Unaccountably the spa hotel, meaning Professor Jorn, stubbornly retained her services, leading to a gradual increase of business given his stamp of approval, and because there really was no adequate alternative. She might be a woman, yet apparently could tot up sums and ledgers like no one else the stuffy coterie of the Great Men of Bad Salzbaum knew.

Frau Dieter wondering why Professor Jorn had stuck by her. Wondering too why he'd so suddenly ditched his garish cravats and his top hat, had her re-draught the contracts presented to his employees to be far more favourable than they had previously been.

*Dark nights of the soul,* young Caro had said to her. *Everyone has them.*

*I will be a better man, if only you will save me.*

Frau Dieter employing Ruan to do a little digging into Professor's Jorn's dark night, which hadn't taken long.

Jorn at the University of Reims Champagne-Ardenne from 1788 to 1792.

1792 the year of the First French Terror, his fellow students dragged from their rooms into the streets, battered and hammered. Not a one of them getting out alive.

Except Jorn, who must have escaped by the merest sliver of the skin of his teeth.

Well, she thought. That would do it.

Jorn not entirely changing overnight from one personality into another.

Jorn still the pernickety pen-pusher he'd always been, still the only one he trusted to do his monthly cellar inventory, still seeking the approval of the mayor and his little cohort of stiff-collared, stiff-minded business men who ran the town.

Subtle changes only as he tried and fought to be a better man, which went against the grain he had so assiduously stuck to since Reims. And yet tried and fought he had, and got there step by step.

Ottelius Jorn spending many nights sitting on a little camping stool listening to the newly installed water organ by the side of the lett, entirely alone, entirely absorbed. Ottelius Jorn spending later nights on the moon-viewing platform gazing through one of the provided telescopes, finding a dim relief in the pale placid face swinging so high above the earth, so removed from all the turmoil men seemed unable to stop themselves repeating and regurgitating in ever newer and more awful forms with every generation.

Ottelius Jorn only once unburdening himself to - of all people - Holger Stoss.

Holger too finding refuge in the ethereal unworldly music of the water-organ, who went out on occasion, when his duties permitted, sat and listened, especially if his day had been more confusing than the one before.

A dark and frigid night in November, hedges sparkling with frost, frozen spider-webs and precipitate.

Water of the lett sleek and black, mirroring the moon and a few glister-edged clouds.

A full year on from the main events that had shifted both their lives from one course to another.

Holger spotting Professor Jorn. About to turn tail, speed back to the mud-baths and Mathilde. Professor Jorn spotting him first, asking him not to go on his account. The two sitting side by side for a few long and uncomfortable minutes as the water turned the organ's wheels and the organ sang.

'I'm not a real Professor,' Jorn spoke into the darkness. 'Might have been, but never was.'

'Me neither,' came Holger Stoss's reply. Professor Jorn smiling, which he rarely did.

'What's it like for you now?' Jorn asked. 'Are you... content?'

*Is there anything I can do for you? What's it like to be losing your mind?*

Holger taking a few minutes to answer. Took him a long while these days to process what was being asked of him. Fine when he was doing what he knew, which was his duties at the mud-baths. Completely at sea when having at something new.

Professor Jorn startled when Holger Stoss came back to life unexpectedly and pointed up into the sky, which was dark as the night surrounding them and wheeled over with an immensity of stars.

'Ever heard of the Dog Days?' Holger asked. Jorn murmuring that no, no he had not.

'See that?' Holger said, Jorn following Holger Stoss's hard-working calloused finger so unlike his own. 'That there's Sirius, brightest star in the night sky, in the constellation Canis Majoris.'

Professor Jorn seeing it, unsettled. Couldn't see how Holger – whose head everyone knew was starting to scramble like eggs in a pan – could still have access to such knowledge.

Holger going on.

Holger explaining.

'Used to know all sorts when I was young,' Holger explained. 'Used to know all them constellations back when I was a sailor and went from one sea to another and back again. Did I ever tell you about when I met my Mathilde?'

Jorn sent off course, for how could he know such a thing? A slight startlement Holger had ever been a sailor. Had presumed Holger had always been here, and now – since Frau Dieter's intervention – always would.

'Point is,' Holger rambled on, 'is that Sirius is always what we sailors fall back on when we're navigating. Brightest star. Easiest to see, wherever you are. And when I crawled out over the ice, after our boat had been crushed, I could see it clear as I'm seeing it now. And it was right over Mathilde's house. Right over. Didn't realise it till ages after.'

Professor Jorn not seeing the point, excusing Holger nonetheless, wondering about his story of boats crushed and the crawling out over the ice and whether this had truly happened, or if Holger's diseased mind had dreamed it all up. An idea dismissed as Holger went on.

'Point is,' Holger began again, 'that once I met Mathilde she became my Sirius, and she's remained my Sirius ever since. And I've been thinking, and I know my head's a mess, but what I've been thinking is this. Who is your Sirius, Mr. Non-Professor? I know I'm a bag of marbles been shook around, but since I've been away from the hedges and in the mud-baths, stuff has cleared a bit. You did me a favour there. Don't have to wake up every morning looking them in the eye. Don't have them constantly poking me here and there where I don't want to go.'

Jorn silent. This the longest, in fact the only, conversation he'd had with Holger Stoss.

Jorn thinking that maybe he'd missed out. Would maybe gain more from being in the company of Holger Stoss than cosying up to the mayor and his crew who only ever talked money and how to make more of it. Profundity then, for who was his Sirius? Jorn not sure he'd ever had one. He'd looked up to his betters in Reims, although was never truly guided by them to better safer places. Quite the opposite. Stick with them and it would have been the worst place imaginable he'd have gone. Certainly he admired his father for building up the hotel and its hedges, teaching him the trade when he'd returned bowed and beaten from the ravages of France. Yet, truthfully, his only Sirius had been his own pretentious self, which surely wasn't what Holger had meant.

'The Dog Days,' Jorn asked. 'What are they? You didn't say.'

Holger letting out a small laugh.

'Sorry, Professor,' old habits dying hard. 'I needs a bit of prompting these days. They're the hottest days of Summer, the burning month we nearly always get. Called Dog Days because Sirius comes into ascendancy at the exact same time. All the old astronomers knew it, as do all navigators.'

'And you used to be a navigator?' Jorn was interested. When he got back to his study he was going to look all this up. Never so intellectually spurred on since he'd been in France.

Holger laughing softly again, and the water-organ rendering a quicker lighter tune as an otter skelped out of the water and ran along the opposite bank before slipping back in again, sending a faint ripple over the moon's pellucid reflection.

'All sailors are navigators,' Holger informed the non-professor, 'as is everyone, in their own way. And everyone needs their Sirius, if they're to find their right direction.'

Holger finding his, by the merest chance, in Mathilde.

Frau Dieter finding hers, by the merest chance, in Fabian Guichot and Fabian Guichot, by the merest chance, in her.

A possibility that would have remained a possibility if Constantine hadn't gone missing, and if Constantine had never been found.

A result Constantine would have been proud of, and with that both Frau Dieter and Fabian Guichot had to be content.

Ottelius Jorn too become at peace, in his own way. Ottelius Jorn trying to stand up to his part of the bargain made in the hedges and become a better man. Holger helping. Professor Jorn meeting up with Holger every now and then, on dark nights when no one else was abroad. Never by arrangement, each gladdened when it happened.

Professor Jorn telling Holger about his sojourn in Reims, how he'd smudged through the greatest revolution Europe had ever seen, how it had so swiftly caught him up when least expected. How close he'd been to dying for no other reason than not being French. How he'd met the devil, who was no devil, in the salt hedges.

Holger talking about his old young days, days clear and bright in his mind when others had become dark and precarious. Telling the Professor about the storms that had whipped his boat up onto the cusps of waves tall as the spa hotel, before flinging them down into the depths; the heart-thumping exhilaration of survival each time they were churned up and back and the boat tipped and dipped beneath the waves before resurfacing.

Telling Professor Jorn of a singular catch of cod netted up from the depths of the Baltic having one fish in amongst the rest no one had ever seen before, glistening red and green and was fully the length of a man. How they'd picked it out and let it go after a brief wrangle with the cook who had wanted to see what it tasted like.

Of another time when they'd come across the gelatinised corpse of a squid which could have spread its tentacles about their entire boat and still had length to spare.

Professor Jorn captivated most of all when Holger spoke of Norway, of his shipwreck, of his rescue, of his meeting Mathilde, of that strange and alien place called Vettie's Giel and the Hill of Torghatten pierced through the one side from the other.

'Oh it were an odd place,' Holger would say. 'Gave me the shivers just to look on it. Mathilde's folk told me it were a gateway from one world to another, if you'd the mind to make it so. A gateway you could pass into and away, or else couldn't hold your nerve and back you came, and back with you came the trolls that wouldn't let you alone your whole life through.'

Holger, on one occasion, saying something more about Vettie's Giel.

Holger talking about his wedding to Mathilde, which he'd told Professor Jorn about many times before. Jorn not minding; Jorn finding his and Holger's nights together comforting as they both repeated their old tales, each time with some variance, some detail added only newly remembered. Like maybe families did, Jorn surmised, when they met up at weddings and funerals, Christmas and christenings. An odd thought for he and Holger to have become family, and yet undoubtedly it was what they'd evolved into on these moonlit organ-singing nights that were theirs alone and no one else's.

'They had a saying,' Holger recalled, 'those folk of Vettie's Giel. They were that cut off, could only be reached by a fearsome bridge what swayed like buggery when you stepped onto it, and took some nerve to get across, I can tell you. Great chasm below, with harsh sharp cliffs and water looking like it were boiling, and its best day was going to be when you mistook a step and tumbled in and it got to boil you right up with it.'

Holger shaking his head, remembering.

Mathilde oh so right to believe that getting Holger's memory on another tack, on a better track, on the days and places he remembered best, would do him well. Curious and perplexed when she'd seen Holger creeping out along the lett after they'd finished their duties at the mud-baths, Holger returning calmer and clearer than he'd been for years. Mathilde following on a couple of occasions, witnessing the mismatch of her husband talking quietly with the stooped form of Professor Jorn camped up on his little stool and her Holger haunched down beside him on the grass.

'This is what they used to say,' she heard Holger telling Ottelius Jorn on the second of those occasions, 'those folk in Vettie's Giel...'

Mathilde having more ears than Hela's shawl as she crouched right down so she couldn't be seen.

'...they used to say,' Holger went on, 'that if you're going to die in the Winter months then you'd best get your own bones down to Bergenstift beforehand, because no one else was going to do it for you.'

Short silence following.

Mathilde holding her breath, no idea where this was going.

'I don't understand,' Professor Jorn said for them both into the darkness. 'What does that mean?'

Holger laughing quietly, and Mathilde hadn't heard Holger laughing for years.

'It means, Mr. Non-Professor,' Holger's short-term memory sporadic, not entirely lost, 'that we're all responsible for ourselves. And you and me, we're not so different. We're both on our way down to Bergenstift. Just got to figure our best way there.'

Bergenstift on Professor Jorn's mind ever since that weird conversation by the lett, compounded by the earlier one about Dog Days and Sirius and the need to find your star.

Professor Jorn quitting his service temporarily a few months afterwards, handing over the running of the spa hotel to his middle-managers the moment he'd been assured Frau Dieter and Fabian Guichot would be in ultimate charge.

'Of course we'll look after everything,' Frau Dieter had said, when he'd asked of her the duty. 'But where are you going? What do you mean to do?'

'I'm going to do what Holger told me to,' he said to her. 'I'm going to get my bones down to Bergenstift before it's too late.'

Frau Dieter not understanding.

Who was this man?

How had he changed from an uptight bureaucrat into a restless heel-kicker who needed to move on?

'Can I ask you something personal?' Professor Jorn had gone on, Frau Dieter straightening her shoulders, raising her chin, certain he was going to ask about Fabian. Which wasn't what he'd asked at all.

'That amulet you wear,' he said. 'What does it mean? Is it supposed to protect you from, or remind you, of something?'

Oh, how to get that explained.

Frau Dieter briefly angered he'd not followed enough of the trial of Mokush, and Ruan Peat's extended testimony during it, to not know what it was. And then surprised he'd even noticed it. Usually the amulet was tucked away within the confines of her dress. Only for a few short days at Christmas did she ever wear it loose and visible, in remembrance of Constantine and the foresight he'd apparently divined, given how she and Fabian had ended up together. A significance she and Fabian treasured.

*It's the sun and the moon, which means Jacob and his wife and their twelve children, the twelve tribes of Israel. The sun being you, Frau Dieter, and Fabian the moon, and us POWs all the stars you've gathered around you.*

Frau Dieter pulling at the silver chain, bringing the small amulet out.

'Sun and moon,' she answered, giving the short version, 'and all the stars they gather about them. A gift from Constantine. A Christmas present. A reminder that those in authority have a duty to look after those who are in their service, as the POWs were in mine.'

Professor Jorn bound to take her statement as a criticism of his harsh treatment of Holger and Mathilde Stoss, never mind his later retraction and the redrafted contracts given to all his other employees.

'The boy Constantine made this?'

Jorn's study of the amulet disturbing, given how it lay nestled and exposed between Frau Dieter's breasts. More disturbing still when he asked: 'Do you mind?' and put out a hand to touch it. Frau Dieter swiftly unclasping the silver chain from about her neck, handing the amulet over to the Professor's long pen-pushing fingers.

'He really made this,' Professor Jorn stated, running his lily-white, lily-soft fingertips over its curves and indentations. 'Sun, moon and stars,' he murmured. 'And he made one for you and another for himself?'

Frau Dieter hesitated, only for a moment, before correcting him. No harm in anyone knowing the truth now.

'And one for Fabian,' she said.

'And one for Fabian,' Jorn repeated.

Memories strong and vivid of being in the cellar, of his instant dismissal of the hedge-man as being of no consequence. The scorn and impatience he'd exhibited. His only concern back then being for the book-finders to poke through the chest and find something of value. Such shame at his complete abnegation of the fact that right there before him had lain a man, a boy, who'd heart and skill enough to whittle such a thing out of wood for his protectors.

Protection they'd been unable to provide.

Making it all the worse for Professor Jorn to realise he'd been privy to certain facts – via his connections to the mayor and thereby to the courts – never made public. Namely the documents Ruan Peat had provided. Glossed over and ignored during the trial of Mokush Polovtsy, his brother Zsolt by then already deceased.

'It was a travesty, that trial,' he said quietly. 'And I'm truly sorry your lad Constantine didn't come out of it better.'

Frau Dieter feeling that old familiar knot in her stomach to think on it.

'He was a hero,' she managed to get out. 'He was trying to do what was right.'

Professor Jorn let out a breath.

'I know it now. God forgive me, I didn't know it then.'

Everything Ruan had shown him, everything Ruan had laid out before him: here the provenance, here the reason, here the deposition of what the book expert Hippolyte Gerhard had told Ruan back in Deventer; here the letter Ruan had from the archivists in Russia. Everything had Ruan shown Professor Jorn in the expectation, the hope, of Jorn speaking up when Ruan could not. And Jorn had not. Jorn had taken the advice of the mayor, or rather the threats: *Speak out and you will not be considered one of ours. Do this and you will be ostracized. We need – Bad Salzbaum needs - quick and decisive judgment. The rest can look after itself.*

The Professor Jorn of that time believing him, letting all lie. For who – when it came down to tacks and financial rivets - gave a damn about the death of an escaped POW deemed of no more worth than the horse-shit you might step in on every single street of Bad Salzbaum? No one, was the answer to that. No one except Frau Dieter, the oddly talking Fabian Guichot, and the book-finders from Deventer – one of whom had had his jaw fractured in two places and couldn't speak on his own behalf. People who, sad to say, didn't count as far as the Bad Salzbaum judiciary, the mayor and his tight little bunch of associates, were concerned. Including Ottelius Jorn.

A travesty of a trial.

One Professor Jorn wished he'd turned from travesty into truth. A time long gone. Spring season now, almost eighteen months since all had been done and dusted.

The plea, the oath, he'd made in the hedges not yet acted upon. Too cowardly a man back then to pursue it. Not so cowardly a man now. A man who had become, since his meeting with his devil in the hedges, no longer afraid to look upon his past. A man who no longer directed his gaze at the mirror on the spa hotel's stairs to check how suave, how business-like he looked. A man who could no longer bear to look into that mirror at all.

And now, eighteen months later - after talking to Holger Stoss, and absorbing into his petrified soul all he had learned about Constantine Honoré, who had lain down his life to stop another revolution as bad as the one Professor had had first-hand experience of in France - a man who had decided his only goal in life, apart from being a better man, was to get to Norway, to Vettie's Giel. See for himself that mountain punched through from one side to the other like nowhere else in the world.

And suddenly Frau Dieter's hands went about his neck, clasped there the silver chain.

'This is for you, for your travels,' she stated, standing back, admiring what she'd strung. 'You were right. It's both protector and reminder. Carry it with you and Constantine will be with you too, and no better person than he to have as your companion.'

Jorn almost crying, realising the enormity of the gift as he could never have done a bare year before.

'Thank you,' he got out. 'I can't think of anything anyone has ever given me so meaningful.'

Meaning every word.

Frau Dieter almost blubbing too, had not Frau Dieter been made of sterner stuff. Frau Dieter merely patting the amulet as it lay on Professor's Jorn's chest.

'He'll do you right, make sure you don't bring back any trolls when you return.'

JORN TAKING HER WORDS with him as he travelled.

How Frau Dieter knew of Holger Stoss's tale about Torghatten Hill, Jorn didn't know; but travel to Vettie's Giel he did: stepped out over the wavering bridge of turf and birch, heart in his mouth, hand on Constantine's amulet as the water churned with menace beneath him exactly as Holger had described; climbed the bird-leg path, braced his back against the rock as he traversed the skinniest parts of it, lay down on his stomach to drag his bag with him on others. Never so frightened since he'd been in France, and never so exhilarated.

Reached the village, skirted it quietly before descending the cliff, crossing over to Torget Island on a flimsy fishing boat borrowed from the several moored on shore. Got over the water, began to climb, pulled himself up the vague access path by his fingertips, pushed himself on with feet and knees. Crawled into the hole, which had to be five hundred feet in length if it was an inch. Walked to the middle and sat in the pierced mountain the whole night through, and not one night but two.

Folk on land seeing him go, shaking their heads - bemused, and a little irritated he'd taken one of their boats without asking - wondering what kind of noodlehead had come into their midst uninvited.

Only one man greeting him on his re-emergence as he rowed back to the mainland: a crook-backed man who invited Jorn into his meagre home, gave him food and water, asked what he'd found whilst he was there, what the mountain had told him. Jorn clutching at Constantine's amulet as he told the stranger he wasn't sure the mountain had told him anything at all.

'It never does,' replied Håkon Tryggvason. 'It's merely a hill with a hole in it. Trick is to make everyone else believe otherwise.'

Håkon Tryggvason well versed in the ploy.

Håkon Tryggvason practically having invented it.

Håkon Tryggvason knowing the only reason he'd sat his own vigil was because he'd wanted away. Couldn't stick Vettie's Giel one moment longer. Needed the time to think his way out of it.

Håkon Tryggvason agog when Ottelius Jorn began to speak of all that had brought him here to Vettie's Giel from Bad Salzbaum – Bad Salzbaum! Håkon could hardly believe his ears - about the boy found in the hedge with his crate of books, the book-finders Jorn had employed who'd overturned his veniality and discovered the real story behind the wood-whittling boy Constantine, the how of and why he had gone into the hedge.

'Which was what?' Håkon couldn't stop the words forming on his lips, couldn't prevent himself from leaning forward, eyes glinting in the bright sun of an early Summer's eve.

'It's the strangest tale,' Ottelius Jorn tried to get all the pieces together. 'It all began with a song...'

And so he went on to tell all he knew: the discovery of the Song of Igor's Campaign, its theft, its arrival in Deventer, the tragedy that had befallen Hippolyte Gerhard.

Håkon having to place his hands between his thighs to keep them from shaking, having difficulty restraining himself from not breaking into Jorn's every second sentence to pump him for particulars. He'd presumed, after the idiot

Polovtsy brothers had managed to lose the cache of books recovered in Bad Salzbaum, that all was over, their noble cause come to a premature end. And it had been a noble cause. Admittedly he'd expected a generous reward from the Polovtsy clan once the Song was in their hands, which was only right and proper given he was the originator of the whole plot. And he'd written a few times in the years following the crate's disappearance, but after wading through several of Zsolt's ramblingly patriotic replies he'd ceased communications, believing it futile to continue.

He should have believed.

Should have trusted in Hela, if not in the damned Polovtsy brothers, for she had a thirst in her desperate to be slaked for a different kind of life, and could never have returned to Vettie's Giel as he had done.

'The upshot of it was,' Ottelius Jorn was saying, 'those Hungarian brothers were on the brink of murdering one of my book-finders, until the strangest thing happened...'

*Oh for pity's sake!* Håkon wanted to shout out. *Just get on with it!*

Ottelius Jorn heading off on a diversion about meeting the devil who was apparently the saving of his soul, or at least the start of it, not that Håkon cared a whit about Ottelius Jorn's soul.

'Which was when we went to the cellar, and knew something was amiss...'

Ottelius Jorn enjoying the apparent frisson his story was engendering in his single listener, who kept his eyes fixed on his with unnerving intensity. Jorn carrying on, emphasizing the mythic intervention of the stranger he'd encountered in the hedges, minimizing his own intervention with the knout.

'And so we caught them,' Jorn ended. 'The two brothers arrested and charged, although only one survived to attend trial.'

And of that trial he was not going to mention a single word, given how deleterious and negligent had been his own conduct during the whole of it.

And of that trial Håkon did not ask.

Håkon letting out a long breath.

'And the woman Hela? The brothers' companion? What became of her?'

Last snatch at the straw of hope.

Håkon barely able to breathe while he waited for the answer, body taut and sprung, a violin string wound so tight it would only shriek and scream if struck by its bow.

Ottelius Jorn rubbing slowly at his nose, caught off guard, for had he ever mentioned the woman's name? He didn't think so. He'd pretty much swept her out of the story, women never prominent in his world except latterly - in the form of Frau Dieter. What he did know were Ruan's suspicions regarding the woman the Polovtsy brothers were somehow connected to: where she would be going, what she was taking with her. And then a sudden revelation, a memory of sitting by the lett with Holger Stoss, and Holger telling him of the visit Mathilde had got from her friend Ussi's daughter. How strange an encounter it had been, how Ruan Peat had latched upon it as an integral part of what had happened to Constantine. The name of that daughter being

Hela. And here, sitting before him, was a man who knew her name and was concerned with what had happened to her.

Ottelius Jorn's lessons in logic and philosophy in Reims, before it had all gone to hell, finally bearing fruit. Scratching through his memory for the man the Moscow archivists had accused of the theft of the Song, amongst other manuscripts, and how it was assumed he'd returned with them to his homeland.

Jorn finally having it.

Jorn letting out a bark of merriment that he'd come all the way to Vettie's Giel and found the one piece missing from Ruan Peat's complicated puzzle.

'It's you,' Jorn said quietly. 'You're Håkon Tryggvason. You're the man started all this going in the first place. You were the one sent the woman to Deventer with the Song.'

If Ottelius Jorn had been instantaneously transmogrified into a troll Håkon Tryggvason could not have been more shocked nor frightened at this completely unexpected unmasking.

'You needn't worry,' Jorn went on, before Håkon could gather wits enough to speak or protest. 'I'll not be telling anyone. Well, maybe one.' Meaning Ruan Peat. Plain vindictive not to mention he'd met the architect of the Bad Salzbaum mystery of the century. 'And your Hela, you needn't worry about her either,' Jorn informed Håkon. 'She got clean away, took the Song and its provenance with her. Although what will happen to both presumably waits to be seen.'

Håkon leaning back in his chair, reassessing both his visitor and that hole pierced through Torghatten Hill.

Wondering if the old tales he'd done so much to bolster might have some truth in them after all: sit vigil, stay your course, and you will be granted a way into a new life. Which had certainly been his experience, his decision then being to go and many years later to return. Except maybe the trolls had come back with him after all. He would never be sure. This stranger apparently knowing everything, as did others. So no more home for him here in Vettie's Giel. Time to move on. Time to take his bones down to Bergenstift and shift them as far away from Vettie's Giel as he could get them.

Just in case.

RUAN PEAT, BACK IN Deventer, already on the scent.

Ruan Peat never one to give up, despite a cracked jaw. Ruan Peat narrowing down the search, informing the Russian archivists of all that had happened in Bad Salzbaum. Bad Salzbaum might not care; he and the Russians archivists of a different mind. A matter of tying up loose ends for Ruan; a matter of national pride for the archivists. Long time for those letters to travel from Deventer to Moscow and back again. Longer for the Russians to converse with the Norwegian authorities. Longer still for the Norwegians to take the bother of going to a place as isolated as Vettie's Giel. Getting there early Winter and no way up the pass, not for them. Not returning until the following Spring, by which time Håkon Tryggvason was long gone.

There one day, disappeared the next.

Folk of Vettie's Giel glad to see the back of him.

# 35

## The Vile And The Despicable

IVOR RE-EMERGED FROM the Palace of Het Loo, missing fingers a constant agitation as he walked his way in near darkness to meet Greta. Het Loo the grandest place he'd ever been, and he knew grand, had been brought up in it. The contrast between Het Loo's opulence and the stinking wastes of Walcheren allowing him to see the grand with eyes other than his own. Specifically Greta's and, like she would have, had found it viscerally distasteful, wasteful and wanting. Swans and ermine be damned: Het Loo decked out room by room with polished wooden floors, red-gold carpets you could sink a fist into; chandeliers the size of two horses yoked together for the ploughing; tapestries and paintings on every wall, as if those walls could not stay up without them. Opulent too casual a word. Splendiferous more apt. A determined depiction of power and wealth more apt still.

Passing through all that pomp and puffery he'd wanted to run up and down those peacocked rooms, rip all those artfully designed tapestries and paintings from their fixings,

438

smash the chandeliers, roll up those expensive rugs and carpets. Kick the lot of them out of the nearest window.

Had wanted to cry out his protests:

*What's all this frippery for?*

*Don't you know the people fighting for you and yours are dying in so many horrible ways I could list them from here to next week and still not get to the end of it?*

*Has it never occurred to you to care about anyone but yourselves?*

Remembered telling Peter Finnerty, on their first meeting, when he'd been so nervous all sorts of nonsense had spurted from his lips, about William IV, stadholder of Holland for a few years a bare half century back, going into battle against the Bishop of Utrecht armed with one hundred and seventy-six pounds of sweetmeats, exclusively for personal use. That same William undoubtedly spending his off-war time here at Het Loo, like all stadholders before and after him since Het Loo had been built.

Felt the weight of that grizzled Yorkshire-man's hand on his shoulders and his voice in his ears:

*Get yerseln out whilst the going's good, lad. No one'll hold it agin you.*

Felt them all, those men under his command, and heard them all - every last man jack of them. Wanted to shout out what they must have wanted to shout out to him, to their commanders, their admirals, their Ministers of War, their stadholders, kings and politicians to just get all this done.

*Get your damn treaties made!*

*Sort out your blasted bloody borders!*

*Sell off all your disgusting shamefully expensive accessories. Give the proceeds to the men who are fighting for you, and the women who are dragging on their coat-tails all across Europe, so those men and women can quit the fight, lead decent ordinary lives like they should always have been allowed to do.*

The pound and hammer of his nausea at how these high-ups feathered their nests and cossetted their days speeding him on his way once he'd left the palace, his success a bitter trophy to take with him: Duke of Brunswick dour and imposing, listening closely to Ivor as the supposed mouthpiece of John, Earl of Chatham. Bad taste in all those high-up mouths how Chatham's plans had gone so disastrously awry in Walcheren he'd been forced to retreat. Two thousand sick piled onto boats along with the few thousand healthy; a further four thousand, who would never leave Walcheren, left to rot away in their pits without a stick or stone to mark their names or graves, to be grassed over and forgotten.

The Duke's eyes fixed on the painting of Mars, Roman God of War, behind Ivor's head. The irony lost on him as Ivor portrayed the grim reality of life on the filthy grounds of Walcheren spewing up ague at every turn, and the deeply unwelcome news that the French had not only taken Antwerp, Ghent and Vlissingen, but were marching swiftly up and down the coast to other ports. Zeebrugge by now undoubtedly under their control, next strike being north into Hollandish strongholds, their aim to fully impose Napoleon's Continental System whether his brother King Louis agreed to it or no. Which he did not; King Louis in vehement opposition to that System because he knew, as did the Duke, how breaking the ties of trade between the Low Countries and England would lead to financial and economic disaster for both.

This new intelligence from Ivor Merrill of how swiftly and determinedly the French were changing tack an eye-opener. Brunswick looking like he'd lifted the silver dome keeping his breakfast warm to find not the devilled kidneys and deliciously buttered scrambled eggs he'd been expecting, instead a hornet's nest swarming and swilling with angry workers threatening not only his breakfast plans but his entire world view.

Decisions quickly made: troops to be recalled from England; stern talks to be had with Louis to bolster ships and defences about the northern ports of Rotterdam and Amsterdam. Agreeing too, as an aside, that if the Servants of Walcheren could be saved, re-housed and rehabilitated, then he would see it done, given the Abbott himself had sent a plea and it was only because of the Servants - Ivor emphatic on this point - that many more men on Walcheren, most notably the officers and the Earl of Chatham himself, hadn't died in despicable circumstance.

Ivor neglecting to mention he was one of the presumed dead.

'You've done well, Captain Merrill,' Brunswick said, at the end of their interview. 'You've done us proud, coming up country on your own recognisance at peril of your life. You will leave tomorrow for England with my command in your pocket.'

Ivor somewhat aghast his repatriation was going to be so sudden, seizing his chance.

'Would you consent to my leave of absence for twenty four hours?'

A faint hope, but if he could get news of his success back to Greta then he needed to take the chance. Brunswick discombobulated, but inclined to leniency.

'I've no idea why you need it, given the import of the situation you've brought to my attention and that you're back where you should be. But, given you have brought it, have risked your life to bring it to me, I will allow you this one night to do what you need to do. You will present yourself here, Captain Merrill, at eight o'clock tomorrow morning on the dot, from where you will be accompanied back to England with several of my retinue.'

Hours given and received with thanks. No small linen bags of hair needed to smooth Ivor's way. Ivor shivering inside his skin as he trudged his way back from Het Loo to the hostelry and Greta. Mad ideas in his head about what he would say to her when he got there: how she was the most singular woman he'd ever met, how she'd changed him, made him the man he'd always wanted to be, how he would gladly lay down his life for hers if she required it, that he...

Words never said.

Ivor arriving at the inn to find Greta sitting companionably with the maddeningly ubiquitous and seemingly indestructible Mick Malloy. All romantic notions knocked out of Ivor's head. Mission statement delivered, mission statement greeted with adulation on all sides.

'For a high one, you've done us proud,' Mick announced, as if he'd thought it could never have been so.

'Well done you,' Greta said, standing up, giving Ivor a quick hug which had him hardening in his horribly vivid breeches which he was going to ditch first chance he got.

And that was that.

Dinner ordered, dinner eaten, wine drunk, casual chit-chat – mostly between Greta and Mick about their days together back in Ireland. Only high-point for Ivor being when Mick slapped his stomach and decided to retire for the night, leaving him and Greta alone for a few minutes at least.

'I'm real proud of you,' Greta said, pushing the last of her pear tart about her plate as if it had some place else to go. Keeping her eyes down, and then suddenly lifting them up. 'In fact you did magnificently, Captain Ivor Merrill. You really did. We couldn't have done any of this without you.'

Captain Ivor Merrill's throat closing up at the compliment, wishing he could say all he wanted, but could not.

'And you,' was all he could get out. 'What will you do now?'

*Oh you're such an idiot, Snivels! Why can't you get your boot out of your mouth and get it said?*

Greta getting to her feet, leaning down to kiss his cheek. 'I've places I need to go,' she said, 'people I need to see.'

Ivor's heart shriveling, too much of a gentleman and a coward to ask where she was going, whom she meant to meet.

Greta giving him a glimmer of hope.

'I knew you would do us proud, as did Peter the first time he met you.' Leaning down, placing her chin upon his head. 'You're a wonder, Ivor Merrill,' she whispered, him feeling her breath on his newly shorn head and his skin shivering with the possibilities of what that touch might mean. 'And if you give me leave,' Greta went on, 'I will seek you out, after I'm done.'

Ivor would have given her all the leave in the world had he been able to get out a single word, which he was not.

And with that she went, and he let her go, and Greta was gone.

GRETA NOT KNOWING WHAT she might find. Greta thinking she might be better off not knowing. Greta thinking she should have stuck to Ivor, take the promised present over the unknown past. Giving her good byes to Mick, who'd done with the French Irish Legion and was heading back to Ireland.

'Not all lost,' he said. 'If there's any fires still to be stoked then I will stoke them.'

'I'll join you once they've turned to flame,' Greta assured, despite wanting more than anything for such not to happen. Mick the first to wish her back, and the first to advise her not to do so. Wanting better for her. Wanting her to have a proper life.

'Don't come on my account,' Mick said, during an embarrassing hug that might very well be their last encounter. 'Go seek what you will find. And if you find better, Greta, then don't you never come back.'

A bit of a choke, that last entanglement. And a bit of a fight as Greta seemed unable to let Mick go and Mick struggled to push her away. Finally had it. Finally caught her at arm's length.

'You've done so much. Too much. More than any person should have been asked to do. And so, Greta Finnerty, I release you into the world. '

Finer words Mick Malloy had never managed in the whole of his life.

Heart spasming as Greta swallowed down his promise, those fine words releasing her from him and him from her.

'I don't know what will happen if I find him,' she said. 'He might not want me. He might find me vile and despicable.'

Mick serious in the moment, although truly he wanted to laugh out loud that anyone could find her so.

'If there are two things you are not,' he stated, gripping hard at her shoulders, 'it's vile and despicable, for you are entirely the opposite. And if I ever find anyone thinks that of you then I don't care who or where they are. I will personally hunt them down and rip out their tongue.'

# 36

## Opals, Rubies, Diamonds

DEVENTER, COLD AND dreich, mid-December.

Ruan not long returned to his workshop from what should have been a scintillating lecture on why the great philosopher René Descartes had chosen to take up abode in their great city instead of his native Paris. A lecture centred on Descartes' social climbing bringing him into conflict with the Duke of Richelieu – never a man with whom to cross swords – and thereafter fleeing Paris, enlisting in the Duke of Bavaria's army. Bit of time to think and travel, major breakthrough resulting: creating a unified system modelled on mathematics and rationality which changed the world, as far as philosophy was concerned.

An intriguing dog-tail of history presented so dully Ruan nodded off at one point and left as soon as he could.

The laudanum not helping.

His trussed-up jaw a painful debilitation precluding speech. The lack of it restful at first, forcing him to spend his days reading, researching or writing. Constantine and Håkon Tryggvason to the fore.

Two weeks in and he was beginning to find it irksome; three weeks, and he wanted to scream out his frustration at not being able to converse, Caro having to do all his talking for him: a cumbersome device that meant writing everything down beforehand. They'd developed a kind of shorthand, yet still everything took so damn long. Thoughts of Hippolyte Gerhard never far from Ruan's mind, of Hippolyte's decision to bring his fretful and disturbing days to an end. Not that Ruan's were by any comparison as fretful and disturbing, were temporary and frustrating, if not permanent.

Ruan sick of the purees and minced-up food he was forced to endure, day-dreaming about crispy chicken skins, the snap of vegetables, salted pork-crackling. Only baby food for him: soup of a hundred different kinds. Caro trying his best to turn them into various spicy dishes, with various spicy breads collapsing the moment they were dunked. Torture to smell the food people bought from street stalls, guzzled on the go. Ruan electing to remain indoors, needing distraction, chasing up the Bad Salzbaum case for something to do.

Ruan sitting at his desk that damp December afternoon, having deserted Descartes as surely as Descartes had deserted Paris, hearing a soft tap at the door.

Caro's tap.

Caro coming in after a few moments, for Ruan could hardly say yea or nay.

'We've a visitor,' Caro said, and Caro could not have looked happier if he'd swallowed the sun and begun to shine with all its radiance. 'You're never going to believe it, Ruan. You're really not.'

And really not, was what Ruan Peat felt. A visitor the last thing he needed. Caro, usually so good at interpreting his feelings, grinning on. Ruan scribbling furiously on his pad and holding it up.

*No one. NO ONE. I don't want to see anyone.*

Caro infuriatingly chipper.

'Don't take this the wrong way, boss, but this is the one and only time I'm going to over-rule you.'

Caro pushing the door full wide, when Ruan's jaw would have dropped had it not been tied into immobility, for there she was: the girl - the woman – he'd tried so hard to obliterate from his mind. Greta Finnerty flooding back into every corner and crevice, crumbling his defences, heart crumping as she stood there looking magnificent, and horribly nervous. Ruan having difficulty standing up.

Greta forewarned, Mick giving her a terse summing up of his sojourn in Bad Salzbaum: *Thought your Ruan Peat might help us if Ivor failed,* he'd said, *only he's been in a bit of a stramash, incurred injuries; could have been a hell of a lot worse.* Greta soul-shaken, riven to the core to read between Mick's militarily clipped lines which meant Ruan had been inches away from being ripped from his life, and therefore ripped from hers. Had wanted to run on swift feet that very minute to Bad Salzbaum to tend him, care for him, declare her need and want of him.

Nothing like the imminent removal of someone from the world to make you realise your world would be a poorer place without them, and a world without Ruan in it a place she didn't want to be. Heart on fire to see him, even if he didn't want to see her. Even if it was the last time she would ever see him.

Distraught to arrive at Bad Salzbaum to find him gone, returned to Deventer.

Mick's words of advice in her head as she made that second journey.

*Don't go barging in on him, Greta. Give him a few weeks. You know how wounded folk are, never want their nearest and dearest to see them at their worst.*

Although she hardly counted as nearest and dearest. Farthest and forgotten being more likely. Kicking her heels for a while, taking the longest route she could from Bad Salzbaum to Deventer. Every day a torture, a weary dread-ridden wandering through a monotonous landscape of windmills and neat villages, until she could stand it no longer. Had to know how he was doing, had to know how things stood between them. If she should take her chances with Ivor instead of him.

Fear and pity fighting for a place in the pit of her stomach as she saw Ruan's lower face hampered and husked by leather strappings, a spoon-sized hole where his mouth should have been. A mouth she'd hoped would have smiled involuntarily when she'd come in. Instead a great blank waste topped by nose, and eyebrows that shot up above dark eyes whose expression she couldn't read. Struggling to get her own face in order. Wanting to blurt out *oh my love, my darling, whatever has happened to you?* Not at all what she said, despite being heart-hirpled, blood-thudded, to see him this way.

'It's good to see you,' she got out, as if speaking to some old uncle she was required, if not delighted, to be introduced to.

Great blank wastes opening up in Ruan for oh, good could hardly describe this moment. It was incandescent, heart-stopping. And so buggering annoying that he couldn't get out a word or raise a smile.

'Are you sure he wants to see me?' Greta murmured to Caro, as if Ruan wasn't there; as if a Ruan robbed of his speech and his ability to express emotion couldn't be trusted to form his own opinion.

'Just wait,' Caro advised as Ruan slumped down at his desk, wrote something on his pad and held it up.

'Opals, rubies, diamonds,' Greta read out the words. 'I don't understand. What does that mean?'

Ruan scribbling again.

'Alone pen?' Greta could not make head nor tail of it.

Ruan obfuscating his words in case this was no more than rapprochement, the mere looking up of an old friend out of duty. Both Ruan and Greta looking to Caro for guidance. Caro able to read people like sailors read sea and sky and Holger's Sirius. Caro regarding the two of them gravely before rolling his eyes.

'You're both such dunderheads,' he exclaimed. 'Why don't you just give each other a hug and be done with it.'

The two dunderheads going a little red about the gills but obeying, walking stiffly towards one another; awkwardly wrapping loose arms about waist and shoulder; hard leather against Greta's cheek, a faint whistle of breath in her ear as Ruan tried to aspirate words from his locked jaws.

*Iuvoo.*

The worst ventriloquist act ever.

*Iuvoo,* he tried again.

Greta none the wiser, until she felt the wetness of Ruan's tears against her skin, the warm snuffle of his mask as he fought to take in breath and cry at the same time, when she traversed the shores of phonetics and landed on the beach of meaning.

'I love you too,' she murmured, at which point the hug became so intimately tight and embarrassing Caro had to turn away, closing the door softly behind him, shaking his head.

*Dunderheads one thing,* was Caro's opinion. *Lovelorn dunderheads the absolute worst.*

'You should have done this years ago!' Caro shouting merrily through the closed door, Ruan and Greta leaving each other go long enough to hold each other out, Greta wiping at both their tear-streaked faces with the edge of her pinafore. Ruan having to start untying the strops at the back of his head to release the buckles because the tears had got in and were dribbling down the sides of his mouth and were intolerably itchy against his stubble.

'Let me,' Greta said, taking over the duty, slim fingers exquisitely gentle and solicitous as she loosed the stays, released the leather, the touch of her fingers against the back of his neck sending dartles of pins and needles meandering through his skin, and again as she dabbed her pinafore at his crying.

'Tell me if it hurts,' she said, taking up the pot of balm from his desk and rubbing it in, the sensation softer than the rose petals that lent the balm its scent. Ruan catching at her fingers, kissing them one by one. Greta's dimples deepening at the intimate caress.

'Hard to believe you chopped off someone's head,' she said, recapping the bottle of balm. 'I'm assuming he was already dead?'

Ruan regarding her with wonderment and curiosity, and then beginning a burbling that grew into laughter. Greta alarmed, putting her hands against his cheeks and chin to stop him fracturing his bones for a second time. An action so natural, so tender, Ruan began to weep again and the whole exercise with the pinafore and balm had to be repeated. Greta shushing him until all was done and she'd got him back into his restraints.

'You're the worst patient,' she commented, 'but you're my patient, so I command you to stop all this blubbing.'

Greta on the outside as practical as ever, if not on the in where she was aglow from head to foot to have seen his face, felt his lips upon her fingertips.

Questions bubbling up on both sides through scribble and speech.

*How did you find me?*
*Where have you been?*
*What have you been doing?*
*I really need to know about this head-chopping business.*

Answers to those questions pushed into the morrow when Ruan shyly put a finger to her lips and opened up another door. Greta's choice whether to go through it or slam it shut. Ruan's heart on the wobble, wondering if he'd gone too far, if it was too soon, if she would consent, if maybe her own wastelands hadn't been as badly empty and barren as had been his own.

Greta wavered, teetered, then took his hand in hers, laced her fingers through his and led him on.

Long evening spent together, naked and wide-eyed on Ruan's bed.

Mechanics a little tricky and bewildering given the delicate nature of Ruan's injuries and their shared ignorance of how all should go; both setting off slow and gentle, spooling spontaneously side by side, skin by skin, limb by limb, until they found their way.

New paths begun, new lives spun the one into the other.

New terrains to tread that would see them far and wide, side by side.

Ruan's jaw healing as Mick had prognosticated, a schedule Greta rigidly adhered to: six weeks allotted for his fractures to start the business of re-bonding; three more before she decreed the strop could be removed and Ruan could start the slow process of building up the muscle mass needed to chew and speak; a further month before he could manage both adequately without stress or strain, crick and pain.

A bleak March afterwards spent travelling to Scotland, to Ruan's old-man house on the shores of Loch Eck.

Mid-April when they arrived and levered the planking from its windows and doors, let in the light. Ruan disheartened to find old-man house as dilapidated as he'd imagined, yet old-man house built well, built for strength and solitude and anything the weather could fling at it. All that needed repairing being repaired; books packed up and sent back to Caro in Deventer. Greta and Ruan remaining until the house was sold.

A honeymoon of sorts: long nights talking quietly of times past and new, sipping wine from the meagre stores in the cellar, sitting companionably by the large glass windows gazing on the grey-green ruffle of the loch and the scrub woods on its farthest side where wild lynx once padded centuries before.

'You don't regret selling this place?' Greta asked, curled up with Ruan on the mildewed sofa they would burn the following morning, along with all the other unserviceable furniture, before they left.

'I don't,' Ruan replied. 'I swore I'd never come back unless you were by my side, and now you are.'

'That's romantic,' Greta said, running her fingers over his healed jaw, an action that still sent scintillations of pleasure and pain running through him. 'If rather weak-hearted. What if I'd never come back?'

Ruan looking out of the windows at the dusk, at the several deer snuffling through the reeds, lapping at the water; a pair of beltie coots marshalling their young to their night-roost; the sleek-slipping arches of playful otter cubs pushing at their boundaries.

Ruan stroking Greta's hair.

So pleased he'd been to leave this old house; so ashamed now how pleased to leave it he'd been back then.

'If you'd not come for me,' he said, 'then I would have come for you. Caro made me swear an oath in Bad Salzbaum that we would.' Ruan resting his head on hers. 'There's always hope until there isn't. Joachim told me that.'

Greta hiccupping on the sip of wine she'd just taken.

'He told it to me too, that conniving Brother.'

The deer moving on, the belties settling to their roost, the otter cubs returning home.

'I think we should find him,' Ruan said, the night drawn dark about them, only sign of the loch being a sliver of moonlight sending a shivering silvered path across its oblivious surface.

'Then find him we will,' Greta agreed, nestling into Ruan.

BROTHER JOACHIM GONE to an astonishing place.

A place that should not exist.

A place that had boggled Ruan and beguiled him, whose name he'd jotted down in the margins of Thomas Campbell's poem on the first English strike against the Danish in Copenhagen harbour.

*Heligoland: this a place I want to go.*

*This a place I mean to see.*

Ruan boggled and beguiled all over again when he learned it was there the Servants had been resettled and rehomed after their dispersal from Walcheren. A place not picked at random; a place brought up by Ivor Merrill during his conversation with the Duke of Brunswick at Het Loo: *It could be extremely useful, from where the Continental System can be breached and broken if the worst happens* – which it did, following Louis's abdication - *and a safe haven for the Servants. A population of over three thousand they can minister to, as well as the English troops already barracked there and the many more we may need there soon.*

A place whose strategic importance the Duke could not deny, no more could he deny the Servants.

Heligoland: forty odd miles off-shore from Holland and Germany soon fulfilling that strategic purpose, become the most important covert trading outpost for both the English and the Dutch in the latter months of 1810 and beyond.

Ruan, Greta and Caro, after an age of tortured negotiations, eventually given leave to visit in the early months of 1811, permit in Ruan's pocket signed by Major Ivor Merrill himself.

Heligoland a place apart, as was Vettie's Giel.

Ruan knowing a lot more about Vettie's Giel since he'd had unexpected word from Ottelius Jorn, who had apparently travelled there on a whim.

*It's desolate,* he had written, *barely accessible. Filled with stone-tumbled valleys and scree-ridden cliffs. And there's a multitude of hares here you wouldn't believe. And something else you'll not believe – I could hardly believe it myself. I've met your Håkon Tryggvason. The very same.*

No mention of tipping the man off and thereby giving him escape.

No mention of the pierced mountain.

Some secrets needing to be kept.

IVOR SNIVELS MERRILL regretting for the rest of his life he'd not had the guts to take that moment to its end, take her face in his hands and declare what she meant to him. Ivor Snivels Merrill a hero once he got back home: the man responsible for keeping Napoleon's Continental System from severing trade between England and Holland, if only for seven months. King Louis abdicating and fleeing Het Loo the following Summer because he absolutely refused to condemn his adopted country to ruination by agreeing to that same system; an abdication and fleeing thereby making such implementations inevitable.

Holland officially annexed by France and Napoleon on 9th July 1810, almost a year to the day after the Earl of Chatham had brought his troops to Walcheren; the canton of Wallis near Oldenburg swiftly following suit, the French Empire thereby taking the largest part of Westphalia and now held the vast majority of ports with access to the English Channel and the North Sea coast.

But seven months was something.

Seven months during which – French Imperialism notwithstanding - several tremendous events occurred to our main players: Captain Ivor Merrill promoted for his duty to his country. Major Ivor Merrill receiving distinction after distinction, mostly due to the loyalty given him by his men because of the care with which he treated those under his command.

Lieutenant-Colonel Ivor Merrill dying in service – never married, never having children - in the last blast against Napoleon at Waterloo, June 18th 1815, the official end of twenty three years of war.

NETSUKE NIGHTS FOR Ruan and Greta spent with Joachim on Heligoland: nights closed, dark and tight when storms drove in, pushing new and different waves hammering upon new and different shores. Nights clear and bright, stars an astonishment flung far and wide. Polaris and Sirius merely the brightest of the enormous many.

'Always knew there was hope for you two,' said Joachim, gazing upwards. No one so pleased as he that Greta and Ruan had been reunited, and no tongue-ripping needed from Mick Malloy - for which Mick had felt some chagrin when he'd got the news.

'You do talk tripe sometimes,' Greta commented.

Joachim smiling, nodding into the darkness, for didn't everyone talk tripe sometimes?

Such was life: sometimes good, sometimes bad, depending on where and how life has led you.

This particular load of tripe turning out just fine.

Last words of the last night, until Caro spoke. Caro looking up into the great wheel of the sky that not even Joachim could explain or quantify, nor give proper account of.

'Don't know about any of you,' Caro said, 'but if this was my last night on earth, my very last night, then this is how I would choose to spend it.'

Ruan and Greta looking up with him, seeing opals, rubies, diamonds.

'Alone pen,' whispered Ruan.

'Alone pen,' Greta whispered back.

No need for explanation. Shorthand long established.

*You are unique and rare, and you are mine.*

Ruan and Greta feet-sky.

And lucky you if you too are feet-sky, have found your opals rubies diamonds.

A great many folk, in a great many places, in circumstances other than your own, will never get the chance.

Here is one on Heligoland, and in Bad Salzbaum another.

# 37

## Last Scene, Last Word

TRIPE-GIRL OF BAD SALZBAUM not a one to look up into the stars, her life not made that way. Couldn't read, couldn't write, couldn't count numbers more than she needed to do her business.

Tripe-girl of Bad Salzbaum humming happily as she stood with the other traders outside the church of St Peter's. Not much to be hoped for in sales given how paltry were the amount of wedding guests, which were almost non-existent. Mathilde and Holger Stoss the only invited guests, Professor Jorn by then away on his travels.

A fact that didn't faze her, and absolutely wasn't going to stop her being there.

Tripe-girl of Bad Salzbaum smoothing down the grey silk of her skirts. They were a little tattered at their hems, but she looked after the rest as best she could.

Tripe-girl of Bad Salzbaum clapping loudly as Frau Dieter – Frau Guichot, as she had a few minutes earlier become – walked sedately down the path of the churchyard on the arm of her new husband. All the other traders beginning to shout out their wares.

'Got fresh veg here!'

'And fresh fruit!'

'New-baked bread and cakes at bargain price, wedding folk, if you're needing them.'

No one needing them.

Fabian about to wave the sellers on, his new wife stilling his arm. His new wife having foreseen this moment. They may not have received many wedding gifts for themselves, but she had one to give. The astonishing Frau Dieter taking a direct line to the tripe-girl.

'I'd like to buy up your entire load,' she announced loudly, 'cart and all.'

Tripe-girl confused, bewildered, bunching her fists in her fine skirts, stammering out her answer.

'My cart? But I'll need it. How will I...'

'You won't need it, my dear,' Frau Dieter said gently, putting a gloved hand to the girl's cheek. 'You will be coming to work for me. Mathilde!' she called, Mathilde bustling up, the only one in on the ruse. Mathilde needing help at the mud-baths, the two of them discussing how best to go about it and this the one decided upon. Most people have their own metaphorical carts of tripe to tote behind them, but smell the real thing and it's the last thing you want to drag through the rest of your life.

Holger coming to the fore, taking the cart from the girl; Mathilde easing the girl away, leading her off to better, longer years than she could ever have expected.

Fabian choking up at this unknown-about gesture. So like his Elise to choose this day to rescue someone else, as she had rescued him.

'You're...magnificent,' he got out on a whisper, circling his arm about his new wife's magnificent waist.

'I had a good teacher,' his wife informed him, putting her fingers to the amulet hanging proud, if a little outré, against Fabian's smart new wedding gear. 'I only wish he was here to see what he caused to be.'

Everyone a song reverberating down the years.

This the end of Constantine's, choruses and claps abundant: Frau Dieter and Fabian Guichot finding their greatest happiness in one another; Greta and Ruan reunited; tripe-girl and the Servants saved; Ottelius Jorn passing through the pierced mountain, coming out the other side the same but different; Håkon Tryggvason setting off for Hungary and Hela, never getting there. Håkon Tryggvason getting lost in Hamburg, where he met exiles from Ireland who had never left and were still ruminating about their cause. Håkon Tryggvason ripe for it, taking their cause as his own; taking up the case of one Peter Finnerty, an Irish journalist jailed on his return to England from Walcheren because he'd been too free with his words of how badly that campaign had gone, how badly the English had treated their captured prisoners from Napoleon's Irish Legion. Håkon Tryggvason at one with the poet Shelley when Shelley dedicated his pamphlet *Poetical Essay on the Existing State of Things* to that same Peter Finnerty, both crying out for the man's release.

Constantine a song sent out into the world, as was the man hundreds of years before him who'd strung down all he could remember about his battle against the Russians by the Donets River, neither knowing what they would cause to happen because of what they'd done.

Songs all around us.

Tip your head, listen, for there are always more to hear.

# Historical Notes

The Walcheren Campaign of 1809 was as catastrophic as described.

Peter Finnerty a real person invited to report on that campaign: an Irish journalist exiled after the failed Uprising of 1798 and later imprisoned following his return to England from Walcheren, nominally for libeling Lord Castlereagh for his mistreatment of Irish Prisoners of War.

Shelley's *Poetical Essay on the Existing State of Things* published in 1811, a polemic against war and English Imperialism in equal measure and dedicated, in large letters on its front cover, to Peter Finnerty in order to raise money for Peter's release.

Thomas Campbell, take a bow. All is as I've said, including his meeting with the ex-Irish in Hamburg and his poems on both them and the blowing up of the Danish fleet by the English in Copenhagen harbour.

Other historical details are as correct as I could make them, including those about Prussia, the Northern Convention, Het Loo, the blowing up of the Danish fleet in Copenhagen harbour in 1801 and again in 1807, the machinations of the Irish Exiles in Hamburg, the taking by the English of Heligoland, and the advance of Napoleon's Continental System.

From Goethe comes the verse:

*Be still, my dearest, be still and still and still, for sleep will surely come...*

The quote from Heinrich von Kleist, *paradise is locked and bolted,* comes from his essay on puppet theatre, *Über das Marionettentheater*, published in 1810. He shot himself the following year, aged 34.

Many thanks to Melissa Gray for the cover.
Do visit my website at www.cliogray.com[1]

---

Milton Keynes UK
Ingram Content Group UK Ltd.
UKHW041907211023
431088UK00001B/1